FINAL
DESCENT

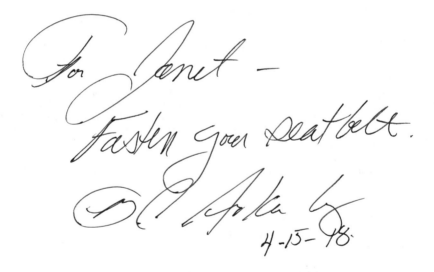

For Janet –
Fasten your seatbelt.

4-15-98

T.D. ARKENBERG

outskirtspress

DENVER, COLORADO

Outskirts Press, Inc.
http://www.outskirtspress.com

ISBN: 978-1-4787-0059-3

Outskirts Press and the "OP" logo are trademarks belonging to Outskirts Press, Inc.

PRINTED IN THE UNITED STATES OF AMERICA

Dedication &
Acknowledgements

I dedicate this book to those who supported me in my personal and professional life, and to the many leaders who pursue results and relationships with equal, uncompromising fervor.

I thank Jim, for his love, friendship, and support. He provided thrust to lift the work, propulsion to drive me forward, and guidance to route me toward my goal. I couldn't ask for a better co-pilot through calm and turbulent skies.

I thank countless friends, whose encouragement provided fuel to keep me airborne over the years, energizing me to reach my destination.

T.D. Arkenberg
2012

Prologue

Current culture romanticizes mid-century, corporate America in much the same way Hollywood, television and books idealize the Wild West.

Post Second World War victors rode spirited stallions through an unprecedented period of expansion and prosperity. With a far horizon and a path clear of fences, the pace was a gallop, not a trot, and never a retreat. The charge—*do more with more*. Opportunities were as plentiful as pre-pioneer buffalo. People were needed to fuel growth. Employees joined a company and retired with a gold watch.

Management theorists dissected organizations and showed the economic and social benefits of enlightened leaders. The nation had united to win a world war. Returning heroes commanded respect as they rejoined the civilian workforce. Command and control were best left on the battlefield.

The skyscrapers of Midtown Manhattan, Chicago's Loop, and of other great American cities still stand as monuments to man's ingenuity and godlike ambitions. But while the wheels of industry still turn, the three-martini lunches, climbs up the corporate ladder and the gold watch have vanished.

By the century's end, the horizon moved closer and economic hurdles fenced in corporate cowboys. Vast pools of cheap labor, global transportation channels, and a growing dependence on foreign resources, including oil, changed the American landscape. Capital and data trade in real time on world markets that never close. Fields that gushed for wildcatters dried up. Fingers found the bottom of the cookie jar. The new battle cry—*do more with less. Circle the wagons!* Reaching the end of the once boundless frontier, the new breed of maverick adapted. The tactics turned to survival: outsource, retrench, downsize, and rightsize.

In our idealized versions of the Wild West, the good guys wore white and the bad guys black. White Hat came to the duel outgunned, often armed only with virtue, a poor match for Black Hat and an arsenal of underhanded tricks. Townspeople, their community's moral fate hanging in the balance, cowered behind wooden storefronts as the clock ticked toward high noon. Some rooted for Black Hat, but most secretly hoped that White Hat could draw a miracle from his holster.

Often, the outcome depended upon the sheriff, a conflicted character torn between fear of Black Hat and allegiance to the badge. The sheriff's intentions remained masked until the climax. Will he turn a blind eye? Will he sink into moral oblivion a broken man? Or, will he find virtue and risk everything to betray Black Hat and allow White Hat, against all odds, to claim victory?

Similar struggles between good and bad take place in twenty-first century corporate America. But the romance is gone and ideals are tarnished. White Hat and Black Hat aren't easily distinguished and a fog of gray shrouds corporate America's Main Street. But the question remains, which side will today's sheriff support?

Chapter 1

Hap Erupts

"You catch the *Times*? Another nail in our coffin—maybe the death blow," snarled Hap Sweeny, Chief Operating Officer of Intercontinental Airlines.

Chad Wilkerson sat, glued to his boss's blazing, metallic blue eyes. The junior executive, whose mop of white hair didn't match his baby face, tapped his foot and pinched his lip. His free hand clutched the edge of the chair like a white-knuckled flyer. No stranger to his boss's throbbing forehead vein and explosive tone, Wilkerson advised colleagues on dealing with the irascible COO, "One doesn't harness a volcano."

Hap didn't want a response. Something else fueled his temper: a recent letter from an old buddy, a guy named Charlie Weber, whose face he pulled from distant memory. Hap first met Charlie forty years before, the day both joined Intercontinental as food runners. The then teenagers shared more than a hire date. Each fudged his age to get the job in order to help a struggling mother, abandoned by an abusive husband. A paycheck meant security. What they found was a family.

In the early years, the two watched each other's back. A young Hap, dodged a third-strike dismissal when his clean-slated pal took the fall for a truckload of spoiled meals, forgotten on a food kitchen dock. When Charlie and his wife lost their first baby, Hap covered for the grieving father by working double shifts for two weeks. Later, when a rare promotion was posted, Charlie passed knowing Hap needed the pay bump for night school. After graduating college, the first in his family to do so, Hap moved into management. He lost track of Charlie who never advanced beyond the airport ramp. *How long had it been, ten, fifteen years?*

Hap's fortunes rose, reaching their zenith with a promotion to Chief Operating Officer under the airline's prior chief. A reputation as a skilled operations man saved him when the current Chairman and Chief Executive Officer, Richard Weston III cleaned house.

Hap occupied a large office on the fortieth floor of headquarters. His second wife decorated the space, constrained by the minimalist modern theme imposed by Weston who viewed the décor as a symbol of efficiency and progressive thinking. "Merely white walls and uncomfortable chairs," Hap said. "Doesn't mean shit when it comes to pushin' an airplane out on time." Frosted glass cabinets reminiscent of a medical dispensary lined the wall opposite the windows of the chrome and glass office. "Christ, where's the red cross?" Hap sniped before dimming the lights to soften the starkness.

He waged a single battle, demanding the wooden desk that served him for more than a decade. A cast iron lamp with amber shade, the brightest light in the office, highlighted the desk's red veins. A son and daughter from his first marriage, and a radiant bride leaning on his tuxedoed arm, smiled from silver frames. The photos gave visitors a glimpse into Hap's connection to humanity. When the second Mrs. Sweeny gave way to the third, his able assistant slipped the new photo into the frame. Hap admired the economic efficiency.

But the resurfacing of Charlie, his former friend, disturbed his sterile sanctuary. The letter's closing words scorched themselves into Hap's memory.

What happened to the wide-eyed kid who loved this airline?
Where's the idealistic maverick hell bent on changing the world?

You forget the people who love this company? I thought your pro-
motion would change things—one of us on top. Now I doubt
Intercontinental will survive—maybe it shouldn't.

Hap pushed Charlie's lament from his mind as he rose from the massive desk. The crown of his scalp, ringed by a laurel of steel gray hair, turned crimson. He paced back and forth, one hand holding a rolled newspaper, the other forming a fist. "*Greedy, reckless,* they called us. Want Congress to put us on a leash." Newspaper whacked the fist. "Passenger Bill of Rights? Heavy-handed crap!"

Hap noticed Wilkerson, jaw clenched, tracking him through narrow black eyes. A source had told him that Wilkerson wanted to talk about a major shake up. Something about axing one department to aggressively expand another—outsourcers who hired cheap vendors and fired pricey employees. Both men knew Weston admired cost cutting efforts, especially reductions in force. Hap understood Weston's fondness for Wilkerson. The junior executive was an ardent disciple of driving efficiencies regardless of the human toll. Wilkerson, the source added, wanted to fire Jim Abernathy, a popular manager with whom he butted heads. He didn't want to kick that hornets' nest without Hap's blessing. *Why should I make Wilkerson's life any easier,* Hap thought to himself.

Hap seethed. "We gotta stop the bastards from pissin' in our pool. We can't afford this Bill. We're on the brink of bankruptcy, *again*. Goes for most of this anemic industry." His mind flashed to meetings with bankers and creditors that consumed his time during the company's tour of Chapter 11. *Assholes! Couldn't fly a kite let alone run an airline.* Few people understood how close Intercontinental came to liquidation. His beloved airline owed its survival to Weston, whose actions earned Hap's loyalty. But Intercontinental wasn't out of the woods.

Hap sank into his chair; fist rapping his temple. "We've

enjoyed freedom for thirty years." He paused, looked across the desk, and scrutinized Wilkerson. A pink face, the picture of an altar boy stared at him—white broadcloth shirt and red silk tie hanging from a porcelain-colored neck. Hap considered him a lightweight, born into a first class seat but acting as if he'd paid every dollar of the fare. Yet, Hap couldn't refuse Weston who demanded he take the silver-spooned, efficiency expert under his wing. Wilkerson's cough drew his glare. "We want *less* regulation!" Hap added. "Goes for foreign restrictions too. Italians can dump money into Detroit, why shouldn't the Germans bailout an American airline?" Bankruptcy taught the craggy-faced ops guy business 101. Companies craved capital the way vampires lusted after blood.

He cupped his chin while maintaining a death grip on the newspaper. "The Bill's a one-way ticket to re-regulation. Media horror stories titillate Congress." Hap stood, paced to the window and back to the desk. "Damn Internet. Sins exposed and replayed to extract every ounce of humiliation."

Wilkerson's fingers moved from his lip and his pug nose, tilted upward. He leaned forward, elbows resting on the desk. "Customers like catching us with our pants down. Everyone loves to hate airlines," he said with the tone of a brown-nosing pupil.

Hap pounded the newspaper on the chair and barked, "Listen! Washington's paying attention to the rabble. Politicians latch onto anything that justifies their existence. We need actions, not excuses!"

Wilkerson flinched. He sat back and nodded vigorously. "Of course, you're right. But Washington seems preoccupied with its own scandals. We hearing any chatter about legislation?"

Hap closed his eyes and tilted his head backward. An image of Congressman Malcolm Klein, Chairman of the House Transportation Committee, popped into his head. After a pause, he responded. "Klein obsesses about airline oversight like a dog with a pork chop. Lobbyists say he's sniffin' for smoking guns."

Wilkerson cocked his head. "He find anything?"

"Not yet. But thank God he's not focused on safety. He and the FAA would love to sink their teeth into our exposed ass. Silence critics who say they're too chummy with the airlines. No, right now, customer service gives him a hard-on."

Wilkerson sat up and wrung his hands. "Like that Northeast Airlines blunder. Thirty ice-covered airplanes stranded on the Philly tarmac for eight hours. A customer's video went viral. Overflowing lavs, crying babies and screaming mothers."

Hap covered his face. "I've seen it. That storm trooper of a flight attendant barked commands and threatened customers. She ran the morning news show gauntlet. A regular drill sergeant."

"Hope she was thoroughly embarrassed," Wilkerson added.

"Embarrassed! She was proud of the footage, a star among co-workers. Oh, the depths to which our industry has plummeted." Hap cringed.

Wilkerson tapped the desk. "At least it wasn't us."

Hap glared. "If that fiasco were the industry's only blunder, we might laugh at Northeast's expense. Klein's daughter and grandson were on that plane. That mess brings the Congressman's wrath on us all. Coulda been us, and you know it. This stuff gnaws at me. Should give you ulcers too."

He pointed a finger at Wilkerson. "Remember last Thanksgiving? Our flight that diverted to Bumblefuck in a blizzard? No staff within 200 miles. Captain abandoned his customers and flew the empty plane back to San Diego. Two days to get a bus in there."

Wilkerson wiped his palms on his trousers. "I played dodge ball with the media for weeks. They dug up something about the Captain having tickets to the Chargers game."

"We got lucky—a light passenger load," Hap said.

"And no videos."

Hap shook his head, recalling the graphic descriptions he read about in the incident reports. "Imagine the conditions inside that terminal after fifty hours. Thank God that New England train crash drew the heat. Free trips and bonus miles bought our customers' silence."

"May not be lucky next time," replied Wilkerson, loosening his tie.

Hap growled, pointing a finger at Wilkerson. "Make sure there is no next time." He flung the paper onto the desk, rose and strutted to the window. The session was over.

Wilkerson retreated through the shadows to the exit. His request to fire Abernathy would have to wait.

Chapter 2

Jim's Paris Diversion

"Bon jour," Jim Abernathy said, disguising his voice with a phony accent as he knocked at the hotel room door. He assumed his wife, Julie, was still in bed, sleeping off her jet lag. Although they were physically in Paris, their biological clocks remained in Chicago where it was in the middle of the night.

He snickered at the sound of her yawning plea coming through the door, "Come back later."

His voice assumed a more nasal quality. "S'il vous plait. Room Sair-veece—café, croissant avec marmalade. Open la porte, pleese." He pressed his ear to the door. He heard the rustling of sheets and pictured Julie scanning the hotel room for him. He knocked again. "Madame Abernathy, s'il vous plait. J'ai votre petit dejeuner. Your, how you say, brake-fast."

"Une moment, por favor." Julie sounded frazzled. She knew enough pieces of European languages to be dangerous. She had accumulated pleasantries and menu necessities from weekend getaways with Jim and a decade as a flight attendant. Her sentences often consisted of fragments from several languages, something he dubbed Englibberish.

Her voice grew louder. "Okay, okay! Hold your caballos!" The doorknob turned and Julie, dressed in her bathrobe, pulled the door open. She flinched at the sight of her husband, his hand in mid knock.

Jim stifled his laugh as he balanced two stacked cups from an American coffee chain in his other hand. "Bon jour," he said with a bow of his head. "Monsieur Abernathy a votre service."

Julie ran her hands through uncombed hair and bent over laughing.

Jim raised his eyebrows. "Eet ees customary, Madame, in France to keese." Julie rose on tiptoes and kissed his lips. "But Madame, local custom demands two, peut-être, three kisses." Jim dropped his accent and puckered his lips.

She kissed him two more times, took one of the cups and stepped backwards before adding, "A horrible Clouseau. So bad, I thought you were real. Besides, it's cheek kissing Mister!"

Jim patted her behind. "Madame submitted willingly."

Julie scoffed. She grabbed him by the lapel and pulled him deeper into the room before kicking the door shut. "Hey! You got me out of bed under false pretenses. Monsieur promised croissant and marmalade." She put a hand on her hip and shifted her weight from one leg to the other.

Jim gasped, placing a hand over his heart. "I'm offended." He reached into the pockets of his leather coat and produced the disputed items. "Dodged that snooty desk clerk."

"Monsieur Sneer?" Julie said, mimicking the clerk's raised upper lip.

Jim chuckled. "We already have two strikes. Requesting an airline discount and declining the breakfast supplement."

Julie laughed as she plucked one of her long blonde hairs from Jim's shoulder. "Airline people may be well traveled, but we're cheap."

"Probably why Monsieur Sneer gave us this *charming* garret." A frown formed on Jim's face as he scanned the room, a hodgepodge of European modern and French provincial. Lace curtains didn't cover the span of windows allowing light to stream in during the day and curious eyes to peer in at night from the hotel across the street.

Julie put a finger to his lips. "It *is* tres charming. I love it.

Think Mimi from *La Boheme*. I'm in Paris with the man I love. No complaints."

He kissed the finger. "That's why I love you. You keep me grounded."

"Not what you said when we met at 35,000 feet." she said with a wink. "Took you to new heights, is how you put it. Remember?"

Jim nodded. "I'm just a sucker for a woman in uniform." He handed his giggling wife a croissant and jar of marmalade.

"Merci, mon cher." Julie put the coffee and food on the dresser before helping him off with his coat. She hugged him and held the embrace.

"Madame, if you're très, très bonne, there's baguette." Thrusting his pelvis forward against her robe he exaggerated his accent. "Eet ees much sought after here in Paree."

"We're both lucky I prefer petite brioche." She measured an inch between her thumb and forefinger.

Jim contorted his face; his shoulders slumped. "C'est la vie."

She grabbed his crotch. "Cheer up Mister. A weekend in Paris will grow that brioche into a baguette."

"Yahoo!" He kissed her cheek. "Sex on every continent should be our goal."

Julie poked him in the ribs. "Isn't it? What else is there to do in Antarctica?"

Jim leaned down and kissed her head. "Gotta love working for an airline. Jetting off anywhere in the world."

Julie squeezed his arm. "You'd bleed jet fuel, Mr. Intercontinental."

Jim Abernathy, a mid-level manager for Intercontinental, sold services like maintenance, baggage running, and customer handling to other airlines using company staff. "Opposite of outsourcing," he boasted to friends, "I've saved hundreds of jobs." He called company honchos, who aggressively farmed out work, *callous, heartless, and short sighted*. Jim often argued with his boss, Chad Wilkerson, whose words were etched into his brain. "Get aggressive, Abernathy! Screw unto others before they screw unto you."

A love of airplanes and exotic locales drew Jim to the industry after grad school. Family ties drove the devotion even deeper. His mother retired from the airline after two decades, a job taken to raise three kids after Jim's dad suffered a fatal heart attack in his early forties. Jim developed an affinity for the employees, especially the front line workers who formed the nucleus of his mother's social circle. He saw the company as an amalgam of its workers rather than glass terminals and titanium flying tubes. While business school classmates coveted careers in consulting and investment banking, Jim dreamed only of joining Intercontinental.

He met Julie onboard one of the company's flights a dozen years before and they married shortly thereafter. After their first introduction, Jim's mother said he'd be nuts to let Julie go. He cherished the fact that the two most important women in his life had become close friends.

Julie spread a bed sheet on the carpet on which the two set down to eat breakfast. The room's only chair had collapsed under the weight of their suitcase. Jim sat cross-legged while Julie lay on her side.

"Didn't hear you leave. Assumed you were on that damn phone again," Julie said, making a face. "They never leave you alone."

Jim dipped his croissant into the jam jar. "I'm lucky I have a job. Many of our friends have been laid off."

Julie cringed. "Wish you'd look someplace else. You've got so much to offer. And I could go back to work, help out," Julie said, caressing his arm. "Intercontinental chews people up and spits 'em out. I don't want that to be you."

"I'm lucky. They like me—*so far*. Besides, A-1 priority's a family. We agreed. I work, you make babies." He patted Julie's stomach. "Deal?"

"If we're lucky to get pregnant, I want our baby to know its papa." Her expression changed as she pressed his hand. "No one's safe there. I don't trust the lot of them. You shouldn't either."

From prior conversations, Jim knew that Julie left unspoken her fear that he'd share his dad's fate. His mom had often told Julie that a stressful job killed his father. "You make it sound dangerous," he said.

"It is. They treat people like dirt. That goes for Weston, Sweeny, and especially your boss, the evil dwarf." Julie poked Jim's chest with the mention of each name.

Jim dipped his finger in the marmalade and held it to his wife's lips. "Ssh. Doctor's orders, Madame Abernathy. Relax, remember? We're in Paris. May just conceive Baby Pierre or Yvette while we're here."

After two miscarriages, Julie begrudgingly accepted her doctor's order of a break from stress as a prescription for a full-term pregnancy. She hated placing the burden of becoming the family's sole breadwinner on Jim's already sagging shoulders. The leave of absence turned into full-blown unemployment when Intercontinental fired all employees on leave during an earlier financial crisis. Although the couple made having a baby their top priority, success eluded them.

Julie squealed. "There it is!"

Jim reached for his crotch. "My baguette?"

Julie rolled her eyes and punched his shoulder. "No goofball, the Eiffel Tower. Monsieur Sneer insisted we had a view, remember?" Julie pointed to the top of the tall window. "Well, there it is."

Jim squinted. "Don't see anything, except the building across the street."

"You're too high," Julie said, pulling down on his shoulder. "Get closer to the floor." He complied, bending down, his head inches from the carpet. "Now, look up. Over the roof line."

Jim wrinkled his nose and looked at Julie's beaming face out of the corner of his eye. "All I see is a satellite dish on the Four Seasons roof." Julie moved closer. He flinched, anticipating a whack for his sarcasm. Instead with a chuckle she grabbed his cheeks and kissed him repeatedly. Jim's eyes enlarged. "What's that for?"

Julie sighed. "Romance. Eating croissants in Paris under the Eiffel Tower with the man I love."

Jim loved her madly. He saw them journeying through life together, growing old one adventure at a time. She didn't need a ritzy suite, expensive clothes, or dazzling jewelry. She shared his wanderlust and love of simple things like movies, long walks, and concerts in the park. She'd make a great mother and he wanted, more than anything, to make that dream come true. Sure work was crazy, and he often felt like he clung to the reins of a whirling, out-of-control carousel horse, but Julie gave him the will to hang on at all costs.

He caressed her, kissing her neck and lips. His hand slipped under her robe. "Madame Abernathy?" he whispered into her ear.

She batted her blue eyes. "Oui Monsieur?"

"Your baguette awaits."

"Ooh la la," she cooed, rolling onto her back.

They made love on the hotel room floor.

Julie's eyes narrowed. "What's that?" She asked, lifting her head.

"If you gotta ask, I'm embarrassed for you," he snickered.

"That noise." Her eyes wandered to the dresser. "It's your phone."

"Maybe they'll go away," he said, pressing his lips to hers. The vibrations persisted.

"Damn it!" Jim pulled himself off of her and she covered her face. "I'm sorry honey," he whispered.

"We never escape that job. They hunt you down everywhere—London, Tokyo, Rio. We toured Italy with a phone pressed against your ear."

Jim shrugged. He mouthed apologies as he reached for the phone. "I know honey, but that's the airline business—24/7—exciting and exasperating. Allows us to weekend in Paris, lunch in New York, and sunbathe in Sydney."

Julie twisted a length of her hair. "I know I sound like an ungrateful bitch, which I promised myself I'd never become. It's just that—"

"We want to start our family. And, this really fucks with our fucking." His mouth slowly formed a smile as his words registered. He blushed.

Julie tilted her head and froze. Then she laughed uncontrollably as she lightly smacked his jaw. He laughed too. She always told him that his kind eyes, angel face, and sweet lips weren't made for swearing.

Jim winked. "Thatta girl. Gotta call Chicago. I'll be quick." He bent down and kissed her forehead.

Julie winked back with exaggeration. "Quick call to Headquarters? Ha!" She shook her head, "Hold on. It's only two in the morning in Chicago."

"But four in the afternoon in Tokyo. I'll call from the lobby. Give Monsieur Sneer another reason to hate me. Already thinks I'm a pest with faxes and my *broken French.*"

"The ugly American," Julie said as she clicked her fingers.

"Sneer's opinion or yours?" Jim furrowed his brow before tickling Julie's abdomen.

"Stop that!" she said between giggles. "Don't start something you can't finish."

"I'll finish you off later," he growled. "You shower and dress. We'll have the day in the City of Love to ourselves." Jim pulled up his trousers and threw on a sweater. He tucked his phone into his pocket.

"The Louvre, Rodin Museum and Eiffel Tower?" Julie asked as she rose from the floor.

"Take you to the roof of the Four Seasons Hotel if you'd like," he said, pointing out the window. He scurried into the hall, grabbing his coffee from the dresser as Julie's slipper bounced off the doorframe. Her laughter followed him into the hall.

As Jim made his way to the lobby, he considered their marriage. They'd been through hell with the failed pregnancies. She called him her rock, a source of emotional strength that saved her from a nervous breakdown. "You'd make a great father," she said. "I want to give you a baby."

He knew they weren't being completely honest with each other. Not wanting to worry her, he seldom talked about the stresses of work. How many times had he lied when he said things were going great? Yet his mother confided that Julie was well aware of the pressures, especially his ruthless boss who'd step on anyone to get ahead. Julie told his mom she knew he didn't want to burden her with his problems.

But how long could Jim hold on at work without cracking? That burning question remained smothered, by husband *and* wife.

⚜

Ninety minutes later, the elevator deposited Julie into the hotel lobby. She found him sequestered in a quiet corner.

"Mmm. You smell good." Jim said, sniffing the air. "I'm on a conference call with Chicago, our people in Tokyo, and a *very* angry customer in Beijing," he whispered, pressing the phone to his chest.

Julie pouted, flashing her puppy dog eyes that he found irresistible. He'd seen that disappointment all too often.

He hit the mute button. "Sorry, honey. I'll catch up for lunch. Our employees are threatening to walk off the job. A jumbo jet might land in Tokyo stranding four hundred and fifty Chinese on the tarmac."

Julie rolled her eyes. "You hope to broker a truce between China and Japan before lunch? Good thing Paris is also called the City of Light."

"Why's that?" Jim asked.

"I won't see you before dark." Julie bent down and pecked his cheek. "Au revoir, my love."

He mouthed *sorry* and *I love you* before blowing Julie a kiss as she pivoted and her black leather boots clicked over the tiled floor and out the front door into the bustling Rue de Rivoli.

Chapter 3

Hap Grabs a Lifeline

"He in there?" Hap asked.

As the secretary's eyes met his, her cheeks reddened to the shade of her lipstick. "He's just finishing up a call." The athletic blonde smiled and returned her attention to the computer screen.

Hap nodded, smoothing the panels of his flannel suit. He scrutinized Weston's secretary with curiosity, grinning as she rolled her lipstick tube out of view. While he wouldn't call himself handsome in the classic definition, he knew his penetrating eyes, confidence, and position of power appealed to women. A healthy diet and strict exercise regimen kept a beer gut, the curse of many men his age, at bay.

As he tapped the desk's privacy ledge, he wondered which Weston would greet him. Would it be the cowboy who bantered with informality, the pompous ass opining on economic theory, or the explosive executive obsessed with inefficiency? The conversation usually careened among all three. Hap adapted. His four-decade career, surviving under a variety of leaders, schooled him in flexibility.

After watching peers slip from favor and finding themselves booted from the airline, Hap learned that survival depended upon owning one expertise, and avoiding attachment to anything...or anyone. His keen knowledge of the operation proved indispensable. A nuts-and-bolts kinda guy, he ran circles around the rest of the stuffed shirts Weston surrounded himself with. The rank and file looked up to Hap, although time and position winnowed personal relationships. Once, he *was* one of them. Not anymore. Unflinching reflexes abandoned anything deemed a liability. Castoffs included colleagues, mentors, paradigms, and values.

Hap comfortably wore the cap of a man feathered by decisions guided by political expediency and ambition. Now at the end of his career, he struggled for an exit strategy that left his life's work, Intercontinental, a strong and indelible company. Although ego remained an important consideration, Hap loved the company and the business. Weston, he understood, had the power to preserve the company...or crush it.

❧

"Come in, Hap." The booming voice belonged to his boss, company Chairman and CEO, Richard Weston III.

Hap never tired of the cavernous office's views: the canyon of skyscrapers lining the river and beyond that, the blue expanse of Lake Michigan. Seated behind the glass desk, Weston directed Hap to the conference table with a tilt of his head and wave of his arm.

Weston rose. He patted Hap on the shoulder before settling into a chair across the table. Custom suits with broad, vertical stripes did their best to conceal a portly physique. As Hap pulled his sleeves over his cufflinks, a smile formed on his lips, picturing the marshmallow-faced boss as the monopoly banker.

"You've seen Monday's editorial," Weston said, looking past his visitor. The skyline reflected in his rimless glasses, the gray eyes seemed to hold dominion over the metropolis.

"And Tuesday's and Wednesday's and..." Hap counted on his fingers.

Weston's head tilted to the left. Neck folds flowed over the white starched collar as he spoke. "Point taken. Irksome, meddling know-nothings think regulation and mandates are miracle cures."

"Haven't seen such an assault on aviation since the mayor's bulldozer scrimmage." Hap nodded toward Meigs Field before resting his hands on the granite, cold to the touch. He waited for Weston to make eye contact.

"Easy to launch salvos from an editorial board room. I won't be bullied." Weston looked toward the towers of the City's two major newspapers. "Airlines, defense firms, oil, and banks are today's targets. Look what happened to tobacco when media and government launched their witch-hunts. Tried, convicted, and sentenced to draconian taxes. Shackled by regulations." Weston crossed his wrists.

"Maybe they'll force us to paint warnings on our planes—*According to the Surgeon General, air travel is harmful to your mental health.*"

Weston laughed, finally turning his gaze from the window to Hap. "Your passion's admirable. You've been indispensable."

Hap nodded. "Driving unpopular changes."

"Together, we protected Intercontinental," Weston said, interlocking his fingers.

Hap felt his cheeks warm. "That's kind."

Weston leaned forward and pounded the table. "And accurate! This airline's a stronger investment today because of us. Couldn't ask for a better pardner."

There it was, Hap thought. *The earnest cowboy. I'm Tonto to his Lone Ranger.*

Hap's eyes widened. He cocked his head. "This isn't a farewell speech is it?" A protracted bankruptcy, combative labor relations and a history of financial turmoil created a revolving door of leaders. Optimism, arrogance, adventure and piles of money enticed would-be saviors across the threshold. Exhaustion, defeat, cynicism and taller stacks of cash drove them out.

Weston's jowls shook as he grinned. "I'm the sixth man to lead this airline in the last decade, an unhealthy trend that's contributed to the precarious position in which we find ourselves. No," he said shaking his head, "my work's not done."

Hap's shoulders relaxed. He may not have always agreed with Weston, but he didn't have the energy to prove himself to yet another CEO. He always wondered what lured the former mining executive to the troubled airline, anyway. Weston had become a legend turning Omega Mining into a global powerhouse. And from all accounts, Omega made him a multi-millionaire when he flipped it to a Brazilian conglomerate hungry for its significant reserves. He had a cushy life, shuttling between a Virginia estate and a Colorado ranch.

Weston removed his glasses and wiped his eyes. "I can't leave. The company's in remission, but not cured. Besides, what boy doesn't love toying with airplanes?" Weston chortled.

Hap offered a mild laugh. He found it difficult to picture Weston as a child. He doubted childish fascination with airplanes motivated him to take the company's reins. "I assumed a lapse of judgment keeps you here. Not sure why you signed on in the first place."

Weston snickered before narrowing his eyes. "Pride, you might say, drove my decision to come—an alchemist seeking gold, a wrangler taming a wild stallion."

"But an airline—a dysfunctional beast. Many say unsalvageable."

"Unsalvageable!" Weston bellowed with laughter. "Absurd. The sum of these parts may prove greater than the whole. Fetch a fortune at auction. A scavenger's delight." Hap cringed at the thought of his airline split into pieces, but hid his distress. He learned to mask his concern whenever his boss talked about the company like it was a chessboard pawn.

Weston replaced his glasses. "Friends called me nuts for

trading country squire for airline baron." Hap leaned forward, craving insight into Weston's inner thoughts. Even after three years of working together, the man remained an enigma. He never let down his guard or engaged in personal chitchat.

Weston inhaled, his chest puffed. "Money wasn't my motivator, although I figured I'd strike gold. Imagine performing a miracle—resurrecting a dinosaur. To be hailed as the man who changed the financial paradigm of an entire industry."

Hap cupped his chin. "An ambitious goal. Alchemists failed, didn't they?" He noticed a flash of ire in Weston's eyes that quickly vanished. "You're rather reflective today," Hap added.

Weston paused before speaking. "I'm fond of you. I respect your operational knowhow. And, I don't hold your forty-years with Intercontinental against you. This culture glorifies the past. Its fatal flaw."

"Your first directive made that perfectly clear." Hap alluded to Weston's executive order to dismantle the company's collection of historic memorabilia, a treasure of artifacts honoring the airline's legacy as one of the nation's aviation pioneers. As the new Chairman, Weston relegated portraits of his predecessors, including the company's beloved founder, to a storage closet. "Not a popular debut."

Weston growled. "I didn't come here to win popularity contests."

"Still, good thing you abandoned plans to sell the entire lot on the Internet," Hap said, adding a laugh.

Weston pointed a plump finger. "You influenced that decision. Would have created a messy distraction. I see that now."

Hap wagged a finger back at his boss. "The greatest PR campaign couldn't have extinguished employee fires."

Weston shrugged. "So you said and I listened, but it had rich symbolic value. I'm here to usher in a new era, to pull down the fences that keep this airline bound by an inglorious and unprofitable past." Weston's voice filled with emotion. "I see you beside me." Clenching the table's edge, he leaned toward Hap. "Make sense? You with me?" Weston frequently employed the pedantic technique. Hap knew his boss wouldn't stop prodding until his captive pupil acquiesced with a nod.

Hap's head bobbed up and down. "You got my full support."

"I know I do, my boy. Now, let's lunch." He rose with effort, huffing. "I asked Kay to have the boys set us up in the Board Dining Room. I've got news that will please you." Weston put his arm around Hap's shoulder and led him out the door.

⁕

The Board Dining Room faced south but gray curtains kept out the mid-day sun. The room's furnishings seemed scaled for a giant's palace. Huge pieces of abstract art covered the walls and a plush beige carpet softened the marble floor. Yellow tea roses appeared to cower in their dainty vase on the massive granite slab that served as the dining table.

As Hap waited for his boss to sit, he studied the linen placemats set with china, crystal, and silverware all emblazoned with the company logo, the letter *I* floating inside a globe. "I'd be content with bottled water and a sandwich."

"Nonsense! I don't do this every day." Weston sat back, waiting for the server to place the napkin on his lap. Other attendants hovered over chafing dishes and bowls brimming with salads on the sideboard.

Hap waved the napkin guy away. He considered an executive catering function frivolous. As the waiter recited the menu, Hap recalled the budget ax that ended many employee traditions: Christmas parties, picnics, anniversary luncheons, and award ceremonies. Most recently, the hatchet claimed the bags of peanuts promoted to customers as a *snack*.

Weston ordered steak and salmon. His appetite didn't

surprise Hap. He assumed that his boss's approach to business left conscience and constitution undisturbed. Hap was surprised, however, by his own hunger. He filled his plate.

Casual bantering consumed the conversation until Weston dismissed the waiters with the flick of his hand. Hap grew intrigued when his boss even excused the attendant tasked with replacing his coffee cup every few minutes to maintain a constant temperature. Alone, the two sat with coffee and a tray of desserts on the table between them. Weston grabbed a custard tart as he spoke. "An excellent lunch. A talented chef is one of the few remaining civilities of the executive suite."

Hap noticed his boss scrutinize him out of the corner of his eye, a look that dared any debate over the extravagance. He learned not to question his boss's pampered lifestyle.

Assembling a plate of fresh fruit, he simply replied. "A fine meal. You have news?"

Weston dabbed the corners of his mouth with his napkin. "Always the ops man—anxious to get to the point," he said, adding a paternal nod. "I've had many recent conversations with the Board regarding shareholders. This is a business, not a charity. A concept lost on employees and unions who gripe about concessions. Christ, they brand us as extortionists, carpetbaggers who used bankruptcy as a pretext to pillage. They complain of sacrifices, forgetting that bankruptcy wiped out shareholders."

Hap rose to pour more coffee, offering the same to his boss who motioned for a fresh cup. "I don't disagree," Hap said, "Employees don't understand capitalism. They grasp the concept of *customer*—"

"But are obsessed with *employee*," Weston interjected with a sneer.

"That can be understood, even excused. It's what they know, who they are. They can't comprehend *investor*. It's too abstract," Hap said, shaking his head.

"Too abstract!" Weston bellowed. "Blissful ignorance. Unions contribute to the unhealthy obsession. They push entitlements to the detriment of investors and customers." Weston's fork pierced a chubby éclair.

"We've been down this path before," Hap said, popping a raspberry into his mouth.

"We're spending millions on our product," Weston said as he chewed.

"You know my opinion. Enhancements are premature. The product may be platinum, but the service is still lead."

Weston's fork clattered onto the plate. "We exited bankruptcy with a plan. I went out on a limb. Convinced jittery creditors and investors we could differentiate our product. I sold *premium* travel with *premium* prices. That's how we escape the tar pit."

"But our own CFO calls air travel a commodity—loyalty to the lowest bidder. The Internet cemented that cold fact. Price drives demand, the same force that affects gold, oil, and pork bellies."

"Cheapskates may fill planes, but I'd blissfully piss off a dozen ninety-nine percenters to hook a single one percenter. Customers who pick airlines for products and services, not price, are the cornerstone of our plan. They pay for *all* of this." Weston's arm arced through the air before he pounded his fist on the table. "We're failing, and employees are to blame!" Hap noticed beads of sweat form between the strands of white hair that crossed Weston's chalky scalp.

"We've all seen the avalanche of letters from disgruntled customers. The media frenzy speaks for itself." Hap's stomach soured. He wished he hadn't eaten so much.

"Occupy my ass! We must silence the drums beating for regulation," Weston added.

Hap rubbed his stomach. "What do you have to make me happy? Frankly, I'm nauseous. Even more depressed."

Weston smiled. Color returned to his pallid cheeks. "We must change employee attitudes and behaviors. Nearly impossible with our cynical bunch. The Board and I want to increase the odds."

"Wilkerson could lead an effort. He has the know-how. Airport employees report to him," Hap said, recalling how he already ordered the know-it-all to fix customer service.

"He may be talented, but he has neither the time nor finesse for this work. We're dealing with people here. The task of aligning employees to our business plan requires sensitivity. Someone seen as sincere. Ideally a person, employees already respect. That disqualifies Wilkerson and every other current vice president." Weston leaned his head back and snorted.

Hap sighed. "Sad."

Weston shot back. "Not *sad*, a reflection of the skills needed to rise from the rubbish heap of bankruptcy. I'm authorizing a new officer to marshal employees to our cause. Attitudes and behaviors *must* change."

Hap froze. "I'm astounded."

Weston patted Hap's arm. "I knew you'd be pleased. You love this company."

"This is the jolt we need." Hap's mind raced to Charlie's letter and the never-ending cascade of other employee complaint letters.

"Frankly, I've no patience or skill to mollycoddle people who wallow in self pity and lament the loss of the good old days," Weston said as his eyes rolled.

Hap concurred with his boss's self-assessment but chose discretion. "An employee champion sends a positive message."

"Take this person under your wing."

Left alone, Hap considered the impact of Weston's news. He pulled the note from his breast pocket. He didn't have to. The letter's last paragraph was etched in memory.

I thought your promotion would change things—one of us on top. Now I doubt Intercontinental will survive—maybe it shouldn't.

The company risked collapse from within if Charlie's feelings were pervasive—a self fulfilling prophecy more dangerous than the media or Washington bureaucrats.

Hap walked to the window and parted the curtains. He stared transfixed in thought until jarred by the reflection glaring back at him. The features were worn, the eyes, desperate. The glowering face of a man weighed down by a deep foreboding about the company's future...and his legacy.

Weston had thrown him and Intercontinental a lifeline—resources for which workers clamored. Would he be able to redeem himself with jaded employees such as the frayed letter's author, his old buddy Charlie?

But questions nagged him. He muttered aloud. "Richard Weston III and employee support! What's he up to?"

Chapter 4

Jim's Hazard—Wilkerson

Jim Abernathy pulled his car under the portico to grab some shade as he waited for his boss to emerge from the private country club. He and Wilkerson had finished a round of golf with an important client and planned to return to the office. Jim used the quiet moment to check in with his wife. He smiled as Julie's face, mugging with Mickey Mouse, filled the phone's screen.

"Honey, that's great news!" he shouted.

"Not sure I'd call heaving in the toilet, great news." The speaker amplified her voice. A loitering valet turned toward the open car window then quickly averted his eyes to a flowerbed.

"You know what I mean." Jim switched off the speaker and lowered his voice.

"Yes, but we've been here before. Last night's fish could be the culprit. Said it smelled funny," Julie moaned.

"I'm optimistic, Mama Abernathy."

"You always are—that's why I love you. Where are you, anyway?"

"In my car, outside Wilkerson's club. I'm playing chauffeur, which from the looks of it is par for this course." His neck arced to a line of waiting luxury sedans with capped drivers.

"Finally suspended tipsy Wilky's license, huh?" Julie snickered.

"He's right here, let me ask. Julie wants to…" He pulled the phone away from his ear in anticipaton of his wife's response.

"Oh no! Tell me you're joking." The panic in her voice buff-ered through the car.

Jim roared as he returned the phone to his ear. "He's inside signing the tab. I volunteered to drive. Wanted a captive audi-ence. Gives me the cold shoulder in the office."

"So you and Chad the Lad spent the morning golfing—male bonding?"

"All business. We shot a round with bigshots from that big Chinese airline customer." He looked toward the club entrance as someone exited. It wasn't his boss.

"I remember. Paris." Julie drew out her words. Jim imag-ined the rolled eyes and adorable little pout.

"That'd be the one—got me into deep kimchi with my boss *and* you."

"Oh Jim, my stomach."

Jim tapped his forehead and wrinkled his nose. "Sorry. Forgot."

"So how'd it go? You make nice nice with the angry Chinese?"

"Their business stays. Wilkerson can be charming when it suits him."

"Really? Never saw that side of him."

"Fairways and putting greens bring out the best in him," Jim said, his eyes fixed on the clubhouse door.

"Not to mention the clubhouse bar—that much I know. I'll never understand how that nitwit got to be a senior vice president. You run circles around him."

"And there you have it ladies and gentlemen, the unbiased opinion of Mrs. Jim Abernathy." Jim used his best sport's an-nouncer imitation then chuckled into the phone.

"You'd make a great vice president and you know it."

"Stop!" He cringed. "Not sure I want to be a VP at Intercontinental."

There was a time when Jim fantasized about a vice president title. He worked hard and loved the company. The promotion would reduce the couple's financial pressures and allow Julie to be a stay-at-home mom without stress. But Jim didn't share all of his misgivings with his wife. She had enough to worry about. However, his mom was another story. As a company retiree, she sympathized with his plight. Last time they spoke, he confided that Intercontinental's officer club wasn't one in which he craved membership. He was beginning not to recognize or even like the place anymore. But with a soon-to-be pregnant wife and a tanking economy, he felt stuck.

Julie spoke up. "You're right. I don't want you to do that to yourself either. It's just that when I see——" Julie stopped.

"Yes?" Jim interrupted the long pause, although he guessed how she'd end the sentence.

"Never mind. Did Chaddy Kathy have anything nice to say? Maybe *thank you* for landing that new million dollar account?"

"Chad Wilkerson? The one who begins every sentence with *I* and ends every one with *me*? Actually, he laid into me pretty good on the drive over." Jim pulled at his hair with his free hand.

"What in God's name for?" Irritation filled Julie's voice. He recognized the tone. The same used when she told him that his devotion to the airline came at the expense of his health and sometimes even the marriage.

"Settle down, grizzly mama. Little cub survived." Jim loved his wife's unwavering support. No matter how horrible things got at work, Julie welcomed him home with a hug, encouraging words and on really bad days, a martini. She was his personal cheerleader.

"Wilkerson thought I should have been in Tokyo. Says I wasted time negotiating. Threats work quicker. I'm soft on employees, swimmin' against the tide, don't you know."

"He said *that?* What more could you have done that you didn't cover on twelve hours of calls? Time spent, mind you, while I toured the Louvre and strolled the Tuilleries, enjoying a romantic weekend in Paris... *by myself!*"

"Something's eating him—probably pressure from his boss. The two can't stand each other. I'm just a convenient whipping boy." Jim noticed more activity at the clubhouse door.

"If Hap Sweeny pooped in Chad Wilkerson's diaper, yippee! I'd gladly kiss Hap's shiny, bald head."

"Gotta run honey. Wilkerson's weaving toward me now. Take care of yourself *and* the baby." Jim grinned, catching his reflection in the rear view mirror. His green eyes danced.

"Keep dreamin'! My money's on spoiled salmon." Julie's groan suggested another trip to the bathroom.

The valet approached Jim's car as a red-faced Wilkerson rocked at the curb like a little boy waiting for the school bus. Jim lowered his window. "Sir, he's with you, right?" The skinny kid with the red jacket thumbed toward Jim's boss. "Mr. Wilkerson insists we stole his car." The kid's voice mixed annoyance and deference, a balance Jim recognized from his days as an airport supervisor. He felt sorry for the valet. Dealing with people like Wilkerson was a thankless task. "I tried to tell him we didn't park his Testarossa or any other Ferrari today for that matter. But, he's insistent." Beads of sweat accumulated on the valet's forehead.

"Thanks. I'll handle it." Jim winked. He unbuckled his seat belt just as his boss zigzagged toward the car. Wilkerson's tiny black eyes peered into the window and his mouth formed a goofy grin. As he fumbled with the door handle, Jim reached across the seat and opened the door.

"You okay?" Jim asked as Wilkerson collapsed into the seat. The valet sighed, whisked around the car and shut the door with a sweeping arm.

"Damn fool claims I drove." Wilkerson waved the skinny kid away. "Stupid car jockey."

"Where are your clubs?" Jim asked, ignoring the comments.

"My clubs?" Wilkerson looked at his feet and craned his neck to the backseat. He ruffled his mop of white hair. "Musta left 'em in the rack. I'll call the pro chop...*shop*. Clubs can use some spiffing, anyway." Wilkerson fumbled in his pocket for his cell phone, connecting to the pro shop only with Jim's assistance.

From the phone exchange, Jim guessed that Wilkerson made a habit of forgetting his clubs. Explained why they sparkled. After securing Wilkerson's seatbelt, Jim put the car in gear and headed down the tree-shaded road to the club exit.

"Like your job?" Wilkerson broke the silence, barking out his question.

"Love it." Jim smiled.

"You're lucky." Wilkerson's window pulsed up and down until it finally lowered.

"Putting people to work is great. Beats downsizing. The revenue's nothing to sneeze at either." Jim's finger tapped the head of the gearshift.

"It's not gonna last." Singing the words, Wilkerson turned from the side window as the car exited onto the main road.

"Excuse me!" Jim noticed his boss's smirk out of the corner of his eye.

"Our costs are out-ra-geous with a capital *G*. We can't compete."

"But, my contracts are profitable. Every last one of them." Jim felt his shoulders tense and his stomach sour. He hoped he was hearing the vodka and not a voice of authority.

"Sure, you'll snatch victories." Wilkerson swatted the air. "But, they'll get harder and harder to find. You're shittin' yourself if you don't see that. *Outsourcing* rocks!"

Jim hated the word. Company leaders bandied it about as freely as a preacher's *amen*. He couldn't let it slide. "Giving work to our employees makes sense. And, makes money?"

"There you go again Jimmy boy. Swimmin' against the tide, blinded by employee sympathies. Sooner or later you'll accept reality. Management doesn't survive by brilliance or innovation. They survive by goin' with the flow. What happens when a fish leaves the school?"

"Graduates?" Jim shook his head. He didn't like arguing with a drunk.

"Becomes a barracuda's lunch, that's what. It's nature's way. The herd outsources, we outsource. The flock cuts benefits, we cut benefits. I'm gonna have to keep my eye on you." Wilkerson wiggled his finger toward Jim, his head weaving with the finger. Jim thought Wilkerson incapable of keeping his eye focused on anything at that moment.

"So, product, service and quality go out the window?" Jim asked.

"You serious? Save your sad little tale for the moms and pops that big boxes clobbered. Cost is king! Mark my words with our damn unions you can kiss your profit margins goodbye. Someone will come along who can do the work faster and cheaper. Hell, with a slight of hand, I could make your profits vanish, poof, zilcho. Simple accounting tricks Jimmy boy." Wilkerson waved his hands and laughed.

"That's depressing." Nauseous, Jim envied Julie's proximity to the toilet.

Wilkerson tapped his temple. "Only if you're unprepared."

"What's the end game for employees?"

Wilkerson's head shot up; his neck pivoted toward Jim. "*Our employees?* The unemployment line. They won't stomach the pay cuts we need to stay alive. They'd just as soon cut off a finger than make concessions. Pride is dangerous, Jimmy boy."

"What about growing the business to keep our people. Don't we owe it to them?" As Jim spoke, he heard his mother's voice. She made him promise when he got the job at Intercontinental to treat all employees, even lowly *peons* like herself with dignity and respect. He spent his career developing such a leadership style—sensitive, considerate, and respectful. He harvested results *and* relationships with equal vigor.

A sniff of vodka brought Jim's attention back to the conversation.

"Dreamer. You and my boss are two peas in a pod—two pissers into the wind," Wilkerson snickered, slurring his words.

"Hap's done pretty good for himself. I could find worse role models." Jim glanced at his boss, unsure of the direction in which he drifted.

"Hap's had forty years to mismanage this airline. He found a golden opportunity to hook me into cleaning up his shit. As the Chairman says, too much pandering to employees, too much managing from the seat of the pants and not enough spine and reason. Hap may be able to fool Richard Weston that he's drunk the Kool Aid, but he can't fool me. Your Hap Sweeny doesn't have the stomach for the tough decisions— *less* heart, *more* head." Wilkerson hiccupped before adding, "Be careful who you align with Jimmy boy—only one of us will survive." Wilkerson's chin dropped to his chest like a slowly deflating balloon animal.

Jim remained silent—the conversation turned dangerous. With any luck, Wilkerson would forget the discussion by tomorrow, if not sooner. Jim turned on the radio with the suggestion they catch up on business news.

As his boss started to snore, Jim worried about becoming a political liability. Wilkerson, he feared, wouldn't have to think too hard to drum up an excuse to fire him.

Chapter 5
Weston's Intentions Unmasked

La Plage, a restaurant whose stunning views of Oak Street Beach inspired its name, sat on the edge of Chicago's Gold Coast where Lake Shore Drive turned east. The master chef from Paris brought the city another three-star restaurant and ensured tables booked full with the city's social, cultural, and political elite.

Richard Weston reserved his favorite table that gave sweeping vistas of the restaurant as well as Lake Michigan. The tuxedoed maitre d'hotel oversaw every detail of the room with his customary aplomb. A variety of palms bathed in discreet lighting, softened the mood and muted the chatter. Yellow-veined marble, classic columns and Mediterranean seascapes evoked the Cote d'Azur.

Weston and Ingrid Shattenworter, the airline's chief of public relations, sipped champagne and picked at small plates of appetizers arranged on the table set for three. Ingrid's responsibilities included government affairs and all communication functions.

Weston rested his glass to pick up a biscuit. Using a tiny mother-of-pearl spoon, he topped the savory with crème fraiche and golden fish eggs. "Shame we took Dom Perignon and caviar off our flights," he said. "First class isn't the same."

"First class hasn't had class for years. Another casualty of 9/11." Ingrid sighed and tossed her head back sending her shoulder-length, platinum hair across her heart-shaped face. A flick of the neck and a brush of a hand restored her hair to await its next journey across her creaseless brow. Ingrid spoke in language styled as meticulously as her hair. Employees viewed her as unapproachable, a museum piece gazed at behind red velvet ropes. She never hurried, waited, or perspired for anyone, except her boss and benefactor.

Weston's gray eyes regarded her through his glasses. "Staff call you, *The Countess,* you know. No doubt because of the German accent."

Dressed in a white knit sweater-dress, she sat with the perfect posture of a porcelain doll. "I'm well aware of my nom de guerre—charming. I prefer to credit my looks and accessories." She lifted her hand over the table and pulsed her long fingers adorned with rings of precious gems. "Majestic infallibility."

Weston smirked. "You sound like the Pope." He leaned forward and whispered, "I understand that a crude variant of *Countess* is often mumbled by those leaving your office." He scrutinized Ingrid's reaction with childish delight. Her cocked head and narrowed eyes told him she processed the wordplay in her adopted language. Her violet eyes grew large and fiery. A spasm jerked her arm, upsetting her champagne glass. He stiffened. Squared shoulders smoothed the rumples of his black suit. He leaned back and raised a palm to deflect a presumed counter attack. Tension gripped the table until Ingrid's arms rose in an Evita-like address.

"I love it, absolutely love it. The Cuntess, ha. I may be a cunt, but I've got bigger balls than all of them." She roared with laughter. Nearby diners turned their heads toward the outburst. Weston waved off the maître d'hôtel who hurried toward the table with furrowed brow.

Weston beckoned the sommelier with a snap of his fingers.

"Another bottle of champagne. And tell our waiter we'll order when our tardy guest arrives."

"Who is this mystery guest?" Ingrid asked.

He knew that his penchant for intrigue captivated and disconcerted her. "Patience, my dear," he said, his cheeks puffing with blintz and sour cream. He studied her with a connoisseur's eye. "I'm surprised I haven't had to share you with another man."

She patted his arm. Her laugh and arched eyebrows were signs that she recognized his subject-changing ploy. "After I met you, I swore off marriage. I'm quite comfortable thanks to a shrewd collection of husbands."

"And divorce attorneys," Weston interjected with a nod.

She sipped from a crystal flute. "I don't need another man...or woman for that matter. Complicates things." She looked to her wrist filled with bracelets. "Besides, I have enough jewelry."

Weston added caviar and chopped egg to a toast point. "People have other needs."

She scoffed. "Casual flings are nothing. Sex is merely biology. Self-sufficiency, and pay-as-you-go, are options. Relationships should yield benefits. Take ours."

Weston considered her words. They were something he might have said. He looked out the window to the lake as he recalled their history, a relationship that went back nearly two decades. They met at Omega Mining when a renegade faction of that corporation's Board plucked Weston from a Canadian minerals conglomerate and appointed him CEO. They tasked him with sealing a merger at any cost to consolidate the international commodities market. Ingrid, in her early forties and recently divorced at the time, worked as secretary and *fixer* to the head of public and investor relations. Weston suspected that she moon-lighted as her boss's mistress.

Weston figured that Ingrid could guide him through company mine fields. His reputation as a swaggering maverick lassoed her allegiance. She didn't disappoint, using a vast network to weed out threats to his mission. Intrigue, he discovered, seduced her and the promise of power was a potent aphrodisiac. Without much effort, he manipulated her into a betrayal. She shared incriminating emails from her boss that revealed a conspiracy to sabotage the merger by artificially depressing Omega's stock price. Weston crushed the plot. With the SEC and financial ruin barking at their heels, his enemies couldn't resign fast enough.

Weston's victory cemented his power at the helm of the commodities giant. He led two publicized efforts to drive up commodity prices and rumors pegged him as the mastermind behind several notorious runs to corner world markets. The schemes included a spike in the price of titanium, the chief component in airframes. Politicians took notice.

The pair's sexual relationship lasted two years until Weston's wife and children joined him in the U.S. He rewarded his co-conspirator handsomely with a bounty that included her former boss's job. Expanded responsibilities gave Ingrid access to high-level people in Washington. She used her position to protect and mold her benefactor into the image he now presented to the world.

"Yes," he said, turning from the window. "We've been good for each other."

Ingrid's nostrils flared. "I should say. I transformed you from rogue to polished powerbroker." A snap of her head sent her hair across her face.

Weston raised an eyebrow as he stared into her eyes. "So, I'm your creation?"

She stiffened. "I introduced you to Washington and Wall

Street. I offered pinstriped legitimacy to the Wild West cowboy."

He scoffed, "Including my manufactured pedigree."

"Don't sneer. Dick Weston became Richard Weston the Third. I tamed the tumbleweed. When Intercontinental's Board coaxed you out of retirement, I never doubted you'd resume our collaboration."

Collaboration sounded too collegial to Weston. Instead, he imagined them as symbiotic partners, who used each other to advance individual agendas. He marveled at her ease in concealing Machiavellian tools under the silk robes of a sophisticated and still sexy, businesswoman. Weston growled as he pressed his trunk of a leg against her calf. She bristled, moving her leg away.

His eyes narrowed. "Don't be a bitter and ungrateful bitch. I launched your glorious evolution from courtesan to Countess, from secretary to Senior Vice President."

The arrival of an escargot appetizer accompanied by a bottle of Chablis preempted her response. Weston grunted his approval of the wine.

Ingrid swirled the glass under her nose. "If you're going to expense this, we should pretend to discuss business. Before our dinner companion arrives."

Weston's outstretched palm invited her to proceed.

"Glad you moved your secretary's desk away from Winny. I never liked shared workstations for executive secretaries. Camaraderie compromises confidentiality."

He nodded as he held his wine to the candle flame. "Can't risk having Hap know my business. People gossip in the canteen over coffee and in the bathroom over a piss."

Ingrid snickered. "You notice our new employee messages?"

"Your propaganda campaign? Just because we use the word *transparency* in every sentence doesn't mean employees believe it."

"We must stick to a message and *repeat, repeat, repeat*." Her words clicked like an automatic rifle. "Employees have simple minds."

Weston's cocktail fork evicted a snail from its pastry home. He didn't buy her premise, but frankly it didn't matter that much. He didn't care what employees thought of him, but he did give a shit how it impacted their jobs. Weston grew weary of the topic and stared toward the lake.

Ingrid cleared her throat. "Our Chief Pilot criticized you. Suggested that financial concerns and management distractions compromise our safety programs."

Weston's head jerked back toward Ingrid. "What? Where, when?"

"So far only in internal meetings. But it questions his loyalty. I'll deal with him. Consider him gone. I'll leave no trail."

Weston nodded his approval.

Ingrid's pencil thin eyebrows arched as she pawed the tablecloth. "Now, tell me about your luncheon with Hap. I imagine he jumped at the offer. Anything to save his beloved airline."

Weston grinned like the Cheshire cat. "Hap's expression was priceless. He looked like he just hit a three hundred-yard drive straight down the fairway."

Ingrid smiled. "So he understands his role?"

"Yes," Weston responded. "But in terms he comprehends."

After clapping, Ingrid held her hands clasped in front of her. "No doubt an inspired performance. Our highest priority to save Intercontinental—duty to our employees and all that crap." She leaned forward. "You did show vulnerability as I suggested?"

"Hap seemed quite taken by my candor and sensitivity." Weston patted his chest and sighed.

Ingrid purred as her finger circled the rim of her wine glass.

"I didn't have to push hard," Weston continued. "Remember, Hap's invested forty years with Intercontinental. He wants to believe... but he's not stupid."

Ingrid tapped the table. "The word's *pragmatic*. Hap's got the survival instincts of a tiger. Don't forget that."

"Still, he's soft for this company. This airline defines him. He's proud of his life's work—probably pondering his legacy." Weston believed he knew how to play Hap. He'd met others like him during his career. While Hap never allowed himself to luxuriate in emotion, he'd embrace this assignment with passion. Ego was involved. Weston had seen sentimentality infect the blood of ruthless executives toward the end of their careers, like an atheist's deathbed conversion.

"At least he's on board. What about the new vice president?"

"Must be the right kind of person. I'll suggest to Hap that you provide counsel." Weston peered at her over his wine glass.

Ingrid nodded. "Understood. Nothing will spoil our plan."

Weston squeezed her hand tightly. "Use your powers. If the project threatens our scheme, smother it mercilessly."

"Even I have limits. At some point you'll have to tell Hap the truth."

"The truth?"

Ingrid rubbed her freed hand. "That you have no intention of running Intercontinental. You want to *sell* the airline, not fix it."

She was right. Weston wasn't the type of captain to go down with his ship. He had no interest in operating an airline. His aspirations soared higher. Intercontinental was merely a pawn to restructure the hemorrhaging industry. He'd gladly sacrifice the company to achieve his loftier ambition. Washington would take note and welcome the savior with confetti, open arms, and an array of opportunities. Senator, Cabinet post, top-tier Ambassador; it didn't matter.

"I'll concoct something," he said. The potential confrontation raced through his mind. He expected Hap to explode if he discovered he was a patsy, spearheading an initiative designed as mere curb appeal to drive a higher sales price. Still, Weston accepted the risk. He needed the window dressing to attract buyers, but more importantly he needed to keep Hap, a man with the power to derail his plans, distracted.

"You could always lie. Say that the company turnaround is your primary goal and a sale merely a last resort," Ingrid said. "Tell him his dear, little employee project is insurance."

Weston sighed. "In a way, it is. Many things could kill a sale."

Ingrid clicked her tongue and shook her head. "If the seller were anyone but Richard Weston III. You *will* sell. Use *your* powers." Ingrid licked caviar from her finger. "You're too big to fail."

Weston leaned across the table, as far as his stomach allowed. "Yet I worry. Hap loves the airline. May quit if he discovers what's really going on. I need his operational expertise, at least for now. Then there's always a threat he sabotages me."

Ingrid smirked. "We've dealt with conspirators before." The deep purple pools of her eyes reflected the dancing candle flame.

Weston smoothed the tablecloth. "If Hap figures things out, I'll play the distressed seller. I'll shrug, pat him on the back, and urge him to see the silver lining."

"And that is?" Ingrid asked.

"His good work allowed us to horse trade from a position of strength. The best deal for *our* beloved company," he said before glaring at her. "Hap had better not stir things up if he knows what's good for him. Goes for all my soldiers."

Ingrid nodded, then craned her neck, scanning the restaurant. "I'm still dying to know who we're dining with."

"The Secretary of Transportation." He studied Ingrid's face for surprise. She remained cool, except for a quick glance toward the window. He caught her checking out her reflection. "If I can't find a U.S. buyer," he continued, "we must overturn foreign ownership restrictions. The current limitations are asinine. Secretary Stevens can help."

"Comes down to a pissing contest between Congress and the President," Ingrid said, before sipping her wine.

"And Klein's the biggest pisser of the bunch. His chairmanship is problematic." Weston snarled. He wished Klein were an easier target.

"He's been a nasty thorn in our side."

"And blissfully, to the current Administration. They're frustrated by his grandstanding on several initiatives."

"What are you getting at?" Ingrid asked.

"Opportunities. Leave that to me." Weston waved her off. "Continue to march your people and lobbyists toward a favorable resolution. I've got other tricks, which shall remain a secret even from you. More insurance."

"I wouldn't respect you if you didn't keep a few secrets… even from me." Her tone was almost convincing, yet he knew that secrets drove her crazy. Her mind, he assumed, probably raced with potential scenarios.

She blinked toward the restaurant foyer. "If you'll excuse me, the Secretary has arrived. I'll escort him to the table."

A wave of his hand signaled consent. Alone, he stared again out the window. The lake's black expanse mesmerized him. He looked to the shoreline where sparkling skyscrapers met the void in a knife-edge separation of light and dark. He viewed business the same way, a black and white world where men and ideas constantly collided. Only cowards and thinkers languished in the gray.

He mumbled to himself. "Dick Weston will succeed. Regardless of the casualties."

Chapter 6

Ingrid and Weston Versus Washington

Chords of *Hail to the Chief* pulsed from Ingrid Shattenworter's handbag. The ring meant one caller, Richard Weston. The head of PR managed her cell phone with Prussian precision. Unique tones heralded Weston, government officials, a stock-broker, and stylist. She relegated others deemed privileged to have her number, to silent mode.

"Christ! What does he want?" Ingrid muttered. She reached to the passenger seat of her roadster, groping in her purse for her earpiece. Her latte teetered in the cup-holder. "Not even seven o'clock. I'll be there in fifteen minutes."

Besides blind loyalty, Ingrid demanded real-time informa-tion from her people. "No surprises—*ever*," she barked at new staffers. Employees who failed didn't get a second chance.

She brushed aside her platinum hair to set the earpiece and answered with poise. "Good morning Richard. I'm nearing the Wabash Avenue Bridge."

～✦～

In his office high above the city, Weston switched to speak-er mode. He rose from his desk, lumbered to the window and scanned the bridge for the bright red SL-600. "Just got off the phone with Klein's chief-of-staff. The Congressman wanted to give me a heads up. I'm being summoned before his commit-tee." The sound of Ingrid groaning pleased him. She should be as pissed as he was.

He dropped into a chair and continued, "Klein's lackey prattled on about the *egregious*—his fancy word—service failures reported by the media. I get to share the hot seat with other CEOs and the Chairman of the Airline Carriers Association."

"How much time do we have?" Ingrid asked.

"None. The grilling is Monday." He gripped the chair. The veins on his hands rose like blue rivers on his snowy flesh. "You should have known this." She was silent. A labored inhale fueled more rant. His eyes squinted on Ingrid's Mercedes. "The twit labeled this a *courtesy* call. Malcolm Klein always calls me personally. The message is clear. I can expect a public flogging." His hands shook. "I detest being bullied."

The threat of public ridicule terrified him. He spent his childhood the butt of endless taunting. The scrawny, mama's boy in the rugged world of Montana cattle country. His own father laughed until he got a mean look in his eye, fueled by whisky and frustration. Then he punched the hell out of little Ritchie *to toughen up the little pansy*.

"Richard, are you there?" Ingrid's raised voice jerked his head to the desk speaker.

"Yes, yes. Go on."

"Klein smells a golden opportunity to parade CEOs in front of the cameras. I'll call Underlicht. We won't let you fail."

Weston's face warmed as he pounded the chair's arm. "I won't be made a fool by any Congressman." Humiliation would dash his political ambitions. His rage surged. "We can't give that committee any excuse to regulate us. That would destroy my plans to sell Intercontinental. I may as well hang the *For Sale* sign on a toxic dump."

"These hearings are staged, Congressional perp walks," Ingrid said.

Weston's fingers pinched the bridge of his nose. "Not a comforting image."

"Klein will paint a picture of chaos. He'll bait the industry into defense mode."

"Disastrous!" Weston bellowed.

"We simply don't snap at the bait. We spin this to our advantage. Besides, you still have friends in the Administration." Ingrid spoke slowly, her voice calm.

Weston rubbed his temples as he slogged toward his marble bathroom with its thirty-five thousand dollar commode. "We can't let Klein wipe his ass with me. I can't get stuck with this airline or I'm finished. The Administration isn't foolish. They won't pull me from a sinking ship—"

"While helpless employees and union leaders flail in the turgid water. Yes, I get it," Ingrid interjected. "*Pathetic.* Let's think." The phone went silent except for muffled street noise and Ingrid's breathing. Finally, she spoke. "Klein's picture of an industry in chaos works to our advantage. Supports your call for consolidation."

"Exactly right," Weston said, encouraged by Ingrid's scheme. She always came through for him. "Pruning deadwood brings financial and operational stability." He lowered his trousers and squatted.

"You make the preemptive strike. Leave the hearing hailed as a visionary."

"I need more than talk," Weston snarled.

"Yes, a shiny distraction for the cats to paw."

"Not too complex. These are congressmen." He pictured her mind racing—the needle of her internal tachometer edging into the red zone.

"I have it!" she bellowed. "A self-policed plan to protect and serve customers. We keep control. We even spin Hap's employee drivel into your message."

Ingrid excelled under pressure. Politics provided an adrenaline rush. Weston valued the messages she crafted from vapor. He recognized her moan in the phone as exhilaration.

"My head's swimming with ideas. Leave everything to me."

"I usually do. But, I can't be embarrassed." His words seethed through clenched teeth. With a grunt, he ordered Ingrid to his office by noon while purging his bowels of the power breakfast shared with an advance scout of the Cabinet vetting committee.

⁂

Ingrid barked at her phone to call Scott Underlicht, her man in charge of government relations and lobbying efforts.

Underlicht answered on the first ring, a perky *good morning* abruptly cut off by his boss's feverish voice. "7:09 and my day's off to an atrocious start. Just got off the phone with the Chairman. He's enraged by a call from Klein's lackey. He's to appear before the House Transportation Committee to defend the industry's service record. I loathe surprises, especially from my boss. I'll be kind and assume your ignorance. How could this happen?" Her hand pounded her car's steering wheel, dislodging a diamond from its platinum setting.

Underlicht stammered. "I... I d...didn't know. I'm sorry. We'll canvas our Hill contacts, at once."

Ingrid looked at her reflection in the car's rearview mirror as she launched into a harsh rebuke. "Listen! The Chairman's performance is critical to our future. Engage our congressional allies, immediately. Weston mustn't be badgered." She clutched the wheel and cursed the pedestrians in the crosswalk. She gunned the engine on the turn.

"I... I understand," Underlicht replied.

"We have seventy-two hours. Meet with Simons of the Airline Carriers Association. He's testifying too. Leverage his position as the industry's voice. Make him the lightning rod."

"Cohesive leadership isn't Simons' strength. He and the ACA are always pandering to individual carriers," Underlicht said.

"Push Simons into the spotlight. He's the perfect scapegoat."

"He won't make it easy."

She bristled. "Remind him who pays for his Armani suits and BMW." Ingrid paused before snapping. "Is that clear?"

"Very clear."

"Good. Simons becomes the target. We join the outcry, pinning the industry's ills on his inept leadership." Ingrid caught her grin in the mirror.

"Blame shifting is a favorite Washington sport."

"The public won't penalize Simons or the Association. Hell, they don't even know the ACA. The perfect patsy. If Klein wants a sacrificial lamb, we serve up Simons," Ingrid said, flipping off a honking cabbie.

"That could work." Underlicht's voice regained its composure.

"Of course it will. Now get over to the ACA. Gather intelligence. Competitors will be in a nervous scramble. We don't need complete victory, we simply need to out finesse everyone else."

Underlicht's upbeat tone sounded forced. "I'll mobilize the team immediately."

"You've got a lot of ground to recover, understand?" She didn't wait for his response. "Weston and I travel to Washington on Sunday. Meet us at the airport. Drive us to our hotel. We'll update him at dinner. Arrange it."

"You can count on…" Underlicht's voice faded.

Ingrid rolled her eyes. "Count on you? Ha! I never give a third chance. I'll gather division heads to mold our message." She accelerated the car through a stale yellow light, narrowly missing a bike messenger. "I'll send you talking points to leak to Klein's committee."

"I'll probe for landmines." Underlicht spoke with the confidence of someone who'd launched the same exercise hundreds of times.

"No more surprises for Weston. Embarrassing CEOs is great sport on Capitol Hill—diverts eyes from Congress' dismal ratings."

"Klein probably has other tricks up his sleeve."

"Malcolm Klein underestimates me." Ingrid's phone went dead as she pulled into the executive garage.

She mumbled under her breath, "Congress isn't the only one with miserable ratings nor is Klein the only one with tricks."

An awakening Headquarters didn't know that a cyclone bore down on it that Friday morning.

<hr/>

As Ingrid swept into her office, her assistant jumped from her desk to catch her boss's fur vest and designer handbag. "Call the team to the conference room. Track people at home. Get into my car. One of my babies escaped." Ingrid waved the damaged ring under her secretary's nose.

Jeannette was immune to her boss's curt directives. An icy blonde cut from 1960's *Vogue*—Jeannette wore sculpted hair and designer clothes. Viewed beside her modern colleagues, she seemed an anachronism who evoked images of classic Hitchcock beauties—more Tippi Hedrin and less Grace Kelly. She wielded her boss's power with the reckless abandon of a teenager shopping with a parent's credit card.

In her office, Ingrid phoned senior vice presidents. The calls were quick, clipped and consistent. She summarized the emergency and ordered her peers to come prepared to present and defend ideas.

At nine o'clock, haggard division heads assembled in Ingrid's conference room to offer ideas for a service pledge that Weston would present to Congress. Ingrid delivered opening remarks towering over the executives, her palms resting on the table. "Failure's *not* an option."

By ten o'clock, Ingrid had her plan—a sketchy blueprint of extorted promises, foggy assumptions, untested components, unspoken requirements, and unidentified resources.

⋙◆⋘

At eleven o'clock, Ingrid burst into Weston's office, arms flourishing the air. "Stroke of luck," she announced. "We uncovered a pledge made to customers a decade ago."

Weston's brow furrowed. "Sounds like a discard found under a sheet in an attic. I will not peddle crap," he barked.

Ingrid shook her head and smiled as she approached his desk. "It's still relevant. A little nip here, tuck there, and we introduce the pledge as a fresh response to customers."

"Sounds like a used car salesman." His trembling hand ruffled some papers.

"Trust me. Our media campaign will be as polished as your Bentley."

Weston sat back. His gray eyes narrowed behind his rimless glasses. "A *pledge* has a certain heartfelt ring to it. The sap Main-Streeters love."

"Dripping with sincerity." Ingrid contorted her face. "It will silence the regulatory hounds."

"With luck, we rid ourselves of this damn company before we must deliver on the thing." His laugh set multiple chins in motion. "How do we ensure this pledge wins acceptance?"

Ingrid grinned as she rubbed her hands together. "Late Sunday, you place a call to Simons of the ACA. Detail the pledge.

Urge his endorsement. Tell him to pressure competitors to adopt it. A united industry will ambush Klein and rally our allies who loathe big government."

"Why wait until Sunday night?"

"Competitors won't have time to respond. Our brethren, naked without an offering of their own, will run to our side like frightened children." She mocked the competitors, feigning a worried expression and cowering shoulders.

Weston beamed. "Brilliant. That hang together or hang apart bullshit. We mark the industry trail."

"And Richard Weston III positions himself as a maverick for change—calling for consolidation, while offering his own version of a Passenger Right's Bill." She lifted her chin and pushed out her chest.

He smirked. "A watered down and unenforceable piece of crap."

"That greases the way for an unencumbered sale of Intercontinental—sliding you right into a juicy appointment." Her hand glided down an invisible ski chute.

Weston pushed himself up from his desk and put his arm around his spin merchant. He whispered into her ear, "Success swings open the Cabinet door, transportation or commerce."

Chapter 7
Weston Won't be Bullied

"Thank you for taking my call." As Weston spoke, his fingers slowed from a frenetic patter to a gentle tap on the arm of the chair. He stared out the window of the Four Seasons suite, his home since taking the helm of Intercontinental three years before. His eyes followed the stream of red lights tracing a slow advance up Michigan Avenue through the gauntlet of hotels and high-end stores toward the indigo blue lake.

"Hope I haven't kept ya waitin'. I'm a public servant after all." The man's gravel voice and exaggerated laugh suggested to Weston an excessive intake of brandy and tobacco.

"I couldn't assume public access extended to weekends or the sanctity of your club."

"True, but you're not the average Joe. Are you, Richard?"

Weston's hearty laugh echoed in the solitary suite. "*Average* isn't bad. My enemies call me much worse and ass-kissers flatter with superlatives. Impossible to live up to either."

Congressman Malcolm Klein inhaled deeply on what Weston assumed was a Cuban cigar. "Politicians share the same fate," Klein said. "Average is a compliment."

"The last person to call me average was a Paris prostitute. Candor, such a French trait. A consequence, I guess, of a no-tipping culture," Weston said with a grin.

"Now you're plungin' into international affairs. Not my area of expertise. I thought you might be callin' about Monday's hearings," Klein said. Something clanked in Weston's ear. He pictured the Congressman swirling a brandy snifter that tapped the receiver. The image annoyed him. His irritation grew as he imagined Klein relishing his powerful advantage.

"Indeed, I couldn't wait until Monday to tell you how excited I am about your spectacle. Practically pissin' my pants." Weston felt emboldened by the crinkled sheet of paper in his pudgy fingers. The document, prepared by an operative, embedded in the Congressman's office, listed anticipated committee questions.

"I assure you, this isn't political theatrics," Klein said. "Public's fed up with the airlines. Service failures are a national epidemic. You forced my hand."

Weston detected growing agitation in Klein's voice as he reached for his own Cuban cigar. "Save the drama for the cameras, Malcolm. We both know the reasons behind these hearings." Weston's nostrils flared. He felt his blood pressure rise. He pictured Klein sitting like almighty God, rendering judgment and poking his prey like a shit-grinning, schoolyard bully.

"You can't dismiss the industry's dismal record," Klein said. His words came over the phone like an evening news sound bite. Weston seethed. He pictured a smirk that undoubtedly accompanied the glib indictment. He predicted Klein would repeat the phrase before the cameras, *ad nauseam*.

Weston volleyed back. "And your motivation's crystal clear—survival and revenge."

"What?" Klein blurted. "Outrageous!"

Weston smiled. He pictured a chorus of withered balding heads turning toward their club brother, Klein at his outburst. "Protecting the little people plays well in an election year. Your personal vendetta is common knowledge. Your poor daughter and grandson, trapped on a plane."

Klein's voice regained its composure. "Their testimonials are compelling. You'll hear them yourself. But they're not unique."

"People will find your indignation insincere. Dormant until family became victims."

"I'm willin' to take that chance. Ignorin' the issues would be irresponsible."

"Tsk, tsk—spare me. Our customer complaint department found hundreds of letters from disgruntled flyers. Care to guess what influential Congressman was copied in on every one, yet did nothing? Tell me, does that sound like a consumer champion?"

"Airin' your dirty laundry would be foolish. You'd be hanged with your own rope," Klein said as his breathing became heavier.

"Am willin' to take that chayance," Weston said, parroting the Congressman's words and cotton country drawl.

"Your funeral."

"Speaking of death, let's talk about your political career." Weston swirled his tumbler of Scotch, tapping the mouthpiece.

Klein cleared his throat, a sound amplified over the phone as a disdainful grunt. "I'm well aware of your ardent support of the current administration. No secret your money's on the President's party in upcomin' mid-terms."

Weston glanced to his lap and a list of PAC contributions Underlicht faxed him earlier in the day. "Malcolm, I hate to point out ingratitude, but Intercontinental has donated handsomely to your campaign."

"I applaud your impartiality."

"It's nothing, merely the ante for a jigger of influence in Washington. Not an exorbitant price to have take my call on a Saturday night."

"Your financial support is appreciated and your irritation concerning Monday's hearing, duly noted. Anything else I can do for you, Richard?"

"You mentioned the mid-term elections."

"It's clear you back the President and his pro business party. If they wrestle control of the House, I can still champion my causes from the minority. My power comes from my tenure, not my position, and certainly not my party."

Weston sneered. "You underestimate me." The phone went quiet. "Malcolm, are you still there?"

"I'm listening."

"I'm not stupid. Your Chairmanship's not my target. No, I'll end your tenure *completely*."

"Ha! An idle threat."

"Not anymore. New campaign finance laws give me fresh opportunities." Weston glanced to the pages of the dossier scattered at his feet. "I'd throw you a nice retirement bash— a nod to all you've done for our industry. Even toss in some airline passes. Take your little lady to Hawaii. And I don't mean Mrs. Klein."

Weston heard the crash of glass against wood and the clatter of ice cubes. Klein's labored breathing and the muted chatter of club conversations were Weston's only clues that the Congressman didn't hang up. Weston continued to poke. He had the bully on the defensive. "Of course no one gives your opponent much chance in the upcoming election—young, idealistic, unconnected, under-funded. Am I correct?"

"Yes. Go on." Klein's voice became more muted.

"Malcolm, no one can deny your dedication to this industry. More hawk than dove but a galvanizing force nonetheless. I don't want to see your run end."

"But?"

"I assure you, ongoing interference is not my aim. Hell, I enjoy watching you stir up trouble for my competitors."

"That's comforting. What do you want?"

"As a concerned citizen, I feel obliged to point out that your motivations are distorted by personal interest. I can't blame you for not seeing that yourself. You're only human. I'm merely asking you to reflect, determine whether your zeal might best be tamed, even redirected. If not, we'd have to take a serious look at your opponent."

"You want me to go easy on Monday?" Klein exhaled.

Weston smirked at the sound of defeat in the Congressman's voice. " I want you to be fair. Let us police ourselves. If we fail, come after us in a year with extended talons. Even then, you'll have better success plucking off the weaklings one-by-one, rather than attacking us together."

❦

After he hung up, Weston sat back and emptied his glass of whisky. He was pleased with his performance. Money was power. It bought information, influence, and silenced bullies. Between Ingrid's schemes and his own ploys, he had scotched this snake. But he knew that other rocks dotted the trail under which more rattlers lurked. Even Klein couldn't be trusted to slither away quietly. Weston looked again out the window. The lake turned black and turgid under an approaching storm.

Chapter 8
Weston Goes to Washington

Scott Underlicht spoke into the phone. "My two-year old requires less supervision." He needed two hands to count the calls fielded from Weston's secretary who finalized arrangements for her boss's trip to Washington with Stepford-wife efficiency. "Wish he'd charter a jet. B...better yet, f...fly another airline. He'd be s...someone else's headache," Underlicht added with a nervous stammer.

The secretary didn't share Underlicht's humor. Her calls created so-called fantasy flights: cabin attendants cherry-picked for appearance and attitude, airplanes spit polished, airports gussied up, over-staffed, and staged with the finest agents. As for delays, unthinkable. Pilots, who as a group, loathed the company's chief, remained sequestered behind cockpit doors, a result of post-9/11 security measures. When Weston traveled, everyone from Hap down fretted on high alert, fearing a call from the choleric Chairman. The *All Clear* text that announced Weston's landing and airport exit brought sighs of relief.

While most CEOs enjoyed pampered lifestyles, a well-rehearsed protocol distorted Weston's view of his own product. Many hands fabricated an ideal travel experience shared by Weston's circle of friends and family. Yet, consumer data and plunging revenues suggested disaster—the loss of top customers. Many corporate clients whose business couldn't be bought with deep discounts, took their travel dollars elsewhere. Weston's frantic calls to discontented chief executives, a last ditch effort to save an account, usually ended with lectures about bad service. Weston was fed up. He'd never find a buyer for the company if customers continued to flee. Besides, his days of groveling to other CEOs were over.

At the most recent board meeting, Weston bellowed from the head of the table:

"We have the best assets in the business. Sinking satisfaction scores and surging complaints can be blamed on one thing: spoiled and malicious employees. We set them up for success and are rewarded with what, I ask you? A perverted sense of entitlement. Sabotage from within is a festering crisis. We must crush dissent or we'll have no buyer."

The impassioned speech earned him the desired outcome—near unanimous approval to proceed with the employee initiative that he subsequently dropped in Hap's lap.

✎❖✎

Moments before Weston's limousine pulled up to the terminal, the airport manager, Brophy, ushered a group of disgruntled customers into a back room. The rabble, upset by a missed cruise due to a cancelled flight, would sour Weston's experience. Instead, the Chairman entered a clean and quiet lobby from which Brophy's assistant whisked him through security to the VIP lounge where Ingrid waited.

"Five minutes, limo to lounge," Weston boasted, his eyes studying his watch.

"Flight's on-time. Leaves from the adjacent gate. All so convenient," purred Ingrid. She sat on a sofa in a quiet corner, cell phone in one hand, and champagne glass in the other. A cashmere sweater and wool slacks conveyed comfort and confidence. "We're all set for tomorrow. I hope you're as charged as I am," she said.

Her exuberance sounded to him like the tone of a warrior lusting for battle. By contrast, he felt stiff—stuffed into a dark wool suit to mask his girth and a crisp white shirt to conceal his sweat. Formality kept customers and employees at safe distances. "You got balls, my dear. Not your keister being grilled," he said. He sank into the sofa beside her and snapped his fingers for the room attendant to fetch champagne and sandwiches.

"Don't worry. We worked all weekend. Underlicht shopped our proposal with Klein's staff. They're onboard." She paused. He felt her studying his expression. "Why the smirk?"

He waved his hand. "Nothing at all. I knew you'd come through." He saw no point in sharing the prior evening's conversation with Klein.

Ingrid spoke. "We reminded the committee of the many constituents employed by the airlines. Mandates are job killers. Offered up the Airline Carriers Association on a silver platter. A bit of staged theatrics."

"Like television wrestling." Weston bit into a sandwich and continued talking as he chewed. "I enjoy watching you bully my enemies."

"*Our* enemies. We're a team." She caressed his arm and bent her head to his. Her tone lost confidence. "Richard?"

"Yes."

"One more thing. It could help us at the hearing."

His arm stiffened. "What?"

"You avoid employees. I understand why. A few bitter troublemakers create a hostile environment for you. Excessive whining and incessant complaining about your compensation. It's all so…absurd," she said, her head nodding. Her expression assumed a look of sympathetic concern.

Weston rolled his eyes. "Spit it out already! What do you want?"

Ingrid inhaled and sat upright. Her words trickled from the side of her mouth. "Talk to employees at the gate, on the airplane."

Weston snapped; a hand clenched the chair's arm. "How can you suggest such a thing? I'll hear the same crap that Klein and his committee are going to throw at me."

"Calm down. Hear me out. Our enemies want to cast you as an arrogant bastard. The callous CEO plays well on television. An easy excuse to impose oversight. I've got a plan."

He felt his face grow red, but an inner voice told him to trust Ingrid's killer instincts. His fixer never failed. "I'm listening."

"We parse these conversations into your testimony. Words of real people. We paint you as a benevolent leader, in tune with employees. Show Klein as a bully. Messing with single working moms and families who need company insurance to care for sick kids."

Weston pouted, still uncomfortable with the proposal. "Schmaltz!" he blurted. "Guessing you got a dozen more soap opera stories."

Ingrid patted his knee. "I understand your concern. But this gives you instant credibility. Humanizes you and the airline. Might even make you...likeable." She gulped.

He flinched. "Don't even think of putting me in a cardigan sweater." He cringed at images of those overused presidential stunts. The reference to a homely sob story while the camera flashed to some poor sop, all smiles in a shiny J.C. Penney suit, seated in the gallery next to the First Lady. "Wasn't my performance as the concerned humanitarian with Hap enough?"

"Trust me."

Weston groaned. "Do I have a choice?"

"Our trip's staffed with sympathetic personnel. I've got prompts to help you. If that fails, we manufacture our own stories."

Weston shook his head. He felt like a child ordered to eat his spinach.

Ingrid continued. "I'll also plant employees in the gallery—regular folks who saved customers' lives; Heimlich, CPR. You'll point them out. I dare Klein to belittle our heroes."

Weston shook. His worst nightmare had come true. He downed the remainder of his drink and snapped his fingers for more.

"Relax. You'll be magnificent. Adoring fans will draft you for a Senate run," she said, handing him a briefing packet as the loud speaker crackled.

Ladies and gentlemen, Flight 877 to Washington Reagan is ready for immediate departure.

Maybe Ingrid had a point. He glanced at his watch and grinned. "Ten minutes early. Like clockwork."

⚜

HDQ waited on pins and needles for the outcome of the Congressional hearings. Such events usually resulted in seat-of-the-pants commitments that rolled down hill for staffers to make good.

"Just escaped that blasted torture chamber," Weston bellowed into the phone from the limo as it headed west on Pennsylvania Avenue toward the Willard Hotel. "You got your work cut out for you, Hap," he said with a glance at Underlicht in the seat opposite him.

As Ingrid's Washington go-to guy dabbed his sweaty forehead, looking like a scared rabbit, Weston recalled his first visit to Washington as the airline's new CEO. A company van filled with spare airplane parts pulled up to the curb. Underlicht opened the door with a shit-faced grin and muttered some crap about frugality being a virtue. Weston gasped, shot him a dirty look, hailed a taxi and abandoned Ingrid and his luggage without a word. The former CEO apparently valued thrift. Didn't take long for word to spread that Weston had other ideas.

"Been expecting your call," Hap snapped into the phone. "I'm in the middle of a crisis. Got a full jumbo jet sitting stranded in Fiji—"

Weston wrinkled his nose. Intercontinental didn't fly to Fiji, but Hap got paid to deal with such issues. He had more pressing news to share. As the limo made a right turn onto 12th Street, the Chairman interrupted Hap to tell his story. "The first two hours of testimony came from disgruntled passengers including Klein's daughter and nine-year-old grandson, Malcolm III. Insufferable nonsense. The snot-nosed brat's already primping for granddaddy's Congressional seat. Oh, the humanity. Ingrid couldn't wait to shed her Pat Nixon wool coat for the Nancy Reagan fur she stashed in the car," Weston said before roaring with laughter.

Hap cleared his throat before saying, "Heard somethin' about an ancient widow whose husband died, trapped on a tarmac."

Weston buried his head in his hand. "Oh God, yes. They wheeled in Mother Machree in all of her American Gothic finery—cotton frock, macramé shawl and straw purse. Her husband was ninety-four, for Christ's sake. Died of natural causes, yet he's the poster child for abused customers."

"And after the sentimental drivel?" Hap asked.

"Played out as Ingrid predicted. We got what we wanted. Most anyways." Weston winked at his mink-clad compatriot wedged in the opposite corner of the limo. "We'll brief the Executive team tomorrow."

"And our pledge?" Hap asked.

"Gobbled it up like Internet campaign contributions."

Ingrid grabbed the phone. "He's being modest, Hap. He ascended as industry spokesperson, consumer champion. The congressmen treated Richard as if he were Moses and our pledge, the Ten Commandments. Klein cowered before the mighty Weston." Laughing hysterically, she handed the phone back to her beaming boss.

"Figured you'd outmaneuver the committee," Hap said.

Weston ignored the insincerity in the tone. "We bought time, but you must act fast to improve service." Politicians, Weston knew, were only stunned temporarily, until the next political wind blew. "You find your employee champion?"

"Got a short list. Gotta find someone credible with employees and agreeable to other officers," Hap said.

Weston's fury surged, primed by five hours before the committee. "Move! Our pledge deflected Congress and will play well on the evening news. But, our employees haven't changed. They'll gladly wipe their ass with our promises. Get going."

"I'll fill it fast..." Hap's voice trailed off. The phone went silent.

"You still there? Hap?" Weston checked the connection.

"I'm here. Merely keeping the airline running."

"Get off your rump! By the way, Ingrid volunteered to co-sponsor the project." Weston cast a mischievous glance at his PR chief, aware of the turd just dropped into Hap's punch bowl.

"What? Ingrid?" Hap's shout could he heard by all of the limo's passengers.

"Anxious to lend support and resources. Entirely at your disposal." While his words proposed collegial support, Weston knew his tone implied an offer Hap couldn't refuse.

"Her employee expertise is daunting, her sensitivity admirable. A valuable resource indeed. Extend my thanks for the generous offer." Hap didn't sugarcoat the sarcasm. Weston chortled into the receiver.

"Gotta get back to my... little issue," Hap said.

"Keep your issue out of the news. I'm still in Washington until tomorrow and don't want to be dragged back before Klein." Weston laughed, ignorant of the severity of the situation.

Chapter 9

Hap Puts Business Before Weston

For once, Hap didn't mind the abrupt hang up. He had made faces at the phone during most of the conversation. "What a ham," Hap said, putting the phone on mute several times to vent at Weston's theatrics. He and Ingrid deserved each other.

Besides, Hap's mind was in Fiji primed by a stream of notes passed under his nose by Winny as he spoke to Weston. He tried to tell his boss. One of the airline's jumbo jets diverted to Fiji on a flight from Sydney to Los Angeles with an ill passenger. All of the cabin attendants except the three most junior fled the plane, telling company officials who tracked them down to a resort, that their actions were justified. The delay pushed their workday beyond contract limits.

The situation had public relations disaster written all over it. Every hotel on the island was booked. With the untenable prospect of four hundred customers trapped on the airplane with no accommodation and no crew to operate the flight, the incident escalated to Hap, the Chief Operating Officer.

Hap ruffled the ring of hair circling his scalp. He'd love to embarrass Weston; let the crisis explode onto the evening news while Moses, the consumer champion, toasted his success with caviar and champagne. Hap grew frustrated with the pedantic outsider who had no desire to understand the business or its employees. *Thinks finding an employee champion is as easy as ordering a pizza*, Hap thought to himself. *Ridiculous.*

Hap had less patience for Ingrid. While he understood her value to Weston, he preferred the Prussian at a distance. Why couldn't she stay in her sandbox? But objections were futile. He comforted himself believing she would bore quickly, disappear or delegate the work to an easily intimidated underling.

Should he let the crisis boil and embarrass Weston? Hap wavered. But he couldn't do that to *his* customers, tarnish *his* airline or embarrass *his* hard working and dedicated employees. He hurled into action, screaming out the office door, "Get me the Ops Director!"

Seconds later, Winny shouted back. "He's on the line."

Hap's nostrils flared as he yelled into the speaker, "Call Fiji. I don't care what it takes, promise the crew anything to get back on that plane—*anything!*"

Chapter 10

The Company Hap Keeps

The Executive Team, or ET as the acronym-addicted airline labeled Weston's direct reports, gathered in the boardroom to await their briefing. The space recently underwent a major renovation as part of Weston's grand plan. "Our Directors must view me as a break from a broken past, a maverick driving the company and industry into the 21st century," Weston told the project's designer.

"Get a load of this place," Hap said after his wolf whistle greeted his first peek into the room. "There goes the bonus pool." His eyes scanned the high-tech lighting, a wall of flat-screen TVs and a myriad of other fancy gadgets.

"In Xanadu did Kubla Khan..." Chief Counsel Lyle Pavlis added with the drama that made him famous as a corporate defense lawyer.

Carrie Patterson, head of HR, gasped. "That's an old movie quote," she said, writhing in her chair. "Love that film. About a guy who loved a sled."

Hap, along with the room's other three occupants, stared at her. He had little patience for the woman. Not because she started her career as a secretary three decades earlier, but because she reached the top of the corporate ladder by boarding the express elevator reserved for suck-ups. He bristled at her promotion to senior vice president. Perhaps the nasty rumors were true. Weston fell under her spell when she dropped to her knees.

"Bricks and mortar are so... passé. A legacy of the last

century," said Tyler Dagger, who spoke without looking up as he scrolled through his smart phone. "But if we must have a Board Room, better to be 4G and nano than strings and Dixie cups. Got enough ancient thinking around here. Don't need dinosaur tech too."

Hap scowled but remained silent. Dagger, Weston's newest recruit, led the company's revenue arm. Dubbed *Wunderkind* by the press, he amassed a small fortune creating an Internet site that provided a marketplace to buy and sell practically anything. Hap referred to the business as an electronic garage sale. And the fact that the company never turned a profit, gave Hap great satisfaction. He wished he could have seen Dagger's face when a new board created by the IPO forced him, the company founder, out.

Weston described the thirty-year-old as a geek savant with the know-how to fix the company's broken revenue model. Long, greasy hair, tattered clothes, and an assortment of colorful sneakers didn't shock his peers, but his quirks did. He refused to shake hands or make eye contact and recoiled from paper, demanding only electronic messages. Ingrid spun the disorder to the company's benefit, featuring Dagger in the airline's magazine as a proud example of a paperless green campaign.

"Probably keeps his piss and fingernails in Mason jars," Hap said after first meeting him. He had little respect for Dagger, a man who cut his teeth on Pac-Man and Star Wars action figures. Dagger didn't dirty his hands in filthy cargo holds or break his back throwing bags. How could you trust someone who avoided a firm handshake, refused to look you in the eye or pick up a dollar bill from the floor? Hap believed Weston hired Dagger to compete with him: the creaseless face of the future versus the furrowed brow of the past.

Hap reached behind him and grabbed a bottle of water from the glass credenza.

"Well, I'm gonna miss the old paneling. Those grimy walls were layered with the cigar smoke of our glorious past."

"Love this," Patterson said, bending over the stainless steel table. "I can see myself."

"Just got my old leather chair to fit my ass too," CFO Bryce Jacobs whined, easing himself into the fighter-jet inspired chair, and rolling from cheek to cheek. The chair's curved design and Jacob's long neck, bent his posture to form the letter *C*.

Hap laughed, guessing a little humility would serve the oafish Jacobs well. Weston's financial architect, who capably led the company into and out of bankruptcy *twice*, was a self-proclaimed misanthrope. Hap told Jacobs that he chewed through staff quicker than passengers picked through bags of pretzel mix. Still, of the entire lot, Jacobs gave him the least heartburn.

Hap scowled at the equipment in front of him, a wireless phone, retractable monitor, and laptop. "Employees are already grousing we outsourced entire departments and sold airplanes to fund Mission Control."

"Don't every one look at me," Jacobs moaned. "We covered our tracks. Scattered the costs like buckshot."

"That's not really true—what Hap suggested, is it?" Patterson asked, twirling her chair back and forth.

Jacobs made a two-finger scout salute. "No." A grin formed on his lips. "But will lounges remain shabby, work areas stay dingy, and equipment continue to break down?"

"*Guilty* as charged," blurted Hap. He didn't care that Weston's Cultural Revolution erased all traces of former regimes. But his stately pleasure dome came at the sacrifice of much-needed infrastructure improvements.

"I'd plead for the court's mercy," said silver-haired Pavlis with a laugh. "Extenuating circumstances. Our fearless leader merely goes with the flow."

Hap's hand wrapped the table. "*With* the flow? He's the leader of the pack." Despite being a Weston crony, Pavlis was palatable. Perhaps because he didn't poke his nose into Hap's airline and offered free legal advice. Pavlis kept Weston out of trouble by hiring the best legal minds money could buy. A career as one of the country's top M&A attorneys filled his toy chest with a Rolls Royce, a forty-foot yacht, and trophy wife, twenty-five years his junior.

As they continued to wait, the quintet bantered with the unease of feuding relatives thrown together at a funeral. The menagerie lacked only Frida Sallinger, whose specific responsibilities were a secret to all but Weston.

The sound of giggles turned heads toward the door. Weston and Ingrid entered the room, engaged in a conversation as if oblivious to the audience anxiously awaiting the curtain's delayed rise. The Chairman took his seat at the head of the table. Ingrid stood to his right with foot tapping and arms folded across her chest until Patterson rose and took another empty seat. Ingrid sat, sliding left-behind papers toward the head of HR. Patterson's lips quivered.

Ingrid and Weston conducted their tag-team briefing with, what Hap considered, the finesse of a Friday night Smackdown. They gave a gushing account of the backroom skirmishes that didn't make the evening news. Self-satisfaction oozed from Weston like a fine layer of sweat.

Hap heard quite enough self-promotion. Time for a verbal wedgie. "Didn't hear squat about TransSky's CEO. Ridgeway's always a favorite, what with his airline's glowing awards and customer ratings. Usually attracts employee cheerleaders. Even Klein has a hard-on for him." As he spoke, he noticed some unspoken message circulate among Ingrid, Jacobs, and Weston. Their eyes and expressions shared a story, even if their mouths remained shut.

Weston gritted his teeth. "TransSky wasn't... asked to attend."

Hap feigned surprise with a dropped jaw, but he chuckled to himself. Leave it to Weston to make a Congressional summons sound like an invitation to tea.

Weston inhaled. "Ladies and Gentlemen, simply put, our customer pledge proved a masterful stroke. We pre-empted Washington's interference." He paused, appearing to scan the room for praise and nods. "But Hap knows this is merely a teaser. Employees *must* keep the promises we made."

Hap knew it wouldn't take long for his boss to turn the uncomfortable spotlight onto him. He bobbed his head and muttered, "Yes, sir."

He'd watched Patterson with amusement as she rose and sank in her chair. She reminded him of a girl playing jump rope, unsure of when to enter. Finally she hopped into the conversation. She spoke fast, "I know I speak for all of us, Richard," she paused, before adding with a smile, "when I say how proud we are of you." Her eyes arced around the table. "I knew you'd emerge as industry leader. Cream to the top. Bravo, Richard. Bravo!" She clapped her hands like a child.

Weston's gray eyes narrowed on her. His lips curled. "You're too kind. We'll need your team to create training around this pledge."

Patterson's pixie head tilted. "For employees?"

Slouched in his chair, Jacobs rolled a pencil toward her. "No. Let's train passengers to be better customers."

Hap stifled his snicker at the sound of exaggerated laughter. He and everyone else turned to the source, Ingrid. Patterson scrunched her face and turned to Weston without responding to the outbursts. "You can count on me, chief. HR will make sure everyone in operations is held accountable."

Hap flinched. "Operations? You gotta be kidding?"

Weston ignored the interruption. "Fine, fine. That's my girl. Quick to take action." Weston then turned toward Hap, his puffy face stern.

Understanding the prompt, Hap announced to his peers. "I'm appointing a new executive to lead a complementary effort to improve employee service."

"Explain." Jacobs barked.

Hap continued. "The pledge is top down, customer driven. My work's bottom up, employee driven."

"Hopefully they meet somewhere in the middle," added Jacobs, who Hap noticed doodled ticker symbols in his notebook's margin. The CFO usually stayed mute about employees and customers unless the topic had a financial component.

Dagger yawned. "That all?"

Weston signaled to Ingrid who brushed back her platinum hair and squared her shoulders. "No. The pledge is only one element. Made the news because of simplicity. *Every* airline called to Washington agreed to create a new role, Chief Passenger Officer, CPO."

"What the heck?" Dagger asked.

Ingrid swatted the air. "The CPO serves as a customer advocate. Monitors the pledge. Champions customer issues. The role links airlines to Klein's committee."

Hap snarled. He glared at Weston rather than his messenger. "What? You abdicated oversight to Congress? More government? Aren't we screwed enough? We got the FAA, DOT, TSA," he said, counting the agencies off on his fingers.

Weston held up a palm. "Union Airlines' CEO sprang the idea in the middle of his testimony. He blindsided us. Airline CEOs can be assholes."

No shit, Hap thought.

"Klein challenged the rest of us. We all had to jump on that wagon," Weston said.

Ingrid shrugged and clicked her tongue. "Much ado about nothing. The CPO is *our* person, monitoring *our* behavior. We play cop *and* robber."

Weston threw up his hands like a preacher. "Hap has a Chief Employee Officer and Dagger, a Chief Passenger Officer."

Jacobs kicked off his size 15 Oxfords, hitting Hap in the shin. "Oh boy! Bottoms up and top down. Batman and Joker may find common ground. Pay top dollar to see that head-on collision," he said, looking first to Dagger, then to Hap with a wink.

Weston shot Jacobs an angry look before he addressed the pair. "The two of you will partner."

"Fat chance," muttered Jacobs keeping his eyes down.

Hap dropped his head into his hands. He felt as trapped as his reflection in the monitor before him. He wanted to fix his airline, but his boss pulled all the strings. Could the employee initiative succeed? Could he work around Weston?

Chapter 11

Hap Improves His Handicap

Grim-faced, Hap sat in his cart fastening and unfastening his golf glove. The starter kept his eyes glued to a walkie-talkie clutched in his gloved hand. *As if watching it will do any good*, Hap thought. What could be holding up the greens keeper? Lingering frost into late April kept screwing up his early tee times. He seethed, vexed that the cold meant they'd be defrosting airplanes again, not just at O'Hare, but all over the Midwest. "There goes the budget, not to mention the damn delays," he muttered aloud.

"Sorry Mr. Sweeny. Shouldn't be much longer." Vapor escaped from the man's mouth.

"What? N...no, I was talking——" Hap stammered, but the starter interrupted him.

"Just need to clear the first few greens and you'll be on your way. Sorry for the inconvenience." The starter shrugged then added, "Golfing alone again this morning?"

"Too early in the season to pull people from warm beds. Besides, the peace and quiet is a welcome break."

"I get that a lot," the man said with a wink. "But you're a hardy soul."

Hap managed a smile for the old guy he came to know over the past few years. He enjoyed the early and late seasons when he could play golf alone without pressure to add a partner or complete a foursome. The solitude gave him time to think away from the pressures of work and home. He needed to review the candidates on his short list. Weston was on his back to appoint the employee champion and he had his own reasons to get the work moving.

A change in the light stirred both men. The sun peeked over the hedges that ran along the course's eastern border on a short bluff above the dark waters of Lake Michigan.

"No leaves yet. Sun should burn the frost off in no time," the starter said. Hap noticed the blue twinkle in the man's eyes when he pointed to the bare treetops. "You won't be rushed. Next foursome won't be here for thirty minutes."

"Thanks Pete." Hap studied the man's face. He hadn't noticed the kindness before. Maybe the nip in the air rosied the cheeks and crinkled the eyes, more than usual. "You don't seem to mind these damp, dark mornings either."

"Ask me again when I'm up to my knees in late season snow," Pete said, pulsing his eyebrows. "But you're spot on. I love it. After retiring, I needed something. A purpose."

"Sounds like your wife wants you out of the house."

Both men laughed but Hap noticed a subtle change in the man's expression.

Pete looked at his feet and kicked the gravel. "Actually Mr. Sweeny, my wife died three years ago."

"Oh, sorry." Hap looked away, pretending to study the course map. He wondered if he ever knew, or simply forgot. Was her name Sarah or Marianne? He wouldn't risk getting it wrong.

"Yeah, thanks. Found myself alone after fifty years. Wife gone, kids scattered around the country. Loads of idle time after decades of eighty-hour work weeks."

Curious, Hap studied the apple face. He forgot what Pete had done for a living—stockbroker, banker—something high profile. Now, merely a glorified greeter. At least he wasn't pushing carts at Walmart. "What about golf? You love the game. Don't you envy us playing and you working?"

"Tried it—got old. It's a lonely sport, most of the time. Talking to the members, knowing their families—that's what I enjoy. Like I said—a purpose. May not be much compared to your exciting life; running an airline, having a beautiful wife. But, it suits me."

A voice crackled over the walkie-talkie. Pete addressed him. "You're good, Mr. Sweeny. Enjoy your round." He tipped his cap and turned.

Hap watched the man shuffle toward the clubhouse. Ending up alone at the end of life, struck him as a cruel reward for hard work. Was Pete as content as he seemed or was it a stoic façade?

He thought again of Charlie, his long lost buddy. His letter of despair over the company and his leadership haunted him. After digging around, Hap learned that Charlie recently lost his wife of forty years to cancer. Her lengthy illness drained their savings and his meager pension left Charlie scrambling for overtime, even during his wife's last few months of hospice care. He pulled his retirement papers with a note to HR that wavered between bitterness and sentimentality. Hap hadn't responded to Charlie's letter—didn't know if he would. He told himself that the old guy probably didn't want to hear from him.

Hap took a few practice swings, his play delayed by a red fox crossing the fairway. He went over the four finalists for the employee project in his head. The list underwent a series of edits as he fished for information on potential candidates.

One name surfaced early, due to the guy's remarkable grasp of employee demographics that a fellow officer called *encyclopedic*. A timely email saved Hap from embarrassment, mistaking knowledge for concern. In a note to Hap, a respected employee of long tenure blamed her abrupt resignation on the man's tyrannical leadership. Hap found many who eagerly corroborated the allegation. Turned out, Mr. Encyclopedia reaped his reputation on the backs of employees. Jekyll to superiors, Hyde to subordinates.

After similar false starts and disappointments, four names remained on Hap's list. Archived appraisals proved useless, recording only accomplishments and silent to leadership style.

"Frightening," Hap fretted aloud as he returned to his cart after hooking his tee shot within inches of the rough. "Mr. Encyclopedia rated *outstanding,* despite being a jerk." Hap blamed the inconsistency on a culture that rewarded results, regardless of the means. He shrugged, acknowledging his own bias toward action, yet he wanted to believe that bad behaviors eventually caught up to assholes, even those like Wilkerson who enjoyed powerful backers.

Intercontinental always had been able to poach good leaders from other airlines. Importing talent was a strategic decision, backed by financial analysis. A study concluded that the company could save money and time, by cutting development programs and hiring talent from the marketplace. CFO, Bryce Jacobs, boasted of the *Just-in-Time* leadership model inspired by Kanban, the Japanese production model.

Hap never supported internal leadership programs. He criticized the formal curriculum as frivolous and pointed to his own rise through the ranks without formal training.

A steep lie on his next approach shot, reminded him of his own balancing act. He had to choose someone acceptable to both employees and fellow officers. Rejection by either group would mean failure.

The first name on his list belonged to Maggie Richards— bright, attractive and articulate. However, she spent most of her career at another airline. Hap assumed employees wanted a known commodity, someone with Intercontinental blood.

They'd call her an outsider, a label used as an indictment of Weston and most of his team. However, Richards would be an easier sell to Hap's fellow officers, who held low opinions of homegrown talent. Weston recruited VPs who boasted that stronger leaders at superior companies weaned them. Weston and his imports disparaged company veterans—*if they had any skill, moxie, or know-how, they'd already be working someplace else.* Hap blamed the words for missing an easy putt.

He blew on his exposed hand as he considered the second name on his list, Marissa Albioni. She impressed him with her long work hours—one of the few with his work ethic. He smiled, recalling the rumblings from her people about barrages of emails on weekends and overnight—probably didn't take vacation either. Promoting her would send a signal that hard work paid off. He closed his eyes, trying to picture her in the role. He grimaced. Her weight was a major liability that he blamed on addictions to soft drinks and vending machines. He recalled sleeves of doughnuts and packages of cookies on her desk.

Obesity, he felt, showed lack of discipline. Weston got a pass because of position, although Hap found his appearance distasteful. Hap rubbed a hand across his flat stomach. Scratch Albioni. Her promotion would reflect poorly on him.

Admiring his third tee shot, he considered the case of Richard Jeffries. An appealing candidate—military discipline. During a ten-year career in the Air Force as a logistics expert, Jeffries made his mark cutting inventories and boosting productivity. His Division reduced pencil pushers to push more soldiers to the frontline; a task Hap believed had similar application for the airline. The company hired Jeffries seven years before, a plan to recruit military officers for supervisor positions—drill sergeants to restore order. Most failed; they scuffled with unions and a bias against outsiders. Rank held little privilege among the apathetic and belligerent work force. Recruits quit or were forced out by mutinous teams, who rebelled against the command and control methods of inexperienced leaders.

Hap considered Jeffries smart, focused, and a proven leader with a rank of Colonel to prove it. While no black mark appeared against his name, the list of mediocre accomplishments catalogued in his personnel file didn't impress Hap. He rubbed his temple after chipping onto the green. Jeffries was too big a risk. Besides he recently assumed a critical project to reduce headcount.

One candidate remained. Hap breezed through the first two shots of a par three. The name popped into his head early due to a stellar reputation earned over twenty years with the company. A good track record, but something about the man gnawed at him. Hap tuned into the chatter that surrounded up-and-comers, and leaders whose buzz reeked of emotion made him uncomfortable. But, he understood, this new role called for someone employees saw as an advocate.

Hap cursed as a simple chip overshot the green and rolled into a sand trap. He'd bogie the hole, if not worse. Maybe this guy was too *out there?* Perhaps his appointment would upset Weston, who cut off anything at the knees that interfered with his shock and awe campaign against labor. Unleashed, a popular zealot could be dangerous without the head or stomach to support decisions that were unpopular with employees. Weston would eat him alive.

Slicing his next tee shot into the trees Hap told himself, "Calm down. Don't be melodramatic." He'd guide the new VP's every move. At the first sign of populist chest beating, he'd make him disappear like that tee shot.

A smile replaced his scowl. He found someone whose passion for employees would breathe life into the effort; someone the Charlie's of the company could rally behind, a voice of hope. Hap Sweeny might no longer be a wide-eyed kid or an idealistic young man, hell bent on changing the world, but he found somebody who was—*Jim Abernathy*.

A degree in Finance would please Weston and Jacobs. Hap looked forward to watching Wilkerson squirm with Abernathy, his former subordinate, messing in his business. While Jim wouldn't have Wilkerson's connections, Hap would open doors for him. Sinking a twenty-foot putt, Hap mused to the still surroundings, "This survivor still has it."

A loud crack above Hap's head broke the stillness. A tardy cry of, *Fore*, forced him to his knees. At that moment, he remembered something—Julie Bannister. The orange dawn reflected in his eyes as he whistled. He spoke aloud. "Of course! Julie Bannister became Julie Abernathy."

Chapter 12

Hap Musters Support

Hap spent the morning shut up in his office, plotting how to sell Jim Abernathy to fellow officers. Their nods would ease Jim's path as he hacked his way through a forest of old wood, stubborn underbrush and poison ivy. And those hazards described only the officers.

On his way to HR, Hap paused to speak to his secretary. Winny Franklin's plain looks and modest wardrobe disguised her influence. She joined the company the same year as Hap, but held her two months of seniority over his head. During spats, Hap often retreated into his office with her words, *seniority has its privileges,* ringing in his ears. He gave in to her more than he liked to admit.

"You don't want time with Weston?" Winny asked, swiveling her chair to face his electric calendar.

Hap stood facing her, a hand cupping his chin. "He knows I'll pick someone who makes me look good."

"He's right. You picked me." She tilted her head back and looked into his face. "Employees give him hives."

He glanced down the hall toward Weston's office then leaned toward Winny and spoke. "But he's not stupid. He's gotta calm the Board and throw Washington a bone."

Winny swiveled her chair to face him. "He'll wait for Ingrid's take on your guy, anyway."

He grinned as he poked her shoulder. "Guy? Not a woman?"

She swatted the air. "Please! Of all the names you've been sniffing, we both know Jim Abernathy's your man."

Winny never ceased to amaze Hap. She was clairvoyant, a good guesser or merely a snoop. But, she kept him grounded. As grounded as he wanted. "You know Jim Abernathy?" he asked, hiding his smile.

"I worked with his mother, great gal. Know his wife, Julie... so do you." Winny shot him her *mother-hen* look. "Jim loves this company—maybe too much. He'll be good for you, Hap. If you let him."

"Not sure how I should take that," he responded as he walked away.

"Take it however you want," Winny mumbled loud enough for him to hear.

<hr />

Carrie Patterson, the head of HR, seldom arrived at the office earlier than 10am. "I'm never off duty," she declared to anyone who'd listen. She entered the building with a cell phone plastered to her ear whether engaged in a conversation or merely listening to dead air. Among employees, Patterson's name provoked rolled eyes and headshakes with many crediting her professional success to a flair for accessorizing.

Once, Patterson met with a group of laid-off employees. Wearing a Prada skirt, eight inches shorter than her age could tastefully accommodate, she perched on a high stool at the front of the room. Her message of shared sacrifice was lost on the swollen-eyed workers.

As Hap approached Patterson's office, an overpowering smell of sweetness hit his nose. The odor, he discovered, came from a huge floral arrangement. Curiosity got the better of him. After looking around, he bent down to read the card— 'You're the Best!' *Probably sent them to herself*, he thought, as he strolled into her office.

After a curt greeting, he sat across the desk from her.

"Remind me why you're here," she said with a vacant stare.

Her fingers poked at her frosted hair, styled in a pixie cut with spiky bangs.

"Abernathy? Isn't he that six footer with wavy blond hair and green eyes?"

Hap glared. "More importantly," he said, "Jim's got twenty years with the company. He's well-rounded in operations and finance." As he spoke, his glance drifted to a stack of fashion magazines on the conference table.

"Don't know him well, but I'm concerned about his fitting in. Looks the part of an officer, but I get the sense he's soft on employees."

"Why, because he married one?" Hap felt his forehead vein awaken.

Patterson cocked her head and smiled. "Oh, Hap. No, office chatter, that's all."

He tried to take his mind off her long, pink fingernails that clicked the desktop. "It's a risk, but we need someone with instant credibility. If he's not right, we toss him out. We're good at that."

"I'm just not sure," she said, batting her eyes. The clicking fingernails continued.

"Maggie Richards is my other candidate," Hap said. He knew Patterson wouldn't support the promotion of a female. *Threatened by the competition*, he thought. His little bomb had another benefit. The fingers stopped tapping as Patterson's back stiffened.

"That woman?" Patterson scoffed. "Abernathy will do. Just keep an eye on him."

Hap left the office relieved at the ease of his victory. He expected more pushback because of the overlap between Jim Abernathy's work and Patterson's HR team. As he retreated from the sickening combination of lilies and perfume he reminded himself that the airline wouldn't need the new role if HR did its job. Patterson, he predicted, would understand soon enough when her team saw Jim tinkering in their toy chest. Then, let the games begin.

⚜

After grabbing a salad and coffee in the employee cafeteria, Hap made his way back to his office before his next meeting. As he rounded a corner, he bumped into a couple of flight attendants carrying coffee. Broad smiles and conformity to uniform standards, ID'd them as new-hires not yet exposed to the frenzied skies or jaded peers. Coffee splattered onto Hap's shirt, but most of the beverages flowed down the front of their crisp uniforms. They bleated several apologies as they assessed the damage.

"You're Hap Sweeny," the female said when she looked up. "We saw you in the video."

It took Hap a second to realize that she referred to a new-hire video, *Service Still Flies*. He cringed when he saw it the first time. Stiff, over-scripted officers mixed pleasantries with a lecture on service expectations. The video introduced employees to Weston with stock footage showing him ringing the Stock Exchange opening bell and presiding over a Board meeting. His own part wasn't half bad.

"Our class loved you best," the male said, practically hyperventilating. "You said—"

The female finished her colleague's sentence. "Without your passionate dedication to serve, Intercontinental's wings will be clipped." She sighed. "Mr. Sweeny, you're the leader we all want to follow." Both of their scrubbed faces beamed.

Hap hadn't heard much of what they said. He scanned his clothes. "Be more careful, especially with coffee. That's your job." A frown etched his face as he walked away.

With heads bowed, the pair walked to their next lecture entitled, *Maintaining Composure and Customer Focus Under Challenging Circumstances.*

❀

As Hap rode the elevator up to his office, he considered his next meeting with Wilkerson. Hap managed him with the light touch of a university dean disciplining the child of a wealthy donor. He granted Weston's fair-haired boy unique freedoms. Loyal staffers embedded in Wilkerson's division allowed Hap to track his actions. If necessary, Hap could pull an emergency brake before he did too much damage.

Although confident he'd twist Wilkerson's arm, he was less certain he'd win a commitment to help Jim. At the very least, Hap wanted to prevent sabotage.

❀

"Get my broker on the phone. Bring me something for coffee stains." Hap barked his orders to Winny, wedged the latest customer reports under his arm and walked into his office.

Standing behind his desk, he grew agitated as he scanned the customer surveys. "Damn," he mumbled. "Worse than last month." Weston and the Board would explode.

They'd point to employees. *At least my stock options are exercisable*, he thought.

"Harold's on the line," Winny shouted from her desk.

Hap plopped into his chair, picked up the phone and changed his tone. "Still on for Saturday? I pushed tee time back to 9. Still expecting frost."

The broker bragged about a new titanium driver and told a joke about a rabbi, a priest, and a banker advising a foreclosed homeowner. Hap laughed even though he hadn't caught the punch line. Instead, he focused on pulling his brokerage statements from the desk. "Wanted to review my orders." Hap's options were exercisable in days, and for a change, were worth something. "Exercise my options," Hap said as his eyes wandered to the customer satisfaction reports. "Every last one."

Winny appeared at the door, arms folded, peering over her bifocals. Hap nodded and spoke into the phone. "Gotta go. See you Saturday, and yes, I'll buy the first round. I think I can afford it." He hung up with a laugh.

Wilkerson entered the office and pointed toward the stain on Hap's shirt. "Another reason I never touch the stuff."

Hap scowled, yelling past his visitor. "Bring me that damned spot remover."

Wilkerson inhaled before launching his comments. "I've been busy fixing customer service. Here's a summary," he said, shoving a document onto the desk.

"I don't have time today," Hap barked. He studied his shirt and held the tie up to his eyes as Winny scurried in with a bottle of some solution and hurried out again. Hap motioned Wilkerson to sit before filling his cup from a carafe kept filled on his desk. He didn't trust people who didn't drink coffee. "I want to talk about Weston's pet project."

Wilkerson nodded. If he was upset at being cut off, he didn't show it.

Hap described the initiative, mentioning Weston and the Board as much as possible to cutoff debate. He fixed on Wilkerson's narrow eyes. "The pledge, your customer work and Dagger's Chief Passenger Officer have similar goals."

"Yeah, employees stand in the way of success," Wilkerson said. "But we're falling over ourselves to fix things. It's a cluster fuck."

Hap nodded. "Big problems require multiple solutions.

Weston's losing patience. He's accountable to investors. Assets must produce."

"I get it. But where do employees fit?" Wilkerson said, running a hand through his mop of white hair.

Hap paused to collect his words. "Employees are blinded by self-interest."

Wilkerson grinned. "Sounds more like Weston's words than yours."

Hap cleared his throat. He felt his cheeks warm. "Well yes, those are his words. He can't stomach their irrational behavior."

Wilkerson wagged his finger. "I don't disagree."

"Weston believes *rational* employees focus on the investor."

Wilkerson leaned forward, resting both elbows on Hap's desk. "Really! Why?"

Hap detected Wilkerson's skepticism. He himself had heard Weston spout his theory enough that it started to make sense. He mustered a confident tone. "Success is defined by profitability—the reason we exist. Employee satisfaction comes from belonging to a successful enterprise. Pride inspires a commitment to serve." Hap waited.

Finally, Wilkerson nodded. "Let me see if I get it. Employees get satisfaction from a successful company. Profits define success. So, employees optimize self-interest by maximizing investor returns. Pride and profitability motivate."

Hap nodded, pointing his finger at the younger man. *Christ,* he thought, *did that crap come out of me?*

Wilkerson sat back, pinching his bottom lip. "Good theory, but it falls apart in real life. How do you convince the axed employee his sacrifice serves the greater good?"

Hap chuckled, "You don't."

Wilkerson assumed a smug little grin as he added, "Perspective depends where you sit...in the lifeboat or floundering in the water."

Hap shrugged. "One always hopes to be in the lifeboat," he said. "Well, that's Weston's view, but he expects us to manage the company."

"He's giving you resources for this employee work. I'm confused," Wilkerson said, shaking his head. "Whatever happened to good old fashioned floggings?" He snickered.

"Think manufacturing. Weston's a miner and you assembled autos." Hap smirked, enjoying the dig to their non-airline pedigrees. "Employees are merely a production input. While pilots and flight attendants may be indispensable, at least for now, others can be replaced—automation, outsourcing."

"Even fly boys and trolley dollies could eventually be outsourced," Wilkerson added.

"Even automated," Hap said. "Good management addresses any problem input."

Hap waited for Wilkerson's nod before continuing. "Same logic applies to employees. The root cause of service failures is a problem with a key input, employees. Bad input gives bad output that hurts profits, investors' bread and butter. Got it?"

Wilkerson nodded. "Makes sense, although employees probably wouldn't like to think of themselves as mere production inputs. Where do customers fit in?"

Hap leaned back and cradled his head in his hands. "According to Weston, sound business models contain a compelling customer value proposition."

"In other words, a company's products and services must satisfy customer needs. That puts customers first, doesn't it?"

Hap shook his head. "Still the investor. The business must first attract capital for product investment."

Wilkerson pinched his bottom lip again. "What about employees?"

Hap leaned over the desk. "My new vice president will focus on them."

"Won't that overlap with HR? Not to mention stepping all over the operating groups." Wilkerson spoke, tapping his foot.

Hap glared. "You consistently gripe that Human Resources isn't meeting your needs."

Wilkerson leaned back. "True, but that doesn't mean this new VP's the answer. What will he or she do?"

Hap grinned. "Work with you and your peers. A rare opportunity to improve service."

Wilkerson stared into his eyes. "I'm unconvinced."

Hap clenched his fist on his lap. He'd hit Wilkerson in his Achilles heel. "Any Chief Operating Officer responsible for customer service would drool over resources to stop the hemorrhaging. Understand?"

Hap grabbed the customer reports. He threw them across the desk toward Wilkerson. "The latest report card from customers. They're at war with our employees and losing. Take a look," Hap said, pointing at the papers that Wilkerson picked up. "Your Division is particularly pathetic. Would you stand before the Board with these scores and explain why you refused their help?"

Wilkerson's eyes looked from the papers to Hap. "Where do I sign up?"

Hap laughed, slapping his thigh. "Good! Now the best news. We're promoting one of your people." He watched the words register on Wilkerson's face.

"Patty Thorsen?" Hap knew that Wilkerson loathed Thorsen, threatened by her long-term friendship with him, even accused her of spying for Hap.

Hap got out of his chair and stood beside Wilkerson. He wanted to deliver the news up close. "No. I've selected, Jim Abernathy. You'll be praised as a consummate team player." He slapped his slack-jawed subordinate on the back. "Congratulations!"

Chapter 13

The Easter Bunny Visits Hap

"Should have our guy today," Hap spoke into the phone, slightly out of breath. He moved from his home's sun porch to the wood-paneled study.

"Christ, I hope so. Employees are out of control." Weston's voice sounded testy. "Just got off a conference call with the Board. Every blasted one of them received a couriered package this morning with a petition for my ouster."

"That's not new," Hap said with a dismissive tone. As he pulled the pocket doors shut, his wife, Amber, shoved a gin and tonic at him. He winked his thanks. From Weston's tone though, one drink wouldn't do it.

Weston continued to bellow, "It's Easter Sunday, for Christ's sake!"

While Weston ranted, Hap held the phone away from his ear. He took a sip of his drink and dropped into the leather desk chair. A courier service that worked holidays impressed him more than his boss's tired lament. *If I had a share of stock every time an employee called for my head, I'd be rich*, he thought.

"What triggered this?" Hap asked.

"Damn pensions, again. These tales of woe are wearing thin."

Hap could have said the same thing about Weston's grumbling. He gazed out the bay window across the well-manicured lawn to his club's seventh green. "What is it you say?" Hap closed his eyes and scratched his temple. "Oh yeah, *unhealthy obsession*."

"Damn right! Their preoccupation paralyzes them. They forget who pulled this company out of the ashes. Still have a paycheck, don't they?"

Hap took another sip of his drink. Would the thousands of workers chucked during restructuring share Weston's lofty opinion of himself? Wilkerson's insight came to mind—depended whether you found yourself in or out of the lifeboat.

Weston continued, "Employees don't give me an ounce of credit for navigating us through bankruptcy."

Hap grabbed binoculars from the credenza. He wanted a closer look at a chip shot onto the green. "Old ground. What lit this fire?"

Weston didn't answer the question but continued his rant. "They've never gone this far. Unions threaten to place ads in national newspapers."

"An ad? What does that do for them?"

"Embarrasses me. Draws public sympathy," Weston snapped.

Still staring through the binoculars, Hap was impressed by the long putt. He tried to identify the putter brand. "Any idea what the ad says?"

Weston's breathing became heavier. "Yes, damn it. A draft was part of the extortion package. A Board member faxed it to the house."

Hap put down the binoculars and leaned back in his chair. Things were getting interesting. "So you gonna tell me, or do I have to guess." He grinned, picturing Weston squirm.

"More car... cartoon than ad," Weston stammered. "Shows a turnip, labeled *Pensions* dripping blood. Squeezed by a caricature of me... as... as the Monopoly banker."

The image of an eight ball dressed up with top hat and monocle amused Hap.

Weston's voice rose. "A red puddle is labeled as my salary. Out-of-context quotes make me out to be an imbecile."

Hap furrowed his brow. "All they want is your resignation?"

Weston shot back. "Course not. A litany of absurdities." A labored inhale preceded his next rant. "We teetered on collapse. Pensions would have buried us. Who'd finance a company funneling new capital to pensions? We needed that money to run the business!"

"Sacrifices would have been easier for our people to swallow if the entire industry followed suit," Hap said, "or every employee group." Padded pensions and retention bonuses for company officers irked front line employees. But Hap didn't bring that up since he'd benefited handsomely from such perks.

"Plain stupidity! You're right, every airline should have cleaned house after September 11th. Calamity gave cover to extract concessions."

"Employees think we had a shaky trigger finger," Hap said as his gaze drifted to the black and white framed photo, now almost 40 years old. He reached forward, picked it up and smiled. He and his ramp buddies, climbing over a new bag tractor. He had a full head of hair then and an easy grin. Happier times. But where was Charlie? Had he taken the picture?

His eyes were drawn to the sound of sliding doors. Amber poked her head through. "Henry's getting ready to drive back to school," she whispered.

Hap shrugged, muting the phone. "Sorry, the big guy's on a roll. It's important."

She rolled her eyes. "Screw him. It *always* is."

He winked. "Tell Henry to be safe and bring home straight A's," he said, pivoting the chair toward the window. He blinked at the loud thud of the doors sliding closed.

Weston was still talking. "It's not as if we didn't create new programs or transition what was left of their old plans to the government. No, what do they do? They harp on what's gone. Yes, I'd call that an *unhealthy obsession!*"

Hap knew all about the employee complaints. Folks planning to retire couldn't tap into the government plan until 65 without severe penalties. But that noise had died down. Most people understood survival.

He pressed Weston again. "Why now?"

Weston paused before answering. "Ingrid created a message to silence critics."

Hap's hand covered his face. The message and messenger ignited the firestorm. Why hadn't Weston and his fixer run the content past him? His forty years accounted for something. But the outsiders thought they had all the answers.

"What's Ingrid's surefire cure?" Hap asked, picking up a pen and rummaging through the drawer for a note pad. His eyes caught the nursing home bill for his mother. *Alone on Easter,* he thought. He brushed the image aside as Weston's rant made him think of a cymbal-banging monkey toy—wound up in a frenzy.

"Some idiot at the employee meeting shouted that I should be embarrassed. Called my salary obscene. Shared sacrifices and all that baloney."

Hap closed his eyes and shook his head. "You didn't let the comment slide, did you?"

"Damn right I didn't! I followed Ingrid's advice. Called the question *ridiculous* and the questioner, *immature.* Dismissed it as whining that takes focus from customers. Reminded them of their option to work until 65. Pointed out our support of legislation to allow pilots to do just that."

"Hit a homerun, huh?" Hap said as Henry's red Z-4 accelerated down the side drive and into the street without a cautionary yield. Hap scowled. *Why was Henry so reckless? Why hadn't he learned to respect the value of money?*

Weston droned on, "Another moron bellowed he'd have to work until eighty. Then some shrew cackled that she'd support a law to force me to retire early. The room went wild!"

Hap grinned, but affected concern. "How horrible for you."

"Envy, that's what it is. Let them become CEO. Their morale isn't my concern. Told them so. Shareholders are my focus. Should be theirs. Ungrateful lunatics!"

Hap wanted to interrupt. Tell Weston what he really thought. Ole top hatted eight-ball deserved what he got for bypassing his counsel. Yet, stirring up discontent wouldn't help his employee initiative. Something else had to be bugging Weston. "Don't take this wrong," Hap said, feeling his shoulder tense. "You normally don't get this worked up by employee chatter."

The response came loud and clear. "Can't afford embarrassment right now."

Unconvinced, Hap tried again. "We've managed these flare ups before. The Board's wrapped up and Ingrid can bury the ad. Worst case? It gets out and we mount a counter campaign." Hearing only a grunt, he furrowed his brow. "What aren't you telling me?"

Weston sighed. "We're facing intense scrutiny. We can't afford missteps."

Hap sensed Weston had other concerns. "Anything else?"

Hap waited, his mind racing to all sorts of scenarios. Finally, Weston's spoke, "We're courting prospective airline partners."

The words stung. Would the company that gave him his identity, his purpose in life, be lost? He felt queasy. "To sell?" He braced for the answer.

Weston paused before answering. "Certainly not. Purely from a marketing angle. Most worry about our employees. They don't want to bed a partner cursed with an infectious disease."

Hap cringed at the comparison of employees to an STD.

"My project will help. Ingrid's coming to dinner to review my candidate." Hap and Amber thought it odd that she had nowhere else to go for Easter.

The phone went dead. Hap studied it for a second before laying it on his desk with a shrug. He emptied his gin and tonic, staring at the foursome putting onto the green. What were the chances he'd win Ingrid's support?

Amber parted the doors. She crossed the darkening room with a drink. The third Mrs. Hap Sweeny was a beauty; raven-haired, twenty years younger than her husband, and in short, a knockout. They had been married for three years, tying the knot one month after his last divorce, and one year after meeting at the club where she worked in member relations.

"You really should have made time for Henry. He left crushed," she said, standing behind her husband and massaging his shoulders.

"Could have fooled me the way he peeled out of the driveway."

"Not the only Sweeny who hides his true emotions behind anger," she said coming around his chair and massaging his shoulders. "He craves time with you, Hap."

"He looks at me the way I looked at..." He shook his head. He wanted to say 'my father' but didn't have the energy for that battle.

Amber squeezed harder on his shoulders. "Try a little harder. You played golf yesterday and again this morning."

"Don't begrudge me the club. It brought us together. Besides, Henry's 22, and a second year senior. By that age, I'd been at Intercontinental for five years." His eyes wandered back to the driveway.

She tapped the top of his bald scalp. "Tina's also left us for the evening. Heading up to Lake Forest with the Henderson boy. She's barely 16. Comes and goes as she pleases. Mostly goes. You should have a talk with her."

He frowned. "That's her mother's job. The settlement outlined responsibilities—Barbara's support parental, mine, financial."

"Barbara's a never-at-home flight attendant and Tina lives under our roof."

"Roof falls in the financial bucket—I'm covered. What do I know of 16 year-old girls, anyway?"

"She won't listen to me. I'm not her mother, as I've been reminded by *both* of you. You're losing them, Hap"

Hap rubbed his hand up the inside of her thigh. She slapped his scalp harder. "Don't start something you can't finish. That Shattenworter woman will be here any minute."

"She'd probably join us—stilettos and Prussian accent."

Amber shuddered. "Gives me the creeps, the way she looks me up and down. But if you crave her riding crop on your bare ass, be my guest! Why is she coming, anyway? We could have had Easter dinner with your mother."

"Now that's a depressing thought. She thinks I'm her bastard husband."

Amber caressed his arm, but he recoiled. She walked to the window to turn on the lamp, adjusting picture frames on the table as she spoke. "But Ingrid, really?"

"Weston wants her in my project. Says she offered. I say, bullshit! He's running scared. He peddles employee tough love to Wall Street." Amber rolled her eyes but he kept talking. "Based on our call, that's not working so well. Damn if Communications isn't as screwed up as HR. I need her—I'll be on my best behavior."

"Does that go for me?" Amber turned, twisting her forefinger into her cheek.

"Kill her with kindness. If she undresses you with her

eyes, say thanks." He paused, eyeing Amber up and and down. "Hmm, I'm likin' that vision."

"Incorrigible! I'll use a riding crop myself," she said, wagging a finger. As she slid through the pocket doors, she muttered under her breath, "Kindness? Love to kill her period."

The Sweenys waited for their tardy guest on the sun porch, watching golf course stragglers. Amber darted back and forth to the kitchen to check the meal, delivered earlier by the club, and incubating in a warming drawer."

"Hope she's okay with lamb—" Amber started to say.

Hap sprayed his drink, "That's precious. The woman's a carnivore."

At dusk, Amber turned on more lights. Hap grew impatient. "I can hear the Countess pontificate now." He affected a German accent, "*This happiness effort*—the words as welcome as dog crap on her designer shoes—*is too pedestrian to consume much of my time. We must simply command leaders to inspire employees or we'll be kaput. Employees must be spoon-fed like children—incapable of complicated messages or appreciating the intellect of Richard Weston III.*"

Amber stood, hands on hips glaring at him. "Shoulda cut you off after three. Behave yourself. It's Easter."

He pouted, batting his dancing blue eyes. "So, crucify me."

"Don't give me any ideas," she said as the doorbell rang.

The commanding Prussian marched into the two-story foyer. Wearing a periwinkle knit suit hugging every curve of her surgically enhanced body, her black pumps clicked on the marble floor. Hap's eyes were drawn to Ingrid's chest where an impressive pearl and diamond pendant swung above her deep and ample cleavage. She greeted the mesmerized couple with a clipped nod of her head. Ingrid's grand entrances enthralled Hap as much as her exits.

"Happy Easter dears. So kind of you to invite me. I don't get out of the city much. A lovely drive, so bucolic. Who knew?"

"It's only the North Shore for God's sake, not the prairie," Hap said with a laugh.

"You were always within sniffing distance of a Starbucks," Amber added.

Ingrid gave a tepid smile. She handed Amber a bouquet of blue Irises and Hap, a basket wrapped in pink cellophane and tied with a purple plaid bow. "Champagne, caviar and pâte. An Easter Bunny with class," she said, straightening her suit.

"Hope it's not rabbit pate," Amber interjected with a snicker before retreating into the kitchen. Hap placed the basket on the entry table and ushered his guest into the vast living room. Ingrid dropped into a plush chair beside the fireplace and sighed. "Sorry for being late—couldn't be helped."

Hap produced two glasses of champagne and sat on the sofa, facing her. "No need to explain. I spoke to our boss. Tells me you two stirred up a hornet's nest in Washington."

Her head clipped to the right, her eyes looked at him under a furrowed brow. "The two of us? You mean Richard of course. I never put myself in front of employees. They don't want to hear me. They need their leaders." She clutched her pendant.

Ingrid's insistence for invisibility with employees was a sore spot for Hap. He believed every company officer had a responsibility to be visible, especially the PR head who created and controlled messaging. He felt Ingrid worked in a vacuum.

He held up his glass to toast. "You'd amaze employees—a gifted orator. Your knowledge of our business strategy is unmatched. You're the scriptwriter."

She shook her head and scoffed, before gulping champagne.

Employees often complained to Hap that conversations with officers were stilted. He blamed guarded messages, narrow channels, and a strategy to exorcise emotion from corporate communications.

"You Mr. Sweeny, are effective in front of employees. Confidence honed from four decades of experience and unsurpassed knowledge of the business. Humble roots cloak you with sincerity." She raised her glass, "To you." She sipped and said, "I know too much. They'd ask questions. I'd be forced to fabricate."

"You make that sound almost disagreeable," Hap said.

"Employees want leaders who know the business. I never claimed to be an airline expert." Her eyes lost the borrowed warmth of her periwinkle suit and assumed the steel gray stare of a cornered cat.

Yet another example being forthcoming with employees, Hap thought, seeing the irony with her transparency campaign. He remembered his mission, charm not arm. He smiled. "You'll handle everything with your usual finesse. Hell, you probably have a package to the Board already…with your spin."

"You overestimate me. The package isn't out yet." She checked her watch. "But will be on its way to their twitching little fingers in twenty minutes." Self-satisfaction filled her words. "Our sizeable advertising spend will smother media channels. We can't control the Internet, but who cares?"

"I knew you'd have everything under control." He refilled her glass as Amber appeared with a tray of canapés before disappearing into the dining room with the vase of Irises. Hap smiled when he noticed Ingrid stare after his wife.

"You wanted to discuss candidates for your Chief Happiness Officer. I loathe that title. It's too, how shall I say—"

"Pedestrian," Hap interjected.

"Emotional…" Her lips curled as she spoke. "Middle America folksy. Wall Street would howl with laughter."

He'd toy with her. "The title's not that bad. We want our

people to feel good."

Her eyes enlarged and her nostrils flared. "Intercontinental is conflicted by global ambitions and Midwestern banality." She tossed her head to the side.

Hap sat forward. He'd heard her frequent laments about *popover country*. The Midwest she said represented *a famine of culture and a bounty of carbohydrates that left brains starving and waistlines bloated*.

"Calm down," he said, trying to mask his grin. "I tossed that *Happiness* crap. Employees might connect to *emotion,* but it's too ambitious of a start."

"I share Richard's opinion that past leadership spoiled employees. I crafted his message." She stood up and edged close to Hap. The pointed toes of her shoes touched his as she looked down at him. "Our airline will not accept anything less than a rational business approach. Investors come first. We won't deviate from that theme." She returned to her seat, crossed her legs, and raised her eyebrows and champagne flute. "If we can agree on that simple point, you have my full support."

Hap nodded, "I'm pragmatic, not delusional. I've kept my job because of more than operational expertise. I support the Chairman's message, but, we must be open to sub-themes. We must recognize employees' need for an emotional link. People think with heads and hearts."

She tapped her foot, the sound muffled by the deep rug. "Impossible, but I'll allow the supposition as long as you don't corrupt the purity of our message. I'm not a stone, Hap, whatever you think. I understand that employees crave connection. But our strategy will change discussions about Intercontinental. Richard and I won't allow anyone to undermine. Is that clear?" Her accent grew more pronounced as her voice rose.

"Ya!" he said playfully, managing a smile. "We can find common ground."

❖

After dinner, Hap and Ingrid moved to his study. The two sat in Queen Anne chairs before a roaring fire. Hap poured cognac which they drank as he reviewed his candidates. At the conclusion, he pronounced emphatically, "Wilkerson and Patterson agree on Abernathy."

She wrinkled her nose and waved the back of her hand toward him. "Let me give you *my* assessment. Maggie Richards brings broader perspective. She's untainted by a long career with Intercontinental. Consequently, she sees the forest. She's bright with good leadership training. The best way to cure a disease is to introduce an external agent. Richard has adopted that approach, importing leadership."

Hap flinched at the second reference to employees and disease that evening.

Ingrid continued. "Yet, Abernathy is a known commodity. He offers immediate credibility to employees. Unblemished record, he gets things done. He's *likable*."

Hap laughed as he stoked the fire then turned to her with poker in hand. "You don't have to say the word as if it's bad salmon."

Ingrid glared at him over her cognac glass. He saw the fire flicker in her eyes. "Does he put likeability above leader-ship?" she asked. "Can he make unpopular decisions? I'm not sure I trust such a likeable man to carry the Chairman's torch. Employees must know their place, behind investors. I'm not sure Richard will approve."

Hap made a pre-emptive strike before she buried a stake in the ground. "Maggie and Jim are equally qualified. My gut tells me Abernathy's knowledge of the airline and his network, allow faster traction. We need quick wins to get employees' attention. We're sitting in a tinderbox. Weston seemed jittery. Look at Washington." He hit his mark. Fury flashed across her face at the reference to Weston's chaotic employee meeting. "Jim can deliver results quicker. Your involvement and message control are your insurance. Maybe you'd like to mentor Abernathy?"

He waited for her to process his words. He figured she'd see his point. Jim would be paralyzed without her communication support. He went in for the kill. "Face it Ingrid, he wouldn't be the first man you castrated." Professionally or otherwise, left unsaid.

She met Hap's stare. "Our respective positions are clear. You understand my concerns and I'm confident of your continued support. If Abernathy is your preference, so be it. As for mentoring him, I leave that to you. Now put that poker down before you brand me, unless that's your intent."

She rose from the chair and smoothed her skirt. "Please thank your gorgeous wife for a delightful evening. And that lamb—delicious. I couldn't get enough."

Hap offered a polite laugh. Did Ingrid mean the roast or his wife? "Amber will be so pleased."

On the way out, Ingrid abruptly turned. "Underlicht will call you to coordinate a Washington visit. Richard and I agree. You can calm the beasts behind that nasty petition. Convince them to drop this distasteful matter." She didn't wait for a reply.

After she left, Hap returned to the study. He sat in the firelight with another cognac. "*Quid pro quo,*" he said. "I mop up their shit, they give me Abernathy."

A loud crackle drew his eyes to the fire. "But why are they so afraid of this Washington rabble, why now?"

Chapter 14

Jim & Julie at Home

The aroma of fresh coffee and voices on a television, lulled Jim awake. He loved Sunday mornings. The leisurely pace that allowed him to catch up on his newspapers, enjoy an unhurried cup of coffee, and spend uninterrupted time with Julie.

Waves of layoffs at Intercontinental had shrunk the workforce but not the workload. Jim's hectic schedule gave the couple little time together during the week—a late dinner, maybe an hour of television before the cycle repeated. Staying connected with family and friends provided another pressure, albeit a pleasant one. They coveted weekends, preserving as much time as possible to spend together and work on their addition.

Julie typically rose first, quietly pushing aside the covers and tiptoeing downstairs. She told Jim he deserved one day to sleep in. Her Sunday ritual began with grinding coffee beans and fetching the bulky newspapers from the end of the suburban driveway.

Most Sundays, he found her nestled in a blanket on the couch watching a home improvement show or a program about babies and kids. Jim called this nesting—just a matter of time before mama bird could put all the mindless programming to good use. Watching cable and other indulgences would be a luxury after the baby came, he realized.

Sedona, the couple's plump golden retriever, was always the last Abernathy to venture downstairs. Having outgrown the agility to jump onto furniture, Sedona adapted to sleeping at the foot of the bed where the carpet muffled her snoring. With their pursuit of a baby, the couple appreciated the new arrangement although thunderstorms gave the dog an adrenaline rush sufficient to mount the bed.

Sunday mornings included long walks into the village for coffee and breakfast. The couple preferred to eat outdoors even on days when the chill required snuggling. Their overstuffed fluff of fur was a kid magnet. Jim loved watching Julie gaze fondly at the giggling rugrats who climbed all over their good-tempered pet.

Jim threw on his sweats, patted the snoring Sedona and headed downstairs. He passed behind Julie curled on the couch, eyes glued to HGTV. With choreography practiced over ten years of marriage, she leaned her head backwards as he bent forward where their lips met in a synchronized kiss.

"Morning sweetie. Your papers are on the table," Julie said before returning her gaze to the television.

Jim closed his eyes and inhaled. "Fresh coffee too. You're the best."

"You expected less. Love you more than you love me."

He squeezed her shoulder. "Love you more."

"Not on Sundays," she said, tilting her head back a second time. Jim snickered when he saw her protruding tongue.

"I'll give you that." He looked at the TV. "What's Mr. tight jeans and Ms. push up bra peddling?" Jim joked that such shows snared viewers who tuned in only to catch cleavage and bulging blue jeans.

"A new show," Julie said. "Kids decorate their bedrooms."

"That's called finger paint, comic books, and dirty clothes piles."

She swatted his hand, still on her shoulder. "Very funny. Seriously, the designers are fabulous. I love watching the kids squeal and cry."

"Sure that's not the parents?" he asked. "How many variations on castles, racecars, stadiums, and dollhouses can there be? Show me a room with a billiard table, mini bar, and plasma screen, and I'll show you a seven-year-old with vision." Jim laughed.

"You're hopeless," Julie said before lowering the volume. "We'll have to redo one of the bedrooms into a nursery."

He was glad she couldn't see his rolled eyes. "So you've told me."

She pivoted around to face him. "But sweetie. You agreed."

He tapped her nose. "I promise we'll do all of that, and the bathroom you want, once we get the green light. There's no shortage of ideas."

"Just money. I understand," she said, dropping her head.

Jim heard the disappointment in his wife's voice. "We'll get there, honey. I don't want you worrying about money, or anything else. Nothing's too expensive for my baby and my baby's baby." He kissed the top of her head. "And, don't even think about getting a job."

He caressed her cheek. He didn't want to talk about their finances and ruin a perfectly good Sunday morning. Yet he felt trapped financially. Their mortgage was underwater—couldn't sell if they wanted. He'd gone over the inventory of debt in his head so many times; two car payments, credit cards, and doctors' bills. They were getting by but a minor hiccup could sink their plans.

Jim walked into the kitchen. Newspapers and an empty mug set on the table brought a smile. Julie made their debts unimportant. Before grabbing the coffee pot, he snatched his blackberry off of the counter with a trepidation that returned every morning when he plugged himself back into his 24/7 world. "All's right with the world," he shouted after scanning the messages. "The airline's cooperating this morning." Julie waved a hand in reply.

Jim sat down and sipped his coffee, flipping first to the business section. Stories highlighted the great recession and stubborn unemployment numbers. Companies, quoted a noted economist, were under pressure to produce earnings— more likely to come from cost cutting than revenue growth. She explained that consumers, fearful of job losses, were hoarding cash. Commodities including oil, attracted investors looking for something more tangible than derivatives and equities. Every economic indicator suggested more struggles for Intercontinental. *Lucky to have a job*, he thought. Unemployed friends shared horror stories of impossible job searches.

The patter of paws down the stairs, and heavy panting, heralded Sedona's arrival. Jim greeted the tail-wagger as she headed toward the French doors. "Morning gorgeous—you're up early."

Julie shouted from the couch, "Sweetie, give me five minutes before our walk. Don't want to miss the big reveal. It's for an adorable, six-year-old girl,"

"Spoiler alert," he yelled back. "Expect a pink fairy castle. But call me if it's a stripper pole." The rising volume of the TV drowned his voice.

⚜

"That company of yours is horrible," Julie said as she raised the zipper of her jacket. Her breath produced puffs of vapor.

"*My* company? You worked there," Jim said, pulling Sedona from a tree in which a cornered squirrel chattered its agitation.

Julie squeezed his arm. "I escaped."

"Lucky you," he said, guessing a hidden agenda. "So what's wrong?"

"What isn't? Bad things to good people."

"Who called this time?" Jim sighed, rolling his eyes. He didn't like friends who took advantage of Julie. They mistook her empathetic ear for that of a therapist. They unloaded their anger by venting to Julie. She didn't need that stress but he knew she couldn't say no.

She slowed, turning toward him. "Nelly and Kim."

"Who?"

"You know," she said. "Nelly Connors, my friend from Headquarters."

Jim nodded. Of course, that Nelly. One of those people who ate and drank Intercontinental. The real soul of the company.

"And Kim," Julie said. "We flew together in my glamour days." She pushed out her chest and wiggled her backside.

He patted her behind. "You're *still* glamorous baby." He turned, waiting for her laugh. "So, both fired, huh?"

"Only Nelly. Layoffs are just part of the problem. Wait until you hear Kim's story."

"And I have some bad news about Shane," Jim said, cringing. He was reluctant to further ignite Julie.

Julie stopped. She grabbed his arm. "Don't tell me."

"Yep, fired," he said looking into her bug eyes. "So much for our peaceful walk, harmonizing with nature."

Julie pointed to a squatting Sedona. "Get a bag. Your precious liitle princess is harmonizing now, fertilizing the Greenbrier's lawn."

Jim handed her the leash before crouching down on the grass. Julie spoke, twirling to avoid Sedona's entangling moves. "It's an epidemic. That place is toxic. You gotta get out of there."

"To where? Honey, we've talked about that," Jim said standing up and grabbing the leash. "This isn't a good time."

"When is a good time?" Julie snapped. Seconds later, she pressed his arm. "I'm sorry," she said with a contrite expression.

He was relieved she caught herself, but the same argument

repeated with increasing frequency. She began to call his loyalty to Intercontinental an *unhealthy obsession*. Maybe she was right. He loved the company since childhood. Could he ever leave?

Jim patted her hand and smiled. "It's okay honey. I like my job most of the time and Wilkerson doesn't bother me, too much."

"Only because he doesn't know what you do," she said, turning to walk down the sidewalk.

Jim deposited the poop bag in a neighbor's garbage. "He's not that bad."

"From what I hear, he spends all his time kissing Weston's ass. And, that's a Herculean task," She snickered. "Is he still planning Hap's retirement?"

Jim shook his head. "Hap's not leaving."

"Not according to Wilkerson. He wants Hap's job so bad he'll do *anything* to get it."

Jim grunted. Julie must have recognized his cue, because she changed the subject. "Tell me about Shane. He and Susan must be devastated. Their kids are in line for college and Susan just got dropped to part-time," she said as they waited to cross a busy street.

"You first. What happened to Nelly?" Jim asked. "She's a lifer—over 30 years?"

"34 ½ to be exact. Furloughed on Friday," Julie shouted as they darted across the street.

Furlough was an airline euphemism like *creeping delay* (Chinese water torture), *inflight snack* (one inhale of pretzel dust), *mishandled bag* (mauled luggage swallowed by a black hole) and *legacy carrier* (bloated dinosaur). *Furlough* had its origins in the industry's early ties to government. The term had a more pleasant ring than *terminate, fire, ax,* or *layoff* although the result was the same.

As they neared the village center, Julie shared Nelly's story. "Sorry if it's butchered," she said. "Took Nelly three sob-filled telephone calls to get it out." Nelly's boss delivered the news after lunch. She was convinced that he manipulated her annual review to give him cover for his decision. He rated her the lowest in her career. His written comments didn't match the score; praise and superlatives suggested higher achievement. Not once during the prior year, had the boss hinted at unsatisfactory work. Facts and fairness were inconsequential. "I assumed Nelly's boss received orders to *cut a head*,"Julie said. "Who didn't matter. Get a load of this crap," Julie continued. "The schmuck told Nelly that he appreciated her *orderly departure*."

Jim scrunched his face. "You gotta be kidding."

"Wish I was, sweetie. Get's better. Told her how lucky she was since she had reached the minimum retirement age. Then gave her thirty minutes to gather her belongings. A rent-a-cop, who needed her help to find the exit, marched her out. After Nelly left, according to her co-workers, the schmuck told them to pick up the slack."

"Her fate could have been theirs," he said. "Poor Nelly. What's she gonna do now, retire?

"She can't," Julie said. "Not with the pension cuts. She has to find another job."

"But escorted out—really? She deserved better after all those years," Jim seethed.

"She's humiliated," Julie said, choking back a tear.

Jim reached for her hand as he held the bucking Sedona with his other. "Finding a job will be tough. The economy sucks, not to mention her age. What happened to Kim?"

"Not as serious as Nelly, but just as frustrating." Julie stopped and wrinkled her nose. "Haven't I depressed you enough?"

Jim inhaled deeply and squeezed her hand. "On a beautiful

spring morning, with the two most important ladies in my life, *no way*."

She entwined her arm with his and pressed her head against his arm. "Sedona and I are lucky."

As they continued their walk, she relayed her friend's story. Kim, a flight attendant, received an automated response from the company's Initiative Center identical to the first three form letters. The note, lacking contact name or number, thanked her for her idea and informed her to expect an update after review and analysis. The closing sentence requested patience. A prominent banner on the company's website promoted the program with such success that employees submitted over 900 suggestions for cost cutting, revenue enhancements and operational improvements in one year.

Kim suggested that the airline stop boarding salt and pepper shakers on every breakfast tray, since morning meals were limited to sweet rolls and doughnuts. After a second submission and form letter response, she elevated the issue to her supervisor who advised her to be patient. After the third form letter, the supervisor agreed to follow up but had no success identifying a contact. He told Kim to resubmit her idea that brought the fourth form letter.

"The shakers continue to be boarded and unused, flight after flight," Julie huffed.

Jim shook his head. He pondered the terrible costs of ignoring employees.

Julie's tone became empathetic. "Kim's hurt, feels she means nothing to the company. Her supervisor feels horrible, but Kim can't help thinking he's inept even though I told her it's not his fault."

"Honey, I'll dig around, but I'm certain the company fired the person in charge of that program over a year ago. They weren't replaced." He couldn't believe the company would continue to solicit ideas and send them into a black hole.

Julie stopped as Sedona jerked Jim forward. "That doesn't surprise me. I wish you could leave that place sweetie."

The couple walked the remaining blocks in silence.

***

Jim and Julie found a sunny table in the village square to drink their coffee and eat their bakery goods. Sedona competed with sparrows and an aggressive squirrel for crumbs of scone and bagel before settling at their feet. Jim adored the way Julie became animated when they talked about their planned additions to home and family.

"Once the baby comes, I want you to work less. Can you scale back your travel?"

Her appeal made her look like a little girl.

"First we have to get pregnant." He tapped her lightly on the nose. "I just don't see things changing. They're talking about more cuts, which means *more* work, *more* travel."

Julie pouted, prompting Jim to add with an upbeat tone. "Cheer up, we have time. Things could improve."

"I'm sorry," she said. "I know you love your job. Tell me about Shane."

Jim sighed. He put down his coffee cup. "Fired last week after 23 years. His manager blamed him for the rotten performance of two vendors under his supervision."

Julie swallowed a piece of scone before speaking. "Wasn't he doing your job in reverse, buying services from others—outsourcing?"

Jim nodded as he launched into his friend's story. Shane tried to improve the quality of the work done by the vendors under his control. Nothing seemed to work. Shane concluded that both companies lacked the resources, profit margins, and expertise to fix their problems. They won their contracts by boasting of low cost structures. "The business equivalent of Internet bait and switch," Jim said. "You know, post a gorgeous face on a dating site that isn't you." They both snickered.

In the past several years, Intercontinental mounted an aggressive campaign to drive down costs of services and products. Bankruptcy gave the airline cover to eliminate burdensome contracts. A new purchasing VP recruited by Weston, extracted costs with unbridled passion. Known as *The Tiger*, she warned the staff that *relationships were dangerous. Familiarity bred compromise and waste.*

Calling complacency a cancer, Purchasing implemented a revolving door strategy—contracts awarded to lowest bidders. The Tiger continuously re-organized her department. She reshuffled and discarded, keeping her staff anxious and alert. Those above her in the food chain, praised her for the graceful manner in which she delivered cost savings. Business units quaked, the pouncing Tiger called forth the ferocity of the CFO, lord of the financial jungle, on any manager deemed uncooperative.

Shane's two lackluster vendors had been low bidders, beating out high-performing, long-term partners. Initially, Shane and his manager voiced concern, doubting the ability of the two companies to perform. Their tepid endorsements eventually came under pressure from *The Tiger* who questioned their commitment. She won, posting the savings on a tally board, memorializing her good work before moving on to her next kill.

"Shane's reward," Jim said. "Constant pressure to bolster floundering performance." When improvement didn't materialize and complaints from customers and leaders including Wilkerson and Hap swelled, hungry shouts of discontent demanded action. Blame needed to be assessed on someone, anyone—a sacrifice at the altar of accountability. Shane's manager offered him up to save his own skin.

"It's a raw deal. They're not giving him any severance. Even denied his unemployment claim." The story made Jim sick. He didn't tell Julie the worst part of the ordeal. Shane's wife was talking divorce. She'd hear that from Susan soon enough.

Julie shook her head. "And what makes you think that won't happen to you?"

Chapter 15

Hap Increases His Odds

"Hap Sweeny, how the hell are you?" The boisterous voice that interrupted the quiet corner of the Washington lounge, belonged to Kyle Richter.

Hap, nursing a double gin and tonic, rose as the baggy-panted man with wrinkled shirt and untamed hair approached. "You're a sight for sore eyes." He waited for the man to free his hands of a coffee cup and briefcase before offering a vigorous handshake. "Thanks for flying down to meet me."

"Your call intrigued me," Richter said, poking Hap's suit jacket.

"Thought it might," Hap said as both men sat. A college kid rocking to his IPod, seemed an unlikely eavesdropper, while a television tuned to a bellowing cable news channel provided cover for the men to talk candidly.

"But I wasn't surprised," Richter said, fumbling in his pockets and producing sugar packets. "What brings you to Washington?"

"Cleaning up Weston's shit. You know the saying—big CEOs, like big dogs—"

"Shit big," Richter snorted as he opened several packs of sugar into his coffee.

Hap sipped his drink. "This was a stinker. Diarrhea of the mouth—created quite the firestorm."

Richter stirred his coffee with his finger. "And you're here to douse the flames, as usual."

Hap shrugged. He was still digesting the employee meeting, the one arranged in barter for Ingrid's agreement not to black ball Jim Abernathy. Something went terribly wrong. But he had little time before his return flight to Chicago, and he needed Richter's help.

Hap winked. "So you expected my call, huh? What else did your crystal ball say?"

Richter laughed. The Boston consultant made a small fortune off of Intercontinental. Prior to establishing his own practice, Richter was a principal for a global firm, Tavistock Partners, known for its barnacle-like attachments to corporate boards and executives. Although he didn't entirely embrace their methods, he enjoyed the financial rewards.

With a stable of well-pedigreed associates, Tavistock prodded CEOs to act—an example of the tail wagging the dog. The firm established credibility by packaging as their own, ideas created at lower levels of a company. Disconnected executives applauded the firm's grasp of their company's pulse, praising as fresh, a regurgitation of homegrown ideas. The accolades resembled the praise showered on the tourist whose recitation of a foreign menu is mistaken for fluency. The firm's founder memorialized his belief that disengaged CEOs provided rich opportunities, in his credo: *Bad Cultures are Good Business.* Tavistock dazzled CEOs who valued prestige above effectiveness; the same way owners of unreliable luxury cars cared little that their status symbols idled in a mechanic's garage.

Richter gave up that game eight years ago. He credited his success in transitioning to an independent consultancy on a large network, keen persuasion skills and a steady stream of billable hours. He enjoyed getting his hands dirty, but didn't lose sleep when results proved elusive. Hap joked that Richter combined a heart of gold with the cold conscience of a consultant.

"I make it my business to stay informed about favorite clients," Richter huffed.

"Sure, sniffing around for a juicy engagement. Time for a new vacation home or cosmetic surgery for your girlfriend," Hap laughed, punching Richter's shoulder.

Richter's mouth fell open, his shoulders stiffened. "I have only the noblest of intentions."

"That mean you're waiving your fee? Finance will be thrilled. They're hammering us to cut purchased services," Hap said with a chuckle.

"Purchased Services! Makes me sound like a high-class hooker," Richter said as he added another sugar packet to his coffee.

Hap nodded. "There are similarities."

"Do tell," Richter said, flourishing his palm.

"Both take any client with money, offer insincere flattery, bill by the hour, and get paid regardless of a happy ending." Hap's chest convulsed with laughter.

Richter glared. "Surprised you missed the fact that we both screw our clients."

Hap grinned. "But consultants are more versatile. They have countless ways to fuck with people."

Richter exploded with laughter. He slapped Hap's knee. "Touch my fee and I'll tell everyone you're a tight wad who adds sawdust to pretzel mix, waters down jet fuel, and replaces first officers with blow-up dolls."

Hap snapped his fingers. "Tried em all. Inflatable pilots had some success but were full of hot air. We pulled the plug."

"Nothing's more prickly than a pilot with a deflated ego," Richter said.

"How about a consultant down to his last billable hour?"

Richter shrugged. "Touché! But seriously, no one's shocked by anything airlines do to save a buck. Who'd have guessed fees for luggage, pillows or blankets?"

"Real money-makers," Hap said. We order pilots to lower cabin temperatures. Blankets sell like hotcakes. One competitor charges customers to piss."

"An incentive to give away beer—great product differentiator and boosts lavatory sales."

Hap pointed at Richter. "Gotta find some way to pay our outrageous consulting fees."

Richter sighed. "I give up. Consulting may be the oldest profession. The serpent that counseled Eve was consultant zero."

"For which advice Adam, and all mankind, paid dearly. Some things never change." Hap enjoyed his relationship with Richter, a welcome break from the barbed-wire fence he raised between himself and people. Confidences were slippery slopes that led to familiarity—dangerous in a culture where enemies exploited vulnerability for political gain.

Richter looked into Hap's eyes. "You didn't fly me down here to insult me."

Hap leaned forward, his tone sincere. "Kyle, I need your help."

"I can see why. The airlines are getting creamed. I caught the Congressional hearings on C-Span. Got a kick out of the lampooned testimony too."

"Weston wasn't amused."

"I bet. Leno joked that Congress urged airline CEOs to take private jets to Washington to avoid delays. Letterman had a spoof about trapped passengers—beverage containers doubled as urine receptacles and seat cushions served as flotation devices and high-fiber snacks." Richter roared with laughter, spilling coffee on his pant leg.

Hap frowned as his finger tapped the tabletop. "And the

actors playing flight attendants barked like Nazi guards."

"You're fodder for the media, comedians and Capitol Hill. Dangerous, especially with bulldog Klein. This is spiraling out of control," Richter said. "Marketing campaigns and public relations' propaganda can't save you."

"Don't underestimate Ingrid. She could convince the media that politicians have integrity."

"And *vice versa.*" Richter chuckled, but his tone turned somber. "It's no laughing matter. No secret either. Your customer and employee ratings are racing to new lows."

Hap took a swig of his drink. "That's why I called. We gotta turn this around."

"I'm listening, but let me ask, why now? Your leadership has never tackled systemic issues."

Hap flinched. "Sure we have."

"Really!" Richter said, bobbing his head. "Besides stopgap efforts thrown together to save somebody's ass?" He paused. Richter's glare made Hap squirm. "Employees are the heart of the business and the core of your problems," Richter added.

Hap sat up, digging his fingers into the armrest. He was embarrassed. "You're right."

"Watching your CEO before Klein, I couldn't believe I was listening to Richard Weston III, pepper his testimony with employee anecdotes. He sounded human. But despite Klein's velvet gloves, I sensed desperation."

Hap nodded. "Classic Weston. Ingrid admitted to staging that piece of showmanship to soften his image. I'm surprised she didn't stuff him in a cardigan and Hush Puppies."

Richter pressed Hap's shoulder. His expression turned dour. "Tell me, have you heard anything about Weston putting Intercontinental up for sale?"

Hap bristled. "No! We're dumping tons of money into the product. He wouldn't burn cash if he planned to sell. And, there's my project. We're not for sale," he said with a scowl.

Richter swatted the air. "I guess you'd know. It's just… well, I've heard things," he stammered. "Including the fact that you've been tapped to lead an employee initiative."

Hap grinned. "You amaze me."

Richter tapped his chair's arm. "Remember that, when you get my bill. So, what is it you need?"

Hap shared the initiative. He described Jim Abernathy, emphasizing Jim's passion for employees. "This initiative must succeed," Hap said. He thought of his old buddy, Charlie. Not to mention feeling like a bloodied gladiator after the just concluded meeting.

Richter interjected. "Sounds like culture change. What's Weston's role?"

Hap sighed. "Merely the banker. We'll have to work around him. That Uncle Dicky act for Congress was a charade. I wouldn't say he hates employees. He just doesn't like them very much."

Richter stiffened. "Then why is he bankrolling this effort?"

"To salvage our sinking business plan."

Richter nodded. "Count me in. Me make you very happy. By the way, you never shared details of your pooper scooper mission."

Hap looked at his watch. "Sorry, but I have to run to my flight."

As he downed the last of his drink and gathered his belongings, a voice over the room's loudspeaker crackled, *We kindly request all passengers on flight 671 to Chicago to see an agent for rebooking.* Hap looked to his phone and groaned. A text from Headquarters notified him that his flight had cancelled for engine issues.

"Figures! Now I'll miss my daughter's recital," he muttered, slumping back into the lounge chair.

Richter beamed. "Now you can tell me about your meeting."

Hap mustered a smile. "You really interested?"

"It's employee related, right? My meter's running. First base isn't free for call girls or consultants." Richter chuckled.

Hap laughed. "A heart of gold but an icy cold conscience."

After getting another drink, Hap launched into a description of Weston's Easter Sunday call and Ingrid's strong-arm tactics that roped him into cleaning up Weston's Washington mess. He shook his head. "A cluster fuck. Instead of dousing the fire, I was prime Jet Fuel A. The place lit up."

"What do you mean?" Richter asked, his eyes widening.

"They came gunning for me, not Weston. They knew about my new pay package. Hasn't been published. Yet, they taunted me with shouts of *bionic man*." Hap noticed Richter's quizzical expression. "A reference to my six-million dollar contract."

Richter nodded. "Where did they get their information?"

Hap shrugged. "No idea. Obviously another leak."

"Another?" Richter's eyes narrowed.

"Where to start? A barrage of anonymous tips. The FAA's reviewing our engine maintenance, the DOT's auditing our complaint letters, and the TSA's hunting for security breaches. All I need now is the SEC on my ass!"

Richter tilted his head. "Those all fall under your area of responsibility," he said. "Don't you find that an odd coincidence?"

Hap brushed off the suggestion with a waved hand and dismissive tone, "My money's on a disgruntled employee. God knows we've plenty."

But something in Richter's face told him the consultant wasn't convinced.

Chapter 16

Jim is Summoned

"Where's Abernathy?" Hap's voice yelled from his desk. Winny scurried into the office. Her bifocals, dangling on a silver chain, bounced against her blouse. "Calm down. Jim's not due for ten minutes. You could have told him why he's being summoned. Poor guy probably didn't sleep a wink."

"Anxiety builds character." Hap's eyes danced as he clutched his coffee mug.

Winny contorted her face. She turned toward the door and muttered, "And, you wonder why we have issues!"

⋘✦⋙

Jim arrived early, flashing a nervous smile at the white-haired assistant who whisked him across the threshold with a hand on his shoulder. With suit, shirt, tie, and shoes standing out among casually dressed peers, Jim dodged nosy inquisitors all morning. He even tamed his wavy blond hair using his wife's hair product. He presented himself, freshly pressed and scrubbed.

Hap rose, leaving the refuge of his desk with extended arm. Jim felt convinced Hap's laser-like stare saw the sweat beads on his forehead and the perspiration stains of his suit. His own hand rose then retreated to his side once he realized that Hap's arm was a guide, not a greeting.

"Take a seat." Hap pointed to a chair at the table with its back to the window. He stood silent with hands crossed. His shirt and face looked equally starched. Jim had never seen such glossy shoes or trousers with creases as sharp as razor blades.

A long pause convinced Jim of impending doom. His own suit felt like it had grown smaller. His mouth dried; his collar chafed. He didn't know where to look. The austere décor of glass and chrome chilled. Oversized artwork unsettled— shapeless pieces of drab color. His darting eyes clicked on the unfamiliar surroundings like a camera shutter, but always the commanding presence dominated the room—breathing, glaring at him.

Jim felt awed by the lair of a man who held absolute power over tens of thousands of employees and influenced an entire industry. Yet, he sensed isolation in the environment; a feeling intensified by the contrast of the dim, sterile office to the light and bustle of activity outside the window.

Hap broke the silence. "Can you guess why you're here?" Neither tone nor facial expression betrayed the interrogator whose eyes remained frozen on Jim.

Jim's hands interlocked on his lap. His wedding band crushed fingers. "No sir."

A smile slowly cracked the granite face. "Don't worry." Hap winked before striding to the table. He sat, his eyes never drifting from Jim's.

Jim sighed. His facial muscles relaxed. "That's a relief."

Hap pushed himself back from the glass table and crossed his legs, one hand resting on an elevated ankle. "You've been with Intercontinental two decades. Many promotions. Very successful, right?"

Jim scrutinized the inquisitor. A nervous cough preceded his reply. "I'd like to think so. I've been lucky—lots of good assignments and great people."

"Your accomplishments are only one reason you caught my attention. Our airline's in a bind. Service stinks and employees couldn't care less. You agree?" The eyes narrowed.

Jim gulped, his stomach tensed. He felt disappointed in leadership himself. Julie's criticisms stung. But, caution dictated he not concur too eagerly, especially to the airline's second in command. Could this be a trap? Why would Hap Sweeny ask a mid-level manager to affirm the failings of the company he led? Didn't that amount to self-incrimination? Jim picked at the suit fabric that crimped under his arms. He spoke slowly, trying to read Hap's reaction. "I've seen customer data. Sadly, their perceptions continue to deteriorate."

Hap poked a finger across the table. "And employees are jaded, angry, disengaged. Don't you agree?"

Jim felt his eyes enlarge. His foot tapped the table leg. He cleared his throat. His voice faltered but he pushed through the words. "Employee surveys suggest that conclusion, yes." As he spoke, he noticed Hap's face redden and a forehead vein throb.

"Hell, the problem goes beyond surveys," Hap blurted. "A fellow I've known for forty years—good guy, backbone of the company—told me we deserve to go out of business. That's like your wife telling you it's time for a divorce. When long-term employees start suggesting we shut down, we're finished." Hap's gaze shifted to the window. "Ever hear of a graveyard spiral?"

"No sir," Jim whispered, "But it doesn't sound good."

Hap laughed. "No it's not good. Happens when a pilot, usually green, loses the horizon and gets disoriented. The plane ends up in an inescapable, spiraling dive." Hap's palm smacked the table. "That could be us."

Did Hap already see Intercontinental spiraling out of control? Jim leaned forward. He became animated. "I know our people. They still care for this company and our customers." He caught himself. He looked across the table to see if he crossed the line. Hap turned from the window. He blinked. Jim felt the eyes soften. A slight tilt of the head signaled a willingness to listen. Hap motioned with his hand for him to continue. Jim inhaled, "It's just that our people are embarrassed. They want to be proud of the company and the uniform that publicly brands them as Intercontinental employees—for better or worse." Jim exhaled. For some reason he expected Hap to smile.

Instead, Hap remained frozen, his lips pursed and brow furrowed. Then he sighed, "Hope you're right. That's why I need your help." Hap's mood melded with the office—both lonely and cold.

A sense of bewilderment swept over Jim. Hap seemed tired, almost afraid. Did a tortured soul lurk behind those formidable eyes and impenetrable face? Instinctively, Jim leaned toward the speaker. Sympathy inflected his tone, "What can I do?" He waited, watching the other man. He sensed movement behind the twitching eyes.

Zeal replaced melancholy as Hap pitched the mission with the fervor of a seasoned salesman. His words came at Jim with jackhammer speed. "You'll have a new role focused on employees. A big investment in our people. Weston and I want someone with company knowledge and compassion. This won't be easy. Maybe the hardest job in the company. We think you're our guy."

"What?" Jim's thoughts jumbled. He loved Intercontinental and its employees. Hap's sudden burst of energy and the exuberant testimonial of his qualifications made his head spin. His hand clutched the side of his face.

"There's no job description," Hap said. "No turnkey staff, not even the hint of a trail."

The light-headedness began to wear off; Jim sensed a disconnect between Hap's upbeat tone and the daunting challenge. He tilted his head. His hands interlocked on the table. "Can you tell me more?"

Hap smiled. "What kind of an employer should we be? What does it mean to work here? Where do we invest to get there?"

Jim rubbed his chin. "Culture change?"

"Of sorts. Human Resources leads traditional culture change. This position is embedded within Operations. You'll report to me."

"Good! I don't want to report into HR." Jim surprised himself with his candor. He looked down at his hands.

"I don't blame you. HR is broken, horribly broken. They're distracted by one reorganization after another. You can keep rearranging the room, but after continued dissatisfaction, even a fool would figure out the answer's new furniture."

At that moment, Jim felt Hap had parted the executive curtain, inviting him backstage for a glimpse of the inner-workings of the executive suite. His confidence grew.

"Patterson's team's adrift," Hap continued. "They've lost credibility. We need someone who enjoys employee respect, who can provide tools and resources."

"Sounds an awful lot like culture change," Jim said.

Hap shook his head. "Culture change may be part of the overall curriculum, but it's advanced coursework. We're in first grade, learning our ABCs. The basics are broken."

Jim sat up. *Hap got it*, he thought. His pulse raced. "I'm assuming we'll have resources to invest in basic equipment and facility improvements."

"And in leadership capabilities, employee development and recognition. Your job is to figure out where to spend." Jim nodded as Hap added, "But we're getting ahead of ourselves. Do you want the job?" Hap's face tensed.

Jim tugged at his tie. "I'm flattered, really I am. But…I… really love my job. And my team," he stammered. "I'd hate to abandon them." His eyes met Hap's stare. He inhaled. "Then there are my concerns."

The last hint of Hap's smile vanished. "Concerns? What concerns?" Hap barked before his lips disappeared.

"Don't get me wrong," Jim said, "this is a fantastic opportunity. I simply haven't seen Intercontinental go the whole ten yards with these efforts."

Hap stiffened and his face reddened. "What do you mean 'these efforts'?"

Jim hesitated, but his confidence rebounded. "We've had mission and vision statements, service rules of 3, 4, and 5, and employee programs too numerous to recall. Nothing ever sticks. Flowers are great, but you can't plant roses in the Great Salt Lake." Jim hoped that Hap would see his point.

Hap leaned over the conference table. He placed his hand on Jim's arm. His words flowed slowly. "Jim, this isn't a question of *if* this can succeed. It *must* succeed. Otherwise our airplanes will sit in the desert and your co-workers will be in the unemployment line. You don't want to put people out of work? People you care about?"

Jim's mind flashed to the image of a graveyard spiral. A catastrophe for friends and family—so many depended upon the company. Julie's and his dream intertwined with Intercontinental's fate.

Hap squeezed Jim's arm. "I stake my career and personal reputation on this effort. You have my support... *and* my word."

Jim took a deep breath. "Your personal pledge means a lot."

"Well?" Hap sat back, the palms of both hands extended upwards.

Jim rubbed his sweaty palms down his trousers. "Where do we go from here?"

"Congratulations." Hap patted Jim firmly on the shoulder.

"I've scheduled a meeting with a consultant, but a great guy. Kyle Richter—probably seen him around. He'll help. You'll have to figure out what your staff looks like. Work with HR on that."

"To blaze a trail?" Jim asked. He had concern that a broken organization as Hap, himself called HR, had the skills and tools to help him hack through the corporate jungle.

"I almost forgot," Hap said. "I've decided to establish a Senior Advisory Board."

Jim didn't know what that meant. More bureaucracy, more hurdles to jump, or worse, more masters to serve? His task was already complicated without adding internal politics. Advisory Boards, especially those made up of big egos never advised. They commanded. "What will they do?"

"Help. They'll be your sounding board, your forum to vet ideas, gain consensus, get resources."

"Who's on this Board?" Jim asked, his exuberance waning.

Hap tapped his forehead. "Me, Ingrid Shattenworter, Carrie Patterson, and operation leaders like Chad Wilkerson and his peers."

"Tyler Dagger and Bryce Jacobs?" Jim asked, knowing that Planning and Finance were key stakeholders who controlled resources and working conditions.

Hap looked away. He rose from the table and walked to the window, his hands in his trouser pockets. His tone changed, matching the chill of the office. "This is *my* initiative—operations focused. Dagger and Jacobs care nothing about employees. I'll make sure you have the right players."

Jim remained skeptical. He considered Hap a skilled survivor He would have to trust the seasoned executive's insight and political instincts—at least for now. Hap turned, extending his arm, this time for a handshake. His eyes flashed with the sun's reflection. "By the way, I neglected to tell you this job comes complete with a vice president title. Congratulations."

Jim's head swam as he staggered from Hap's office. He stumbled on the carpet and found himself face–to-face with Winny. Her broad smile put him at ease.

"Congratulations," she whispered, flashing a thumbs-up.

Jim forced an embarrassed laugh. "Thanks. If I could get off on the right foot."

"No worries. You're more sure footed than most of the vice presidents around here." She winked. "Let me know how I can help."

"For starters, tell me how to break the news to my wife." Swept with buyer's remorse, Jim gritted his teeth. Julie would kill him. He should have consulted her.

"She'll be as proud of you as your mom. You'll see." Winny batted her hand toward him. He felt Winny's eyes follow him to the elevators and thought he heard her mumble, "Little chick, that's the least of your problems."

Jim's mind raced back to Julie and her fears of his survival in the toxic environment. "But I can fix things," he uttered aloud, catching the stare of another secretary. He thought of his new mission. Optimism surged, fed by restored faith in his company and leadership. He had no reason to expect anything but full support from front line employees all the way up the line. *But what did Winny mean?*

Chapter 17

Hap's Dealt a Mixed Hand

Seconds after the elevator doors shut on Jim Abernathy, Winny poked her head through Hap's office door. "Jacobs wants to talk about the budget. Managed to dial all by himself if you can believe that."

The secretary's irreverent barbs endeared her to Hap. While he shared similar opinions of his peers, his sarcasm lived vicariously through Winny's unfiltered wit. Both of her hands rested on her hips. "God forbid his high and mightiness should walk the thirty yards from his office."

Hap stifled a laugh as he waved her away. "Better shut the door." He winced as he eyed the phone. He didn't enjoy talking to the CFO who spoke about company finances with the detachment of a contract killer. All too often, Hap found his operating divisions in his sights. "What's up?" Hap asked, holding the phone while scrolling through emails.

Jacobs' bass voice droned without inflection. "We've got problems. Oil futures are skyrocketing."

"I recall you mentioning that increases were possible, but not to worry."

"Time to worry. Oil's up $10 a barrel today."

"Why?" Hap said as he frantically toggled to a financial website.

"Speculators. Money is abandoning equities. It's a feeding frenzy."

Hap sighed. "And who said greed is good?"

"I for one. We just got dealt a bad hand this time. Oil's

unpredictable. One sniff of opportunity and the vultures swoop."

Hap scowled. Would he ever get used to Jacobs' matter-of-fact attitude toward company misfortune? He switched to speaker-mode and rose. His chair crashed backwards into the credenza with a thud. "How bad is it?"

"Bad! Each dollar increase boosts our annual operating costs by fifty million." Hap did the simple math in his head as Jacobs grunted over the phone. "Kiss a half-billion of profit good-bye. Bye-bye bonus."

Hap's thoughts sped to his stock options. He prayed that his stockbroker had already executed the order. He bent over the computer, scrambling for stock quotes as Jacobs' monotone lumbered on. "It could get worse."

"What about our hedges? Surely, *your* people saw this coming." His interrogatory tone surprised him.

As he expected, Jacobs bristled. Blame came quickly at the airline where mistakes scored leaders. "*My* people are doing exactly what the Board and the executive team on which you sit, told them to do."

Hap rolled his eyes, "And that would be?"

"We're only hedged ten percent. Creditors didn't want us using *their* cash to gamble."

During bankruptcy, the creditors committee used court-appointed powers to protect cash even if it meant shortsighted decisions and poor service. Hap understood their rationale, but didn't like it. Hap paced. One hand stroked his face and the other tucked into the front pocket of his trousers. "Can we buy hedges now?"

Jacobs resumed his monotone. "Too late. Too much uncertainty. Oil could shoot to $100 a barrel or dive to $40. I'm calling an emergency session with the executive team. The Board will be looking for answers."

Hap stopped in his tracks. His eyes narrowed onto the computer screen. *Stock down $12.* He fumbled for the mute button and bellowed for Winny to call his broker. "Ask Harold if he executed!" he shouted.

"You there? Hap?" Jacobs asked.

"Yes, yes, go on," Hap said after un-muting the phone.

"Wall Street demands a swift response—sacrificial lambs. They want specifics, warm-blooded, two-legged specifics," Jacobs said.

The indifferent tone struck Hap as cold-hearted. An image of Jacobs with an executioner's mask flashed into his head. But still Hap knew the CFO was right. With oil outside of their control, Wall Street would look for them to cut heads quickly. Maybe there was another solution? Hap spoke into the phone, "Aren't our competitors in the same fix? Could the answer be as easy as raising fares?"

"Logical, but there's a hitch," Jacobs replied.

"What hitch?" Hap dropped into his chair, purposely avoiding the computer screen and the stock's free fall.

"Lone-Star Airlines," Jacobs said.

Hap scowled. "Their airplanes burn fuel, don't they?"

"They're sittin' pretty. Hedged for the next three years. By frickin' dumb luck, Lone Star becomes the industry price leader. We raise fares, they don't. Guess who snares the customers?"

"Surely they're not that stupid. This is their golden opportunity to reap ungodly profits. Higher revenues, lower costs—jackpot!" Hap sounded manic.

"Dagger doesn't see that happening."

Hap yelled at the phone. "Lone Star may be not be bright, but their shareholders are. Management can't squander a chance to raise fares and bank extraordinary profits. Stockholders won't allow management to act like idiots."

"Lone Star operates from a different playbook. They'll leverage the fuel crisis for long term strategic gain."

"And piss away a windfall?" The words clipped from Hap's lips. "Someone should knock some sense into them."

"Be my guest. Don't let price fixing, collusion and the Justice Department stop you."

Hap flipped off the phone. "So Lone Star just sits there while we suffer."

"Watching the rest of us retrench—eliminate routes, shed aircraft and wrestle with bloated overhead."

"That's insane!"

"They want to grow market share. Unwillingness to price gouge feeds customer goodwill. One analyst is already blogging that Lone Star will benefit from sustained growth. Stability avoids knee-jerk distractions."

"I still can't believe shareholders will allow management to rob them. It's criminal," Hap seethed. Wall Street had it backward. They treated Lone Star executives like geniuses while crucifying Intercontinental's leaders.

"Weston shares your view if that's any consolation. But it doesn't change our immediate task. Slash costs. Start with ten, fifteen, and twenty percent reduction scenarios." Jacobs hung up.

"Shit!" Hap buried his head in his hands. Winny dashed in and out again without a word. He looked down at her scribbled note. *Execution confirmed—Net $5.50. ?????*

He laughed at her question marks, clapped his hands and leaned back in his chair. Again he did the simple math in his head—$5.50 times 100,000. Euphoria swept over him. He muttered aloud. "Win some, lose some. Greed isn't only good, it's fantastic." His eyes rested on Jim's personnel file and his smile vanished.

Chapter 18

Jim Makes His Bed of Roses

Jim found himself in his office. He didn't remember how he got there or how long he'd been sitting behind his desk. He stared at the opposite wall. Blotches of color came into focus as vintage company ads and dozens of pictures—proud and happy snippets of his Intercontinental career.

His team would be happy for him, but celebration would fizzle. Who'd be their new boss? Would Wilkerson use the promotion to ax the department? Jim didn't have the answers. With elbows resting on the desk, he cradled his head. His eyes found the photo of Julie and him taken at a team picnic in their backyard. They were holding onto each other in a fit of unbridled laughter. The photo also captured his mom, smiling in the background, wearing a company T-shirt. She held a hot dog that tempted Sedona with a raised nose. On tough days Jim found refuge in the family portrait.

He rubbed his eyes. Under normal circumstances, Julie would be proud. In light of recent conversations, he wasn't so sure. But he had to tell her. As he reached for the phone, a rapid tap drew his gaze to the door. In a flash of green, Cal Gladden pushed himself into the office and swung the door closed with his rear end. He plopped down without a word, placed his super-sized soda cup on the desk, folded his arms, and peered over bifocals. Thinning brown hair and an attempt to cover a bald spot with the longhair flyover technique, made him look older than he was.

"Why Mr. Gladden, it's after two." Jim pointed to the

plastic cup. "Another two-hour lunch?"

Cal stared in silence. His crinkled eyes twinkled, his lips twitched. Jim knew the signals. The office blabbermouth had a secret he couldn't hold in. Jim broke the silence. "What gives with that shit-eating grin? You finally get that promotion or did another vice president get booted?"

Cal raised his palm. "Let me ask the questions. Who do we both know who got booted *into* a vice presidency?" His thick, black eyebrows pulsed.

Jim sat back and folded his arms. He hoped Cal was merely on a fishing expedition. He pressed his lips together.

"I hate when people with good news play dumb—annoyin' and downright unsportsmanlike," Cal said, leaning closer and folding his hands on the desk. He enjoyed a vast network. Information flowed to him as freely as it gushed away.

"You'd sleep with Weston himself for gossip," Jim said with a laugh.

Cal swatted his palm at Jim. "The Chairman? That's nothin'. I'd sleep with his wife for dirt, and she's even bigger than his royal portly self." Cal paused, assumed a serious expression and winked before adding, "What makes you think I haven't already sacrificed my virtue to his plumpness?"

Jim roared with laughter. He couldn't help himself. Cal always delivered smiles. His humor medicated an environment where stress was viral. The two friends often swapped company war stories and shared frustrations with irreverence. Jim pushed himself back from the desk and spoke. "I give up. I know you think you know something—spill."

Cal leaned closer. "Maybe, I should show more respect to a company *officer*. I wouldn't want to be insubordinate." He sat back, his back stiffened and his expression hardened. Then he saluted. "Permission to sit in your presence, sir?"

"Cut that out." Jim said, shaking his head.

Cal wagged his finger. "That suit's a dead giveaway—*The Man's* uniform. Fraternizin' with enlisted men's a no-no." He pulled at his own shirt, a kelly-green polo, embroidered with the company logo.

Jim tugged his shirt cuffs. He had been in such a fog he had forgotten to take off his jacket. "Okay, what have you heard?"

Cal's eyes widened as he began. "Rumors began swirling about you and Maggie Richards after the Executive suite started sniffing around." He stopped. His eyes narrowed on Jim. "Hey Jimmy don't give me that look. Our spies know their spies who know… you get the picture. No secrets. Everyone concluded that you were both getting canned because of terrible food ratings and the mess in Washington."

Jim popped up in his chair. "That's absurd! Maggie and I don't have anything to do with those things."

"Don't look so shocked. So our system isn't perfect. It's more fun that way. But what the frick? You've been around long enough to know that blame is an art, not a science. Those areas are swarming with problems. Someone has to take the fall—might as well be you two." Cal pointed an Uncle Sam finger at Jim who merely sighed and shook his head. Silence, he knew, provided a vacuum that Cal couldn't tolerate for long. As expected, his friend's chatter filled the void.

"You know the company credo Jimmy—blame, name, shame, and game. For every snafu, *blame* must be assessed. Whispers increase until a culprit's name goes viral. The hungry mob *shames* the name into accepting blame. Guilt and innocence are inconsequential. Voila! The system is *gamed*, the name disappears—fired, quits or if connected, promoted. Just like the Air Force."

"Sadly, I know the protocol. Nothing gets fixed. But the action-clamorers get served someone's head. So what does this have to do with Maggie and me?"

"As it turns out Jimmy boy, nothin' at all. Merely a fleetin' diversion, a momentary thrill for blood-thirsty spectators craving a gory sacrifice."

Jim's eyebrows arched. "Hmm… you sound disappointed."

Cal shrugged. "The brass had loftier plans." His hands sounded a drum role on the desk. "Introducing our newest Veep—in charge of some stuff?"

Jim sighed, "Stuff? That the best you can do?"

Cal narrowed his eyes. His hands circled an imaginary crystal ball over which he hunched. "It's foggy—something about employee happiness, culture, investments." He looked up and grinned. "In the ballpark?"

Jim nodded, prompting Cal to add, "Great! In that case, I'd like a huge raise, shorter hours, bigger office, super-sized soda machines, and softer toilet paper."

Jim roared with laughter. "You'd have better luck with Santa Claus. I know I'll regret this…"

"Regret is why we have alcohol and drugs," Cal interrupted. The pulsing fingers of his extended palm prodded Jim to continue.

Jim flashed a don't-mess-with-me face. "Swear you won't breathe a word to anyone, *please*. I haven't even called Julie yet. I don't know if she'll kiss me or kill me."

"If there's any doubt, send flowers—roses not lilies. Now blab. I won't breath a word—swear." Cal crossed his heart and sat at attention.

"I mean it, Cal. My team will be crushed if they don't hear the news from me. PR and my new boss will have my head. You know Ingrid is anal about controlling information. I wouldn't be the first person skewered by that woman." He tapped his index finger on the desk.

"Your illustrious career would be over before it began. The Cuntess reigns supreme—wouldn't want to find myself on Shattenworter's shit or should I say, shat list. You have my word as friend and co-conspirator. Now spill." Cal sipped on his straw. His eyes lit up like a child's.

Jim felt his muscles relax. Sharing his news brought him relief. He inhaled deeply before speaking. "Hap made me responsible for employee investments." He saw a puzzled look on Cal's face so he continued. "I'm in charge of making this a good place to work. Like culture change but not really."

Cal beamed. "You're perfect. That's HR, right? I hear Carrie Patterson plays with the best of the boys and I do mean play." Cal accentuated the sucking sound with his straw.

Jim wiped his brow. He ignored the sophomoric bait. "God, no! Can you name one good thing to come out of Human Resources?"

"Fired HR people. Problem is, they keep cloning themselves so we never come out ahead. A dirty trick," Cal interjected with a smirk.

Jim laughed. "I'll report to Hap. How cool is that? If anyone can make this work, it's the Chief Operating Officer. He's probably the only senior leader who knows the business. Imagine what I can learn from him." He described as much of the job as he could remember, talking fast and using his hands. His confidence surged. He stopped when he noticed Cal's face contorted. "What's that look?" he asked.

Cal rubbed his chin. "Doesn't it worry you that Intercontinental has never sustained any of these efforts? I can list the failed programs in the five years I've been around."

Jim leaned back in his chair. "Hap assured me I'll have the support of the Board *and* Weston. Ask him next time you find yourself in bed together." Jim winked.

Cal folded his arms and wrinkled his nose. "Outta your league, Jimmy boy. Best leave innuendo and locker room humor to this old pro," he said with a chuckle. "Seriously, do you recall any employee effort that didn't come with the promise, *this isn't the flavor of the month or the program du jour? Walk the talk, talk the walk and blah, blah, blah.* Those words are the smooch of death, young man." Cal puckered his lips and made a kissing sound.

Jim could see why Cal's military career was cut short. But he couldn't be cynical, not now. He wanted to believe—he needed to believe. He cleared his throat and spoke with determination. "Hap says our survival depends on my success. He's staking his reputation and career on it. Believe me, I asked the same questions, just a bit more delicately."

Cal sat back in his chair, his eyes enlarged. "Whoa boy! That speech for me or Julie?" The mention of his wife's name made Jim wince. Cal added, "I'm fine as long as you feel that Hap's got your back."

"He made me a VP didn't he?" Jim protested.

"Watch out for friendly fire is all I'm sayin'. You know the risks of being an officer around here—shorter shelf life than milk. Most strut about with bulls-eyes on their backs. Just a matter of time before they get picked off. The lucky ones shove a peer into the rifle's scope."

Cal rose and tiptoed behind him. Jim looked over his shoulder with a bewildered look. "What are you doing now?"

Cal patted him on the back and said, "No bull's eye—*yet.*"

Jim swatted his friend. "Sit down or leave." He pointed to the door.

Cal shrugged. "Wishful thinking." He plopped back into the chair. "Hap's record isn't good."

Jim frowned. "What's that supposed to mean?"

"More than a few under his command have had careers cut short—even friends. Except for the perks, I'm not sure I'd want to be a veep."

"Your tune might change when you're asked." But Jim

knew Cal had a point. Vice presidents faced a revolving door, hinges greased by insecure colleagues, and political infighting. The officers didn't go in for Kumbaya or group hugs.

Cal shook his head. "No my friend, junior veeps dart about like frightened rabbits, and the senior ones hide their insecurities behind arrogance. The proverbial sheep in wolves' clothing. Not my thing." Cal slurped only air from the empty soda container.

Jim shrugged. "Julie's in your camp. Of course I've dreamed of being an officer, who hasn't? Do I have my doubts—you betcha. But this new position solves my dilemma. That's the beauty."

"You really think so?"

Jim nodded vigorously. "I've been asked to change Intercontinental. Make it a company where I can be proud to be an officer. A better place for all employees."

"May require a miracle or two."

"I'll be doing a lot of praying," Jim said.

Cal patted Jim's arm. "Don't want to see you get hurt. Think of that poor schmuck condemned to roll a rock uphill, only to have it roll back every time. In the military that's called BOHICA...*bend over, here it comes again.*"

"If that happens, maybe I'll just let the rock roll back and crush me. I'll give it my all, or die trying."

Cal nodded. "That's called a suicide mission."

Maybe Cal was right, but he saw it differently. A way forward or a way out—none of this in-between crap. He couldn't stay in neutral, not anymore. "If I succeed, this will be a great place to work."

"And if you don't?" Cal gave him an over-the-bifocal glare.

"I'm toast, but I'll be ejected from a bad place. That's a no-lose proposition."

"Good attitude Jimmy Boy. Hope it lasts. Now how'd you

like to hear some dirt on your old boss Wilkerson? My sources tell me that he's behind some nasty business."

Jim rolled his eyes and held up his palm, "Maybe later."

"Suit yourself. Gotta take a super-size pee anyway." Cal rose and pitched the soda cup into the wastebasket. "And take off that jacket. You're not dead yet."

Jim grabbed his friend's arm. "Remember, not a peep. Now get lost! I gotta order roses...and pray."

Chapter 19

Hap Spars With His Nemesis

"They'll eat me alive," Weston bellowed to his four subordinates huddled in the conference room with its sweeping view of the city. "They want answers to our fuel fiasco." Weston's Savile Row suit billowed in the gust created as his fist crashed down onto the table.

"Richard's correct," Ingrid said as she picked lint from the sleeve of her cornflower blue suit. "We've branded ourselves as financially responsible. We've publicly repudiated the unrestrained joyrides of Richard's predecessors." She arched a pencil-thin eyebrow and snapped her head with Prussian precision adding, "Our analysts' call must dazzle The Street."

"I'm well aware of our task. I'm the CFO," Bryce Jacobs huffed. His irritability surged alongside oil prices while his oversized features sagged under the stress—baggy eyes, sinking jowls, and slouched shoulders. Employee whispers joined the louder union chorus in alleging that Jacobs dropped the ball when he failed to predict the spike in oil prices. Pressure on him mounted. The screws mercilessly turned by Weston and Ingrid accompanied the jeers of institutional investors who demanded immediate action to stop the stock's free fall. Blame had been assessed with the name of Jacobs.

Sheer luck saved the CFO from the wrath of his fellow officers. Most like he and Hap, had standing brokerage orders to cash out options the moment they became exercisable—in this case, mere hours before the stock tanked. Rather than being shunned, Jacobs emerged a prize commodity. Wealth preservation galvanized the pack, bestowing absolute author-ity on the man who could restore the stock price.

Ingrid leaned forward, her palms resting on the icy gran-ite. "I know you're the CFO—indebted to you for stating the obvious. But, Richard is king. People look to him for answers."

She sat back, her spine rigid as she swept a bejeweled hand across the table. "Gentlemen, you must feed the analysts. I'll keep score and add Richard's voice." She caressed Weston's arm. Hap watched as she removed a long strand of auburn hair from the CEO's suit, examined it and dropped it to the plush carpet.

Kay, Weston's secretary appeared at the door holding an imaginary phone to her ear. After acknowledging the prompt, the CEO rose from the table, and grunted to those seated, "Best give Ingrid what she wants."

Hap waited until Weston's pinstriped frame lumbered out the door before he spoke. "Perfuming the proverbial pig." He grabbed a bottle of water off the table.

Ingrid glared at him.

"Round up the usual suspects," Jacobs added in his monotone.

"Don't you have an unproductive quip or cliché to con-tribute?" She flipped her platinum hair in the direction of the room's remaining occupant, Tyler Dagger who slouched in a chair at the end of the table.

"We've done this exercise before, it's not difficult," Dagger said with disdain. One hand held a smart phone while the oth-er clutched a bottle of organic tea with a sanitary wipe.

Even across the room, Hap smelled the nauseating con-fluence of chamomile and antiseptic. He jumped to his feet, folded his arms and glared at Dagger. He felt his face grow warm. "Of course it's easy—for *you*. I have the biggest slice of pie. That's where we'll cut—we always do. You sit there in your sweatshirt and whine about your inability to increase revenues."

Hap paced the length of the room, his hands tucked into his trouser pockets. He was tired of Dagger dismissing the sacrifices borne by operations and sick of the excuse that pricing and sales couldn't boost revenue. Dagger took credit for booms but pointed fingers during busts. The Executive Team was an army of one and he was fed up. "Self-serving, bullshit," he muttered, undaunted by the turned heads.

Dagger sighed loudly as his fingers pecked at his phone. "Perhaps you'd like a lesson in Econ 101. I can sketch simple supply and demand curves in your notebook." Dagger stopped texting to wag a finger toward Hap's papers. Then he inhaled and met Hap's stare. "If you delivered a good product, we might command a price premium."

Hap seethed, convinced that the grimy little bastard as he called him, took advantage of their boss's absence to grandstand. All in the room were aware that Weston frowned on displays of disrespect among his underlings, labeling them childish histrionics.

"If you developed realistic plans and products, we'd have a shot at success," Hap volleyed back, his eyes narrowing on his nemesis as he clutched an empty chair back.

Dagger's eyes returned to his phone as he responded. "Customers pay us to get them from point A to point B, not sit on the tarmac. We could fly more segments if we could eliminate wasted time on the ground. Too bad Operations excels at keeping airplanes grounded with delays and cancels. Don't fault the architect for shoddy workmanship."

Hap marched to a spot opposite Dagger and leaned across the table. He knew that Dagger called him an industry dinosaur and placed blame for much of the company's failures at the COO's doorstep. "I'd like to see you turn an airplane packed with 400 customers, bags and cargo—empty it, and fill it up again with 400 new people and bags in under fifty minutes. *You* set *my* employees up for failure," Hap shouted before kicking a chair. "I'd love to show you how you impact Operations." As he uttered the words, he saw Weston re-enter the room.

Weston looked from Hap to Dagger and smiled. "That's what I like to hear—collaboration. I hope that same spirit inspired you with tangible offerings for Wall Street." He plopped into his chair, glanced at Ingrid and asked, "Have the boys been behaving?"

"Boys will be boys! They'll deliver," she said, tugging at her teardrop pearl pendant. The room gasped as she then blurted, "I've got it. *All* of you will host the call."

"Won't that be clumsy and crowded?" Weston asked.

"I agree," Hap said as he returned to his chair and began tapping the table with a pen.

"As do I," added Dagger. "We need a crisp message not a Greek chorus."

Ingrid sneered. Her hands clenched the arms of her chair. "I lead Public Relations."

"Now who's stating the obvious?" Jacobs mumbled under his breath.

Hap stifled a laugh as Ingrid glared at the CFO. She growled, "We don't have time for childish banter. My plan will work." She winked at Weston.

Hap saw through Ingrid's plan. Broader participation would take pressure off of Weston and her. He had seen her often use the threat of the public spotlight to stir creative juices and extort cooperation. He stroked his chin and cleared his throat before speaking. "I'll deliver cost savings, but Wall Street doesn't want to hear from me."

"Ingrid's idea is brilliant," Jacobs interjected with a slap to his thigh. All eyes shot to the CFO who added, "Wall Street wants a comprehensive response. You've all forgotten that until this oil shock, everyone focused on service failures. We've made promises to Congress—expensive promises."

Hap scowled. He had never known Jacobs to promote collaboration or offer to share the spotlight. He suspected Jacobs wanted to drag others into the line of fire to diminish his own chances of a direct hit because of his failed fuel strategy.

Weston twiddled his pudgy fingers. After a moment, he nodded as he spoke. "Yes, the employee and passenger officers support my story and polish our image. Leave it to the finance guy to remind us about customers and employees. We take the call together. End of discussion."

Ingrid clapped her hands, "Gentlemen, we reconvene tomorrow with your cost cutting plans. That only allows me one day to package."

Although he hated Jacobs' maneuver, hearing that Jim's work remained on Weston's priority list encouraged him. He expected Weston and Jacobs to abort the nascent mission. In the past, such initiatives would be low hanging fruit plucked for quick savings.

As he waited for Dagger to leave, Hap noticed Weston motion to Ingrid and Jacobs to remain. Maybe he had detected a shared look among the same three when Weston's call came in. Hap exited the room, but stood with his back to the open door, thumbing through his notebook pretending to look for something.

"I'm assuming that was Ridgeway on the phone," Hap heard Jacobs say, an obvious reference to TransSky CEO, Steven Ridgeway.

"Any closer to a decision?" Ingrid asked. Hap assumed a constant clicking was the tap of her fingernails on the granite slab.

Jacobs droned in, "More to the point, are they *still* interested?"

Hap held his breath, eager for the reply.

Weston answered, his words slow, "Still interested? Yes! The question is at what price? They're not oblivious to the drop in our stock price. They've experienced the same, although as Ridgeway boasted, they're more favorably hedged. Their stock sputtered, but is rebounding as details of their hedges emerge." Hap chuckled, imagining Weston narrowing his gray eyes on Jacobs at the mention of a hedge.

"Price is merely a matter of negotiation. What about their other concerns the..." Ingrid's fast-paced tempo came to a halt with Weston's exaggerated cough. In an instant, Hap saw a flash out of the corner of his eye. Long bejeweled fingers clutched the doorframe and pushed it shut with thud. Hap's back felt a whoosh of air that carried with it the scent of Ingrid's perfume.

He walked away processing the conversation. Something Richter said made him uneasy. But then he remembered Weston's own words on that frantic call to his home on Easter. Of course, that had to be it—the topic was marketing partners.

Chapter 20

Jim's Night of Wine and Roses

Jim cut the engine but remained in the car. Finding the right words to tell Julie about his promotion consumed his thoughts to the point of distraction. He narrowly missed being hit by a cab as he rushed to the station and almost boarded the wrong train. Now he had to muster the nerve to enter the house and break the news. Under normal circumstances, the promotion would be cause for celebration. But Julie had made her feelings known. She warned him to make an exit strategy from the toxic environment. She shared tales of discarded friends, trampled loyalties, and current employees who complained of soulless leadership focused on results—relationships be damned. It pained her, she said, to see him worked to exhaustion by a callous boss driven by personal ambition.

Jim took a deep breath and exited the car. "Let's hope the roses did the trick," his voice echoed in the empty garage. As he opened the house door, his nose filled with the comforting scent of garlic and onions. "Mmm! Something smells great," he yelled through the empty kitchen. Sedona barked from another room and her paws tapped the wood floor in a mad dash to the door.

Julie's voice came from the dining room. "Hello sweetie. It's your favorite—lasagna."

"Yum. But that doesn't excuse your wifely duties. You're supposed to meet me at the door with a kiss," he replied. He crouched beside the dog that collapsed at his feet to expose her soft belly for pets.

"I stole a trick from Intercontinental's playbook. I out-sourced your welcome kiss to Sedona." Giggles peppered Julie's reply.

"At least it's not some guy with bad breath and body odor," Jim chuckled. "Wow, promise me you won't outsource *that*," he exclaimed when he looked up. Julie stood in the archway with a glass of wine wearing her beige sweater dress that showed every curve of her frame.

"Eyes up here," she said, pointing to her face. She walked toward him and rose on tiptoes to offer him a kiss. "Let's hope you feel that way when my figure goes," she said, handing him the wineglass.

"No worries—it's for life, baby." He patted her behind. "And what a life it is."

She tilted her head back and looked in his eyes. "Glad you like—the life and bootie."

He winked then held the wine under his nose. "What a celebration—lasagna, a great vintage and my favorite dress."

"Speaking of tomato sauce and red wine, grab my apron, would you," she said, pointing to the counter.

He pulsed his eyebrows and handed her the green garment. "A sin to cover that up." He teased her ear with his tongue. "I know what I'm having for dessert."

She swatted him away as she mixed the salad dressing. "I should have known the roses were merely a ploy to get me into bed. You'll have to settle for a cannoli." She bit into a celery stalk, inches from his grinning face.

He'd forgotten about the roses. He craned his neck around the room but didn't see a vase. "You did get the flowers? Hope you like them."

"Love them." Julie tugged at his tie. He bent down and met her lips. She caressed his chest. "Almost as much as I love you." Then he saw her hand dart behind his back. He jumped when she pinched his rear end. Her expression changed. "You're a rat. I'm furious."

"B, b, but," he stammered. At last, she found her opening. He braced.

She pressed her finger to his lips. "But nothing. Go change. Get comfortable. We'll discuss it over dinner. I don't want the food to get cold."

As he headed upstairs to change, Jim asked himself how Julie could have found out about the promotion. He planned to break the news over dinner. He owed her the chance to explode in his presence. A telephone confession would have been easier but cowardly. It would have been cruel to make her sulk around the house alone—and dangerous. Emotions incubated without dialogue. He rubbed the spot where Julie pinched him.

He hung up his suit and pushed aside his jeans for a pair of khakis given Julie's killer outfit. It couldn't have been the flowers. He instructed the florist to sign the card, 'Just Because I Love You, Sunshine'. Perhaps Cal blabbed, maybe to his wife or a co-worker who then called Julie. He couldn't get over how well she seemed to be taking the news. He laughed at the possibility that she concocted the warm reception as a ploy to get him drunk before smothering him in lasagna. "Cal was right about one thing," he mumbled to himself as he splashed on aftershave, "roses are magic."

As Jim descended the staircase, he stopped and gazed over the banister. Julie was lighting the candles. How lucky he was to have a gorgeous and understanding wife. He crept down the stairs and snuck up behind her. He nuzzled her neck with his nose, recognizing the perfume he bought her in Paris. "Mmm, you smell good," he said.

Julie turned and thrust the candle lighter at him. "Down boy. Now sit."

"Everything's beautiful," he said, taking his seat. The table was set with their fine china, arranged at right angles. The roses sat in the middle of the table, their blood red hues highlighted by the flickering candles in the dimmed room.

"We had to mark the occasion," Julie said with a wink.

"You're amazing. To be honest, I wasn't sure how you'd react." He inhaled, soaking in the smell of perfume and roses that combined with the food and wine.

She shrugged. "Actually, I broke down."

"What?" He said, stiffening. He detected her eyes moisten. Perhaps this is where she'd let him have it. But would she choose anger or tears? He didn't know which would make him suffer more.

"I cried, hysterically," she said between sniffles. "Probably all the pent up anxiety."

His hand squeezed hers. "I'm sorry you had to be alone."

She looked into his eyes. "Sweetie, I thought a lot today. They say wistfulness and weeping are normal."

"That's understandable. It's a big step—life changing for both of us."

Julie nodded. "That's what I mean. I guess I could blame my reaction on raging hormones. It's ironic, a paradox really."

Jim tilted his head. "A paradox?"

"We have lots of plans. Financial security is important."

He nodded. "Absolutely!" Obviously, Julie had concluded that his vice presidency meant more security and a chance to accomplish all of their plans.

He watched her inhale. She squeezed his hand tighter and looked like she was forcing herself to smile. "But, I'm convinced more than ever, that it's time for you to quit."

Jim gasped. "What? Leave Intercontinental?" His hand pulled away.

"I want you to leave that awful place. I know it's odd,

especially now, but they devour people. Promise me you'll start looking for a new job. Hell, quit tomorrow. You deserve to be happy too."

"I don't understand," he said before taking a gulp of wine.

"With all our goals, I knew you wouldn't leave. You'd feel forced to stay, trapped for our family." She refilled his wineglass. "I realized that after my mom called you about the baby."

"Baby—your mother?" He blurted.

"I'm assuming she phoned you." Julie pointed to the roses with her fork. "She's the only one I told after the kit tested positive—twice." He saw the puzzled expression on her face.

His mind raced. His eyes scanned every inch of her face. Why hadn't he noticed that she wasn't drinking any wine? He attributed her hormonal lament to PMS. What an idiot! Of course... she was pregnant. He rose from his chair, knelt beside her and embraced her. Tears flowed down his cheeks. "I love you so much, Mrs. Abernathy."

"I don't understand," she said, running her fingers through his hair.

He squeezed tighter. "We're having a baby. That's all that's important. Blame my stupidity on *my* raging hormones. I love you, sunshine."

Jim kissed his wife as Sedona, tail wagging, snuggled up beside them. His news would wait until morning—after he consumed an entire bottle of wine by himself.

Chapter 21
Jim's Co-Pilot

Jim was anxious to meet the man Hap touted as the best co-pilot for the employee initiative, lacing his endorsement with uncharacteristic superlatives. For the rendezvous, Jim chose a table in the corner of the cafeteria. Another closed-door session in his office would set off alarms with his team. For some reason, Ingrid and his new boss hadn't given the green light to announce the promotion. He didn't know how much longer he could muzzle Cal, who begged him to lift his gag order.

Scanning the room for his visitor, Jim took inventory. Formica tables and multi-colored vinyl chairs mended with duct tape, scattered over chipped and yellowing linoleum. The murky windows opened onto an alley that faced the mailroom of the neighboring building. Some clever person paired exotic destination posters with hygiene placards: hands under a faucet and Iguazu Falls; a hairnet and Greece's Medusa bust; rodents scurrying from properly secured trash and Hong Kong's year of the rat. Jim appreciated the humor but hoped his new position came with funds to spruce up employee areas throughout the company.

While Jim never met Kyle Richter, the two had exchanged physical descriptions. From the kind voice and self-deprecating humor over the phone, Jim already formed a favorable opinion of the man. Although the consultant dismissed his website photo as fantasy meets Photoshop, Jim felt confident he couldn't miss a sixtyish man with wavy white hair, pinstriped suit and orange tie.

But the man who entered the cafeteria with the bright salmon tie didn't match Jim's image of a sleek, East Coast consultant. The rumpled suit, tussled hair, steel wool eyebrows and scuffed shoes reminded Jim of a former accounting professor. The consultant's appearance was atypical of the polished powerbrokers who usually surrounded Hap—packs of Brooks Brothers' clones.

Richter returned Jim's wave. As he approached the table, he stumbled over his overstuffed briefcase trolley. Heads turned at the screech of metal as the consultant grabbed a chair to avoid a fall. Jim couldn't decide what was louder—Richter's commotion or his flashy tie.

Jim jumped to his feet. "You okay?"

Richter flashed a smile and extended his hand, seemingly unfazed by his ungraceful entrance. "I'd trip over my own shoelaces if I didn't wear loafers. You must be Jim."

Jim shook the hand gingerly. "You sure you're okay?"

Richter shimmied, tested his spine and dusted himself off. "Good as new. How 'bout some coffee before we get started."

"I'll get it," Jim said, motioning Richter to sit. "Relax." He feared Richter would draw more unwelcome attention or scald himself and he didn't want to spend his afternoon filling out accident reports for the legal department. Jim began to worry about his co-pilot. If Richter couldn't navigate across the cafeteria, how could he help Jim drive change through the airline? Wrong Way Corrigan, sprung to mind.

"Guess we can manage without Hap. Gives us a chance to calibrate," Richter announced when Jim returned with two coffee cups.

Although Jim was anxious to start tapping Richter's expertise, he found himself drawn into exchanging biographies, work histories, even favorite authors, hobbies, and cocktails. The friendly banter contrasted with the stilted sessions Jim shared with his new boss. Since his promotion, Jim saw Hap vacillate between enthusiasm and caution, like a first-time parachutist eager for the fall yet reluctant to jump. Perhaps Richter could suggest ways to penetrate Hap's prickly veneer.

Before long, Jim felt at ease, appreciating Richter's sense of humor and sincerity. Jim opened up. His account of his promotion, his wife's apprehensions and the farcical mix up in sharing the news with Julie brought the consultant to tears of laughter.

"But your wife's okay with the new job?" Richter asked after regaining composure.

"Sure, sure," Jim said. He relayed how he finally broke the news. He had gotten up early that next morning, not an easy feat after drinking an entire bottle of wine. He prepared a big breakfast to take to his wife. "The breakfast tray made her a captive audience."

Richter nodded. "Ah, but there was the silverware and the threat of impalement by sausage link."

Jim laughed. "The two roses produced a calming effect."

"So that's where you had her?" Richter asked.

"Not exactly." Jim explained how he talked about the baby and all the plans for their family. "We want to give our baby only the best—we've waited so long."

"With three kids, I can attest to the expense."

Jim shrugged. "In a way, the new baby gave me the leverage to drop the bomb. She cried, asked me to reconsider."

"But you prevailed."

"I hope so. I tried to make her see the upside: financial security and the chance to help our friends who still work here," Jim explained. Yet he remained unsure if Julie had totally bought in. He wasn't comfortable, not yet, of sharing his wife's mistrust of company leaders with the man who Hap called friend. Something in Richter's expression prompted

Jim to add, "Julie *is* supportive. No doubts there." He sipped his coffee, studying Richter's reaction over the brim of his cup.

"Good. This company elicits visceral reactions from employees, customers—everyone really. That's one of our challenges," Richter said. Jim watched as the consultant's tie dipped into his coffee. Richter wrung out the liquid and carried on the conversation with only a minor shrug. "Well, congratulations Papa!" He blurted, slapping Jim on the back.

As the two huddled over some papers, a shadow stopped their conversation. Khakis pressed against the table edge. Jim looked up to find Cal Gladden, a spectacle in day-glow orange, grinning from ear to ear and holding a super-sized soda cup.

Jim's eyes popped. "Why am I not surprised?"

"Fine way to greet a pal. You two are the talk of the salad bar," Cal said with a wink as he extended his hand toward Richter and introduced himself.

"Cal has an uncanny ability to sniff out secret meetings just like he can rattle off details about any airplane he sees in the sky," Jim added.

"That's right; model, routing and operator. I'm practically omniscient," Cal said, beaming.

"I've told him he belongs in a carnival," Jim chuckled.

"You said circus," Cal interjected.

Richter laughed then added, "Impressive skills."

"Cal's an unabashed airline geek whose grasp of company business springs from old-fashioned nosiness," Jim said, pretending to punch his buddy in the gut.

Cal folded his arms and stuck out his tongue. "Fine way for a veep to act." He put his hand on Jim's shoulder. "Mr. Richter, insults notwithstandin', you're working with one hell of a great guy here. No one better for the job."

Richter smiled. "So I've been told."

Cal flourished an imaginary sword at Jim. "You'll be slaying lots of dragons, kid. Some will call you crazy, including me. But, I support you 100%."

Jim grinned. As Cal exited the cafeteria, he turned to Richter. "He's a good guy."

Richter's tone became serious. "You'll need cheerleaders like Cal, plenty of them to maintain your humor. This work is lonely, hard. Dragon slaying's pretty accurate."

Jim leaned closer to the consultant. "You've done a lot of this type of work, haven't you? Is it as impossible as all the books say?" Jim had done a lot of reading since landing the job. Most books listed common obstacles preventing organizational change, but a company's idiosyncrasies were the biggest variable.

"The odds are 50/50 *at best*."

Jim gritted his teeth. "Not very promising."

"Who drives culture?" Richter asked.

Jim thought for a moment. "Ultimately company leaders."

"Precisely! And ever notice that most management teams look like clones of each other—a homogenous mass of sameness?"

Jim laughed. "We had one CEO who started a suspender craze and another who created legions of Harley enthusiasts."

"Fashion, grooming choices, and music follow the same trend ingrained into us in youth—*follow the leader*. The same thing happens in reverse, what I call the narcissus effect."

Jim found himself captivated. It dawned on him that Richter had fallen into consultant speak seamlessly. He rested his chin in his hand and listened.

Richter continued, "The fact that most executives hire mirror images of themselves, makes it hard to turn organizations. But it's not the most difficult challenge."

Jim interjected, "Dare I ask?"

"You need to know this. Current leaders enjoy success with the status quo."

Jim shrugged. "Sounds obvious"

"The truth usually is. Without a push, why would someone choose to leave a place where they've found success? You've *arrived*—now *leave.*"

"How do we create that push?" Jim asked, beginning to understand the challenge.

Richter pointed upward. "Starts at the top. Moses didn't ascend from a well with the Commandments. Leaders change when their CEO does. That's key, a leader who preaches the new culture with the passion of a television evangelist."

"I don't see Richard Weston shouting, *Hallelujah Brother.*" Jim grimaced. Would he fail before he began?

Richter paused. He patted Jim's arm. "Hap's your champion young man, not a bad surrogate to captain this effort."

"And Weston?"

"At worst, invisible—at best, silently encouraging the work forward," Richter said.

Jim gasped. "At best, he's silent? Where does that put our odds?"

"Afraid you'd ask, dear boy," Richter said, picking at his eyebrow. He inhaled. "Without Weston, your odds are zero."

Jim slumped. He felt sick. Julie was right.

Richter patted Jim's head. "I'm not done. You and Hap are alike—passionate. Passion gives us 25%. The full weight of Hap's support brings us back to 50%, if not more. We're back to even odds."

Jim sat up and sighed. "Not good. But your *we* and *us* are comforting. And *we do* enjoy Hap's support—I don't feel so alone."

Richter smiled. "I hope I haven't discouraged you."

Jim laughed. "Teamwork and blunt honesty are good things. Even long shots win races." He hesitated for a moment. How would Richter respond? He decided to take the risk. "You're not Tavistock material… that's meant as a compliment."

The consultant peered over his cup. His bushy eyebrows rose. He put down the cup and laughed as he slapped his thigh. "And a fine compliment it is. I won't deny my pedigree opens doors. Most people think I left Tavistock to start my own consultancy. They assumed ideals and integrity drove me away."

Jim sipped his coffee, riveted by Richter's candor.

Richter recounted how he left Tavistock to assume the helm of his family's business, at the time the largest remaining textile producer in the country. With his father nearing eighty, he convinced the family to abandon the company's operating philosophy that he labeled, outdated and a sure path to obscurity. "With a dazzling business plan and a velvet plow, I pushed my father aside."

He described his grandiose plans to expand globally through aggressive borrowing. "Leverage is to borrow as commode is to crapper," he chuckled. Cost reductions including a squeeze on suppliers, would service the ballooning debt. He moved production and finishing off shore, shuttering their North American mills. "Pounding his shoe, today's capitalist predicts that any company not outsourcing will be buried," Richter added. "My father thought differently."

Richter replaced leaders at all levels adopting the *best practice* of annual herd thinning. Managers who had risen through the ranks but were unskilled in new techniques as well as those who fraternized too closely with workers to remain impartial were shown the door.

Richter wrung his hands. "It took exactly three years to run the business and my life into the ground." By firing veteran managers, he lost expertise and tribal knowledge—even survivors opted out. He destroyed the culture responsible for generating quality and fostering dedication. Replacement vendors that agreed to lower prices proved unreliable. Some shut down as a result of undercutting their own cost structures to win bidding wars. The supply chain became a revolving door that distracted management focus from production, employees, and customers—the stuff that mattered. Defect-riddled offshore production, corrupted the product. "Customers fled. Called us a commodity. A bitter union campaign finally tore the company apart."

"That was the end?" Jim's voice was kind. He sensed the account pained Richter, the confession, a form of penance.

"Cash flows dwindled, we couldn't service the debt. I spent six months selling what I could to salvage some value for the family. Ironically, former Tavistock colleagues flew to my door. They drooled making pitches to nurse the company to health, even if only temporarily to snag a buyer—"

"But you kicked them out," Jim interrupted.

"Didn't have to. When they learned we were broke, they scattered quicker than drunks from an empty bottle."

Both laughed, but Jim detected a change in Richter's demeanor. His eyes glazed and his tone became somber. "The business came to an ignominious end. My father died soon after, a broken man. My wife disliked what I'd become. I couldn't blame her—I hated myself. My second strike out at the marriage game."

"I'm sorry." Jim moved his hand toward the consultant's arm but avoided contact.

Richter patted the offered hand. "The lowest point of my life. Single-handedly, I destroyed a successful business and wounded an entire family. Humiliation and failure are great teachers."

"So that's when you started your new business," Jim said.

Richter nodded. "I hoped to save others from my mistakes while making a little money."

Jim smiled. He made up his mind to trust Kyle Richter, won over by the man's heart of gold.

Chapter 22

Ingrid Schemes

"Get Orkin." Ingrid's pearl-white fingernails tapped the black lacquered desk. Her Chanel clad secretary nodded and pivoted sharply on Jimmy Choo heels, arcing her pendant before it came to rest in her cleavage.

Ingrid waited. Her hand stroked her hair as she stared at her reflection in the clock perched on a corner of the antique desk. In the past few weeks, she maneuvered the airline through turgid Congressional waters and led the call to fortify the barricades against Wall Street's attack. Her words crafted company creed and litany. She and Weston would stand together to achieve their goal, the sale of Intercontinental. The dusty lavender lips curled upward as the gilt clock ticked in the silent office.

Meg Orkin, Ingrid's Director of Factual Information gave a courtesy knock but pushed through the doorway. Her gangly legs pecked across the Oriental rug. She plopped into the French empire armchair clutching a steno pad, the same shade of red as her pageboy haircut.

Ingrid flashed her wide smile. "I need your help."

Orkin sat to attention. "Of course. What can I do?" she asked, flipping open the notepad and readying her pencil. Ingrid credited Orkin's proficiency to a Midwestern ethic that elevated work above personal appearance.

Ingrid inhaled. "We're stretched. As usual, I'm at the heart of it all." She sighed with dramatic exasperation. "First there's the customer pledge. Then Underlicht's work in Washington.

Now I'm the architect of our cost cutting plan—financial triage."

Orkin began to speak when Ingrid's palm shot up with a gasp. Ingrid yelled, "Jeanette!"

The patter of heels clicked toward the office door, halting with the secretary's appearance and bow. Ingrid shouted, "Tell Jacobs we need more cash in Underlicht's hands, *today!*" A backhanded swoosh dismissed the secretary whose heels clicked away.

Ingrid turned to Orkin. She held her hand up and rubbed her thumb repeatedly over her fingertips. "Politics has always been green."

Orkin cackled. She suffered from short outbursts and eye spasms when she spoke that gave the impression of a squawking chicken. Ingrid conditioned herself to the tics in the same way urban dwellers ignored the rattle of elevated trains. "Do you want me to help with our lobbyist?" Orkin asked, tugging the hem of her dress.

Ingrid wrinkled her nose and shook her head.

"With the customer pledge?" Orkin asked.

Ingrid glared at her. "No dear. But the posters are brilliant, if I must say so myself."

Orkin nodded. "Employees should get the message."

"Don't blame me if they don't. I shudder to think what managers would tell employees without my talking points. It's the same with Dagger's Chief Passenger Officer. I must script that role as well."

"Has that job been defined?"

"Our passenger champion will give a public face to the pledge. We'll parade him around the morning news programs, stage spontaneous photo ops during weather calamities, and give him a blog."

"A catalyst for change," Orkin said.

"God no—there's no money to throw at it. More like a mascot," Ingrid scoffed.

Orkin twiddled her idle pencil. "You mentioned cost cutting. Is that where I come in? My hands have calluses tilling those fields."

Ingrid glared again. "No dear. I'll ready Richard myself. It's a balancing act. Wall Street expects scorched earth while employees want a field of dreams."

"That's a magic act," Orkin cackled.

Ingrid grinned. "We'll spin feed employees as always. By the way, identify three staffers to cut—low performer, dead wood, troublemaker. You know the routine."

"What?" Orkin squawked, her feet tapped the floor. "How can I cut with all of our work?" She pecked her head with the pencil.

"Don't panic Everyone must sacrifice. Richard must bare his claws for shareholders. Layoffs play well to Wall Street."

"I can't make you look good with less people." Orkin's voice trembled.

"Don't fret my dear. Our work is critical. But we must play the game. We simply backfill with consultants." Consultants didn't appear on personnel rosters—the manpower equivalent of off-balance sheet financing.

Orkin's feet stopped their frenetic patter. "That's a relief," she said as the steno pad dropped to the hollow of her lap.

"Yes dear, you'll have your invisible worker bees. We look like team players but hog the ball so to speak." Ingrid laughed. "My budget's above scrutiny."

"No one would dare." Orkin smiled.

"A win-win. We cut our clunkers under cover of duress then overwork consultants until the financial tempest clears. Then we hire newer models, eager to please."

"The corporate circle of life. What do you have in store

for me, then?" Orkin's eyes enlarged as she rubbed her hands together before picking up her notebook.

"Hap is leading an effort to align employees around our business plan. Bad behaviors continue to sink our market value," Ingrid said before launching into a discussion of Weston's strategy. She didn't disclose anything about selling the airline, focusing only on the business plan. "We can't extract thousands from customers with five-star promises and thrift store delivery."

Orkin froze. She looked up from her writing. "You've forged that message and…" She bit a fingertip and her voice stalled.

"And?" Ingrid asked.

"Employees may doubt Weston's sincerity," Orkin said, peering over her glasses.

Ingrid's eyebrows arched. Her eyes narrowed on Orkin. "This isn't Richard's work. We push Hap into the spotlight. He's the only senior executive with any credibility among our people."

"What about Hap's new vice president? Employees will have to trust him or her. You need a Capraesque hero or a damn good actor."

"Hap settled on a Tim Abernathy. Claims he has passion," Ingrid said, rolling her eyes.

"It's Jim, Jim Abernathy. I know him—nice guy with a good reputation. I'm not sure he has the horsepower to change our culture—he's a lawnmower, we need a bulldozer." An exaggerated cackle echoed in the office.

Ingrid gasped. "I'm not asking you to *help* Abernathy. Your mission is to thwart him."

"Thwart?" Orkin asked.

"Employee sympathies must not be allowed to infect investor confidence."

The conversation paused before Orkin nodded. "I under-stand. Where do I fit in?"

"Provide communication support. Pretend it's like any other initiative. Our help is expected. Hap will demand our resources." Ingrid waited until Orkin finished writing and looked up. She pointed a finger and spoke firmly. "Control the message, the audience, and the tempo. Richard's absence should not be mistaken as carte blanche for Hap and Abernathy. We breathe life into projects or smother them. You've done so yourself, remember?"

"I haven't forgotten. But the work hasn't always been plea-surable." Orkin's head bowed. Since Ingrid's arrival, Orkin drew blackout curtains around her emotions.

"Your pleasure's not my concern." Ingrid frowned.

"Of course not." Orkin's eyes grew large. "You want me to ensure Jim operates within limits, fencing his initiatives and messages—filtering his work."

"A-plus! I'll be working closely with Hap should Abernathy give you any trouble. Hap hopes this work can succeed—he's delusional. But I understand his sympathetic blinders. Don't give Hap an opportunity to question your support, or for that matter, mine." Ingrid leaned over the desk as she delivered that command. "You will be my eyes and ears." Her eyebrows arched. "We understand each other? Nothing must derail our plans. Is that clear?" Her violet eyes flashed.

Orkin nodded. She was one of the few staffers from the prior administration to survive Ingrid's purges, adopting her new supervisor's credo—*always make the boss look good*—*no questions asked.* "I always defend *your* interests," she said.

"Intercontinental's and above all *Richard's* interests dear girl, please. Your dedication is admirable." Ingrid adjusted her sleeve of bracelets.

"I try to please." Orkin cackled. She paused then added, "We've worked together for a few years. You must have an additional tactic or two? I can't baby sit Jim every minute."

"Of course not," Ingrid laughed. Her fingernails tapped her desk rapidly. "We need an insider, someone Abernathy trusts. I'll tell Hap that I'm giving Abernathy a permanent communications specialist. He'll be waiting forever, a victim of our budget woes." Ingrid rubbed her eye, a show of faux sympathy. "Until then I give him a drone who acts the part but reports to me."

"We push where the work and messages support your strategy and pull back where they don't," Orkin said, jotting in her steno pad.

"Bright girl. There's more. You will propose an overarching communication philosophy to Abernathy—*see, experience, hear,* or whatever your creative mind devises."

"Another stall technique?"

Ingrid nodded. "We don't broadly communicate Abernathy's work until we have vetted it. More insurance, preventing premature release of anything we deem dangerous."

"Like live television tape delays."

"Please, a nobler spin—*we build trust by under promising and over delivering.* When you and Abernathy present this approach to Hap, I'll sing the praises of abandoning the days of smoke and mirrors." Orkin squawked. Ingrid continued. "If Abernathy gets out of control, we simply make him disappear with little or no collateral damage. As if the work never existed." Her eyes danced and she clapped her hands, signaling satisfaction and the end of the meeting.

As Orkin exited the office, Ingrid called after her, "By the way dear, I really like that frock. The colors suit you—nothing too vibrant. You're from Iowa, aren't you? Not everyone could get away with muted florals and what looks to be an antique cardigan—precious." A final back sweep of her hand gestured her protégé out the door.

Alone in the office, Ingrid turned to the ticking clock and growled aloud, "Abernathy will get only enough rope to muzzle nasty rhetoric and curb bad behavior. Anything more…" She jerked her hand as if tugging a leash.

Chapter 23

Human Resources' Sandbox

As Ingrid plotted to corral Jim's ambitions, Carrie Patterson summoned one of her directors to discuss Human Resources' support. Sharlee Guerrin's Doctorate in Organizational Psychology plugged the holes in the company's leadership development program that Weston called an abyss. After data showed the airline in the industry's cellar for most reportable categories, Weston bellowed at Patterson to fix the problem. *A goddamn clusterfuck. I can recruit, but once they're hired, they're your frickin' problem.*

In her three-month tenure, Guerrin discovered that she was smarter than her boss. Exposure to C-level leaders with meaty assignments would showcase her skills and propel her upward. She saw herself nudging Patterson aside, convinced the airline needed a licensed therapist rather than a bubble-headed Barbie. She guessed she'd quickly outshine her boss—a circus Chihuahua could do that, she reasoned. She tuned into Patterson's insecurities and toned down her appearance with thick glasses, simple makeup, and sensible suits. She even pinned up her blonde hair.

Patterson's call for a meeting to discuss a Hap Sweeny project excited Guerrin as she hadn't yet met the airline's number two man and industry legend. She arrived early and kept counting the roses in the vase outside her boss's office as she waited.

"Come in," Patterson called with a mousy squeal. She waved her subordinate away from the desk to the crushed velvet chairs, one-piece units fitted with kidney-shaped work surfaces. Scooting into one with a notepad, Patterson beamed. "Aren't these divine? Absolute whimsy. They're part of my vision for a modern HR."When the chairs first arrived, Patterson announced with the pomp of a ship christening, "HR awakens to a new dawn." Her team stared slack-jawed at the burnt-orange, amber, and pea green café chairs. Patterson had recently attended a seminar in Paris. In addition to Vuitton and Chanel accessories, she took away from the trip a warning. HR organizations needed to become approachable, transparent and integrated into the core business or risk irrelevance and even outsourcing.

"I just love your cute, comfy chairs," Guerrin said, although she loathed them. Like many, she considered them juvenile and unprofessional. She'd rid the office of the coffeehouse castoffs and the pink shag carpet once she sabotaged her boss.

"They're relaxing—but not for everyone. I'm naughty to gossip." Patterson's voice dropped to a whisper, "Marissa Albioni got stuck. Maintenance pried off the tabletop to dislodge her—soda spilled all over her stretch pants." Patterson giggled. "I'd be in big trouble if the Chairman ever dropped in." She drew an imaginary circle in the air with her index finger and puffed out her cheeks.

Guerrin pushed along the conversation with a courtesy nod. "Tell me about Hap Sweeny's project."

Patterson's account of the employee initiative took no more than five incoherent minutes after which Guerrin felt even more confused. "Hap promoted Jim Abernathy to Chief Employee Officer," Patterson said. "But not a word to anyone until it's been announced. Ingrid would have my head." She slid her finger across her throat.

"What's Abernathy's background?" Guerrin asked.

"Tall, wavy blond hair, green eyes." Patterson winked.

"Married though—I checked his file," she said, continuing to giggle.

Guerrin furrowed her brow. She'd have better luck conducting her own reconnaissance. "Is he connected to that customer pledge? Posters are popping up all over the building—quite adolescent."

Patterson grinned, wiggling in her seat. "I know the answer. We discussed that at the Chairman's staff meeting. Hap's employee work is bottoms up while Dagger's customer project is top down." She wrinkled her nose and tapped the tabletop with her hot pink fingernails before pausing. "Maybe it's the other way around," she added.

Guerrin leaned toward her boss. Surely there'd be more details—these efforts were huge. But the office remained quiet. She followed Patterson's eyes as they wandered to a bird on the window ledge. After a few moments, Guerrin tapped her pen on the table. "Carrie, Carrie, what does that mean?"

Patterson's head shook. She turned to Guerrin with puckered lips and a scowl. "How should I know? That's why we appointed new vice presidents—that's their job."

Guerrin pulled at her turtleneck. She needed to vent her rising body temperature. "Where do I fit?" she asked.

"Abernathy's building an organization. He needs our help."

"To do what exactly?" Guerrin asked, uneasy with the term *employee work*.

Patterson counted off her fingers as she spoke. "Job descriptions, titles, recruiting, interviewing, and compensation levels. I'm shocked you wouldn't know HR's role." Guerrin bit her lips as Patterson added, "I want you to be the HR coordinator."

"Maybe you'd like to create the job titles—that's your specialty," Guerrin said with a smirk. She detested her own title, Director of Developmental Needs. It conjured up images of flannel-suited executives on short yellow buses. She scuttled efforts to change the title after learning that Patterson was the proud author.

Patterson cocked her head and bit her pinky. "Hmm. Love to, but far too busy."

"I'm to work with Abernathy, *not* Hap Sweeny. Is that what you're saying?" Guerrin asked as she glanced at Patterson's notebook. The margins were scrawled with bird doodles.

Patterson flinched. "*I'm* Hap's interface—officer to officer."

Guerrin felt herself begin to perspire. She struggled to remove her wool jacket, confined by the chair. "Did Hap provide a vision for this work?"

Patterson's hand fluttered in front of her face. "Briefly, broad terms. Let me see—recognition, leadership, training, skill building, career management... stuff like that."

Guerrin sputtered, her voice rose. "That's my job!"

Patterson gasped, her eyes bugged out. She wagged her finger. "You're responsible for developmental needs, your title says so. Let's avoid turf wars—so unprofessional."

Guerrin's face felt like it was on fire. She pointed a finger back at her boss as she stammered. "Training, skill building, and career management *are* development. Everything you listed is Human Resources work—*your* turf."

"Not recognition. That I can say for certain." Patterson's waving pink pen met Guerrin's finger.

"Because there is no recognition—chopped years ago I've been told. People strategy belongs to HR." Guerrin gripped the table, her knuckles whitened. "Development is *my* sandbox."

"Oh my. I didn't connect the dots," Patterson said, biting her fingernails.

Guerrin clutched her own throat, fearing her impulses to choke her boss. She took a deep breath. "Can you approach the Chairman, express concern? Maybe change his mind?"

"No! He bullied Hap to act fast. That flight has departed." Panic filled Patterson's voice. She continued to nibble her fingers.

Guerrin stared into Patterson's eyes as she thought how she could hijack the plan. She lowered her volume to a whisper. "I have an idea."

Patterson leaned forward. Her elbows rested on the table as her hands cradled her China-doll face. "I'm all ears."

"Abernathy needs our help to create a team. We're in the driver seat."

Patterson frowned. "I still don't like where we're headed."

"Think! Legislators who craft ethics reforms, bankers who design financial regulations. We stack the deck."

Patterson tilted her head. After a few seconds she batted her eyes. "Like chubbies at a buffet—I get it. What else?"

"We mold his jobs—limit scope, prevent overlap. We keep strategy and force Abernathy to implement *our* plans. We position his team as obstacle busters—*our* enforcers. We're paired like horse and cowboy."

Patterson's pen scratched her pixie cut. "Which one are we?"

"The cowboy. We hold the reins—direct every movement of the horse."

Patterson shrugged. "I like horses. I think Abernathy will too. Frankly implementation isn't one of our strengths."

Guerrin nodded. Her confidence surged. "We keep the juicy stuff—strategy, theory, big picture things, and unload the crap onto Abernathy. While we hobnob with executives, he's blowing up balloons, and cutting cake with the masses."

Patterson perched on the chair's edge. Her eyes riveted on Guerrin. "A reasonable division of labor."

"No one will be able to pin implementation failures on us again. We can join those who leer and wag fingers at Jim

Abernathy." Guerrin mimicked the gestures.

Patterson giggled. "Brilliant!"

Guerrin watched Patterson's expression change from joy to concern. "What's wrong?" she asked.

Patterson's fingers tapped her plump lips. "What happens if his team doesn't like our plan?"

"That's the diabolical beauty. We control job grades, pay levels and recruiting. We'll impose ourselves into interviews and final selections. We maneuver Abernathy into a submissive role."

Patterson sat up. "Explain that to me."

"The jobs and salary we impose will attract only second stringers, also-rans with no fire power. Abernathy will be shooting blanks." She waited for Patterson to stop writing before adding, "We pull all the strings."

"Fantastic. What next?"

"Gather your team. We'll prime them for this fight."

Patterson scribbled furiously. "Then what?"

"We woo Abernathy."

"I thought we didn't like him."

Guerrin stifled a laugh. "We need to keep him close. I'll approach him with open arms to offer full support. We convince him HR is family, *his* family."

"A family where we call the shots," Patterson said as she bobbed her head.

Guerrin tapped Patterson's arm. "You've got it. Leave this to me. I need you to convince Hap that we're aligned with Abernathy. Tell him we'll muster every resource to help." Her mind churned as she shimmied from the orange pod toward the door.

Patterson called after her. "Watch your calendar. I'm assembling the girls for a skill building session." She held up her well-manicured hands beside over-done eyes "It's a make-up party. Great products to boost your career. You can't find them at your average cosmetics counter."

Guerrin smiled through gritted teeth. "The modern HR," she said, quickening a retreat from the office. Once outside, she muttered, "We're under attack and she worries about lip gloss and mascara. *Us girls* will be tickled cherry blossom pink… yippee. The woman is nuts. Developmental needs? I have the prime candidate."

But Guerrin's mind returned to her plan to turn Jim Abernathy into HR's eunuch.

Chapter 24
Jim Gets Unexpected News

Jim's quiet commute on the 7:19 express came to a screeching halt with the rap on his shoulder. Without time to look from his newspaper, a hand and a leg pushed him toward the window. "Scoot your ass over. Nerve hoggin' two seats."

As his coffee splattered onto his raincoat and the padded bench seat, Jim recognized the voice of Cal Gladden. "Good morning to you too. Rather early isn't it," Jim said, folding his paper and noticing two gray-haired ladies in babushkas frown at Cal. "I didn't know you took this train."

"Don't, but knew you did. I searched every car." Cal pressed a gigantic plastic cup into Jim's free hand before taking off his bomber jacket emblazoned with airline patches. Dropping into the seat, Cal grabbed his soda and spoke. "You promised I'd have the promotion exclusive—the *quid pro quo* for my silence. If I didn't love you Jimmy, I'd have already flooded Facebook and numbed my fingers tweeting." Cal punched Jim's shoulder. "Anyway—congrats—officially."

"Shh! Lower your voice." Jim looked around the compartment—the women in babushkas had stopped chattering and stared at them. He turned to Cal. "What are you talking about? I never got the green light." Jim hid his anxiety behind a nervous laugh. "I hope you're kidding," he said, studying his buddy's face for a sign.

Cal frowned as he dabbed his elevated backside with a napkin. "You wet the seat? No joke Jimmy. On *my* part. Maybe you're punkin' your old friend?"

Jim's voice trembled. "What are you babbling about?"

"I'm a newsy. My blackberry beeped around midnight. The company issued a press release announcing new veeps. Weren't you warned?"

"That would have been the decent thing for the Cuntess to do." Jim's face reddened. His anger mounted. He met the babushkas' stares with a glare.

Cal winked and elbowed him. "Hey pal, control yourself. You're a VP."

"Vice presidents are initiated with secret handshakes and ways to bad mouth our littermates." Jim pivoted in his seat, his newspaper falling to the floor. "What did the goddamn press release say?"

Cal looked to his feet and shifted his shoes before scanning the aisle. "Better check with the train's lost and found," he whispered.

Jim's eyes narrowed. "For what?"

Cal's eyebrows pulsed. He poked Jim. "Somebody lost his rose-colored glasses."

Jim rolled his eyes. "*And* his sense of humor. Start talking."

Cal dug into his khakis and pulled out his phone. He scrolled his messages. After a tap of a key, he began to read. "Intercontinental Airlines reaffirms its commitment to investors, customers, and... employees."

Jim sighed. "Why are employees always last?"

"At least they're mentioned. It rattles on about some buck hired from Tavistock—the old bullshit about Javitz. Poor zlub leaves to pursue other interests."

Jim's jaw fell. "They deep-sixed Javitz? I didn't know he left?"

"Probably doesn't either. Still have a meetin' on my calendar with the late great Javitz." Cal slurped on his straw.

Jim shook his head. "Our vice presidents have shorter shelf lives than inflight snacks. Poor Javitz—outlived his expertise."

"Or pissed somebody off. You do realize, Jimmy, you're only the second officer who ascended from inside the airline since Weston arrived? He prefers imported cheese."

"Who replaced Javitz?" Jim asked.

"Someone named WASPity, WASPity, WASP the Third. You know the type—Ivy League, father a diplomat, uncle in the Cabinet. Goes by Trey—country club jargon for the Third. Why do blue bloods always have sappy nicknames for themselves and their houses?"

Jim ignored the question. "What else does it say?" he asked, eyeing the screen.

"Here, read for yourself. It's my turn to eavesdrop on our busy buddies." Cal handed Jim his phone, then turned to stare at the babushkas who looked away and began gabbing with each other.

As Jim read, he grimaced. The release sanctified Trey and reaffirmed the company's fiscal discipline: *without investors there would be no airline.* Trey's pedigree included Wharton and a decade in mergers and acquisitions.

Jim griped into Cal's ear. "Practically a commercial for Tavistock."

Cal swatted him away. "Not now Jimmy, the bitties have some juicy stuff—swingers in accounting. I'm trying to figure out where they work."

"You're hopeless," Jim said, returning his attention to the phone. The release next mentioned the new chief customer officer laced with hyperbole. It referenced the customer pledge Jim had seen posted around the building.

Jim spoke aloud. "Dagger's hired another e-commerce junkie, a mirror image of himself for the customer job."

"Yeah—some whiz kid who made a fortune selling shoes,

or was it vacuums. Maybe you can sweet-talk him into replacing those yellow canvas boats you wear—so unbecomin' of a veep." Cal contorted his face and kicked Jim's feet as the babushkas giggled.

"After they boot someone in the ass," Jim said with a kick to Cal's shin. "Thought you said I'm mentioned."

"Wah, wah! Keep reading—second to last paragraph—*success depends on realigning or reeducating employees.* Says you'll report to Hap—labels you a company veteran who likes employees. Keep goin'." Cal's index finger scrolled the air.

Jim gasped. "*Likes* employees? What am I, Mr. Rogers?"

Cal laughed. "Barney the dinosaur popped into my head. I like you, you like me—Kumbaya."

"Patronizing crap," Jim mumbled. "Employees shouldn't be an afterthought."

"You sound like a communist. Don't be so glum, the new customer guru got only two paragraphs to your one—longer paragraphs, but still only two." Cal nudged Jim, tussling his hair.

Jim groaned. "They ran out of space after Trey's autobiography."

"That's a fact. Four paragraphs for Trey of Green Gables and a fifth for Tavistock. You can't fart around here without a consultant gettin' credit," Cal said.

"And, billing for it. Maybe my team hasn't heard about my promotion yet," Jim said, although he knew personnel news spread fast.

Jim 's attempt to ditch his buddy in the crush of commuters at the station failed. He hoped to preserve the sanctity of his morning ritual, especially today—a brisk walk to soak in the city and collect his thoughts before diving into work.

Instead, Cal tagged along, a pattern of running to catch up then fading back.

"Sad news…" Cal began to say as he wheezed. "About Nelly Connors."

"Yeah—almost thirty-five years of service and dumped into the street. Wham, bam, thank you ma'am," Jim called over his shoulder.

"Rotten shame. Isn't she a friend of your wife?" Cal yelled forward. He almost tripped over a concrete planter ogling a short-skirted passerby.

"One of her best buds. Mentored Julie in catering—kept her from quitting many times. Julie says if Nelly hadn't encouraged, we'd never have married."

He didn't tell Cal that Nelly had been a recent irritant between husband and wife. Although Jim liked Nelly, he felt she was taking advantage of the friendship. Since her dismissal, she'd been calling Julie three, sometimes four, times a day sobbing. Jim blamed Nelly for stirring up Julie who started to needle him again about quitting.

"Then you guys must really be devastated," Cal said, gasping for air.

"Julie plans to see her later this week and hold her hand as she looks for a new job."

Jim didn't see or hear Cal anymore. He turned to see his buddy several paces behind, face flushed. "Told you to take the bus, I walk fast," Jim said. Cal remained bent over. His head shook. Jim hoped he wasn't having a heart attack.

"Then you haven't heard," Cal said.

Jim put a hand to his hip. "Heard what?"

Cal scurried forward and pressed Jim's arm. "Nelly's in the hospital. Suicide attempt last night—sleeping pills."

Jim's mouth dropped open. He felt like he'd been punched in the gut. He gripped his forehead. "Because of that place?"

Jim nodded toward Intercontinental Tower, two blocks ahead.

Cal shrugged. "So everyone assumes."

Guilt surged within Jim. Julie had been the poor woman's lifeline and he resented the intrusion. Had Nelly sensed his aggravation when he answered the phone? Had he been cold or rude? He couldn't remember. He thought of Julie, no doubt distraught. He had to rush to the office and call her. "Poor Nelly. Work isn't that important."

Cal sighed. "Unless Intercontinental *is* your life."

⚜

Jim's hope of discretion vanished the moment the revolving door deposited him into the white marble lobby. By the time he reached his office, he had run a gauntlet of a half-dozen congratulatory wishes, four pats on the back, three hugs, two high fives, and one peck on the cheek. He politely accepted the well wishes but avoided lengthy conversations. He focused on reaching his office to call Julie and check on his team. He predicted a morning of triage and tears. He couldn't shake the news of Nelly and its impact on Julie.

An eerie stillness greeted him when he reached his department. A talk radio program droned from one cube, classical music from another. Steaming coffee mugs suggested a recent exodus. Inside his office, Jim dropped his workbag onto the desk. His phone blinked with messages. An apology from communications would be expecting too much, he thought. He fished his cell phone from his bag—three missed calls from Julie and one message. Bantering with Cal, he hadn't heard the phone ring. He fumbled with the buttons as he scrambled to hear Julie's message.

Julie's voice was frantic, borderline hysterical. Her sob-riddled message informed him about Nelly. Julie planned to rush to the hospital. She said she loved Jim before a breathy pause. Then, her tone chilled—*I blame Intercontinental.* His calls home and to her mobile went to voice mail.

Jim dropped into his chair and stared at the white walls. The blinking red light of his desk phone roused him. The digital voice informed him of a full mailbox.

Kyle Richter left a pleasant message in reference to the Press Release. *Sincerest congratulations. I look forward to collaborating in support of employees. Let's meet.*

In his message, Hap spoke matter-of-factly, *we pushed the announcement to pre-empt today's analysts' call. The premature release couldn't be helped—bigger objectives had to be considered.* Jim imagined Hap talking in the same monotone to his wife: *Honey, the premature ejaculation was unavoidable—look at the big picture.* Jim forced himself to laugh. It felt good.

Meg Orkin from Ingrid's staff left the last message. She had the same drone and stilted rhythm of the phone's digital voice. *Congratulations. Employees have a champion. Ingrid wants me to help you. I have the perfect communication strategy to chip away at employee cynicism.* A cackle punctuated her message which ended with—*Talk to Hap if you have issues with the press release. Let's meet soon.* Jim imitated Orkin's cackle as he hit the delete button and scowled at the phone.

⚜

Sometime after noon, Jim returned to his office. Julie was still unreachable. He returned Richter's call.

After pleasantries, Richter asked, "Everything okay? You don't sound like someone promoted to vice president."

Jim cradled his head. "I just met with my team—fears and tears."

"Rough, huh?" The consultant's tone, sympathetic.

Jim described his frustration with being blind-sided by the announcement but avoided mention of Nelly. "I tracked my people down to the cafeteria where I found angry and somber faces that screamed betrayal. I confessed knowing for some time. Told them I'd been sworn to secrecy."

"I'm sorry. They must know you're not to blame. It's symptomatic of your dysfunctional culture."

"Senior leaders didn't give a shit about my relationship with my team. Exactly the kind of crap that must change. Relationships matter, people matter." Jim kicked a metal wastebasket, his mind troubled by images of his team as well as Julie and Nelly.

"There's the Jim I know—fire in the belly for employees. Wanna know something?"

Jim recognized Richter's attempt to buoy his spirits. "What's that?" Jim asked.

"Employees are smart. They'll respond to your sincerity. I'd bet money your team has already forgiven you. Most will want to join your mission."

Jim laughed. "True. A few popped their heads into my office. Said I'm not allowed to leave without them."

"You're a relationship builder. Hang in there, friend. I'll see you next week. Call day or night."

"You kept me from imploding."

"Just the first of many dragons, I'm afraid."

Jim closed his eyes. "And demons."

Chapter 25

The Medium is the Message

*W*elcome to *Money Matters, your Sunday business magazine. I'm your host Seymour Clifton. After a recap of the week's top stories, we'll see two approaches to economic stress. First, American Cellular, opening outlets, adding jobs, and investing in employees. Then, we takeoff with Intercontinental Airlines and chart its flight plan for turbulent skies—1,500 layoffs and cost slashing. Now, to the week's headlines…*

Money Matters aired live. The mid-town Manhattan studio buzzed despite the early hour. The *green room*, painted Wedgwood blue, purred with soft jazz. Black and white still shots spanning three decades of banter between Seymour Clifton and finance titans covered the wall above a well-provisioned sideboard.

American Cellular CEO Gail Schadden and her companion sat in leather chairs near the entrance. After polite hellos, the Intercontinental entourage paraded to the couches in a sunny corner with views of the Chrysler Building and the Brooklyn Bridge.

Two flat screens let panelists and their guests monitor the program. A pimple-faced page, uniformed in gray pants and blue blazer, sat expressionless, bursting forth periodically with a countdown, the info fed from a radio and earpiece.

"Get me a plate and coffee," Weston barked to Ingrid. He plopped down, but barely dented the contemporary sofa. He snarled. "More uncomfortable than it looks. Must be coach."

Bryce Jacobs lumbered from the buffet with a brimming

plate. "But the food is first class." Despite a noble effort to disguise his oafish frame, Jacobs' suit shrugged in defeat.

Ingrid's heels clipped along the floor in tiny steps as she balanced two plates stacked with food. She held them safely away from her suede jacket and yellow knit dress. Weston's chubby fingers snatched both from her. "I only needed one. Coffee," he grunted. His glare ushered Ingrid toward the urn.

Ingrid dropped her glazed python bag at Weston's feet. Her nostrils flared but she smiled as she strolled past the two female executives who interrupted their conversation at the sound of Weston's bark.

"Maybe he'd like some hot sauce in his damn coffee," Ingrid mumbled under her breath as she pulled the spigot.

"Five minutes, Ms. Schadden." The page's shrill outburst turned heads.

"Creepy little prick," muttered Jacobs.

"He'd be great at the airport. Could prod our employee slackers," Dagger added.

Hap stiffened. His brow wrinkled. Ingrid looked from Dagger to Hap and frowned. "The page is female," she said. "Seems well suited for her current position." She wriggled onto the couch between the adversaries. "Neither the time nor place to snipe. Besides, from her sloth-like posture and boorishness, I see promise in Planning, *not* Operations." She elbowed Dagger as Hap snickered.

Dagger recoiled before asking, "Everything all set at Headquarters?"

Ingrid nodded. "People cling to their Sundays but Underlicht says everyone's in my conference room."

Jacobs fidgeted. He pulled his collar as he twisted his neck. "Remind me how this works."

"I monitor the program," Ingrid said, pointing toward a TV. "As do our people in Chicago. When Seymour Clifton asks a question, Chicago texts a response." In prepping for the appearance, Ingrid warned everyone to be poised and professional since analysts formulated investment opinions from the show.

Jacobs rolled his eyes. "Why me?"

Ingrid curled her lip. "We've been over this. The camera will focus on Richard. That makes you the best person to screen the texts and interject if needed." She considered it clumsy, but the producers wouldn't let them use radios and earpieces to feed answers.

"Ingenious! You always make me look good," Weston said with a wink for Ingrid. He wiped sticky fingers on the sofa before pointing to the CFO. "Jacobs, you're on point." Jacobs groaned as he shook his head from side to side. He glanced down at his phone, dwarfed in his massive hand.

"*Two minutes*, Ms Schadden." The androgynous sentinel sounded the alarm. The female CEO and her companion rose to join the program's host on the set. Commercials for denture cleanser and adult diapers flashed on the screens.

"Good luck. Don't agitate Clifton for me. He can be an ornery bastard," Weston shouted as he dabbed lemon curd from his lips. Schadden turned with a wave and smile.

Hap watched the women exit the room as he spoke. "Attractive *and* smart. I own her company's stock—consistently outperforms despite telecommunications' woes."

"Ms. Candy Pants squanders efficiency," Jacobs griped. "She refuses to offshore. Claims long-time vendors and suppliers add value." Jacobs blew through pursed lips. "I'll give ya, attractive, but smart? *Hell no.*"

Weston patted Jacobs on the shoulder. "Hope Clifton goes easy. The capitalist's, capitalist is a shareholder hawk. He's skewered Fed Chairmen and Treasury Secretaries."

Ingrid added, "United Biscuit stock tanked after he bit

into their CEO's ass. Clifton's on-air rant gets credit for their shareholder revolt and hostile takeover."

Jacobs snickered. "That's the way the cookie crumbled."

Ingrid ignored the CFO. She added, "The tirade became an Internet sensation."

Weston struggled for the TV remote, inches from his stubby fingers. He snapped, "Turn up the volume. Let's hear how perky Ms. Schadden defends herself."

Ingrid batted her eyes at the monitor. "Poor dear."

"Twelve minutes Misters Weston and Jacobs," shouted the sentry as the group turned to the monitors.

"*Gail, I'd like to discuss your philosophy that some have called unorthodox in this harsh economy.*"

"*Leadership is my passion. And, you can't talk about leadership without emphasizing employees.*"

Weston and Ingrid exchanged smirks.

"*Your critics argue that American Cellular's employee focus short-changes shareholders. On shoring and a reluctance to shed heads or cut benefits are cited as examples. Let me read a quote from one CEO — 'Gail Schadden is committing corporate suicide'.*" Clifton folded his hands and leaned forward.

Ingrid turned to Weston, "Is he quoting you?"

Jacobs raised a fist. "He's got her by the balls."

The Intercontinental delegation fell silent, eyes riveted to the screen. Jacobs pushed himself to the sofa's edge while Weston flailed his arms in a plea to lift him to his feet. Weston clapped his hands and wobbled closer to the flat screen. "Here we go."

"*I've heard it all. The rabble who believe a company focuses on employees only to the detriment of shareholders. I believe companies can focus on shareholders to the detriment of employees and for that matter, customers. Sure we're employee centric—damned proud. But we're also customer and shareholder centric.*"

"Impossible!" roared Weston. His spittle sprayed the monitor.

Clifton shook his pen in the air. *"Aren't promises not to outsource or cut costs kowtowing to employees at the expense of shareholders?"*

"She's cornered now." Ingrid seemed surprised by her snort. She rested her chin on Weston's shoulder.

Schadden smoothed her jacket and smiled. *"We don't play one group off another. We harmonize all three. But, it all starts with employees doesn't it?"*

The green room's occupants froze. Everyone turned to Weston who stiffened.

"Some might disagree. They'd say that investors sow the seeds for any business." Clifton's eyes narrowed.

Weston squeezed Ingrid's arm. "Here-Here."

"Or that a market must exist before that, putting customers first. You can argue for both. But, I'm telling you employees make us successful. We invest in them, and they deliver. Employees aren't liabilities. We're a service provider—we need engaged, enabled and empowered employees to deliver exceptional service. My philosophy is quite simple."

Clifton held up his index finger. *"Employees first?"*

Weston and Jacobs grinned. Ingrid sighed.

Schadden shook her head. *"That's the nonsense I hear from those who think we're simply out to make employees happy. If your goal is happiness, you're doomed."*

"I'm surprised. Sounds contrary to everything you've said."

Jacobs joined Weston and Ingrid at the monitor. "Damned right! She's back-pedaling and he's calling her out," he said.

"Not if you listened to my message, or better yet, listen to your people. Employees are your best consultants—cheaper too. Open your ears. They understand profit, and you know what else?"

Clifton tilted his head, his tone softened. *"I'm captivated."*

"*Employees want what management and shareholders want—a successful company. They want tools and training to serve customers. They yearn to understand how they contribute to company success. That's alignment, connection, satisfaction, and engagement. Powerful motivators, more durable than happiness.*"

"*It's working. Your market share is growing and your stock outperforms peers,*" Clifton said with a wink to the camera.

"*Satisfaction means profit. Loyal customers need less advertising, promotions, and discounts. Loyal employees mean lower recruiting costs, less new-hire training, and higher productivity. That's how we deliver shareholder value.*"

"*That's the harmony you mentioned—leaving your shareholders humming a happy tune. We have to go to commercial. When we return, Gail talks leadership.*"

Hap grinned. "Boy, sure chewed her up and spit her out. Poor dear, licking her wounds and tending to bruised balls." Ingrid turned to Hap with gritted teeth.

"We'd have seen a different outcome if she had a penis," said Weston.

"Or was a homely, oversized matron. Men are suckers for pretty faces and perky boobs even if they come courtesy of Botox and silicone." Ingrid thrust out her chest and pulled her cheekbones taut.

Jacobs adjusted his jacket and tie. "Bunch of crap, packaged in a nice wrapper. I'd hate to see American Cellular's stock tomorrow."

"Someone turn that blasted sound off. I've heard enough," Weston bellowed. As Ingrid muted the televisions, she unintentionally activated close captioning.

"Five minutes, Misters Weston and Jacobs." The page smiled, the tone animated.

Hap's eyes remained glued to the words wrapping along the bottom of the monitors as Ingrid brushed crumbs from the folds of Weston's suit.

"*We're back with Gail Schadden. You've talked about employees, now tell us about leadership.*"

"*We ask a lot from our leaders. They must harmonize with our culture—support employees. We link all of our systems including employee and customer feedback to assess leaders. We look at the whole picture.*"

Clifton sat back. "*Don't you want results driven leaders?*"

"*We want sustainable results. Some leaders bully to deliver numbers. Others, afraid of failure, crowd out their people to retain control. They either can't or won't coach. They put personal success above teamwork and the company's broader wellbeing. No, we want the whole package. Leaders who deliver results and relationships.*"

"*I'm told you personally teach leadership modules.*"

"*With great pleasure. I'm not only the CEO, I'm the CCO.*" Schadden winked.

"*What's that?*" Clifton asked, wrinkling his nose.

"*Chief Culture Officer. Culture starts with me. Leaders value what I value.*"

"*So, everyone at American Cellular is perfect?*" Clifton posed the question with a wink and a pat on his guest's arm.

Schadden laughed. "*We're like any organization. We have people who don't get it. If you're willing to learn, we're committed to teach and coach. But, if you tune out our message, it's time to look for another job. Misaligned leaders are toxic. We don't plaster pithy sayings onto posters and pat ourselves on the back. We lead by example.*"

Clifton patted her arm. "*You've enlightened me. To many CEOs, employees are a dirty word. Your passion is refreshing. I wish you and American Cellular the very best. I'm betting you'll have many calls from prospective employees and customers tomorrow.*"

Schadden smiled. "*I hope I've convinced you to become a customer.*"

"*And investor—you've made a compelling case for both. When we*" *return, Intercontinental Airlines CEO Richard Weston III and Chief Financial Officer, Bryce Jacobs."*

"Two minute warning, Misters Weston and Jacobs."

With backs to the monitors, the grim faced trio glared at the page. Hap snickered.

Chapter 26

Grounds for Discourse

Coupons and cute guys enticed Lindy Price to suggest Grounds for Discourse under the Wabash L for the rendezvous. She waited inside, the back of her rain-splattered coat pressed against the crimson curtains at the café's entrance. From what she could see, the décor pleased her—pendant lights, wood floors, ocher walls and several hotties. She hummed the chorus of a familiar aria.

Lindy collapsed her umbrella into her purse as Chris Goodfeld pushed open the door. He shook water from his coat before hugging his teammate. "Love the smell of coffee. Especially on a day like this," he said.

"And baked goods," added Lindy with lifted nose.

The past Friday had been a blur in which Intercontinental announced massive layoffs as well as the promotion of three new officers including the pair's boss, Jim Abernathy. The entire team felt abandoned, set adrift just as tsunami alarms sounded. The two set the meeting as a chance to regroup before the new workweek. As was the practice among senior leaders, most honest conversations took place away from the office.

"Alto, slim, caramel latte whip." The stubble-faced barista repeated Lindy's order with a Latin accent.

"If... if a... that's small, low-fat with whip cream?" she stammered.

He winked. "Yes ma'am."

"And a non-fat oatmeal thingamajig," she said, pointing to the muffins. Is that a skinny Quaker?" She returned the wink and they both laughed.

Chris smiled at the flirtation and nudged Lindy.

She hissed, "Oh please. I could be his mother or," peeking over the counter, "older sister." She pressed her face against the pastry case. "How about you? My treat. I've got coupons."

"Just regular coffee, if they sell it—large with cream," Chris said. He nodded to the arriving muffin. "Skinny huh?"

Lindy sighed. "My endless struggle to squeeze into my old uniform. If we're all axed, I'm bouncin' back to the airport." Lindy handed money and coupons to the grinning hunk who directed them to the pick-up counter.

Chris laughed as he took the plate. "They'll never fire you. You do good work."

Lindy scrunched her face until her eyes crinkled. "*Doin's* not the issue. Problem's my *mouth*. When I see bone-headed moves, I can't help myself."

"You? I'm shocked." Chris staggered backward; hand clutched chest.

"Oh, shut up," she said, pulling him forward by his sleeve. "Acting doesn't suit you. I'm the drama queen. And watch that muffin."

"Everyone loves your honesty, especially Jim."

"True. What you see is what you get, maybe a little too much," she said pinching her waist. "Liposuction's an option."

Chris shook his head. "Stop. Everyone loves you the way you are."

"Love doesn't get you far at Intercontinental. Our newly orphaned team could get screwed. *If*, and it's a big if, we survive those monster layoffs, Wilkerson might decide to replace Jim with some clown. Someone who door mats the team to get ahead." She dropped a couple of singles in the jar drawing a salute of the barista's beret.

"So much for coupons," Chris said.

"Didn't want him to think I was a tightwad," she whispered.

Chris laughed. "Anyone ever mention that you fret too much?"

"Constantly. Jim thought I was having a stroke on Friday when he found us in the cafeteria. Wanted me to take a cab home. I guess being booted out of headquarters wouldn't be the worst thing given the way the company is going." With extended arms, Lindy pressed her wrists together with imaginary handcuffs. She marched toward the steaming coffee. "Take me away."

Chris pushed the muffin plate into her hand. "You're not going anywhere, unless it's with Jim."

"Everyone wants to work for him. I had a dozen calls over the weekend asking about his new department, as if I should know," Lindy said, shrugging her shoulders.

They picked up their coffees and scanned the café for a table. "Here comes Jenny Rodriguez," Chris said, spotting the co-worker out the window.

"I asked her to join us," Lindy said. "Figured she'd know something. She used to work for Jim. They're friends."

"Rumors suggest more." Chris raised an eyebrow. "Who could blame him?"

Jenny walked in wearing a glossy-red coat with matching hat and umbrella. She paused at the entrance to twist her polka dot fur-trimmed boots on the entry mat. Lindy elbowed Chris and they both laughed as most in the café stared at the newcomer.

"You look adorable—put my drab London Fog to shame. We've ordered," Lindy said to Jenny after meeting her at the cashier. "I've got a coupon somewhere." With plate balanced on cup, she rummaged through her purse.

Jenny enjoyed a long tenure at the airline, proving indispensable to a string of bosses. The smart ones rewarded her with promotions and flexibility. Jim realized his good fortune when he found Jenny on his team the first time. Their paths crossed whenever he had an opening in his group.

Jenny navigated to Lindy and Chris. After setting down her coffee, a yogurt parfait and a plate piled with doughnuts, she took off her coat and sat on the banquette beside Lindy. "I love this place," she said. "That gorgeous cashier comped the doughnuts as a welcome. They look yummy. What'd he give you guys?"

Chris and Lindy eyed each other and smiled.

"I hate you," Lindy blurted. Chris flinched.

Jenny gasped. "What!"

Lindy pointed at the plate. "The figure of a model, yet you eat that."

Jenny giggled. "Great metabolism and home gym. You both look mahvelous by the way. Here, have some." Jenny circled her plate over the table.

"Can't. Job security's on the line," Lindy said, kicking Chris under the table.

Jenny cocked her head before refocusing. "So much to talk about—Jim's new job, those stupid posters, Nelly Connors…"

"…Layoffs, Weston and Jacobs on *Money Matters*," Chris added.

Jenny giggled. "Didn't catch it—hubby and I slept in and had breakfast in bed. I made French toast stuffed with Bavarian cream. Yummy!"

"I hate you even more," Lindy shrieked. "You didn't miss much—mostly a rehash of Friday's bombshells."

"How'd ole moon face and the giant do? You know Weston asked me to work for him," Jenny said. Lindy and Chris went slack-jaw. "Why are you both looking at me that way? I said no," Jenny continued. "I have my standards. Now if Hap had asked—"

Chris kicked Lindy under the table before saying, "Weston looked like he'd eaten a bad piece of fish—pasty, stiff."

"Somebody else who should be counting calories," Lindy interjected, puffing her cheeks.

Jenny chuckled. "I love you, Lindy Price." She spooned into the parfait.

Lindy crinkled her eyes. "Big bird didn't say much."

"Stared at his crotch," Chris said, imitating Jacob's bowed head.

Lindy spewed coffee. "The show's host asked Weston about employee investments. After seconds of dead air, Jacobs jerked up like a jack-in-the-box, stared into his hand and stammered something about new seats and layoffs."

Chris added, "Weston laughed. You know, that my-yacht's-bigger-than-your-yacht kinda laugh. He said Jacobs mixed up initiatives. The host busted a gut when Weston added that his CFO flustered easily whenever he discussed spending."

"After that, Jacobs clammed up," Lindy said. "Stopped looking at his lap too."

"Layoffs! That's not investment, it's divestment," Jenny protested.

Lindy shrugged. "According to Weston, job slashing eliminates clutter. Streamlining helps employees focus. Guess we should be begging for layoffs instead of raises."

"A poopy answer," Jenny said, scraping the last yogurt from the cup.

"Clifton agreed," Lindy added. "He asked Weston if millionaires rejoiced at losing their fortunes, happy to focus on less zeros."

Chris chuckled. "Pouted until Jacobs whispered in his ear. Then he became downright giddy when he pulled Jim's new position out of his big ass."

Lindy cupped her chin. "But floundered again when pressed for details. Weston kept trying to nudge the conversation to finance but Clifton shut him down. He wanted to talk about employees and leadership."

"That lady CEO got him primed. Had Clifton eating out of her hand. Eye candy too," Chris said with a boyish grin.

Lindy leaned forward. "I loved what she said about leaders, responsible *to and for* employees. She gets it—unlike our goofballs."

"Weston didn't have a chance," Chris smirked. "Thought he'd pop his buttons when Clifton asked if he should scuttle his Intercontinental stock."

"I almost felt sorry for him. Clifton poked like a bully," Lindy said before flinching at their expressions. "Why those looks? I said *almost*, didn't I? I know he's a jerk."

Jenny pulled out her lipstick and a mirror. "Let's talk about something else. I don't want to get depressed before setting foot in the office. I won't make it to Tuesday!"

"You'll be on a sugar high till Thursday, kiddo," Lindy said, smiling toward Jenny's nearly empty dish.

Jenny's face brightened. "Let's talk about Jim. Just love that man. This employee stuff sounds positive for a change."

Lindy kicked Chris under the table as she spoke. "We thought maybe you talked to him this weekend. Got any scuttlebutt?"

Jenny blushed. "We don't talk out of work."

After synchronized sighs, Lindy and Chris summarized what they knew. Chris added. "Jim doesn't have many details. He's working with a consultant. Once that's done, he'll build the team—design then build."

"Logic, fancy that," Jenny said. Take my boss. The woman creates work. Doesn't plan, just barks orders. Whips up frenzies like farts in a frying pan. Has us whirling in different directions like one of those spinning sprinklers." Jenny's finger circled the air.

Lindy grimaced. "But she delivers. The higher-ups love that."

"Dig a hundred wells, you're bound to strike oil," Jenny shrugged. "She's cruel. Public humiliation's her weapon of choice. My co-worker's afraid she'll be skewered. Has diarrhea before every staff meeting. Girl Scout honor," Jenny added.

Lindy chuckled. "Scares the shit out of people, huh?"

"How do you cope?" Chris asked.

Jenny shrugged. "She likes me."

Lindy wagged her finger. "She's not stupid. You make her look good."

"Maybe. Besides, I don't want to be called Ms. Poopy Pants. Let's get back to Jim. I can't think of anyone more perfect to push employee issues."

"That's the unanimous opinion. Management finally gets one right. Jim's the eternal optimist but I'm not sure he knows what he's up against." Lindy sighed.

Chris patted Jenny's arm. "I have to think he'll find a way to recruit you."

A smile swept across Jenny's face. "Best boss ever."

"Compared to your current one?" Chris chuckled.

"Pleazzze. Next to her, this doughnut's a great boss." Jenny waved a glazed cruller in the air. "Jim's the only manager who measures success by his peoples' success."

Chris sighed. "We just have to figure out how to get on his new team."

Lindy clasped her hands in prayer. "Or beg for jobs with American Cellular."

Chapter 27

Tick Tock, Strikes Jim's Clock

Jim walked into the empty kitchen as the grandfather clock struck the last of its ten chimes. The dark house was otherwise quiet. His girls must be asleep he thought. The pregnancy made Julie tired and moody and Sedona bonded with the expectant mother. Jim often found them together, napping on the couch or cuddling on the bed when he came home. Late nights at the office had become the norm.

He flicked on the light expecting to find Julie's note. *Sorry he had to work late, apologies for heading to bed, instructions for heating dinner plated in the fridge.* Scribbled 'Xs' and 'Os' always brought a smile, even after the toughest of days. He excused the missing note as exhaustion. Poor thing, he sympathized. After dropping his bag and throwing his coat over a stool, he took a few seconds to process what he saw at the far end of the counter. His heart raced as he walked over and lifted the bottle. He frowned at the cork, foil peel, and opener.

"How could she? No matter how upset she is about Nelly," he mumbled as he checked the amount of wine missing from the bottle.

Julie's voice preceded her shadowy figure that emerged from the dark study. "Everyone's reckless these days," she said coldly. "Tsk, tsk, hurting themselves and others." There was sadness in her voice, but his ears picked up something else. An edge, maybe bitterness, maybe anger.

"Oh Julie, but you shouldn't be…" He stopped. His jaw dropped. "What in God's name is that?" he asked, pointing to her hands. One held a wineglass and the other cradled a tabby cat against her nightgown.

"The wine upsets you. Doesn't it, silly boy?" She raised the glass in a toast.

"I'm talking about the cat. Where did it come from?" He asked as he walked over to grab the glass. Both Julie and the cat hissed.

Julie turned, deflecting his advance. "Leave us alone."

"But the baby, Julie. What were you thinking?" For the first time, he noticed Sedona who peered from the study. With drooped head and soulful eyes, she seemed bewildered by the upheaval in her placid domain.

Julie's red eyes blinked toward him. "But, I have been thinking of the baby—"

He cut her off. "...Then how..."

She ignored him and talked over his words. "...And thinking about you, and Nelly, and us." She stared into his eyes. "All I've been doing is thinking. It hurts. I want to be numb." Her eyes followed the swirling red liquid. "Here's to us." She raised her glass.

He took a deep breath. Worry mixed with anger. "I'm sorry about Nelly, honey, I really am. I know I haven't been home as much as I should..." Julie interrupted with a scoff that emboldened his tone. "You shouldn't be drinking."

She glared at his wagging finger, a look of defiance. Neither spoke. After several seconds of the standoff, she closed her eyes. Her shoulders slumped and she staggered backward to lean against the counter. She shook her head. Tears welled in her eyes. "I stared at the bottle for an hour. Finally got the nerve to open it. Another hour passed before I poured the glass. Turned off the lights so I didn't have to look at it any more. That damn clock kept goading me. Do something. Forget your pain." She set the glass next to the bottle and hugged the cat to her chest and started to sob. "I couldn't. I didn't want to hurt the baby too."

Jim swelled with relief. He wanted to hold her. She pushed him away but he pulled her to his chest. She and the cat submitted. He wished he could squeeze out her anguish. He kissed her head and he felt her muscles relax. A meow interrupted his concentration. "Where did you get that cat?" he asked.

"It's Nelly's—Amelia," Julie said. She took a step backward and nuzzled the cat with her chin. "Nelly doesn't have anyone else." Jim had always loved Julie's compassion. She wouldn't kill a bug she could shoo outside and she made him stop the car for stray animals. He understood that caring for the cat channeled Julie's concern for her friend.

"How's Nelly?" Jim asked, caressing Julie's cheek.

Julie backed away. Her eyes flashed with anger. "She almost died."

He shook his head. "I'm so, so sorry. I wish it could have been somehow avoided."

Julie cocked her head. Her expression hardened.

"What's wrong honey?" he asked, frightened by the look.

"You sound like that damn company. *We regret, simply unavoidable, unforeseen, unfortunate, but necessary and blah, blah, blah.*" She looked at his feet. "Looks like you've been treading in Ingrid's shit. You reek of it." The cat jumped from Julie's arms and scampered away.

"Don't lump me in with that bunch," he said, raising his palm.

"You are that bunch. Don't you get it? Join the pack or die."

Jim extended his arms pressed Julie's hands. "Let's not argue. I know you're upset. How's Nelly?"

Julie sniffled. "She's in an induced coma. The mixture of pills shut down her organs. They don't know the extent of the damage."

Jim pressed his forehead. "That's horrible—poor thing."

"Her Doctors aren't sure she's going to make it," Julie said, choking back tears. Jim pulled her to him and kissed her neck. He didn't know why, but the smell of her hair made him tear up. Sedona wagged her tail and pushed her nose between their legs.

Julie pushed away and disappeared into the study, emerging with a box of tissues. She spoke. "I warned you. That place is toxic. They discarded Nelly like a worn out coat. Worse, treated her like a criminal. Thirty-five years and denied the dignity of a graceful exit. She had ten minutes to cram three and a half decades of life into a box. No party, no thank yous, no time to prepare. The pills filled the void."

"She deserved better."

"When I picked up Amelia, I found Nelly's company awards lined up on her dining room table. Damn right she deserved better. Did you send that email?" Julie asked. She had texted Jim earlier in the day to send an update to Nelly's work colleagues. His face fell, he closed his eyes.

"Of course you didn't. Nelly gave her life to Intercontinental and by God they won't rest until they get every last drop of blood from her."

"Honey, I'm so sorry. I've been swamped. Hap wants me to present to the Board." Hap told him that Board support would keep the employee initiatives alive. While he didn't say it, Jim felt Hap believed the Board would be a stronger ally than Weston.

Julie glared at him. "I want to be happy for you, I really do."

"But?" He asked, bracing for another onslaught.

"Enough is enough. We have a lot to think about. If you won't consider that, I will."

"Consider what?"

She dabbed her eyes. "I love you. But I can't sit back and

watch you destroy yourself. How long before you're ambushed like Nelly?"

"I'm not Nelly. I have you and the baby, thank God."

"They'll find your vulnerability. And when they do." She slapped the counter.

"But honey, I promise."

"You promised to take me to several doctor appointments, promised to celebrate your mom's birthday. You promised to share this pregnancy with me. But I sit here every night by myself. Didn't you say we'd make the big decisions together? Your goddamned job was sprung on me." As Julie's voice rose, Sedona scurried back to the study. "I feel like I'm having this baby by myself."

"Corporate America isn't the romantic world of the movies. Water coolers, office parties and two-hour martini lunches don't exist. Nine to five is a myth. Seventy-hour workweeks are the norm, doing the job of two or three people. It's kill or be killed. Bad things happen everywhere. Wise up. I have to earn a living."

She folded her arms tightly across her chest. "It's too late for Nelly, Shane, and dozens of other good, decent people destroyed by that place."

"But I can help those still there. I can make a difference. Hap's behind me."

"For how long? When it comes to you or Hap—and it will, who do you think he'll choose?"

"He's backing me up. You don't know him like I do." He dismissed her smirk as scorn for his naiveté. "What do you want me to do?"

"Leave before it's too late. Follow your dream—start your own company."

"Doing what?"

"Sell coffee if that makes you happy. You could write.

You've got the talent—training manuals or travelogues. That's always been your passion."

He swatted the air. "That's dreaming."

"No different than thinking you can fix a culture where the CEO doesn't give a shit about employees. A work-around is what you called him, right? Save yourself…save us."

"And abandon everyone who's counting on me? Without a fight? I've got to try to fix things. Hap has faith in me. He's given me Richter."

"Richter sounds like a great guy, but they'll find his Achilles' heel if they haven't already. How loyal will your mighty consultant be when the deep pockets don't like what they see?"

She began to turn when Jim grabbed her, leaned into her face, and said, "I love you so much. I don't want to lose you." She let him kiss her.

Chapter 28

Jim Stumbles into IROPS

Intercontinental is paging all customers off cancelled flight 877 to Bermuda. Proceed to the passenger assistance counter.

Intercontinental 1354 to San Francisco is delayed. Passengers should check monitors for the new departure gate.

Passengers on Intercontinental 62 to Honolulu are instructed to proceed to gate 30 for an immediate departure. Doors are closing.

Jim parked in the O'Hare lot reserved for badged employees. Horizontal rain pelted him while wind gusts turned the umbrella into farcical prop as he sought cover in a bus shelter named for one of the airline's destinations. He flicked water from trousers and shoes before sitting on a splintered bench under a heat lamp. Homemade ads for roommates, used cars and diet pills diverted him as he waited.

The shuttle eventually arrived. After stops at *Paris, Hong Kong, and London*, the rickety bus groaned a path across taxiways where it dodged jumbo jets and service vehicles. Jim sat wide-eyed, pumped by a dose of the real airline. Jet fuel smells, take-off roars, and airplane underbellies primed the cast from cleaners to captains. At the terminal, Jim's adrenaline surged with the same rush he imagined happened on a movie set when the director shouted *action*.

Announcements droned as Jim ascended from the bowels of the building into the steel and glass monolith. Frenzy gripped the concourse where noises, smells and a kaleidoscope of colors converged. Extensive experience during IROPS, the insiders' term for irregular operations, sensitized Jim to customer behavior. Hurry suggested purpose but blank faces and furtive looks into teeming gate rooms betrayed anxiety. Thunderclaps and lightning silenced the refugees before a chorus of profanity arose from the agitated masses. Ears perked and breathing stalled with each crackle of the public address system. Departure calls spirited the hopeless while frustration creased the brows of the forlorn legions ordered to the assistance counter, IROPS purgatory.

Jim saw frazzled passengers drive agents to the refuge of gate room podiums. Lines snaked into the concourse, coalescing into a shapeless amalgamation that hissed its collective discontent. IROPS vexed customer and employee alike.

Jim admired the grit of staff that manned their stations, rain or shine. They dealt in the present; caught whatever was thrown. They didn't have the luxury to punt decisions forward, delegate to subordinates or bury problems in abandoned stacks. Corporate, he thought, would drown outside their cubicle havens.

Despite severe conditions forecasted to last the day, Kyle Richter's flight had a priority tag courtesy of its three-dozen connections to Asia. IROPS played like high stakes poker with International connections *difficult* to re-route, and elite customers *easy* to piss off, the face cards. Aunt Gert, en route from Fort Wayne to Scranton was the two of clubs while Weston and his cronies, the deck's aces.

As Jim weaved down the concourse, he considered how IROPS confounded the airline's million dollar systems. Immediacy trumped planning. Procedures were as grounded as mobile homes in a tornado.

"Jim… Jim… Jim Abernathy!" The shout came from his left. Having worked at O'Hare, he wasn't surprised to hear his name. He craned his neck to find the caller.

"Over here. Newark." A bare arm flailed above the heads crowding the podium. The LED sign above the gate room flashed, *Newark—Delayed*.

Behind the podium, Jim found Kelly Green, an agent he supervised years before. He almost didn't recognize her. Mousey brown bangs gave way to bright red spikes. A purple serpent inked its way down her forearm, its pink tongue flicking at a red apple. Faux leopard, cat-eye glasses secured by a ball bearing chain completed the metamorphosis from farm girl to urban rebel.

Kelly proved Jim's hypothesis that airline jobs were magic. You could be anyone, go anywhere; a jet set lifestyle. Employees changed personas easily. Cabin aisles and concourses became catwalks to strut new identities. As a new supervisor, Jim hadn't been familiar with the practice among some workers to assume aliases for privacy. The company didn't mind as long as employees wore nametags. Co-workers knew S.P. Fairy as Sugar Plum while others adopted more intuitive monikers, S. Claus, H. Doody, E. Presley and a herd of flight attendants named Bambi. Once, Jim caught flak from an agent he accidentally paged by his real identity, a surname that belonged to a notorious crime family wiped out in a hit.

An entertaining mix of customers shared the stage including the blonde who strolled through O'Hare's lobby wearing only a mink. Supreme Court justices, Senators and stars of screen and sports crossed paths at O'Hare, America's busiest intersection. Every day at the airport was an adventure, irregular the new normal.

Jim liked Kelly the second she bucked her peers to welcome the green supervisor from HDQ. He admired her technical and soft skills. With her coaching, he survived the hazing from agents and other supervisors and quickly made a home on swing shift.

Shifts developed distinct personalities. As soccer moms, suburbia and mini-vans defined days, hip-hop, tattoos and piercings described swing. Despite frequent calamity, swing got the job done. Customers and employees, both edgy, bonded. A local dive bar provided after-shift group therapy. The scrappiness of swing shifters hooked Jim.

Most seasoned employees, however, avoided swing because the tightly wound airline snapped in late afternoon. Strings of four-hour mandatory overtime got old fast. Kelly was part of the unique breed who lingered on the shift after seniority could spring them to days.

"Kelly Green, that you in there? Your name's the least colorful thing about you now," Jim said with a broad smile.

"Finally. Your fuckin' supervisor." The growl came from someplace on Jim's right as Kelly abandoned the podium to hug him.

"I'm so glad to see you. Sorry to drag you into this. It's *Newark*," she whispered into his ear and prolonged the embrace.

Over Kelly's shoulder, Jim saw a barrel-chested man advance. "Fuckin' time ya showed up," the man in the rumpled suit said.

Jim glanced at the departure screen. 11:20 hadn't departed—current time, almost 3. Newark customers stung on good days. "Yes sir, name's Jim Abernathy. How can I help?" Jim extended his hand.

The man didn't reciprocate. "I don't want ya name. I anda hundert of my closest friends want answers." The man arced his arm around the gate room. As he edged closer, Jim smelled garlic and onions, a byproduct of the pizza box clutched in his hands.

As Jim stepped back, he noticed the man's bulging red

neck and throbbing temple vein. Calming the guy would be priority—lowered the odds of mouth-to-mouth resuscitation. Experience taught Jim to contain the conversation to the complainer, to lower his voice even as the customer raised his and to request a moratorium on swearing. Keeping cool while the complainer spiraled out of control restrained an anxious mob.

Kelly spoke. "Mr. Esposito's upset we can't quote a departure time. I got here fifty minutes ago. Found the podium abandoned. Said the last agent staggered away. They've requested a supervisor for an hour. Can't reach mine either. Control center told me to hang on but that was twenty minutes ago."

Esposito interrupted, "No one can tell us a goddamned thing."

"Mr. Esposito, I apologize for the situation. Let me make some calls. I'll get some information. Okay?"

A sneering Esposito wagged a finger inches from Kelly's nose. "I'm still pissed that Lady Gaga here wouldn't help us."

"Mr. Esposito, one more thing." Jim inhaled before leaning into the guy's ear. "Treat Ms. Green with the same respect I treat you. If you can't, our business is over. You won't be going anywhere today. Is that clear?" Jim stepped back. His broad smile intended more for the simmering onlookers.

Esposito nodded. His head bowed to the carpet. Jim took the mike to apologize and explained his intent to talk to pilot and control center. The crowd exhaled. Jim concluded, "Ms. Green is one of our best and brightest. She'll take good care of you, if you let her."

✦

Jim exited the airplane and returned to the podium with the pilot who he introduced to Kelly. The three huddled on a plan before addressing the crowd in a show of solidarity.

"Jim," a voice called. Jim smelled pizza and turned to find Esposito.

"Sorry for losin' my cool. Thought you'd disappear on that airplane. Sorry about takin' frustrations out on Ms. Green. It's not her fault. If only I could get to that CEO of yours. I'd give some good ole Jersey feedback." He extended a hand and the two shook.

As Jim exited the gate room, Kelly tugged at his sleeve. "You're still my hero. I'd love to chat about this place. It's changed since you were here. *Everything's* broken— phones, printers, computers, trust, you name it. It's embarrassing. Supervisors don't support us. They're scared to death, bullied for results. We're orphans."

Jim squeezed her arm. "I'm so sorry. I'd love to talk. Hopefully, help's on the way."

"One more thing," she said. Then rose on tiptoes to kiss his cheek.

Jim blushed. "What's that for?"

"For everything. Not raggin' about my tattoo. The nice things you said. Treating me like I mattered. I can't remember the last time management stood up for me. Sometimes..."she said with a sigh, "I just wanna give up."

As Kelly scurried away, Jim detected her eyes swelling behind the rose-tinted glasses.

He found Richter's gate as the flight purged its passengers. After a seemingly endless parade, the white-haired Richter emerged from the jet bridge, the last to deplane. He bantered with a flight attendant. Jim recognized the same suit worn to their first meeting but his eyes wandered to the dark circle fanning out from the consultant's left lapel. Jim watched Richter's hand shoot into the air in an animated exclamation that sent his trolley and computer bouncing to the floor. Jim darted to assist.

Richter grinned. "Ah, my friend. We finally made it." The bright orange tie and brown loafers made Jim smile. Richter shook his head. "Been one of those days." He motioned to the auburn-haired woman in the airline's teal blue uniform. "This fine company representative is Samantha."

As Jim and Samantha shook hands, Richter continued, "I spilled my entire cup of coffee. Darn turbulence. Samantha kindly administered club soda triage." The flight attendant's raised eyebrows told Jim that unstable air had little to do with the consultant's mishap. "Had to give her feedback. Magnificent flight, despite the delay," he added.

"Magnificent?" Jim asked, winking at Samantha.

Richter gushed. "Exceptional updates. A real team effort in Boston—suits *and* uniforms. Actually made us feel like guests instead of just saying that overused word."

Jim's eyes widened. "Why Boston?"

Samantha answered, "I'd like to say it's me and *all* my flights are faaan-tastic." She posed dramatically, one hand clasping her hip, the other flourishing the air with an imaginary serving tray. She relaxed her pose and added. "Truth is, we're a team."

"What does that look like?" Jim asked, studying Samantha with folded arms.

Her tone sharpened. She frowned. "You're not going to blab our little secret to HDQ are you? Whenever *they* get involved, it's nothing but bad news."

"Promise." Jim crossed his chest. "Last thing I wanna do is spoil what's working."

"That's what they all say. But you're cute, I'll take my chances. Respect and camaraderie. Managers support us. It's that simple."

Richter's fingers rifled his uncombed hair. "Is this a local initiative?"

Before she could respond, Jim asked. "Did management

tell employees how to act?"

"Heavens no! Nothing's more powerful than watching managers; the suits as you adorably call them, solve problems and laugh together. We mimic them."

"Sounds organic, viral," Richter responded in consultant speak.

"Huh?" she asked.

"Spontaneous, popping up all at once," Richter said, his cheeks turning pink.

"For the most part," she said. She glanced at her watch. "I'd love to keep chatting, gents, but I must fly. Ciao." She walked away but a moment later called back. "Gents, I've got a marv idea. Come visit. See for yourselves. Take one of my flights. Guaranteed to be faaan-tastic. Ciao Bellos." She blew a kiss.

Chapter 29

Jim Debuts

"Abernathy, but Jim with a J, not T... on my way... only a few blocks. At the bridge... yes on foot. Got it. I'll find you right a..." The call disconnected. As Jim tucked his phone away, his mind churned to the evening ahead—his officer debut, an introduction to Weston and now a personal summons from the Countess. Anxiety mixed with adventure as he hurried to the dinner.

The evening's warmth came courtesy of the westerly breeze that buffered the icy emissaries off Lake Michigan. The setting sun, unobstructed by the wall of skyscrapers that lined Wacker Drive, speckled the river with light. Jim welcomed Daylight Savings Time. A night of abbreviated sleep was a bargain for sunshine that advanced into the evening like a scout clearing summer's path. However, the thermometer seldom kept pace with the sun's northward march, chilling most spring fevers.

Jim glided across the bridge and mumbled under his breath. "Wow! Ingrid Shattenworter has my number. Two weeks ago, she didn't know who the hell I was and now, she's calling *me*. Called me Tim, but called nonetheless." He resisted an urge to whistle as he considered the conversation. She showed a good sense of humor. Called him pedestrian. He wrinkled his brow. "At least I hope she was joking,"

Several secretaries provided advice for his first officer event. Dinners were business- casual unless advised otherwise. Suit overdone, jacket and tie, acceptable but unnecessary. Jim chose semi-conservative, jacket and flannel trousers.

Early in his career as an intern for a stodgy accounting firm, a partner embarrassed Jim for not wearing a dark suit. With martini breath, the pompous Suit offered a pay advance in front of Jim's peers should he be strapped for cash. Jim fought back tears on the commute home, recalling taunts suffered from bullies as a chubby kid. A spurt to six two ended the teasing, but the experience wounded him. He had no tolerance for bullies. He wondered whether the firm ever figured out why he passed on their permanent position. People do sweat the small stuff, he reasoned. He laughed, remembering a Calism. *A bunch of little crap clogs the toilet as effectively as one big dump.*

He hurried across the bridge, dodging photo snapping tourists and a homeless guy, who cheerfully greeted commuters by name. Ingrid's urgency surprised him. Had he already messed up? He didn't suppose she wanted to apologize for the press release blindside. He approached *Magnus Angus*, a restaurant that catered to rowdy conventioneers, free-spending tourists and businesspeople with expense accounts. Everything oversized: half-quart martinis, 48-ounce steaks, platter-sized desserts and sky-high prices—the city of big shoulders and waistlines.

As Jim neared, he recognized company VPs who hopped out of taxis or idled in the valet queue. He hadn't considered cabbing the six blocks from the office, especially on such a great night. *You're entering a new world. Study, take notes,* he reminded himself. Meeting with or working for an officer was one thing, rubbing shoulders as a peer, another thing altogether.

Jim reached the door as two vice presidents paid their cabbie. The man, handsome with wavy hair and an out-of-season tan, produced a wad of cash from a wallet fished from his pocket. He flicked off a twenty. "Jeanne, give this to the driver.

He can keep the change. Get a receipt."

The woman climbed out. With a smirk, she chided her colleague. "Jerry, you should have seen him light up with that outrageous tip. Wish I had Sales' expense accounts. Haven't you heard we're cutting costs?" She rubbed his arm playfully and a toss of her head swept chestnut brown hair from her face.

"If you don't squeal, I'll keep mum about that extra night you slipped into your New York trip. Hope you enjoyed that new musical."

"You're shameless. I mentioned that in confidence." She pressed her index finger to the man's lips.

"No worries. Look where we're dining." He swept his hand toward the restaurant's green awning. "Not exactly Hamburgers Are Us. You need twenty bucks for the crapper. Or, no toilet paper or hand towels." He laughed at the revulsion that flashed across her face. "Keep away from our pals from finance."

"Why?" she asked with hand on hip.

He held up his hands like a prepped surgeon. "Tightwads. Never tip."

She swatted his linen jacket. "You're shameless, simply shameless."

Laughing, they disappeared into the restaurant without as much as a nod to Jim who greeted them with a smile as he held open the door. His head shook at the irony. The company expected managers like him to scold employees who submitted breakfast receipts in excess of five dollars and treat reimbursement requests for lunch as mortal sins. "*Manager?*" He exclaimed. "Keep repeating. *You're an officer.* Eyes, ears open."

The hostess directed him down to a private dining room. As he descended the stairwell, he heard two heated voices. Columns hid their faces, but he watched martini glasses quiver on their table. Customer chatter and piped in music muffled the conversation. Still, he guessed one of the men was former boss, Chad Wilkerson. *"Butt out. I don't give a rat's ass what you think. You have no proof... I don't need to play dirty to sabotage him. I can be dangerous..."* A bartender thundered down the stairs with three bottles of vodka and pushed him along. Jim sought the men's room as a refuge to muster courage and make one last nervous pit stop.

"Congratulations! I'm positively ecstatic." The booming voice belonged to Betty Jankowski. She saw Jim when she emerged from the restroom. She ran a hand down her wool skirt before she offered it. "Only water. Better yet, gimme a hug. More hygienic." She laughed deeply. Jim smelled cigarette as she drew him close.

Betty got her vice presidency after her predecessor got fired. Considered a call center lifer, Betty started on the phones in the sixties when index cards, clotheslines and poster boards tracked flight reservations. Her promotion, heralded as a *one-of-your-own, rose through the ranks* selection was a peace offering to calm the fury whipped up by the unpopular predecessor. Standing six feet, heels put her nearly at Jim's height.

Jim wiped his sweaty palms on his trousers. "At last, a friendly face."

"In case you haven't noticed, sweetie, you and I are misfits," she whispered. "I won't be around long."

Jim cocked his head. "What?"

She spun him around and rested her chin on his shoulder. "Look at the faces—mostly outsiders. You and I grew up here. The only homegrown VPs on Weston's watch." She pivoted him back around. "You got your work cut out for you sweetie, but you're the drop dead best person for the job." She squeezed his shoulder.

"Can we sit together? This is my first dinner."

"Haven't you heard?" She laughed. "Virgins sit with Weston."

"Huh?"

"Officers, new officers."

Jim swallowed hard. His palms moistened. "Hap didn't say anything."

She roared even louder. "Guessin' he didn't mention your speech, either."

Jim stiffened. His eyes bugged. "You're pulling my leg. New officer hazing?"

She slapped him on the back. "Afraid not, sweetie. Won't get any tears from me. I had the same root canal. Good luck. Extra points for pulling a Bush in Japan." Smokers' cough punctuated her boisterous laugh.

"Huh?"

"Heaving into Weston's lap." Her laugh faded as she disappeared into the bar.

Jim remembered Ingrid's summons and panicked. He scanned the room, his eyes dodging scurrying servers with trays of hors d'oeuvres and cocktails.

"Jim?"

He turned to see a tiny hand that matched the squeaky voice extend toward him. It was cold and bony to the touch. "Carrie Patterson," the woman said. "Pleased to meet you."

"We've met. We both served on that employee travel committee a few years back." Jim caught himself staring. He hadn't seen her up close for years. The lips too large, lipstick, and too perfect nails, the same shade of red. Hair and face, too stiff to be real.

"You can't possibly expect me to remember. My God, it's freezing in here." She shivered, pawing his wool jacket like a cat.

"I'm comfortable," Jim said, guessing that her ultra mini-skirt and sleeveless blouse weren't chosen for warmth.

"Leather's supposed to be warm." She slid her hands down

her hips. "HR and I support you 100%." The lips, plump like cocktail wieners, opened and closed mechanically—words spoken without expression.

Jim nodded. "Sharlee Guerrin's already called. We set up time to talk."

"Keep her involved and informed. Wouldn't want to trip over each other, would we?" He shook his head as she continued. "You'll find HR all over the work you hope to do. Let's not duplicate efforts." Her lips twitched but remained horizontal.

Jim didn't think that her face could structurally support a smile. He responded, "Couldn't agree more. There's so much employee work to keep us all busy for a *long, long* time. So much to do. Where to begin?" Jim laughed nervously but regretted his words immediately. Would she take offense with the inference of her team's incompetence?

Patterson tried to pucker her lips but stamped her tiny foot instead. Watching her reaction, Jim remembered Hap's words—*Human Resources was broke.* But Jim saw his mission differently. Patterson probably wouldn't agree. Jim continued, "I'm sure your team's excited about the extra horsepower I bring. It'll be great partnering with them."

"Really? We'll see." Patterson turned, her tiny feet clicked in pursuit of the Chief Counsel who slunk into the room behind her. Her concern reminded him of a dog that discards an old bone, ignoring it until a rival shows interest. Then, teeth are bared.

Before Jim digested the conversation, the perfumed arm of Charlotte Singleton, sheathed in white angora, spun him around and planted a kiss on his cheek.

"Hello dahlink. Congrats. You escaped Chad the cad's evil little clutches." Her hands formed into claws. Jody Cantelone stood at Charlotte's side and waited her turn to hug him.

He gushed, "Good to see you both. Thanks for the warm welcome."

"Damn good to see *you* here. We so need someone like you. Ops suffers and HR sucks." Jody didn't mince words.

Charlotte squeezed his arm. "As you know dahlink, Wilky, doesn't get the whole employee thing either. Damn queasy around the little darlings."

"Fuckin' squeamish around us too. Just shoot me," added Jody. She grabbed Jim's arm and pulled him toward her. She whispered in his ear. "Careful. Wilkerson's a little prick with a big ego. Don't trust him."

"How'd he take my departure?" Jim asked.

Jody shrugged. "Blames you for all his screw ups."

Charlotte stiffened. "Speak of the weasel. Not sure why his head's not up Weston's ass. Sorry dahlink, there's a martini calling me and a scotch and soda screaming for Jody. Good luck with your speech. I recommend liquoring up."

"Thanks for the tips." Jim had forgotten about the speech. He still hadn't found Ingrid. His stomach knotted. He watched Wilkerson's white head steer toward him. Heels added two inches to Wilkerson's height. As Jim waited, a conversation between two officers unfolded behind him. Jeanne, the business trip padder bantered with gaunt Chief Budget Officer Tate Gregory, a stereotypical numbers cruncher with the demeanor of an undertaker.

Jeanne spoke slowly. "I know what you want, but across the board cuts are ridiculous. Merely rewards big spenders."

"But, surgical reductions are hard. We don't have time." Gregory spoke in a soft, monotone drone.

"Don't tell anyone I told you, but Sales throws money away, shamelessly. Dig into Jerry's expenses." They disappeared into a corner where Jim watched Jeanne work

Gregory with strokes, giggles, and batted eyes.

Wilkerson finally reached him. His ruddy face tilted upward. "What did Charlotte and Jody want?"

"To say hello."

Wilkerson slipped his phone into his trousers and extended an arm, giving one of those awkward handshakes with a wrist roll. Jim applied counter pressure, forcing Wilkerson's passive-aggressive wrist back to neutral ground. "I've got tons of employee work underway," Wilkerson said as he nursed a vodka and lemon.

Jim wrinkled his nose. "You never mentioned anything before."

Wilkerson pinched his bottom lip and frowned. "Course I did. You'll be amazed. You'll have your hands full elsewhere. Schedule time. I'll brief you. May want to export my work. Richard supports me. Extremely impressed." As Wilkerson shook his drink toward Weston, some of its contents splashed to the carpet.

"I'll help everyone. Even those who don't think they need it." Jim winked. "Sometimes the Division head's the last to know."

Wilkerson sneered. "Finance is giving you a budget."

Jim made a champion's fist. "Finally! Hap hasn't mentioned resources. Glad to hear I'll have money."

"Down, Rocky. Don't expect much. We're all cutting. That's why I'm stumping for my employee projects."

Jim thought about covering his wallet but folded his arms instead. "Such as?"

"Streamlining the airports... re-engineering."

"Sounds like business as usual. That wouldn't fall into my investment portfolio."

"Course it does. Efficiency benefits employees. Think Garanimals or paint by number." Wilkerson toasted his glass but clanked Jim's empty hand.

Jim stepped backwards. He told himself not to snap at the condescending crap or get drawn into an argument. Not at his debut. "You want me to re-engineer your airports?"

Wilkerson flinched. "Course not. That's why we have consultants."

Jim scratched his temple. "How do you want me involved?"

"You're far too busy. I'll be kind." Wilkerson tried to punch Jim's shoulder but missed. "I only need a teensy eensy bit of money. The project won't survive without your support. Hap'll see my point." Wilkerson's little black eyes glared.

"How much?" Jim sighed. Would Hap side with the senior or junior officer?

Wilkerson cleared his throat. "A million dollars. But I'm sure I can negotiate down a smidge."

Jim's jaw dropped. "Let me see my budget first."

"Take your time. I don't need money for a few weeks." He looked past Jim. "The Chairman's free. I'll mention our agreement." Wilkerson's stiff turtleneck pushed his pug nose in the air as he staggered toward Weston.

Jim winced at the drive-by. He concealed himself next to a column to scan for Ingrid. He declined the passing trays of crab cakes and satay; his stomach couldn't handle it. A firm hand grabbed his shoulder.

He turned to find Hap's steel eyes. "Been looking for you. Betty Jankowski slurred a scolding. Says I never gave you direction."

Jim's back pressed against the column as Hap inched forward. "Everybody's mentioned a speech."

Hap smiled. "It's nothing. Just a short talk, new officer ritual. You won't be alone. We're introducing two other vice presidents tonight."

Jim pulled at his lapels. "What's the subject? How long?"

"Short. Three to five minutes, tops. After we sit, I'll say a few words, introduce you. Simply talk about your focus. What it means to be a new officer. Then, Weston speaks and we eat. Simple as that." Hap snapped his fingers.

Jim inhaled. "Okay."

"I placed you between Weston and Jacobs. Maybe a little employee karma will rub off. Get a drink." Hap bowed and darted away. Jim grabbed a beer off a passing tray.

A large man, his round pockmarked face dotted with perspiration beads, approached. "You Abernathy?" Stains arced under the arms of the man's heavy suit.

"That's me. And you?" Jim extended his hand. The gesture not reciprocated.

"Underlicht, Scott Underlicht; Ingrid's man in Washington. She wants you, *yesterday*." The voice was gruff.

"Been lo.. looking for her." Jim's voice trembled as his eyes darted around the room in search of the platinum head.

"Upstairs." Underlicht grunted and nodded toward the ceiling.

"What?" As Jim leaned closer, the scent of musty wool hit his nose.

"First floor. Front door." Underlicht's right hand formed a lump in his pocket. The scene reminded Jim of *film noire*. A menacing thug prods the hero who gets pummeled by a gun butt.

Jim led the way, guessing he didn't have a choice. He attempted small talk over his shoulder. "So, you're based in Washington."

"Yup. Hit town today. Didn't expect Chicago to be so damn hot in spring."

"A pleasant break. Winters are killers."

"Depends on your perspective." Underlicht lumbered up the last few stairs to the main floor. Sweaty fingers stained the mahogany-paneled walls as he maneuvered up the narrow stairway.

Jim wiped the back of his neck, moist from Underlicht's heavy breathing. "You'd be more comfortable without your coat."

Underlicht snickered. His words came like a German-accented robot. "Jackets, vorn at all times. Form as vital as substance."

Jim pointed to the necktie in Underlicht's pocket. "But ties are optional?"

"Ordered to ditch it. Blend in. I've said too much." Underlicht pointed to an alcove draped with green curtains. Jim expected a sinister laugh and a violent push but thanked his escort for parting the drapes.

Hit by a blast of jasmine, Jim entered a surreal scene. Ingrid sat in a high-backed chair with carved arms and ornate legs that met the floor with what looked to be lion's paws. The room's single spotlight highlighted the facets of her amethyst pendant and made the diamonds and purple stones of her earrings sparkle.

Her eyes didn't stray from a compact mirror as she applied lipstick. "I'm terribly sorry." She paused. Jim's imagination accelerated into overdrive. She added, "Abernathy, there's no place for you here."

Jim stammered. "Ex...excuse me?"

She glared. "There's only one chair."

He laughed nervously as he scanned the room. "Oh. That's okay."

"I've been exceedingly patient. I've been calling you. Has the new officer experience swept you off your feet?" Her eyebrows arched.

Jim fumbled for the mobile in his trouser pocket, horrified to find a black display. "Must have switched off by accident. I looked for you, downstairs."

"Thirty minutes? I underestimated this establishment's

size. A virtual maze of a warehouse." Her violet eyes narrowed on him. "Let's move on. You won't be careless again."

His hand dug into his jacket pocket to hide a sweaty palm. "Promise."

With an exaggerated smile from lavender lips she spoke, "You have my undying support. I'm so eager to help that I've volunteered to co-sponsor. Hap and I will *both* direct."

"Thank you," Jim said, wondering why hadn't Hap mentioned anything.

"I'll give you access to my personal director for all your communication needs."

"That's very generous."

She shook her head. "Amateur."

Jim stammered. "Ex...excuse me?"

"We can't tolerate amateurs. This work needs the finesse of a professional like Meg Orkin, my personal assistant. You'll have to sacrifice access for quality. That's reasonable?" Her eyes narrowed, her face framed by the platinum hair that fell to her shoulders.

His head bobbed rapidly. "Of course."

"I knew you'd see it my way. Hap boasted of your intelligence."

"He did?" Jim waited but Ingrid remained silent. She stared above his head.

"Now run off and enjoy your debut." She shushed him away with the back of her hand. "Be sure to tell Hap of our little chat."

Jim nodded. "Just have to get through my speech."

"That reminds me." Her voice rose from a whisper to a command. "Clear messages through Meg. That's not too much to ask in return for our help."

Jim backed out of the alcove. He fought the urge to bow. He wondered if the stroke of midnight would find him whisked back to his old life. He chugged the rest of his beer. Maybe exile to his pre-officer life would be a blessing on many fronts.

Jim descended to the dining room. As his speech gelled in his muddled brain, he saw Gregory again. Now, engaged in a spirited discussion with Jerry, the big tipper. Jim chuckled at Jerry's smooth talk. "Sales runs a tight ship. Brings cash in the door. You don't want to cut off the hand that feeds you. Especially in this economy. You may want to audit Jeanne's compliance with travel policy. Heard her division is looseygoosey. Would net you real savings. But, don't tell anyone I told you."

Chapter 30

Jim Finds Common Ground

"I'm a block away. It's next to the drug store, right?" Jim yelled into his phone as the L screeched into the station above the crowded sidewalk. "Huh? Oh, you got coupons."

He bounded across the street as the light turned yellow. He dodged a taxi and practically fell into the café. As he parted the entry curtains, Lindy's unmistakable squeal pinpointed his former team. He missed that camaraderie, especially after the officer dinner and two days of meetings that droned on like a time-share pitch. While his old team worked like dogs, they never squandered an opportunity to blow off steam with a laugh or a pat on the back for each other. They waved to him.

As Lindy hugged him, she slipped a coupon into his hand. "Here ya go, Chief. I'm buyin'. I promise to behave. Wouldn't want a VP kicked out of a coffee shop. Morality clauses and all." She elbowed him in the stomach.

Jim unzipped his leather jacket. "Morality clause? Those went out with hats and ethics. Dare I ask what you're hootin' about?"

She pointed to the floor. "I'm goin' straight to hell."

"Spill," Jim said with a chuckle.

"A lap toddler threw up on our hoity Chairman La Di Da the Third on a recent flight, first class of course." Jim shrugged. Lindy continued, "Wait. Gets better. They tried to move him to the only open seat; a middle in coach. But, his royal portly highness couldn't squeeze between two linebacker types. Pouted all the way to Atlanta. Deplaned with baby puke on his bottom." Lindy's curly head bent over in laughter. "The flight attendants showered the kid with honorary wings and gave the mom a bottle of champagne." She removed her glasses to wipe away tears.

Jim grabbed his coffee and scone and said to the amused barista. "She's right, she is going to hell."

"Bet she's got coupons when she gets there," the barista said with a wink.

Lindy squeezed his arm. "You're adorable Felipe." Then turning to Jim, she added with a giggle, "They call me the coupon queen."

As Jim and Lindy reached the table, Chris and Daniel greeted in unison, "How'd it go?"

Jim draped his jacket on the chair. "Okay. At least, I think so."

Lindy flailed her arms and plopped down to her coffee and sweet rolls. "First things first Dad. How's Julie and Baby to be?"

Jim inhaled. He ran his hands down the legs of his corduroys. "Good, real good." He paused before deciding to add, "Julie drove up north to stay with her mom for a few weeks. You know, before she's too far along." He saw their looks and felt compelled to give some explanation. "She's still upset by the whole Nelly thing. And, of course I'm working all kinds of ungodly hours. Her trip made sense." He added the last bit, not sure if it was for their benefit or his.

Lindy smiled feebly as she rubbed his arm. Perhaps she sensed his unease. "Good Chief. Let us know if you need anything. We love you guys to pieces." He nodded as he pressed her hand.

Lindy winked. "So, Chief, your officer debut was a smashing success?" Jim noticed her plate and chuckled. She blushed. "I know. My diet. But, it's *casual* Friday, not *fat-free* Friday. I'm wearin' guilt-free mama jeans." She pulled the elastic waist-band. "Now, give us the scoop on the officer dinner. Spill."

"Did ya learn the secret handshake?" Chris asked.

Daniel didn't let him answer. Stroking his chin, he said, "If we look real hard, bet we find ourselves a used pod." He pinched Jim's arm. "Our good ole Jim snatched away by Vice President, James Abernathy the Third."

Jim punched Daniel's shoulder. "Very funny. You'll have to decide for yourselves." But maybe Daniel was onto something, he thought. Was ole Jim at risk of vanishing?

Lindy wriggled in her seat. "We're waiting."

"The meeting could be improved."

"That's pod-Jim's way of saying it sucked," Daniel said.

Lindy's eyes bugged. "Zombie-fests, we've heard. Grown men and women afraid to speak."

"No argument here," Jim said.

"Spill." Lindy's beckoning palm coaxed words from his mouth.

He scanned the café but didn't see anyone he knew. He spoke softly. "Set up's all wrong. Rows of tables face a podium. Speaker after droning speaker click through slides we've seen. Weston and his cabal perch in the front row, next to the door. His comings and goings flustered presenters."

Chris sat back and folded his arms. "That's probably intentional."

"The spotlight's reserved for underperformers. Exercise in humiliation. Hardly any participation except for a *hear, hear* or a *quite right* from Weston and his cronies."

Lindy wrung her hands. "Sounds ghastly."

He lowered his voice further. "I'm waiting to see if a division head, who shall remain nameless, survives to the next meeting. She stammered through a presentation littered with *mea culpas* and fixes. Did everything but fall on her sword."

Lindy slapped the table. "*Nameless? Unfair!* We lured you to coffee under transparent pretense to *spill*. Heard Weston scolds," Lindy said as she dunked a roll into her coffee.

After a look around, Jim whispered, "Like a Puritan preacher. Hell fire and brimstone with leers from flint gray eyes and quivers from three chins. He repeats—*With me? Understand? Make sense?* You'd laugh *or cry* to see fifty executives nod like terrified churchgoers."

"And, if you don't nod..." Daniel's index finger sliced the air in front of his throat.

"Heck, you can be sure I nodded." Jim bobbed his head with exaggeration.

"We'll buy you one of those bobble-head dogs for practice." Chris mimicked the dashboard accessory.

Lindy shuddered. "Brings to mind Sister Mary Agnes and her yardstick—whack."

Jim laughed. "Only a first impression, but the meeting wasted brain power. Why gather us from around the globe to rehash old news without discussion? Get this, Dagger offered Cubs tickets to anyone who'd ask a question."

Daniel shook his head. "Pathetic. Next it'll be cattle prods."

Jim shrugged. "It's the culture they created. They don't see it."

"It's a long way from your smiley face cookie awards and our bare-all staff meetings," said Chris.

"Yeah, and we were a helluva lot more productive," added Daniel.

Lindy rested her elbows on the table. "Dinner any better, Chief?"

"I know. *Spill*." Jim raised his coffee cup. "I recommend *Magnus Angus*. Good food, great views."

"We can get reviews online. Free coffee should buy us the dirt." Daniel tapped the table with a grin.

Jim chuckled. He could laugh about it now. He tried to tell Julie but she complained of being too tired to talk about *his* work. "Had the best seat in the house. Wedged between Weston and Jacobs."

"Aargh!" Lindy squealed.

"Stimulating!" Daniel added. "As you passed the butter, did you ask Weston if he's selling the company?"

"Or ask Jacobs for the pepper and a primer on how he's guided us into bankruptcy, *twice?*" Chris asked before biting off a chunk of bagel.

Jim shook his head. "Hap had ulterior motives."

Lindy picked at Daniel's plate. "Hoped you'd rub off on them, huh, Chief?"

He shrugged. "No secret they don't warm to employee issues."

"Issues! Employees period!" Daniel exclaimed. "Flight attendants keep asking why Weston hates them. Never talks to crews. Refuses to eat or drink anything, unless a travel companion samples it first. Probably afraid they'll poison him." As a former flight attendant, Daniel tapped into the jumpseat rumor mill. Jim liked access to the frontline's pulse even if Daniel sometimes indulged in hyperbole.

Lindy shook her head. "How sad. But Daniel, do spill. Do flight attendants really doctor the coffees of rude customers with eye drops? Fact, or crap?"

Daniel flinched. "Please. Flight attendants are safety professionals." Lindy glared at him until he added with raised palm, "I plead the fifth."

Lindy frowned. "You're no help. Jim, tell us more."

He continued, "I think Hap wants Weston to see that I'm not planning to lead an employee coup. I said as much in my speech."

"Speech? You gave a speech." Chris asked. The three perked up.

They laughed at Jim's story of being blindsided. He shared details of the other two new officers. "The customer guy, you know, Internet whiz kid. Had a PowerPoint complete with sound effects and giveaways. Trey, a Tavistock retread, came in a three-piece suit and bored everyone but Weston and Jacobs. His prepared remarks went on for fifteen minutes. I thought Weston would crap his pants with shouts of *hear, hear* and *atta boy* as Trey railed against socialist policy makers."

"Jesus Christ. What'd you say after that?" Daniel asked.

"Kept changing my mind as I sat there downing beers. I really didn't know what I was going to say until I stood up."

"So, tell us," Lindy said. "Whatever you said, bet it was great."

"Spoke from the heart. That's all I had. Talked about my love for Intercontinental, our employees. Talked about being a second-generation, Intercontinental junkie, growing up with the airline. Thanked my mom."

"Jesus Christ!" Cried Daniel. "Mom and apple pie. Bet that made Weston squirm."

"Couldn't see his face. He and Jacobs stopped breathing though when I mentioned the best merger in aviation history." Jim's eyes danced.

"So the rumors are true," Daniel said.

Jim snickered. "I was referring to the fact that Intercontinental brought Julie and me together—*our* merger, *our* marriage."

"Aw..." Lindy pinched Jim's cheek. "And your little dividend's on its way."

"Betty Jankowski said it brought a tear to her eye," Jim said.

"I'm cryin'," added Lindy as she dabbed her eyes.

"Went on to say that my mission is *not* to make employees happy."

Lindy's mouth fell open. "Whadda ya mean that's not your job?"

Jim rubbed her shoulder. He felt it stiffen. "Calm down. Employees want to contribute, be valued, have pride in the company. They want satisfaction more than *happiness*. With me? Understand? Make sense?"

The three bobbed their heads. Chris was first to realize the Weston parody. "Stop that!" he said, punching Jim's shoulder.

"Thought so. Pod-Jim," added Daniel.

Lindy raised her right arm, her hand in a fist. "Our employee champion. How'd everyone react?"

"Good applause. Mostly from folks who've been around awhile. Jody Cantelone screamed *hear, hear, atta boy*. Weston turned to me with a scowl—*recognize that voice,* he barked. I lied, said no. Ingrid glared at me, like I had spinach in my teeth."

Daniel raised an eyebrow. "Weston and Jacobs didn't kick your shins or impale you with a cocktail fork?"

"Or spike your coffee with eye drops?" Lindy shook Jim's cup as she stuck her tongue out at Daniel.

"They were polite. For all I know, they cursed me under their breath as they cut into their surf and turf. Truth is, they didn't talk to me much. They fell all over Trey and kept asking the whiz kid for stock tips on Internet startups."

"Did Weston address the group, Chief?" Lindy asked.

"Pontificated. Talked about fiduciary responsibility to shareholders. I felt his hot breath on my head as he talked about officers' unwavering duty to investors. When he finished, Ingrid led the room in a toast to his vision."

"Hmm. You didn't see his comments as a challenge to you?" Daniel asked, slapping Lindy's hand from his plate.

"I'm a realist. Weston won't change his message for me."

"You gotta hope you can influence him," Chris said.

"I wouldn't have taken this job if Hap didn't assure me Weston and the Board want employee alignment."

Daniel added. "Sure he didn't mean re-education camps? Ingrid'd make a great Commandant."

Jim shuddered. "A bit drastic even for Weston. He's a businessman. He wants the company to succeed, even if primarily for investors."

"And his overweight ego," Daniel said.

"Agreed. But succeed nonetheless. Weston's smart. He knows employees are key," Jim said.

"Let's hope so," said Chris.

"That's how I reconcile my focus with his. I fulfill my duty to shareholders by helping employees succeed."

Lindy saluted him. "Fearless Leader!"

"Preachin' to the choir here," Chris said with a shrug. "It's your new peeps that you gotta get to listen."

"He's right. You're only one person. Others will have to get on board, including our Chairman," Lindy said.

"*Especially* the Chairman," Daniel added.

"I gotta believe that's possible." Jim looked into their faces. He could have been talking to Julie.

Lindy spoke. "You got a lot ridin' on faith. Don't get us wrong, Jim. We believe in you. Hell, everyone wants to work for you. We're just wondrin', who's gonna support *you?*"

Chapter 31

Jim Fastens His Seatbelt

*Sit down. We can't close the door or pushback until everyone's in a
seat and all bags are stowed. Don't get me angry.*

Jim and Richter boarded with the rest of first class. After
squeezing carry-ons into the closet, they settled into
their first row seats. "Drives me nuts when the overhead
bins are filled with crew bags," Richter said, turning to Jim.

Business people with attaché cases and garment bags
trudged down the aisle interspersed with families towing wide-
eyed toddlers and vacationers wearing sweat pants and jerseys
and hauling overstuffed bags. Leis, tank tops, flip-flops, straw
hats, and sunburns tagged passengers connecting from Hawaii.

Despite having his shoulder jostled and bumped, Jim
watched the colorful parade with a smile. "God I love this
business."

Richter nodded. "You sound like Hap."

"We connect the world."

"Now you sound like a commercial."

"Hope I'm not too annoying?"

Richter patted Jim's arm. "On the contrary my boy. Makes
our job easier."

"Visiting Boston was a great idea," Jim said.

"Gets me home and gives us a chance to see what Samantha
was talking about," Richter answered.

"Boston's one thing, but changing the entire company isn't
going to be easy."

Richter nodded as he grabbed a seatbelt. "If it were as simple as following instructions, company engineers could implement."

Jim chuckled. "*An Idiot's Guide to Culture Change* would send an entire army of consultants to the unemployment line," he said, nudging Richter.

Richter scoffed. "My breed mutates faster than viruses. We've withstood decades of eradication efforts. We attach to insecure, yet lucrative hosts." Richter lunged, grabbing Jim's arm. He laughed when Jim jumped.

"You've found an eager host. You have something I need," Jim said, kicking off his shoes.

Richter stared at him. "What's that?"

Jim slumped. "Hap's ear."

Richter's hand tapped Jim's. "That'll come, young man. He's just cautious. But smart enough to know a good thing when he sees it. And that's you."

Raised voices interrupted their conversation. They looked back to see a minor scuffle between the purser and a small elderly woman in the front of the economy section. The sudden appearance of a husky businessman separated the quarrelers. With a huff and a sneer to the purser, the man lifted a bag from the floor into the overhead. He slammed the bin and returned to his seat. "*Thank you,*" the frail passenger called after him. "*That's a gentleman.*" The purser clicked his tongue and wagged a finger. "*Now sit down and behave. I don't want to have to ask the captain to remove you.*"

"Wait." Kyle pulled Jim down into the seat. "We're going to Boston to learn. This flight is a great laboratory to study employees in their native habitat."

Jim nodded toward the purser. "That guy's a menace. Most of our people have strong bonds with customers. More so than with management." The purser reminded Jim of a donkey—big ears, buckteeth and droopy eyes.

"How employees behave without supervision is very telling. Strong cultures extend beyond watchful eyes. Confront the jackass later," Richter whispered.

"I intend to. Besides. I'm dying for a cup of coffee and our purser looks like the type who packs eye drops."

Richter arched his bushy eyebrows. "Eye drops?"

Jim shook his head. "Foodservice 101. Never criticize wait staff until *after* the food arrives. Trust me."

"He can't be from Boston. Dear Samantha would recoil at his behavior," Richter said.

"Even good teams have slackers."

Richter tapped his armrest. "The best cultures self-police. Peers force out misfits. Ever hear *Don't fit, Quit?*"

Jim shook his head. "No, but sounds catchy."

"Weak cultures allow deadbeats to survive alongside stars like Samantha. Most organizations never achieve that type of transcendence. Applies to leaders too."

Jim scowled. "Worse are the deadbeats who inspire copycats."

"That's the danger. Strong doesn't necessarily imply good. *Don't fit, Quit* can drive out the best and brightest in a culture dominated by bullies and Philistines."

A few stragglers boarded. The purser returned to the front galley joined by a second flight attendant who bounced with a cheerleader's exuberance. From their seats, Jim and Richter eavesdropped.

"'So,' I says, 'Lady, I'm no skycap. We're here for safety. I'd be happy to send your bag to the cargo hold. You shouldn't have booked the bulkhead,'" the donkey brayed.

"What'd she say?" asked the cheerleader.

"'Aren't flight attendants paid to assist customers?' Then I says shakin' my head, 'You got assist all wrong. I'm happy to assist taggin'' *the bag and checkin' it below. Pick it up in Boston's baggage claim if that's what you want.'"*

"You didn't. What'd she do?"

"As I bent down to tag the bag, I went all sugary sweet on her. She starts breathin' hard and wimpers, 'I can't. I have a close connection. I'll miss my flight. Wah, wah, wah.' Then Mr. Do-gooder butts in."

"I'd never have the nerve."

"Gotta stick up for yourself. I'm not paid enough to take sarcasm and condescendin' attitude. No'one's lookin' out for Roger but good ole Roger himself."

The cheerleader responded with a high-five. *"Good for you."*

With hand on hip, the donkey rocked his head. "Stick with me kid. I'll show you how to handle people. Gettin' impossible to do our jobs. How can we offer pre-departure drinks while greetin' customers and watchin' the door? Am I right?"

"You're right," the cheerleader said.

Jim dug his fingernails into the armrest. In the time wasted to kvetch, the donkey and cheerleader could have served the entire plane. "I want coffee," he mumbled.

The banter continued. The donkey brayed, asked for and received concurrence from the cheerleader who affirmed the wild assertions.

Richter leaned toward Jim. "Our dear little ingénue is being schooled by the jaded veteran. The Socratic method thrives at thirty-five thousand feet."

Jim sighed. "Disturbing."

"Especially if management doesn't intervene. If those two are treated equally, you can guess whose behavior becomes the norm. The path of least resistance."

Jim dropped his tray table with a thud. He hoped the action triggered the coffee service. "Unless she's hardwired with the service gene."

"Oh Lord, the Holy Grail, the panacea for poor service.

Most companies wring their hands, lamenting that elusive gene," Richter said, rolling his eyes.

"You're skeptical."

"Blaming deficient DNA for bad service is a convenient excuse peddled by mediocre companies. Lazy CEOs think good service is simply a matter of finding the right genetic cluster. Horseshit!"

Jim motioned toward the galley. "Even if our ingénue has the magic gene, you're saying she couldn't resist the jackass's influence?"

Richter fished the seatbelt out from under his rear end. "Didn't your mother warn you about hanging with the wrong crowd? Same thing, especially when management fails to reward star performers."

"There's always training."

"Training can't do the trick alone. You need good leaders and strong reward systems." Richter gave the twisted seatbelt a dirty look.

"That's all part of my plan," Jim said, pulling his hair. His confidence wavered. Everything he hoped to fix, under closer inspection, had dependencies and interdependencies. Bulldozing the culture and starting from scratch might be easier.

Richter cleared his throat. "Don't forget Hap's advice." He held up the two seat belt ends with a helpless pout.

Jim secured the buckle. "Metrics! How could I forget?" Hap's terse delivery reminded Jim of the The Graduate. One word: Plastics.

"Warned loud and clear. Weston's support depends on your ability to calculate a return on investment. Measuring everything's a quirk of your culture."

"Explains why training, recognition and development are always scrapped in a budget crises. It's impossible to find numbers to justify new uniforms."

"New uniforms?" Richter turned toward Jim.

Jim shrugged. "Any employee expenditure. Our emperor has new clothes and the Countess reigns from Versailles, but we need *numbers* to justify basics."

"Someone needs to muster the courage to tell your emperor that his employees have *no* clothes and remind the Countess of the fate that befell the last residents of Versailles."

"Me?" Jim's shoulders stiffened.

"No! Someone with power." He patted Jim's arm. "Hap's the guy, but he needs ammunition. Finding a way to measure your work won't be easy, but you gotta try. Your CFO's another one who doesn't see the value of your mission."

Jim scratched his forehead. "I know. Calls it fluff."

"You have to speak a language he understands. Numbers."

"Let me guess. You can help with that too." Jim rubbed his fingers together. How long before Richter's fare meter caught the attention of Weston and Jacobs?

"Shouldn't we do a pre-departure beverage for first class?" The cheerleader asked as she grabbed a tray and cocktail napkins off the galley counter.

"If you insist." The donkey whined and clicked his tongue.

Jim wiggled upright. "At last, coffee."

"Rats, they're ready to close us up," said the cheerleader, looking down the jet bridge.

"Darn. We'll have to wait until we're in the air. Unless we're lucky and turbulence keeps us seated." The donkey smirked as he reached for the cabin mike.

"Morning ladies and gents. Welcome aboard flight 768 to Boston. I'm your purser, Roger. On behalf of your Newark crew, I'd like to remind you we're here primarily for safety but it's our pleasure to serve."

Richter and Jim snickered.

"Know what?" Richter asked

"I'm afraid to answer."

"We might learn something from a visit to Newark."

"Couldn't you have said Rio or Rome? But, next time, I bring my own coffee." Jim tugged his seatbelt snug.

"Holy shit!" Richter cried.

Jim jumped. He turned to Richter. "What's wrong?"

"I pressed the call button instead of my reading lamp. Roger'll throw me off the plane—or worse, *eye drops!*"

Chapter 32

Jim Meets the Steering Committee

"Oh gosh, Winny. Thanks for your help." Out of breath, Jim addressed Hap's secretary. His hands rested on the privacy ledge where she kept a bottomless bowl of candy as well as Hap's incoming mail. Winny was one of the few people who came through for him. Most people avoided his calls or delegated his requests to an unproductive subordinate. The worst were those eager to help as long as Jim relinquished all authority. He couldn't thank Winny enough for pulling strings to commandeer the board dining room for the inaugural meeting of the employee steering committee. His first foray into upper echelon company politics made him nervous.

Winny peered over the rims of her glasses. "My, you look handsome."

Jim brushed his hand down his jacket. "My lucky suit, fresh from the cleaners." In Julie's absence, a department store salesman had accessorized the new shirt and tie. He even managed to polish his shoes despite Sedona's constant nudging to play. He understood that the dog, like him, was out of sorts with Julie gone.

Winny winked. "Still an army of one?"

His eyes fell to the candy dish. His face warmed and his stomach soured. "Julie's still at her mom's."

Winny cleared her throat. "I meant your staff."

"Oh. Still solo I'm afraid, but I hope to settle that with the committee." As he laughed nervously, his eyes came to rest on correspondence on FAA letterhead. Just below Winny's date stamp, **FINAL NOTICE – PROPOSED FINE** appeared in bold type. He averted his eyes but the words *multi-million dollar* and *flagrant disregard* registered in his mind.

Winny thumped an index finger on a stack of papers. "Don't be nervous. Your committee should look to you for answers. They're clueless about employees. Forgotten that they were all once just low level peons."

Jim flinched. Her words reminded him of his mother's counsel. He responded, "Kyle Richter says the same thing. He's been a tremendous help."

She removed her glasses and fixed her warm blue eyes on him. "May I not be struck by lightning for saying this," she said pausing. "*Listen* to the consultant." She puckered her mouth as if the words were distasteful. She added. "I like Richter. Hap does too. May not look the part," she said with a chuckle. "He works wonders shuttling between offices. Gets the spoiled children to play nice, nice."

He was glad Winny shared a favorable opinion of Richter. He said a lot to the man in confidence and hoped his trust wasn't misplaced. "He's coached me on building a team despite roadblocks from HR," Jim said.

Winny nodded. "He's not threatening. These people have egos with a capital *A* for..." She whispered the last word. "Asshole."

Although Jim tended to agree with her assessment, he let it pass. He grabbed a foiled chocolate. "Richter's quirks disarm resistance."

"He's successful because they assume he can't be," Winny said.

Jim's voice lowered. "I'm assuming Hap's wise to Richter's technique."

Winny glanced toward the open door. "I love my boss, but he values results, *above everything*. Richter delivers—has conversations senior officers aren't comfortable having. That goes for..." Her voice faded as she nodded toward the office.

"I've seen Richter interact with employees. Very effective. Many officers can't or won't do the same."

"Most consultants shove papers in my face. Bark for copies, meetings and conference calls. The most insipid are those just past the scared shitless stage. I call them passive aggressive." She paused, forming an impish grin. "No, I call them assholes too." She held a finger to her lips as her eyes twinkled.

Jim glanced at his watch. "Gotta run. We start in fifteen minutes."

She tapped his hand before he turned. "Call me if you need anything."

Winny watched the gray suit walk away. She whispered to herself. *I like the confident stride. You've survived your first months— admirable. But little chick, you still have no idea what's ahead. The committee should listen to you, but will they?*

<hr />

As Richter picked from a food tray on the buffet, his gaze wandered upward to the portrait of the Board of Directors. "They seem to begrudge me the tuna sandwich and cookie," he said. Jim laughed as Richter turned to him and added, "We're in pretty good shape, young man."

Jim checked his watch. "Sure hope so. It's Hap's agenda. Pre-reads went out last night." Jim sighed. "But group dynamics are unpredictable."

Richter swallowed the remainder of his sandwich. "Especially with this group. Observe Carrie Patterson's confidence melt with Ingrid in the room. Note the unspoken tension between Hap and Wilkerson. I can't put my finger on it, but I'd swear an alliance has formed between Ingrid and Wilkerson." He grabbed bottled water and plopped down in a seat closest to the chair Hap would likely occupy. "Everyone confirm?"

"Almost. Ingrid never RSVP'd and as you know, Dagger and Jacobs weren't invited," Jim answered, tidying the food trays and water. Was that his job? He didn't know. Thank God for Richter's inside scoop that always sounded like a scouting report. Otherwise, he'd be totally lost."

Richter rolled his eyes. He deposited the remainder of the cookie in his mouth as a flash of lightning lit up the room followed by a thunderclap. Jim jumped.

"Calm down," Richter said, rising from his seat to close the sheers that covered the wall of windows beaded by rain. The room had an unobstructed view of Lake Michigan's turgid gray waters.

Jim tapped his forehead. "Almost forgot, Betty Jankowski isn't on the committee either."

Richter flicked crumbs from his chartreuse tie. "That's a lot of employees excluded from scope." He shrugged. "Still, we've surfaced the issue. We can only press so much."

Jim nodded. "Hap scowls and narrows his eyes whenever we push. The unmistakable message—*drop it*."

Richter tugged at his bushy eyebrows. "But why not Jankowski's call centers?"

"She's tainted. Reports to Dagger," Jim said.

Richter shook his head. "Like the Hatfields and McCoys. And Papa Weston does nothing to broker peace."

Jim looked up from his task of arranging handouts. "I've reached out to Betty. I'll keep her informed."

"Good. A role model for your boss," Richter said, patting Jim's shoulder before returning to his seat.

"She appreciated my gesture. She prays Hap will absorb her organization."

"Why?"

Jim straightened the chairs. "Betty's a lifer—over forty years. She respects Hap."

"And not Dagger?" Richter asked, cupping his chin.

Jim lowered his voice. "Says he and his cohorts aren't invested...emotionally."

"Did she elaborate?"

"Now don't be offended," Jim said, waiting for his words to register before proceeding. "Betty sees them as, ahem, consultants. Carpetbaggers, with a short-term mission to create value, cash out and move on." He studied Richter's reaction.

Richter shrugged. "Sounds like consultants to me. I've heard rumors Weston isn't interested in running an airline either."

"That feeling is widespread. He doesn't do much to dispel the perception," Jim said.

A motion at the door drew their attention and shut their mouths. Hap's booming voice broke the silence. "*Perception?* My Chief Employee Officer and over-priced consultant are dealing in perceptions? I prefer to live in the real world, cruel as it may be." Hap scowled as he navigated to the water. His frown anchored a face bearing the weight of heavy concern. His eyes mirrored the raw afternoon.

Richter sat up in his chair. "Good afternoon to you too. You know the old adage, perception is reality."

Hap made a disagreeable face. His starched shirt and creased trousers rustled as he walked to the head of the table. "Perceptions distort the truth. They're costly. We need to educate employees. It's bad enough we have real issues, but layering on perceptions creates a cluster fuck." He frowned at his watch and snapped. "It's two o'clock. Where is everyone?"

Jim noticed the FAA letterhead clutched in Hap's hand. He spoke. "My watch shows two more minutes. Never heard from Ingrid."

Hap rolled his eyes toward Richter. "My dedicated co-sponsor? Weston assumes she'll be an active contributor."

Richter scoffed. His expression conveyed to Jim an unspoken understanding. Jim noticed that Richter and Hap often spoke in shorthand whereas Jim felt he could use an interpreter in conversations with his boss.

At that moment, Shannon Brady entered the room and took the seat next to Richter. Brady led Intercontinental's flight attendant division. She was one of Hap's first management changes, prodded by Weston to infuse the company with blood from successful airlines. Her star rose as she oversaw major cost and productivity enhancements. Jim marked her an ally. She had been receptive to the work, pledging support in exchange for a role in shaping initiatives.

Carrie Patterson appeared next. Jim hadn't seen her for weeks as she delegated all Human Resource support to Sharlee Guerrin, who welded herself onto him. In fact, Guerrin came on strong, offering assistance at *all* hours. Her flowing blonde hair, designer wardrobe and killer looks proved a distraction he could do without. Her fervent concern for his wellbeing in light of Julie's absence bordered on seduction.

Glancing at his watch, Hap glowered at Patterson as she strutted across the room to scan the finger sandwiches and cookies. The silver belt of her red, ultra-mini sweater dress jangled, as did the mock stirrups of her patent leather boots.

"Mr. Sweeny," Patterson said. "You can't spoil my mood. I'm having a simply marvelous day. I'm on the verge of a major breakthrough, a game-changer that pushes the envelope on employee culture." She picked at a tray before selecting a sandwich. The crisp sound of cucumber snapped between her teeth, matched the look shot at Jim.

Hap buried his head in his hands. "What might that be?"

Patterson gushed. "Pet insurance and concierge service.

Fifi can have her cholesterol checked while master orders opera tickets or a flat screen TV, *wholesale.*"

With her look around the room, Jim felt she was pimping for applause. None came. He marveled at her ability to talk on any subject, comedy or tragedy without altering her expression. Brady and Richter stifled laughter.

Hap's lips curled upward. "Congratulations. We'll happily promote that as another Human Resources' enhancement. Now, take a seat." Hap directed her to a chair next to Jim. "We can't wait."

Chad Wilkerson entered, eyes glued to the phone in his palm. Without looking up, he took a cookie. He sat at the far end of the table isolated by several empty chairs on either side. Jim slid a pile of handouts across the table. Wilkerson leaned over and elevated his chair before returning Hap's stare. He responded with the tone of a bratty child. "Couldn't be helped. Weston's flight was in danger of delay. Had to authorize a plane swap. Customers on the shanghaied aircraft aren't all too happy." His little boy grin seemed to say to Jim, *Oh well.* After a nibble on his cookie, Wilkerson added, "Everything's breaking. The FAA won't be happy." His tiny black eyes danced. Hap's nostrils flared and his grip tightened on the letter in his hand.

Ingrid made a grand entrance. She enunciated with Prussian precision, "Good afternoon fellow employee huggers." A clipped nod sent her hair sweeping across her face and back again in one graceful motion. Her pink and black suit hugged her figure and her strand of pearls undulated with the movement of her chest. She sat next to Shannon Brady. Jim caught the sneer she directed at Wilkerson who attended more to his phone than to her entrance.

Jim pointed toward the refreshment trays. "Glad you could join us. I wasn't sure. Sandwiches and cookies are on the buffet."

"Why wouldn't I be here? I'm co-sponsor." Ingrid's pencil-thin eyebrow arched toward Patterson's half-eaten sandwich. With a backhanded gesture to the buffet, she added, "I never eat from a communal tray unless I'm desperate, or it's offered by a white-gloved server. Can we begin?"

Clutching a red steno pad, Meg Orkin scurried into the room. Brushing behind Jim, she gently tapped his shoulder, plucked a handful of cookies and sat across from her boss. She looked at Wilkerson and emitted her signature cackle. Hap glared from Orkin to Ingrid insinuating an explanation. All other eyes traveled the same path.

Ingrid rolled her eyes. "I've asked Orkin to join our happy little team of goodwill ambassadors. She can shape our message and has already partnered with him." Her head clipped toward Jim. "Isn't that so, Abernathy with a *J*?"

Jim scanned the other faces before nodding. "We've worked closely in the last few weeks."

"There you go." Ingrid threw both hands up, a large diamond and ruby ring shimmered in the room's spotlights. "A model of camaraderie."

Patterson wriggled in her chair, struggling to form her words. "I, I, I—"

Ingrid glanced at her, holding up an index finger. "One moment, dear."

"But—" Patterson turned red. Jim felt the nervous patter of her tiny feet. Richter's accurate prediction of the meltdown impressed him.

Ingrid thrust her palm in Patterson's direction. "Halt!" She addressed Hap and Jim. "As the traditional voice of the employee, Communications has clear, established channels." She turned toward Jim. "Orkin informs me the two of you have collaborated on a strategy. Is that so?"

He stammered. "Yes...We—"

Ingrid cut him off. "Orkin warned me of your modesty—misplaced in a vice president. *You* shaped the plan," she said, wagging a finger at Jim. "I hate to steal your thunder but it's too brilliant not to share immediately."

Hap scowled at Ingrid. "You obviously intend to share the strategy. Proceed."

"Correct me if I corrupt *Abernathy's* idea. Look—Like—Listen." She turned to Orkin. "Clarify!"

The Straw-blonde Director sat up in her seat, straightening her cardigan and cotton frock. "Employees are jaded and cynical." Ingrid glared while Orkin cackled. "*Jim* believes employees are promised out. *Jim* believes we need to show results and only then, broadcast. A twist on the old, under-promise and over-deliver." She smiled and then added hastily, "Jim believes."

Ingrid grinned at Jim. "Isn't that right, Abernathy?"

"I get it," Hap interjected with a crooked smile. "Jim believes."

Jim didn't flinch. He felt like a ventriloquist's dummy. He smelled the setup but didn't quite know why. He looked across the table to Richter as he responded. "Correct. Actions speak louder than words."

Hap rubbed his forehead. "Richter, what do you think? You believe?"

Richter's response came slowly. "The pace may be a bit cautious. But the strategy…is workable." He looked at Ingrid and Orkin before turning to Jim. "On the other hand, if we can get our message of hope out faster, we should."

"Can I talk now?" Patterson looked from Ingrid to Hap, who gestured her to proceed.

"If she," Patterson said pointing to Orkin, "can be part of the team, I want to add Sharlee Guerrin. She's worked on Jim's staffing plan. Human Resources is the traditional voice of the employee and…" She glanced furtively at Ingrid before fixing her eyes on Hap.

With an agitated hand, Hap motioned her again. "And?"

She paused, her plump lips quivered. "We have a lot to say on the subject—the subject of employees, I mean."

The irony amused Jim. While both Communications and HR claimed to be the voice of the employee, employees complained they had no voice. And if they did, no one would listen, least of all HR or Communications.

Hap pointed to Richter who seemed to understand the prompt. "I concede Patterson's point, however in my experience, steering committees work best when kept to small, manageable numbers of like authority levels. Max-mix isn't effective." His hand crumpled his tie.

Bolstered by Richter's counsel, Hap spoke decisively. "Listen to Richter. If Orkin joins, we can't reject Guerrin and then who?" Nods supported Hap's position. Orkin cackled before bowing her head in her steno pad jotting notes feverishly.

Ingrid glared at each nodding head before she spoke. "Fine! However, you must agree to include Orkin, this Guerrin and whomever else when their expertise is required."

Patterson's eyes darted behind her immovable façade. "Does that mean Guerrin can come? I'm…I'm not clear," she stammered.

Richter spoke very slowly, enunciating each word. "Guerrin can come to meetings where her input will be beneficial to the discussion. Do you understand?"

Patterson bobbed her head. "Yes." She paused before adding, "I think so."

Jim presented his scope. Richter supported the proposal with professional citations and Hap interjected to remove challenges and keep the discussion focused.

Ingrid bristled, tugging at her bracelet. "I cannot stress

enough my vehement opposition to including Communications as a remediation focus."

Hap replied, "With all due respect, surveys identify Communications as the prime source of employee dissatisfaction."

Wilkerson and Brady concurred, offering feedback from their teams.

"Unacceptable," snapped Ingrid. "Communication is simply misunderstood—too broad for employees to comprehend. Let's not even mention survey ambiguity."

Patterson turned to Richter. "I can ask staff to review the surveys, especially if Ingrid can't interpret them. I have a PhD."

Richter spit his coffee.

Hap grinned. He offered Richter a napkin. "Unless she's been hiding her academic prowess, I think Patterson means her staff person in charge of surveys has a Doctorate."

Patterson's head pulsed up and down, her eyes darting around the table. "Yes, yes. The Doctor's input would be beneficial to the discussion, right?"

Ingrid's nails scratched the granite tabletop. Hap looked with urgency to Jim and Richter. Ingrid inhaled and drew up her shoulders, her attack signal.

Richter interjected. "I see Ingrid's point. But the fact remains employees perceive deficiencies with communication capabilities. To ignore those perceptions would shroud our entire initiative in skepticism."

Ingrid waved off his comments. "Pshaw."

Orkin stepped into the conversation. "Capabilities? Hmm. Good word. What about a focus on communication capabilities and technology for a global workforce?"

"I see," offered Jim, "it's not the message. It's the messenger and the hardware—operator error." Orkin cackled and her eyes enlarged. Jim considered the compromise bullshit although Orkin's finesse in defusing her boss impressed him.

"Pre-cise-ly," said Ingrid, pausing on each syllable.

Jim addressed Ingrid. "You'll support communication technology and capability building for leaders?"

Ingrid's face and shoulders relaxed. "Of course. We understand our role, after all. Our hands are tied by the antiquated technology and deplorable communication skills of our supervisors."

Jim took what he could get. He noticed the look of relief that swept over Hap's face at the de-escalation of tension with Ingrid. Jim would save his political capital for his planned organization that he proposed next. Richter coached him to demonstrate how expected results drove team structure. The consultant also predicted Patterson's objection, suggesting a shimmering centerpiece to distract her.

Patterson, as if on cue, chirped. "Guerrin warned me about this."

Jim recalled a recent late night visit to his office from Guerrin. Carrying a bottle of wine and two Styrofoam cups, she professed concern he'd burn out. She demanded with batting eyes that he relinquish his staff design to her, a trained professional. "I want to help you," she said, squeezing his hand. "It's a thankless task." The spent bottle of wine gave him the courage to decline and withstand the tearful pawing and raging tantrum that ensued. He gave his secretary credit for cleaning up the broken glass and wine stains as if she were watering plants or setting out his mail.

Hap turned to Patterson with a look that demanded clarification even though Jim knew that Richter had briefed Hap beforehand on the issues.

Patterson wriggled to raise herself in her seat. Her bony fingers shook as she put on reading glasses and fumbled through her notes. She inhaled. Her words sounded stilted as she read. "HR recommends job titles and pay levels to attract front line supervisors for developmental opportunities. Artificially high..." She paused in mid-sentence to separate pages that looked to Jim, stuck together with red nail polish. She continued. "Artificially high job levels, demotivate. We're looking out for Jim's best interests." Jim sighed, Richter tapped the table, and Hap yawned. Patterson looked up, seemingly distracted by the sounds. She added, "I probably shouldn't say this here..." she motioned toward Jim, "but looking deeper, we concluded he shouldn't even be a vice president." Jim's eyes bugged; he went slack-jawed. Hap scowled but before he could say anything, Patterson patted Jim's arm. "But no one's going to take the title away from you now."

Wilkerson smirked. Hap's vein throbbed as Patterson returned to her reading. "Applicants seek responsibilities commensurate with posted levels. If reality is less challenging, they lose interest, grow frustrated. Seek concurrence..." She cocked her head. Failing to wrinkle her nose, she tapped her feet instead. "These are Guerrin's notes," she said with a blush. "Should have said, don't you all agree? We can't do that to employees or we're part of the problem, not the solution."

Jim's mind raced immediately to Frida Sallinger, Weston's Senior Vice President and glorified gopher who seemed quite content sitting idly in her magnificent office behind an immaculate desk, or driving her big Mercedes around the city. Sallinger, a forty-year company veteran, wasn't swiftly jettisoned when new talent made her redundant. Weston pulled her onto his staff where she served in a lofty-titled, highly paid, yet invisible position. Her ill-defined responsibilities careened from aide-de-camp to enforcer, making her the subject of sneers and speculation by employees, shareholders and fellow officers. Other than whispers of sexual dalliances with Weston, Ingrid, or both, the most pervasive rumor conjectured she knew dirty little secrets that cement-ed Weston's power over key leaders and the Board. While Ingrid was Weston's public fixer, Sallinger lurked in the shadows.

Poor, miserable Sallinger, Jim thought to himself. I've as-sumed she had the world by the balls. Based on Patterson's description of highly paid, under worked employees, I'll ex-tend my sympathies next time I run into her at the health club or at Neiman Marcus. So brave to hide her frustrations behind that deeply tanned face and carefree smile. No wonder she can't put in a full day's work, the poor wretch must wrestle with depression.

Hap's voice rose, his face still red. "Is that any worse than being promoted into a job, well above your capabilities?" He didn't wait for an answer. "This Committee has unanimous-ly agreed to aggressive deliverables. Your proposal would under-skill Jim's team. Constrain him with junior titles and entry-level salaries. Weston and the Board approved Jim's position and this work." Hap slapped his hand firmly on the proposed staffing plan, cutting off debate.

Patterson crouched in her chair. She mumbled, "If only Guerrin were here. She could have convinced you."

Hap winked at Jim. "The Committee blesses your frame-work and gives approval for the organization. Now, we want action. Measurable results. Fast. You've got my approval to fill... half your jobs."

Richter and Jim said in unison, "Half!"

Hap stared with narrowed eyes. "We've got major budget woes. Fuel and cash concerns. We must be cautious."

Hap rose to leave but the mention of budget animated the room. Wilkerson and Brady each staked a claim to portions of Jim's budget, seeking to replace money lost as part of the airline's austerity program.

"Jim, work that out." With a wave of his hand and a frown, Hap delegated the diplomatic chore to his new vice president to arm wrestle with senior counterparts. He yelled over his shoulder. "Meeting adjourned."

Chapter 33
Jim's Deluxe Office in the Sky

"Call security." Jim formed his hands into a bullhorn. At the door stood his paunchy friend in an orange polo shirt with a green company logo. Cal Gladden's hands clutched a shopping bag and a super-sized soda. A bright yellow tie completed his curious ensemble.

Cal's eyes arced around the office as he let out a wolf whistle. "So this is the junior executive special, the deluxe cubicle in the sky. Nice view," he said before turning his attention to the interior. "But the furnishings scream blue-light special."

Jim shrugged. "What can I say? Facilities suggested I scavenge the building for furniture."

Cal went slack-jawed. "You're kidding! Did ya turn up a fired Veep clingin' to a credenza? The great unwashed like me are left to the mercy of that officious bureaucrat called Wanda, but I thought junior execs had it made. I've seen the big wigs' cribs. The Countess dressed hers up like Versailles. Took a lot of customer butts to pay for that—at least four first class asses to Beijing and a few to Rio. Pardon my French, but your shit could be had for a super saver to South Bend."

Jim shook his head. "Real nice. I'm okay with cast offs. It's prudent."

"With the way we churn vice presidents, we could go into the second hand business—furniture and officers."

"Wanda tipped my secretary to call dibs on Ken Javitz's old desk."

Cal froze. "Javitz's chair's still warm. Bad karma, Jimmy.

You don't need that shit."

"Karma's the least of my worries," Jim said, making his way to Cal's side.

"Jimmy boy, I'm disappointed. You forgot your ole buddies in the single digits? Expected a trail of breadcrumbs as you ascended to the high thirties. You're within sniffin' distance of the High Cs up on forty." Cal raised his nose and smelled the air with exaggerated sound effects. "Ah rank."

Jim patted Cal's shoulders. "Ever think I didn't want you to find me?" Jim chuckled before motioning Cal to the conference table where he emptied his hands.

"That's no way for the *employee* veep to talk. To think, I gussied up." Cal flipped his tie into the air. "Came bearing gifts too."

Jim leaned forward to get a better look at the tie. "You mug a clown?"

Cal smoothed his tie. "Paid the Heavenly Lemonade guy five bucks for this gem. You don't like the winged lemon? Authentic, genuine plastic."

"Does it squirt juice?" Jim asked before eyeing the bag. "Can only imagine what's in there."

Cal rummaged inside the bag. "Humph! Office warmin' gifts. Better sit down Jimmy." Jim sat and folded his arms on the table as Cal produced the first item. "So you never go hungry for new ideas," he said. "Writable toilet paper and pen. Most veeps produce their best work in the head." Jim accepted the roll with a snort.

Cal rustled in the bag a second time. "To freely ingest leadership's bitter rhetoric without nausea, a bottle of antacid… *extra strength*."

Jim grabbed the bottle. "That I need. With budget cuts, political skirmishes, deadlines and late nights, I'm already sick to my stomach."

Cal snickered as he produced the next offering. "To deal with enemies," he announced, shoving two items into Jim's face, "rat poison and eye drops. Your vision will be clear to see enemies while a sprinkle of powder dispatches pesky varmints."

"Nice, very nice," Jim said, reaching for the bag.

Cal swatted his hand. "Not so fast, Mr. Veep—to inspire joy, drown your sorrows or both...champagne. Congrats! Drink it. Don't christen this place. Jimmy, I've said it before, you're the best man for the job."

Jim took the bottle and extended his hand to shake. "Thanks, Cal. Love to crack it open now. It's been tough."

Cal dropped onto a chair. "Sorry to hear, and I mean that. Dragon slayin' business pretty rough, huh?" Cal flourished his straw as if it were a sword.

Jim wiped the spray of soda off the table. "Want the good or bad first?"

Cal pulsed his eyebrows. "You know me. I luxuriate in other's misfortune."

"I see the horns now." Jim's gaze drifted to Cal's forehead and comb-over.

"Nothin' personal. I'm an equal opportunity prick. Told you this work wouldn't be easy. I want to hear how right I was." Cal sucked the straw, peering over his eyeglasses.

Jim's eyes challenged Cal. "Thought maybe you'd bet against your cynical tendencies and be satisfied with a healthier culture."

Cal swatted the air. "Can't help myself. It's hard to leap to a brave new world when your footin' is on the slippery slopes of the current environment."

Jim sighed. "Christ! Richter nailed it. Takes great effort to convince leaders to change. New cultures are formed by the outcasts, misfits and persecuted, not the entrenched elite. I didn't anticipate resistance from other levels."

Cal grimaced. "Hope you don't see me as a roadblock or worse, a saboteur. I wouldn't do that."

Jim shook his head sternly. "Not intentionally."

"What?" Cal's face turned crimson.

Jim cradled his head. "I'm not questioning your friendship. I'm beginning to see that folks might not welcome my mission—reluctant rescuees or worse, unintended obstructionists."

"I'll reform. Promise," Cal said, holding up his hand.

Jim smiled and winked. "No worries."

Cal's shoulders relaxed. "I've missed our chats, Jimmy. No one sees you. You don't take the train or eat in the cafeteria. You forget the little people?"

"Et tu Brute?"

"Huh?"

"Forget it, Cal. I park in the underground garage or take early trains and I've been eating lunch right here. I've been swamped." Jim paused and leaned back in his chair. "Hey you don't eat in the cafeteria either!"

"Irrelevant! By the way, the cafeteria and lower floors are in hopeless states of disrepair. Leadership doesn't recognize how bad it is. Outta sight, outta mind."

Jim rose to close the door before returning to his chair. "Are you going to bring me every gripe? You've already emailed your self-serving wish list." He held up a hand and counted on his fingers. "Let's see, a huge raise, shorter hours, bigger office and super-size soda dispensers."

"Don't forget softer toilet paper in the men's room. I've seen none of it, damn it! What have you been doing?" Cal punched Jim's shoulder.

Jim threw the toilet paper roll. "Catch. Request fulfilled." They both laughed. Jim continued. "I know about the lower floors. I'll try to find money."

"Lavender-scented urinal cakes don't count as refurbishment," Cal whined.

"You're lucky Finance didn't order stall doors removed to increase productivity."

Cal huffed. "Stall doors! Overrated. I'm an exhibitionist. Too much shit happens behind closed doors around here, anyway."

Jim laughed. "So much is broke. I've been swamped with notes from employees about old and broken tools. The problem is staggering. Here, I'll share one." With a backhanded sweep, Jim grabbed and email off his desk and began to read.

"Dear Employee Officer,

HELP! Last Sunday, we hustled to dispatch our early flight. The weekend was a ballbuster. Heavy loads, bounced passengers...non-stop activity, due to a huge convention. We had no wriggle room.

Our regional manager promised pizza if we got our flights out on time. Our 6 a.m. airplane looped back to us throughout the day, meanin' we'd be hammered if we delayed the morning flight. Some call 'em boomerang flights—what goes around, comes around. I say sins of the morning shift shall be visited upon swing.

At quarter to six, plane fully loaded with souls and bags, our push back tractor, vintage 1955, known, dependin' on one's age as Marilyn, Dolly, or Angelina—yep *big* headlights—crapped out.

Times are tough. We don't ask much. Heck, we prodded the old gal to work well beyond normal life expectancy. Our lead mechanic and Dolly's caregiver—same vintage—tearfully announced she was gone, despite efforts to resuscitate.

The station log reflected that a loyal partner died in the line of duty."

"That for real?" Cal asked, grabbing the paper.

"Fraid so. Tracked down the paperwork. Procedures required a call to their manager and a fax to HDQ within two hours to explain the delay." Jim snatched another paper from his desk and pointed to a time stamp. "At 8AM, employees sent a detailed report to the office of the Ops Director."

"You speak with the Director?"

Jim frowned. "Yep—on Tuesday. She knew nothing. We found the report still sitting on her fancy fax machine, piled high with weekend incident reports."

"Miffwick!" Cal exclaimed.

"Huh!"

"Military term, M-F-W-I-C. *Who's in Charge?* You can guess the *MF*."

Jim laughed. "Sure can. We have an army of workers chanting Miffwick."

"Don't envy you, Jimmy. Wouldn't know where to start. Other than my wish list, that is. You satisfy one employee, you piss off the other hundred, you can't help."

"Our leaders live in a bubble. They park in a heated garage for God's sake. Most people in this glass tower are clueless when it comes to employee working conditions," Jim said, tapping the just-read note.

Cal pouted. "There goes my soda dispenser."

"The heated garage is simply a metaphor for perks and resources that keep officers clueless. Weston's penchant for importing fresh talent widens the reality gap."

"Always knew you were a closet socialist, Jimmy. Don't be naïve. Rank has and always will have its privileges. Auto execs drive free cars and bankers enjoy low-interest mortgages and blah, blah, blah. Perks never trickle down to the little people. Most bleeding heart liberals drip blue blood, *Mister Vice President*." Cal grabbed Jim's wrist and examined his veins.

"They spew egalitarian nonsense from the comfort of a heated toilet seat. The military isn't a democracy and neither is corporate America."

Jim pulled his arm free. "Perks and compensation aren't the root causes of our cultural ills. Simply easy targets."

"Union leadership stirs those pots with fervor." Cal swirled an invisible spoon.

"Exploiting a convenient hobgoblin to fire up members. Discontent and disengagement run deep—wouldn't take a big spark to ignite this place," Jim said.

"But pay and benefit cuts are real."

"Employees are more frustrated with unreliable products and broken tools. That note didn't mention pay, did it?" Cal shook his head as Jim continued. "Executive comp and perks divert attention from the real issues."

Cal pointed upward. "So you support the mega million pay packages for the top brass?"

"Not if we can't replace fifty-year old equipment. I'm just saying, we've lost sight of employee needs. Leaders should load their plate only after everyone else has eaten."

Cal patted Jim's back. "You're here to sort that out. What's the good news?"

"Scored a victory over HR with Richter's guidance and Hap's power."

"Good for you," Cal said, offering a high five.

Jim didn't reciprocate, shrugging instead. "But I only got half of the team I need."

"Half? That's like playing baseball without the infield."

"Hap blamed fuel prices, other cost pressures, and a looming cash crunch."

Cal smoothed his comb-over. "Senseless to hand you a mission and withhold necessary resources. Remember the schlep picked to centralize employee services?"

Jim stared out the window. "Julie reminded me of him too. Quit after two years of torture—fed up with defending his mission and fighting for resources with the very people who selected him."

"The flak was merciless. Employee services are still a mess." Cal's tone was sarcastic.

Jim turned back to his visitor. "I remain optimistic." As the words came out, Jim chafed. His mind reviewed a litany of pressures: an under resourced team, a scalped recognition budget, a raid on the funds needed to fix worn out facilities and equipment. Greedy peers assaulted his meager budget like frenzied crows, circling road kill and protected their turfs like hungry dogs. At the same time, Hap and the Steering Committee were demanding results.

"Is your team, or rather half team, functional?" Cal asked.

"Yep, no thanks to HR's best efforts to handicap me with inexperienced workers. Had to fend off Sharlee Guerrin's advances."

"The slinky dame with non-stop legs? Send her my way." Cal sucked in his gut and smoothed his comb-over.

Jim cleared his throat. "Anyway, I secured the A-team. Strong, idealistic and passionate for employees and company."

"Sounds like someone else I know," Cal said with a wink. "Heard you scored Lindy Price and Patty Thorsen. Surprised you didn't snare Jenny Rodriguez too. She'd kill to work for you, again. She's a gem and so adorable."

"Jenny's boss warned her to steer clear of my department—referenced the Titanic. Intercontinental's cultural sea is littered with icebergs, don't you know."

"Hell, Weston's shaped like one, probably as dangerous—scary what's below that surface. But, Jenny's boss is a fellow veep. Whatever happened to *score one for the Gipper* or *all hail the conquering hero?*

Jim sighed. "Replaced by *everyone for themselves*. She told Jenny to hug the metal."

Cal contorted his face. "Hug the metal! What the hell does that mean?"

"Stick close to airplanes. Those jobs are safe."

Cal shook his head. "Warned you about the folly of employee causes. You Jimmy boy may as well be hugging a tree... with Dutch elm disease."

"I respect Jenny's decision. Another colleague who also forgot the Gipper sent a scathing email accusing me of *poaching* his people. Questioned my integrity and threatened to raise my *questionable judgment* to Hap," Jim said, using his fingers to put imaginary quotes around the words. "Yet another teammate rejected my request to interview a staff member, citing her strategic imperatives."

"So much for camaraderie. And yet you sit here Jimmy boy, with a smile on your face and no razor blade at your wrist. You're delusional." Cal pressed his hand against Jim's forehead.

"The promise of a better company still inspires me." Jim waved his arm over to his desk strewn with congratulatory cards. "Look. Add hundreds of emails. Each message represents hope. I now have a staff who believes in our mission."

"They believe in you, Jimmy." Cal poked his chest.

"And I can't let them down. But if all fails, I now have an exit strategy." Jim showcased the box of rat poison in his palm.

Cal chuckled. "So who else have you poached or should I say, pried their clinging fingers from the rivets of a fuselage?"

"Dave Ramirez. He'll standardize tools, facilities and equipment."

Cal snapped his fingers. "My guy for the soda dispenser and bigger office."

"I'll warn him about you. I'll warn them *all* about you. Dave's bright, a quick study. Guess he almost got fired for a bad decision he could have avoided if he asked employee experts. He's a zealous convert."

Cal flourished his straw. "Another dragon slayer. Anyone else?"

"Evy Dial, a PhD out of Research & Development. She'll create metrics to measure our work."

"To gauge success or baffle Finance with bullshit?"

"All of the above. I gotta link our work to corporate goals, financial and operational."

"To compete with the metal huggers."

Jim nodded. "Also hired a woman from outside, Mary Tucker. She's got recognition. Her budget was gutted before she set foot on the property."

"Her glass is neither half full nor half empty, it's just a teeny weeny little shot glass," Cal said. "Why'd you go external?'

"Tell me about our last recognition program?"

Cal closed his eyes. "Don't recall any. Some argue that a regular paycheck is sufficient reward."

"Not very motivational. Sad I had to hire from outside to find someone with current skills. That's the team."

"Lean. Advantage dragons," Cal said, drawing Jim's glare. Cal cleared his throat. "I'm just sayin'. I'll give you plucky though. Hire quickly."

"That's my plan. Thanks for the office warmers," Jim said as he gathered loose pages from his desk. "Gotta run to the first dragon slayer round table."

Cal cupped his chin. "Think my file cabinet counts?"

"What?"

"Huggable metal," Cal said, sticking out his tongue. "By the way, when will we see announcements about your work?"

Jim flashed a thumb's up. "Hooray! Our Communication strategy is working."

Cal cocked his head. "What?"

"Never mind. That would take another hour. After which I'd down the champagne, rat poison, and eye drops. Sorry I never asked about you. What are you working on?"

Cal grimaced. "Not sure you want to hear."

Jim scoffed. "Oh come on. Make my day."

"Don't say I didn't warn you. Planning's puttin' together proposals to shrink the company into profitability, again. Usual suspects—route eliminations, outsourcing, and staff cuts. Heard Weston wants to shed 1,500 jobs." Cal then flourished the air in front of him with an imaginary sword. "Tavistock to the rescue."

Chapter 34

Jim Runs into Headwinds

"Gotta second? Wanna review my schedule." Jim said to his secretary before disappearing back into his office.

With Winny's clout, in a few short weeks his office assumed a comfortable appearance despite a mish mash of scavenged furniture. Two leather chairs, floor plants and clay red walls drew visitors' eyes away from Javitz' old desk and worn desk chair while airplane models including one made of building blocks invited play. A matted press release of his promotion along with his former team's photo and well wishes sat framed on the floor waiting to be hung.

Books from consultants fishing for business lined a beat-up bookcase. Jim referred to the library as literary bait. He had no idea the culture field had so many experts... corporate shrinks. With the airline cash-strapped, the fishing expeditions would result in empty hooks, but Jim devoured the material searching for free help.

Wall posters depicted the glorious past: vintage aircraft above Rio, Waikiki, and the Manhattan skyline. A promo piece from the fifties heralded coast-to-coast flying in less than ten hours aboard a double-deck Stratocruiser. Meticulously uniformed stewardesses with pillbox hats and heels offered five-course meals on china and crystal. In a club-like setting, suited men mingled with women wearing dresses, accessorized with pearls, fur stoles and leather handbags.

A lumbering clipper over the unfinished San Francisco Bay Bridge evoked special memories. As a kid, Jim's dad tucked him into bed with the radio call—*China clipper calling Alameda, come in Alameda.* Jim knew his dad, if he were alive, would be proud of his success.

While his office achieved harmony, Jim's vice president mantle still rested uneasily on his shoulders. As he dropped into his chair to await his secretary, his eyes rested on a photo of Julie on a Hawaiian beach. They made the trip shortly after receiving news of his promotion and the baby knowing job demands and a high-risk pregnancy would ground them for months. The impromptu weekend seemed years, not weeks before. Her smile soothed him on tough days despite being a reminder of the sputtering relationship.

Julie sounded upbeat when she phoned over the weekend announcing plans to return home to be near her doctor during the last trimester. Jim considered the news promising, but wished she didn't end the call voicing her intent to sleep in the guest room.

"You rang?" The squeaky voice belonged to Mona Schmidt, a secretarial temp. A relic of the sixties, her ever-present sneakers struck Jim as ironic since she only hurried to catch her nightly train.

A permanent secretary was impossible due to the company's financial crisis. Jim's plea for help brought him Mona in a rare show of collaboration between HR and Communications. Mona spent six weeks assisting Ingrid's secretary Jeanette before being offered to Jim. He couldn't believe she survived six hours. He pictured Ingrid shoving her into a taxi, kicking the door shut and commanding the cabbie to drive—*schnell.* He dreamed of the day he could send her packing along with her lava lamp and *Make Love Not War* poster.

His eyebrow arched as Mona entered empty-handed, her purple peasant dress billowing below her hips. "Might be a good idea to grab a pen and notebook," he said.

"My bad." Mona grabbed paper off his printer and rummaged his desk for a pencil. "All cool," she said, holding up the two items. She sat, her sneakered feet crossed at the ankles.

Jim sipped his coffee urging himself to be patient. "How are things going?"

Bracelets of glass beads clanked as Mona's hand rose to push gray-streaked hair from her eyes. "Groovy. Lindy makes copies and Dave books your travel. I dig this team."

Jim asked her to schedule updates with staff and Richter, confirm meeting dates with the Steering Committee and Hap and finally to order flowers for Julie's homecoming. He cringed as Mona's pencil pressed into his re-varnished desktop. Mona stopped writing. She looked up. "Hells Bells. Your boss."

"What about Hap?"

"Lemme see," she said, pulling the ends of her hair. "I remember. He wants you to call him. ASAP."

Jim grabbed the phone. "When did he call?"

Mona's fingers rubbed her temple. "Hmm. Late yesterday or earlier today," she said, wrinkling her nose. "Got it. Today. Sure of it. Put him on hold when Jeanette buzzed my other line to confirm lunch."

Jim's eyes enlarged. "Hap's not only busy, he's my boss. You know the saying—never disappoint the boss."

Mona shook her head, long earrings hitting her cheeks. "Can't say I do. My bad, but gotta go anyway. Can't keep Jeanette waiting. She's as uptight as her boss, Ms. Shadden..wood.. erer—Ingrid. But I shouldn't complain. They've both been nice.

Lunch is Jeanette's treat." She turned before exiting. "Your ears will be burning. They're *very* interested in our work."

⁂

"Food poisoning?" Jim blurted. He jotted notes as Hap described a picnic incident over the phone. Employee calls to news outlets alleged poisoning by management.

"You got it." Hap's tone stern. "We're fielding calls looking for comment. Let me read the more interesting copy, *Hot Dog! Intercontinental's Novel Approach to Trim Payroll—Flash, Airline Food Toxic—Korporate Kool-Aid Kalamity!*"

Jim squirmed. He felt Hap's scowl through the line. "I'll—"

Hap cut him off. "I'm not looking for excuses. Weston's hot. Bellows that bad publicity is bad for business. Find out what went wrong. Fix it."

"Yes sir." Jim hung up. When would he gain his boss' trust and confidence?

⋙✦⋘

"You gals just chillin'?" Mona asked Patty Thorsen and Lindy Price as the two took seats outside Jim's closed door.

Patty's eyes fixed on Mona. "We have a three o'clock. Confirmed with you this morning."

"You're not lyin'!" Mona exclaimed, pointing to her computer screen.

Lindy winked and mouthed a *thank you* to Mona. Patty stomped her foot.

Mona yawned before saying, "He's on a conference call. Tryin' to mop up a mess. Mr. Sweeny balled him out this morning about mass poisonings at the airport. A fiasco, says Jeanette and Ms. Ingrid. Jim shoulda handled it better."

Patty took a deep breath. "Three employees, I repeat *three* had minor stomachaches. A misguided media call blew the incident out of proportion."

Mona covered her mouth. "My bad. Only repeatin' what I heard."

"A dangerous habit. All of us would appreciate your discretion and a little less drama. We have enough on our plates justifying our existence without wasting time on mindless gossip," Patty said before turning a reddening face toward the window.

Lindy peered over her glasses. "Mona, I really like your hair."

Mona stroked her head. "Thanks. He's off the phone. By the way," she added with an exaggerated wink. "Good news on the home front. Mrs. A's comin' home."

Lindy pushed a trembling Patty into Jim's office. Jim sat at his desk, head resting in his hands. He ushered them to the conference table. Patty shut the door. With a gesture to the outer office, she whispered, "Our flower child must go. She'll single-handedly destroy this team's goodwill. She's inept and a gossip." With hands on hips, Patty pivoted toward Lindy. "And you. Always have to be Ms. Congeniality. That hair of hers is a rat's nest."

Lindy shrugged. She pointed to her own unruly curls, the subject of much self-deprecating humor. "She looked crushed," Lindy said. Patty's eyes enlarged.

Jim spoke. He couldn't hide the weariness in his voice. "I've come to the same conclusion. But, she's our only support."

Patty rubbed Jim's shoulder. "Sorry," she said. "You're having a bad day with the media circus. You don't need another issue."

Lindy fanned her notebook. "Not counting *our* issues. Just have to suck those up."

Jim managed a smile. He plucked notes and a pen from the desk and strode to the table. "Hap wants a remediation plan on his desk at dawn."

Patty rolled her eyes. "Three people get cramps! That man has more important things to worry about. A multi-million dollar fine and a spy in his organization." She pointed at Lindy whose mouth dropped open. "Not a peep," Patty said before turning to Jim. "Hap hasn't met a crisis he didn't like, no matter how small. When I see him, I'll tell him."

Jim envied Patty's candid relationship with Hap. Many assumed Patty hit the *pink ceiling* since nurturers like her didn't win promotions, not at Intercontinental. Yet leaders such as Hap and Wilkerson elbowed their way to her side because she symbolized a leadership ideal they believed bathed them in a light favorable to employees—respect by association.

Jim held up a palm and said, "Careful. I'm treading on thin ice."

Patty ran fingers through her hair. "You warned us we'd face resistance. Boy, you didn't exaggerate. Our work is called *fluff*. We're known as cake and balloon people."

Lindy's finger tapped the table. "But on a positive note, I can't tell you how many employees have stopped by my office. They're thrilled we exist. A beacon of hope." Lindy beamed before slouching. "Although they doubt we'll last a year." Patty scowled and Jim laughed.

"Let me tell you why we're needed," Lindy said before launching into a story. An employee contacted her after receiving a third letter from Payroll denying reimbursement for a company error regarding transfer and moving expenses. Although Payroll admitted the mistake, they refused to pay claiming they had no budget for such issues. By his third appeal, Payroll dug in its heels. Their last letter warned of serious repercussions if he continued to harass them.

"That poor man answers customer calls, day in and day out, urged by his supervisor to show empathy and flexibility," Lindy said with a sigh.

"Did you help him?" Jim asked.

"Yes." Lindy turned bright red, her eyes averted to the window.

"I know that look. Spill," Patty said.

Lindy looked sheepishly at Jim. "I reimbursed him from our budget."

"Great!" Jim exclaimed. "I would have done the same thing."

Lindy grinned. "Know what Human Resources said?"

Patty shook her head. "Guessin' it wasn't *thank you.*"

Lindy's nostrils flared and her hands trembled. "They feared he'd tell other employees and open a flood gate of requests. Christ, I goddamn hoped he told other employees his employer has a heart."

"Not to mention integrity," Jim added. His spirits surged. He was elated to have passionate people like Lindy on his team. "Employees flock to you. Your ability to connect is a gift," he said, squeezing her hand.

Patty wagged her finger at Lindy. "Pace yourself, Mother Theresa. We have fifty thousand employees. They'll all beat paths to your office. We'll be broke in a week."

Jim's face lit up. "Lindy should have a blog."

Lindy stiffened. Her face contorted. "A blog? What the heck for?"

"Time you joined the jet age Ms. Earhart," Patty said.

Jim nodded. "You can reach thousands of employees without being tied up in meetings for the next ten years. You're a natural," he said, slapping the table. Now tell me about your weeks."

Lindy flipped her notebook open. "Every division's under budget pressure. All service training has been eliminated—*again!*"

Jim grimaced. "Figures. Wouldn't be so bad if we produced widgets but we sell expensive services."

Lindy thumped the table with her pen. "There's one exception. Wilkerson developed apology training. Brady's flight attendant division wants in too since so much is broke on our airplanes. The modules include scripted apologies. Lots of role-play. They've asked me to play a crazed customer."

"Pathetic!" Patty interjected. "The training, not the typecasting. Employees will whip out flashcards with canned regrets."

Jim agreed. "That's Wilkerson's manufacturing background. An *I'm sorry* rolls off the tongue every minute."

Patty sighed. "Of course we'll give employees goals and quotas. Let's focus on fixing problems not streamlining the apology process."

"Miffwick!" Jim exclaimed. "Never mind," he added upon seeing their blank stares.

Patty spoke. "Leadership will be another battle. HR sees leadership as their exclusive bailiwick. Lindy and I met with Sharlee Guerrin and a team of consultants embedded within her organization. They circled the wagons."

Lindy leaned over the table. "You shoulda seen us, Patty and me in a room with a dozen HR types. I never saw so many decks or heard so much double speak. We were repeatedly reminded of everyone's PhDs, don't you know."

Jim pointed to the women. "Hap's not impressed. That's why we're here."

Patty grinned and patted Jim's arm. "Oh my dear, let's discuss our spineless champion. Each of Hap's leaders has an opinion on what you should be doing. Better watch your back."

Lindy placed her glasses on the table. "We always blame low level managers for our failures." She threw both hands in the air, her voice trembling. "I'm passionate."

Jim spoke, "You're passionate about everything. That's why we love you."

Lindy's eyes swelled. "We have waves of frustrated managers. They're choosing to return to non-supervisory roles."

Jim reached for a box of tissues on his desk. "Precisely why leadership must be a priority."

Lindy pulled three tissues. "You'll have to arm wrestle HR. Hap's got the power to drive this work."

"He's reluctant to exercise that prerogative. I can't figure it out. Richter thinks he's confounded by corporate politics. Hap wants a consensus but prefers I test the waters."

"Good grief! Hap Sweeny better find his balls, fast," Patty blurted.

❦

Mary Tucker returned from the airport where she attended a briefing on the food poisoning incident. She joined Jim at his conference table. "Never seen anything like this. Employees gleefully feed company mishaps to the media."

Jim shook his head. "Anger escalates rapidly into aggression. Unhappy employees coined the term sabotage."

Jim's search for a recognition leader dovetailed with Mary's desire to leave the hotel industry. She brought fresh thinking unfettered by company history or emotional bonds. Jim knew suspicion greeted newcomers who hadn't suffered the scars that glued employees together. Outsiders succumbed quickly.

As Mary twisted the pink band at her wrist, Mona interrupted. Jim's face fell after reading the note she passed him. *Sorry sweetie—you'll have one less ally. After forty years, my turn to be scrapped—off to Paris for R&R. Au Revoir mon ami & bonne chance. I'll drink a magnum of champagne in your honor. Betty J.*

"Everything okay?" Mary asked.

Jim crumpled the paper and threw it on his desk. Julie's photo stared back at him.

"Nothing tops the case of the poisoned potato salad." He took a deep breath. "Brief me on the rest of your work."

"Where to begin? One contingent wants my budget, but not my input. Another group sent wish lists demanding immediate attention. The third lot wants neither my money nor my involvement with one camp completely mistrusting head-quarters and the other seeing no value in recognition. Lastly, did I say—*what budget?*"

Jim studied Mary's face. She smiled but he knew even she was growing weary of the hurdles that seemed to block every path forward. He spoke. "You're dealing with people who've fasted so long, they don't know how to eat."

Mary shrugged. "I'm a big girl. Many employees approached me at the airport. They want our help. Check this out," Mary said tossing something onto the table.

"What is it?" Jim asked picking up a gold-plated keychain with the company logo on one side and an inscription *U R Key 2 R Success* on the other.

"An airport employee gave it to me. He's a top elite customer check-in agent in terms of compliment letters."

"Wow, impressive. But where'd he get this?" Jim asked, holding up the cheap trinket.

"In his mailbox with a post it note from his supervisor."

Jim scrunched his face. "What'd it say?"

"That he sold more upgrades than any other agent. Over one million dollars in the first quarter alone. The keychain was his acknowledgment. He didn't know whether to laugh or cry."

"That's terrible," Jim said. "Elite Check-in agents are drilled to recognize top customers. Too bad we failed to set an example. Shoved in a mail box for Christ sake."

Mary's gaze drifted to the window. "I thought about jumping—"

"Out the window?"

She turned and looked at him with a half-smile. "On a plane at the airport. Escaping to Paris."

Jim gasped. "Anywhere but there. Every employee on the verge of quitting heads to Paris for their last hurrah."

Mary winked. "I promise to send a postcard."

Chapter 35

Jim Seeks Domestic Bliss

A hastily scratched note from his secretary assured Jim she had ordered flowers, reconfirmed with the florist, not once but twice. His insistence on the confirmation wasn't because he mistrusted the flower shop. He crumpled the note with a smile for Mona's annotation—little pink hearts dotted the *i's.*

With luck and a healthy trot, he'd catch the 6:33, the last evening express before the hourly locals. That train would put him in his garage by 7:30—early enough to grab dinner with Julie. He left a voice message at the house welcoming his girl home and suggesting they go out for dinner. Unsure of her mindset, he was cautious not to use the word *celebrate* or sound overly confident about her return. "Don't push," he coached himself. But, he found it hard to hide his elation with the homecoming of his wife and baby-to-be. Jim dashed out of the office.

He ran the last few blocks to the station, ignoring the incoming calls that sent repeated vibrations to his front pocket. He listened only for the slot-machine ring tone, symbolizing his biggest jackpot, Julie. He'd glance at any messages on the train. His priority tonight was the repair of his own human relations.

At his request, his mother-in-law phoned when Julie left her house. His wife texted midway from an oasis north of Milwaukee, and a second time from a fast-food joint inside the Illinois border. The messages weren't effusive but thankfully, not cold nor distant either. Maybe he was just hopeful.

The couple had three months until the baby arrived, the furthest along Julie got with any of her pregnancies. But the doctor expressed caution; they weren't out of the woods. He recommended her return to Chicago and ordered weekly check-ups.

Jim expressed a desire to accompany Julie on the drive, but her strong-will surfaced. She hit him with the—*I'm pregnant, not helpless*—rebuke that became a familiar refrain but agreed to delay the journey if the forecast merely hinted at storms. Thankfully, the skies were clear and the airline's meteorologists, who Jim pestered for days, tracked the nearest weather to a mild disturbance over western Iowa. Since the morning, the weather updates streamed hourly.

He rehearsed his homecoming speech, over and over. With his A-team in place, he'd delegate more. Julie knew Lindy and Patty; their cachets offered instant credibility. But Julie would probably joke that he'd spend more time coaxing Lindy off a ledge than the other way around. Topics he'd avoid would be equally important. Why mention the assaults on his budget or even his new manager's threat to quit and flee to Paris? He wished he could boast that everyone embraced the culture change but she wouldn't believe him. A number of insiders, he figured, probably informed her about his team's difficulties already. It would be useless to pretend things were going well. If only he possessed Ingrid's knack for spinning sad tales into fantasy.

Jim's sprint down the platform gave him the momentum needed to board the train just as the conductor closed the doors. As usual, the last express was packed with other prudent commuters wanting to avoid the slower trains. Sweaty from his jog, Jim didn't even look for a vacant seat; standing with circulating air was preferable to the hot, vinyl benches.

From the vestibule, Jim spied the back of Cal Gladden's glistening scalp and comb over in the adjoining compartment. A super-sized soda confirmed his identity. Jim watched with amusement as his buddy sipped from a straw while his young blonde seatmate buried her head in a book, squirming as close to the window as she could manage. Gossip and Cal's obsessive need to talk shop, didn't facilitate the kind of escape Jim needed to mentally prepare for his rendezvous with Julie.

❧❖❧

Jim noticed the outside house lights. Maybe he read too much into it, but a warm feeling arose knowing that Julie made it safely home and turned the lights on for his arrival. In her absence, he missed the domestic ritual.

A mixture of nervousness, fear, and exhilaration swept over him, just like their first date and wedding day. Shunning his appeals to meet, nearly three months elapsed since he'd seen her. A refusal to take his calls during the first two weeks tortured him altogether while her mother's thorough updates were the price he demanded to refrain from camping on his in-law's front lawn. For the past two months, he and Julie spoke two or three times a week. It may have been wishful thinking, but he sensed a difference in Julie's tone in the last few calls. Perhaps even a full-blown thaw.

"Tread lightly, Jimmy boy. Don't smother her." He talked aloud as he pulled his car into the garage, spirits surging at the sight of Julie's red SUV parked in its usual spot.

He debated which restaurant to suggest. Their favorite spot for cozy dinners including the past two Valentine's seemed too presumptuous. On the other hand, she might roll her eyes at the ritzy place with the stuffy wait staff. And, he certainly couldn't risk minimizing the occasion by underwhelming her with a trip to their favorite pizza joint or chain restaurant. He

decided to let her pick, warning himself against drawing con-
clusions from her selection.

Similar angst filled his choice of flowers—red roses too
desperate, carnations too cheap and azaleas reminiscent of
maiden aunts. He rejected Mona's suggestion of daisies as too
ordinary.

Hopefully, he wouldn't find Julie locked in the guest room
with Nelly's cat as a hissing sentinel. She certainly wouldn't be
so foolish to drink wine this close to the due date. He quickly
dismissed that thought as unfair. Since that earlier night that
seemed a lifetime ago, Julie showed nothing but commitment
and concern for their baby.

As he walked into the kitchen, Sedona ran to him with tail
wagging. The dog's eyes flashed desperation and her clinginess
suggested that Nelly's cat already imposed dominion over the
shaggy-haired retriever. He lifted his nose and sighed. The house
smelled great, a combination of garlic and onions. Oh how he
missed Julie's cooking for the past three months. Sedona probably did too. He grew accustomed to dining on a sandwich and
chips scarfed down on the evening commute, either on the train
or more likely in the car on the highway since his erratic hours
didn't mesh with public transport. He became a company slave
and couldn't be captive to the train schedule as well.

The sight of Julie standing barefoot at the stove stirring
a pot made his heart race. He felt his palms grow clammy.
Julie turned to him and smiled. "You made the train. A pleasant surprise." Her tone neither sarcastic nor cold was more
matter-of-fact and noncommittal. Her smile felt sincere. She
seemed content.

Jim forgot to consider that three months of pregnancy
would transform his wife. In his mind she remained frozen in
time, his memory fixed on that horrible afternoon she drove
off to her mother's house. After allowing him a quick kiss on

the cheek, she climbed into the SUV with that cat in her arms. They both sobbed, each managing a polite wave before the car disappeared down the street.

Julie was bigger of course, yet her radiance struck him— the simple beauty of her long blonde hair and face without make-up. She looked more beautiful than he remembered. He crossed the kitchen with outstretched arms.

"Careful," Julie said, lifting the wooden spoon. "Let's not splatter your jacket." He settled for a kiss on her cheek instead. She smiled and squeezed his arm. "Making one of your favorites, spaghetti and meatballs."

"Not the recipe you charmed out of that chef in Positano?" Jim asked, sniffing the air over the saucepot.

"While you flirted with the blouse-popping waitress? Yes, *that* recipe," Julie said, tapping the spoon on the pot rim.

"I told you, simply a ruse for you to connive your way into the kitchen."

"I say now what I said then…" With exaggeration, she enlarged her eyes and glared at him. They both laughed.

"Smells great." He again buried his nose in the pot and dipped a finger in the sauce.

"Pasta's good for me. Doctor wants me to put on a bit more weight."

He froze. "Nothing's wrong?" Concern rose in Jim's voice. His breathing stalled.

Julie rubbed his arm. "No, no. Shouldn't have even mentioned it. He wants me to bulk up, based on my history. Everything's fine."

He scrutinized her face, comforted by the absence of worry. "I'll put out plates," Jim said with a glance to the empty kitchen table.

"Thought we'd eat in the dining room. It's already set," Julie answered.

Jim sat on a counter stool, admiring the back of his gorgeous wife. Serenity and a feeling that everything would be all right, swept over him. "So good to have you home, honey."

She nodded, still facing the stove. "Thanks for the hydrangeas. They're perfect."

He looked around, but didn't see them. "You can plant them in the garden."

Julie nodded. "Why don't you go up and get changed? The garlic bread will be ready when you're done. We can have it with the salad."

"You know I love that," he said, rising from the stool. A peak into the dining room found the table set, blue hydrangeas off to one corner. He resisted the urge to hum one of Mona's songs as he climbed the stairs, all smiles. With Julie back and his team in place, life was back on track.

As he re-entered the kitchen, he found Julie straining the pasta. "Careful honey, don't scald yourself."

"I'm pregnant, not helpless," she said, peering at him with s slight grin. "Can you open the wine? I'm assuming you want some."

"Don't need any," he said.

A hand landed on her hip. "Nonsense! Just because I can't, doesn't mean you shouldn't. Go ahead."

Dinner progressed well. Sedona reclined in her old spot at their feet, waiting for something to pass quietly from Jim's hand as Julie pretended not to notice. The cat watched the domestic scene from a perch behind the stair railings. Julie shared stories about her family and asked after Jim's mom. Except for an update on Nelly's condition, Intercontinental didn't come up as if by some unspoken agreement between the couple.

As Jim cleared plates, Julie brought out a large container of tiramisu she said she bought along with fresh bread at the village's Italian bakery. He wanted to squeeze her when her face assumed a guilty-little-girl expression as she divvied up huge portions onto two plates. "My sweet tooth," she confessed, "is most appreciative for doctor's orders."

She declined Jim's offer of a cappuccino, explaining that she had to cut her coffee intake. "The tiramisu probably contains a fatal dose of caffeine already. But worth the indulgence for tonight," she said, licking her lips.

Jim beamed. "Have I told you how happy I am to have you home?"

"A few times," she said with a wink. "It's good to be home. I've missed our beautiful house, Sedona and, of course, my Jimmy." Her eyes were kind.

"I'm so glad to hear you say that," Jim responded. He took her sigh as a cue to discuss the progress at work—his new team and Hap's support in the face of budget pressures. Julie listened with head bobs, smiles, and narrowed eyes, but she didn't interrupt.

At last she broke her silence. "Heard the budget took a toll on more of our friends. We get newspapers in central Wisconsin, Internet too," she said with a chuckle and a swirl of her water glass. After a pause, Julie raised an eyebrow. "Are you happy, Jim?"

He couldn't get the words out fast enough. "At the moment, I'm ecstatic you're home."

She tilted her head. Her expression became more serious. "That's not what I meant. Are you happy with your work, happy with your boss's support, and happy with your progress?"

No one had asked him if he were happy and he certainly never considered it. Pressures were too numerous to luxuriate in self-indulgence. He paused before responding, finally stammering. "G…guess I'm happy. Content… satisfied may be better words. Of course, I want everything to move faster. Hap to be more supportive. Wish I had unlimited resources.

But, that's life." He shrugged, a bit uncomfortable with the subtle change in mood brought on by the discussion of work.

"How about you?" Jim asked before taking a big sip of wine.

When her words finally came, they were slow. "For a long time, the answer has been no. Been miserable with my self-imposed exile. Devastated by Nelly's lack of progress and, although you might not believe me... concerned by the struggles I know you face every day."

Her empathy moved him. He reached for her arm. "And our baby?"

She sighed, practically giggled. "Thrilled. At last, I'm a mom." She patted his hand while rubbing her belly.

"And me?"

"Jim," she said. "You are who you are. I'm okay with that now. I've made peace with... the fact that my Jimmy is gone. Happy? No, but content." She nodded.

He pulled his hand away slowly. His back stiffened. "What does that mean?"

Her eyes met his. "After the baby comes, I want a divorce."

Chapter 36
Jim Seeks Guidance

"I'm not the *I told you so type*, but—"

"You told me so," Jim said. He cradled his head, his elbow resting on his mom's kitchen table. Two, no three days had passed since Julie dropped the bombshell. He'd lost track of time, moving forward in a fog of self-loathing, anger, and questions, lots and lots of questions. But no answers.

"Sweetie," she said, setting down her wineglass, "you're my son. I love you."

He made a pre-emptive strike. "But..."

His mom shrugged. "I love Julie like a daughter."

At least she didn't play the martyred grandmother card. In the early weeks of Julie's pregnancy, he came home to find the two cooing over baby outfits and other items for the nursery. The fact that the two women idolized each other pleased him, *most of the time*. Occasionally, he rolled his eyes, threw up his hands, and griped that the axis of evil had nothin' on the pact between mother and wife. Surrender was easier and smarter.

He reached for the wine bottle and filled both glasses. "I know you love her," he said. "And that makes me happy." He took a gulp of wine. "If only she were a bitch."

She slapped his hand. "Hush now. You don't mean that. You wouldn't have married her. You're just sore 'cause you know she's right."

Here it comes, he thought, the lecture about being a rotten shit. Diving into work, day and night, seven days a week when Julie needed him most. Hadn't he played the *what-if game* over and over in his head since Julie's pronouncement? "Of course she's right—to a point. But she blames me for Nelly's attempted suicide, blames me."

His mom's eyes enlarged, her left eyebrow rose. He knew the look. "Stop that. She doesn't blame you for anything. You blame yourself." Her finger tapped the table.

He sighed, closed his eyes and tilted his neck back. Perhaps she was right. Guilt weighed on him like a backpack full of rocks. He couldn't shake the hangover-like numbness that gripped his head. As a company officer, why hadn't he done more, and quicker, to save people like Nelly and their friend Chris?

Had he helped anyone? His team spent more time trying to get invited to meetings and impose themselves into initiatives than doing anything. Why didn't he have the guts to barge into offices and demand action, set the employee agenda instead of being Mr. Nice Guy? Playing by the rules was paralyzing, an inch forward, two feet backward; retreat instead of advance. He was no hero. He was the outsider who criticized the club but finding himself inside, shook hands, cozied up to the buffet and sat down to enjoy the view. Now he could add his family to the list of people harmed by his inaction.

"I don't know what to do, Mom." He found compassion in her eyes. "I'm lost without her."

She squeezed his hand. "I'm assuming you told her that."

He nodded. "I sobbed, like a baby. Told her I loved her, told her I didn't want to lose her, told her…" He stopped when she held up a finger.

"Listen sweetie, I'm no marriage shrink and I'm certainly no consultant. But what's that you bragged your buddy Richter said?"

Jim flinched. Work was the last thing he wanted to discuss. As for Richter, he had dozens of sayings. What did any of them have to do with their marriage? He shook his head. "Gimme a hint."

"You threw out quotes like a door-to-door Bible thumper," she said, plucking at her short white hair. "Can't talk yourself... outta... behaving." She shook her head back and forth as if she were trying to jar the words from her brain. "Talk's cheap is the gist. Told you I'm no consultant." She took a gulp of wine.

He chuckled. Perhaps not a consultant, but decades of working for Intercontinental as a passenger agent taught her tons about people. "Makes sense. But what does that have to do with me?"

She poked his temple. "Think, sweetie. Take your own medicine. You just gave me a litany of the things you told Julie."

"Yeah," he said, looking at her from the corners of his eyes.

"You're always telling me that those knuckleheads at the top of the airline talk a blue streak but do nothin'. That Ingrid woman for one. Well, employees are no dummies. Weren't in my day and aren't now. They won't believe anything they can't see, touch or smell. Julie's no different."

His eyes narrowed. "What are you saying?"

"Your wife wants action not words. You can recite all that la-di-da Hallmark crap, but seein' is believin'."

His mom was right. He'd broken many promises. He thought Julie understood why. Maybe she did understand, but that didn't mean she accepted it. Understanding didn't erase the hurt. He lost sight of Julie's needs. "But my job, Mom. You of all people know how that place runs."

"Chews people up and spits 'em out. You gotta decide who you want to be when you grow up, James Andrew Abernathy."

He rubbed his eyes. "Thought I had that all figured out." He exhaled; his shoulders slumped. "Maybe I don't know shit."

The chest poke made him sit up. "I know you don't want

to be Richard Weston. No son of mine could want *that* for Christ's sake. But do you wanna be Hap Sweeny?" She stopped and looked into his eyes. He didn't have the answer, yes, no, maybe. He wasn't sure. She continued, "Well if you do, keep goin' the way you are. Hap's two wives ahead, plays a mean round of golf, and drives a fancy car." She emptied her wine. "You don't know this. Julie was embarrassed. Didn't want to hurt you. She dated Hap… years ago. Work was just one of his mistresses… but the most important."

Jim ran his fingers through his hair. He and Julie made a pact not to discuss prior lovers. He couldn't think about it now. He had his work cut out for him. Before he could figure out how to keep Julie, he had to figure out some things about himself, including what he truly wanted out of life. Hap and most of the executives made it clear you couldn't split loyalty between work and family and keep both. None of the circle at the top had what Jim considered a triple-A rated home life.

"You got some heavy thinkin' to do, young man. You're gonna be a daddy before you know it. For that matter, I'm gonna be a grandmother. I waited long enough for that title. I want my grandbaby in my life."

The gramma card played at last. But his mom was right. They all waited so long for this baby. Julie had done her part. He couldn't screw it up.

As his mom rose from the table, she bent down, kissed his cheek and gave him a big hug. "I love you, sweetie. You'll do the right thing. You always do."

Chapter 37

Jim is Summoned Again

"Shit! Can't be late," Jim mumbled. Winny told him to rush to the airport. Said Hap called it urgent, his time limited to a short window. It wasn't like Winny to caution him against sharing information. Perhaps this was big, Weston convening a clandestine Board meeting. Special meetings generally resulted in big changes. Reorganizations, shakeups, acquisitions—hopefully not another bankruptcy.

Jim paced, waiting for the employee shuttle to the terminal. Rumors and gossip garnered on the ride provided intelligence on the state of the airline. Tone conveyed as much as subject matter. He felt vice presidents should ride the shuttle instead of reading employee surveys. However, fear of the unbridled masses kept most officers off the dilapidated busses.

At last, a grimy shuttle plodded through the gate. Repeated glances at his watch didn't expedite its meander from Athens to Hong Kong to Cape Town. Flight crews and ground staff alighted and boarded with roller boards and backpacks unhurried. The lumbering bus finally approached. His shirt dripping with perspiration, Jim was anxious to escape the heat and humidity. A chubby flight attendant hobbled off the bus with a suitcase and overstuffed shopping bag. "Damn air conditioning's still out," she griped to Jim and the others waiting to board.

Jim glanced through the hot compartment without recognizing anyone. Wicking away sweat, he grabbed a seat near the rear exit behind a young man and woman. On account of their attire, he pegged them as supervisors, a position for which he had fondness having been one, himself. Two flight attendants sitting to his left examined jewelry and designer knockoffs purchased from a colleague, fresh from a Beijing layover.

Wiping his brow, Jim listened to the two supervisors. "Listen Alice," the young man said. "Not sure how you lasted two years with flight attendants. Maybe it's different over there. I've had it with my manager. Not sure I'll last two months in Passenger Service -- much easier being an agent."

"You sang a different tune as an agent," the girl named Alice said.

The man nodded. "Yeah, a dufus of a boss, stupid rules and stupider decisions."

"Nobody listened, you said. Derrick, you can make a difference with your team." She punched him in the arm before rubbing shoulders.

"If only. Wanna hear the counseling I got yesterday?" He didn't wait for an answer. He turned to look at her. "Accused of spending *too* much time with my people. Believe that crap?"

Alice pulled a magazine from her tote and fanned herself. "I don't have any time to spend with flight attendants. Too many to supervise and they're usually airborne. We're under the budget knife again. I connect only with troublemakers." She sighed.

Derrick spoke fast. Sweat dripped down his neck. "I tried to get to know my team. Backgrounds, families, career goals— stuff a supervisor should know, a human one anyhow."

As the bus filled, the heat became intolerable. Jet fumes and blasts of warm air off the steamy tarmac blew through the open windows. Inside, body odor and fast food mixed with perfume and shower soap. Resting the magazine on her lap, Alice spoke. "I remember when I started as an agent. I was so overwhelmed. Not the glam I expected. Like drinkin' from a fire hose. You never forget your first irregular operations."

"I wanted to lessen my team's anxiety. My manager called me to her office. Told me to cut the personal chitchat."

Alice flinched. "What?"

"There she sat, munchin' on cheese curls. Had the nerve to lecture me. *Conversations should be business focused—supervisors are spread thin—drive results,* she says." Derrick assumed a nasal affectation when mimicking his supervisor. "Then she winks, boasts of a *magic technique.*" The husky man dabbed his face.

"Can't wait for this." Alice alternated fanning herself and her overheated colleague.

"*Every agent is guilty of somethin'*, she says."

Alice clicked her tongue. "That's pretty cynical."

"Here's more pearls from the orange stained lips. *Assume guilt. We don't have the luxury to police every action. Stand opposite an agent. With hands on hips, shake your head and scowl.*"

Alice grimaced. "Even if they're not doing anything wrong?"

"*Irrelevant*, she said. Under observation, self-conscious agents will comply with guidelines and service standards. *Works wonders*, she bragged. Encouraged me to follow her lead, *if* I wanted to be successful."

"You won't, will you?" Alice said, squeezing his arm.

"I can't respect that kinda leader. Gotta be careful. Big bosses think she's great."

A cheer at the front of the bus diverted Jim's attention. From the ensuing chatter, he learned that the hollers were for a retiring pilot about to take his final trip. The spontaneous outpouring of high fives and applause touched him. He recognized the beaming captain as a cult hero, the *wing-pin champion.* He recalled the story.

The beloved gold wings for kids disappeared without explanation. This pilot wanted answers but found only dead ends.

Purchasing said the pins cost too much—the pilot sourced them at a steep discount. Managers said the pins carried liabilities—the pilot contacted Legal who dismissed that argument. The pins triumphantly returned. The pilot emerged an employee hero, a bureaucracy buster in the culture of *no*.

The bus pulled under the terminal's shady underbelly where most employees got off. The rustle and open door refreshed the stale air and refocused Jim on his mission. The hotel was the next stop. Nerves unsettled his stomach and questions crept into his mind. What did Hap want? Maybe it was good news. Perhaps Jim would get approval to hire the rest of his team and clearance to spend more money. Just as quickly, pessimism swept those thoughts away. Would he get fired?

The bus lurched forward after ingesting homebound workers. As it rolled into the blistering sun, rumblings of the broken air conditioning stole any pockets of breathable air. Two burly mechanics dripping in their uniforms, took the seats vacated by the flight attendants. They bantered about suits from the FAA swarming around the airport like flies around the lav service truck. "Hear we're in for millions of fines," one said. "Yup. Heads'll role, probably even Hap Sweeny's," replied the other.

A few of the newcomers recognized Jim with a nod and wave but clogged aisles and thirst for the latest gossip failed to generate any conversations. The bus reached the hotel. Jim crossed the bustling lobby and sun-drenched atrium for the escalator to the spot where Winny told him to wait.

The circular mezzanine contained conference rooms named for industry fossils: Braniff, Pan Am, TWA, Western. Despite the dim lighting, Jim quickly found the Eastern Airlines room. As he settled into a cushioned chair to wait for his boss, Jim guessed that the hotel found it easier to embrace the industry's romantic past than to keep up with the dynamic landscape of current players.

A familiar form darted from the corridor leading from the rest rooms. The small figure with upturned nose and pompous strut belonged to Wilkerson. The leather-soled shoes clicking rapidly across the floor reminded Jim of a child rushing to Sunday school. In the months since Jim joined Hap's team, Wilkerson never exhibited anything resembling camaraderie. His interactions were limited to condescending emails demanding updates and snipes during staff meetings. Jim waited. He sensed Wilkerson assessing alternate escape paths. Jim opted for a pre-emptive strike. As he stood up, he spoke. "Hello Wilkerson. You attending the Board meeting?"

"Here for the same reason you are," Wilkerson replied. His look of surprise seemed phony. "Hap's meeting with each of us during meeting breaks. We're done." He didn't look into Jim's eyes but kept his moppish head of white hair directed at the floor.

"D... done?" Jim stammered.

Wilkerson grinned. "Finished. I already met with Hap."

"Oh," Jim said, feeling his shoulders relax. "Must be important. What's going on?"

"Hap'll fill you in," Wilkerson snapped reproachfully. "Kiss another chunk of your budget good-bye." He looked up into Jim's crestfallen face for the first time. "Hap's decision. He's still in charge, *for now*. Gotta run." In the scant light from the room's chandelier, Jim detected Wilkerson's black bb-like eyes dance.

Jim sank back into the chair, his arms folded to ward off the chilly air. He addressed the empty foyer. *Resources vanish. It's like grasping clouds. My position's a sham.*

The door of a far conference room opened. Five dark-suited men exited into the shadowy hall, their polished shoes picking up speckles of light. Jim recognized the towering outline of Bryce Jacobs behind the portly silhouette of Richard

Weston. He held his breath as they strode toward him, pairing off with men he didn't know. The fifth and final figure was Hap Sweeny, his trim and crisp form unmistakable.

Jim watched as Weston and Jacobs gestured with animation, downright jovial as they led their respective conversations. Their partners nodded, offering only brief responses. Hap trailed. His shoulders sagged as he plodded down the dark corridor, head bowed to the oriental carpet.

As the group neared, Jim stood. Anticipating a greeting, maybe even an introduction, he smoothed his shirt and trousers. The men stopped outside the conference room into which he expected them to disappear. As Weston looked into his eyes, Jim saw recognition on the CEO's creaseless face. But Weston retreated back into his conversation, his voice dropped to a whisper. Jacobs turned his back to Jim, his words muffled. Still, Jim discerned *acquisition*, *valuation* and *integration* before Hap, expressionless and haggard, drew up behind the others. He acknowledged Jim's presence with an uplifted finger.

Weston's voice regained a normal volume. His chins quivered like vanilla pudding. "Gentlemen, a very productive session. Thank you for flying in. We made great progress meeting face-to-face."

One of the shadowed forms spoke. "Details remain, such as survey updates, but we inch forward. I remain optimistic. Next time, though, we meet in our hometown. Do your folks good to get acclimated."

"Deal," Weston gushed. "But I'm thinking New York for the final round." He slapped the man's back before they said their good-byes.

The two strangers smiled at Jim as they passed on their way to the escalator. He turned his attention back to the conference room door in time to see Weston's puffy hand grasp Hap's shoulder and his eyes draw close. "Buck up now," Weston said. "Don't ruin it for yourself. Understand? With me?"

Hap stared back at Weston with cold eyes and expression like granite. Weston's grip rippled Hap's jacket. After a pause, Hap nodded, almost mechanically. The grip relaxed and he tapped Hap's shoulder. "Thatta boy."

After Jacobs joined the two for a huddle, he and Weston stepped into the conference room. Before the door closed on them, Jim heard Weston mutter, "Let's do this."

Hap approached as Jim noticed someone seated in the shadows. He recognized the rising silhouette as Ingrid, her perfume camouflaged by large vases of summer flowers. She prowled forward, her mint-green linen suit blending with the plush carpet. Jim froze, seeing a sinister grin under violet eyes that became pools of blackness in the dim light. Without a word, she rubbed her hand along Hap's arm as she passed. Jim watched her expression transform effortlessly into a look of sympathy as Hap bristled. A mirror to the left of the gilded conference room door captured the fiendish grin's return before Ingrid slunk into the room.

Hap dropped into a chair, rubbing his suit where Ingrid pressed her hand. "This won't take long." Jim studied his boss's face as he lowered himself into a chair. He waited as Hap glanced to the closed door before speaking. "Pressure mounts. Fuel continues to soar. Revenues will sour fast." Hap scowled toward the escalator. "Why anyone would want to buy an airline is beyond me."

"That the reason for the special meeting?" Jim asked, looking to the conference room.

Hap's fingers tapped his chair. His eyes narrowed. "A multitude of issues," he said. "I've cut recognition by one million. We can't afford that extravagance now. We must conserve cash. Tavistock will lead a *Lights Out* exercise. Brace for more reductions and staff cuts." Steely eyes fixed on Jim at the mention of layoffs. "The situation is dire. I expect your support."

"*Lights Out* sounds final," Jim said with a shrug. He wondered if the ringing in his ears was the sound of an iceberg sheering the hull. He felt a sinking pang in his stomach.

The vein on Hap's forehead throbbed. "We must cut anything not essential to run the airline. This is survival."

"Are... are you pulling the plug on... all the employee work?" Jim stammered.

Hap shook his head. "That's a different conversation. No, your work continues, *for now.* But, scale back. We need results. Weston's impatient."

"He is? Didn't think he knew my work existed." Jim's tone blended interest and irritation.

Hap scowled, his tone stern. "I keep him informed. He knows as much as he wants to know. I told you he doesn't want to be involved with employees, merely wants results."

"Measured in?" Jim asked.

"Satisfaction scores. The elimination of negative employee rhetoric."

"Richter preaches patience. Says you can't *talk* yourself outta something into which you *behaved* badly?" Jim laughed at his mom's attempt to remember the phrase.

Hap's forehead furrowed. "What the hell does that mean?" he snapped.

Jim felt his anxiety give way to anger. "Talk's cheap. Action's what matters," he answered glaring at Hap. "Culture change doesn't come with a flip of a switch especially without the Chairman. We spent weeks re-writing a thank-you letter from Weston to employees. After wringing out every ounce of emotion and gratitude, Ingrid informed us Weston *couldn't get comfortable.* Can't say thank you?"

Hap gritted his teeth. He turned from Jim to the conference room. "I told you not to confuse your efforts with culture change. You're setting your sights too high."

Jim felt his lips quiver. "I look to you and the Steering Committee for changes to my scope," he said in a huff.

Hap looked at Jim. His expression and tone softened. "The company's a spinning top. Everything's up for grabs. I hear what you say about Weston—unfortunate, but reality. Keep working. Short term, quick wins. Direction's good, *for now*. I'm behind you," Hap said with a look at his watch. "We're done."

Hap rose and headed for the conference room. After two steps, he turned. "Carrie Patterson's gone. You'll see the announcement tonight. Frida Sallinger's taking over HR while leading the search for a replacement."

While Jim couldn't say he was sorry to see Patterson go, he was surprised by the abruptness of the departure. He couldn't help feeling rapid change was merely beginning. The words *for now, for now*, echoed in his ears like a call to the lifeboats.

Chapter 38
Hap's Perfumed Surprise

Hap turned his back on Jim in the chilly mezzanine of the airport hotel. He walked toward the gilded door of the Eastern Airlines conference room into which Weston, Jacobs, and Ingrid had disappeared to join Intercontinental's waiting Board of Directors. He glanced into the mirror to the left of the door and stopped to scrutinize Jim's reaction to the additional cuts. A vice president, Hap felt, must learn to cope with turbulence as he did. He saw the current ordeal as a good test of Jim's mettle.

The mirror reflected bewilderment. Jim, dropping into the overstuffed chair, cast his eyes down to the carpet. Sensing anger, Hap seethed, his eyes narrowed, forehead creased and scowl returned. He wasn't touching Jim's precious title, merely asking him to surrender budget and sacrifice a few staff. Consternation over such a simple task spurred doubts about his decision to promote him. However, he had bigger priorities. He'd test Jim's grit for the job later.

Hap inhaled deeply, squared his shoulders and pulled open the gold handles of the double-door. The dusky room belched anticipation. Its occupants huddled in droning clusters. The eyes of those scattered around the table blinked toward him before returning to peck at phones.

At the back of the room near the white clothed refreshment tables and silver coffee urns, Jacobs congregated with the sub-committee created to shepherd the sale. The CFO's frame loomed large, his broad, sloping shoulders towering over a devoted flock. Hap only learned of the secret committee's existence that morning. He sneered at them.

He noticed Weston's round silhouette partially eclipsed by Ingrid who stood perfectly erect in profile, her back to the conference table. One board member studied her derriere, eyebrows rising each time her weight shifted and her buttocks, which filled the linen suit, undulated. The prudish head of an insurance conglomerate didn't notice Hap's voyeuristic interest or the frown directed at him from the Board's lone female.

Weston and Ingrid conferred with a third person. With only his back visible, Hap assumed him to be from the Board. Yet, something about his stance seemed familiar. Hap admired the well-tailored, silk suit; guessed Italian, hand-made—stylish, but not flamboyant. As the man nodded with great fervor, meticulously groomed hair fell back into place, effortlessly.

When Ingrid took a step backwards, Weston's face, fleshy and pale as the moon, emerged from eclipse. His puffy eyes turned from his conversation partners; an emotionless gaze rested upon Hap, frozen at the door. With extended arms, Weston corralled his companions. Ingrid also turned to the door and flashed what Hap considered to be, a manufactured smile. The mystery figure recoiled at Weston's touch. Even though the man's face remained obscured, Hap instantly recognized him as his nemesis, Tyler Dagger.

"What the hell is Dagger doing here?" Hap muttered aloud, his face and scalp warming. Dagger wasn't present at the morning session when the sale bomb dropped on Hap. Weston insisted Board meetings be orchestrated with painstaking detail—no surprises including no crashers except those Weston or Ingrid contrived themselves. Nausea swelled within him as he speculated on Dagger's unannounced appearance and the stunning transformation. Hap never saw the geek's hair combed, let alone styled with a four hundred dollar haircut. The five thousand dollar suit replaced baggy khakis, flannel shirt and high-tops with Velcro fasteners. He considered Dagger's metamorphosis extraordinary if not ludicrous.

Déjà vu stung. Hap recalled the day, seven years before, when Weston's predecessor introduced a nervous but proud Hap Sweeny to the Board as the airline's new Chief Operating Officer. For his debut, Hap submitted to the machinations of a style coach, whose dark eyes, swarthy complexion, and monochrome wardrobe conjured up images of a magician. His Svengali, he remembered, got stumped by his bald scalp and became downright bitchy when Hap vetoed a shaved head. Hap cringed at the memory of the shiny dove-gray suit and pointed Italian shoes that made him feel as stilted as a wedding cake groom; a freakin' queer on a pedestal.

With a face betraying anxiety and mounting ire, Hap inched toward the trio as if in slow motion. Weston pushed past Dagger, pulling Ingrid with him. They intercepted Hap before he reached his polished target, affecting airs of normalcy. Standing between the rivals, Weston's massive frame screened curious onlookers and muffled the conversation. Arcing her neck, Ingrid beamed to the entire room drawing their stares. Her platinum hair cascaded across her face. She planted her snakeskin, peep toe pumps at Hap's toes, pivoted forward, clutched his shoulders, and kissed him on both cheeks before announcing loudly, "Dear Hap, so good to see you."

Weston looked at him with narrowed eyes. "I can't have a scene in front of my Board. Not yet," he said with a smile masking gritted teeth.

Momentarily shaken by the theatrical ambush, Hap regained his resolve. With finger wagging toward Dagger and teeth clenched, he stammered, "What... what the hell is... is *he* doing here, pimped up like a slick, Italian gigolo? Perfuming the pig. It's transparent and... asinine!" Hap's voice rose, drawing an audience of concerned faces.

He watched Ingrid survey the room as if logging reactions and identifying threats. She raised a palm to Dagger who made a move toward them.

Weston patted Hap's shoulder, his voice lowered to a whisper. "My boy, I know this has been a heckuva day. Can't be easy learnin' we're closin' in on the sale of your darlin' airline. Face-to-face horse-tradin' with TransSky makes it real. I'm sensitive to your feelin's." Hap bristled at the fake sincerity. Weston traded in chaps and a twang for pinstripes and a Park Avenue accent too long ago for the homespun crap to be believable. Hap turned toward Dagger.

Weston tilted his head. His accent moved east as the hand on Hap's shoulder pinched like a vise, the grasp rippling the fabric of his suit. "Come, come my boy. Let's take this outside where we can talk. Don't grandstand inebriated with emotion. You've built a fine reputation. Lauded for composure while others devolve into calamity and chaos. Hallmark of the consummate Chief Operating Officer, isn't that so?"

As Weston spoke, Hap barely noticed Ingrid entwine her arm with his. With little effort, she pivoted him away from Dagger and toward the door. She nodded in sync with Weston's points while pressing herself closer. He felt himself becoming intoxicated by her perfume as her grip tightened. As she maneuvered, Weston applied pressure to his back. Before he knew it, the pair manipulated him out the exit.

Hap found himself in the tomb-like reception area wedged between Weston and Ingrid. His eyes were drawn to the atrium where sunlight beamed down on Jim's fair-haired head before his slumped-shouldered form disappeared down the escalator. Hap shivered in the foyer's chilly darkness.

"Isn't that your man, Abernathy? He's certainly not progressing as we intended," Weston huffed, his head also turned toward the escalators.

Hap stiffened. He extricated himself from their clutches, removing Ingrid's arm with the care one would use to extract a tick. "Jim says culture change requires leadership support at *every level*." He jabbed with words, restraining the fist he preferred.

Weston folded his arms across his chest. "He must have been delighted then, when I scolded officers a few short weeks ago. Told them, if you recall, that employee engagement didn't rest on Abernathy's shoulders alone. Collective responsibility, I said. Got heads nodding too."

"Firm support from the pinnacle of leadership," Ingrid interjected. "Doesn't get higher than that."

He wanted to wretch. Did she really believe that baloney served up as she batted her eyes and pawed her benefactor? His glare moved from Weston to Ingrid and back again. "A stray, stale comment isn't a compelling campaign!" he blurted. "Now, let's talk about Dagger."

Any jovial affectation remaining on Weston's face vanished. His features and tone hardened. "That's exactly what we'll talk about. I suggest we find a vacant room." He raised a single finger and pushed it within inches of Hap's face. "And I didn't mention Abernathy to make small talk. Your employee cheerleader and his reckless detours are dangerous."

Weston squeezed Ingrid's arm and pushed her toward the Board meeting. "Get to work, my dear." She brushed her hands down the front of her suit and squared her shoulders. Her face lost its hardness and she fabricated a smile before disappearing behind the gilded door.

Hap and Weston walked silently, retracing their steps back to the room where they sealed the airline's fate only an hour before. Above his own pounding heart, Hap heard only the sound of Weston's labored breathing. The Chairman stopped.

Hap took it as a cue to pull the burnished handle of the conference room door. His eyes drifted to the gold-lettered plaque above the entry—*Intercontinental*. He could only laugh as he entered the pitch-black room.

Weston lowered himself into the chair at the head of the table and remained silent as Hap groped along the brocade wallpaper until he found and flipped the light switch. He turned from the wall. With only a few spotlights illuminated over the table, an ethereal light bathed Weston, accentuating his white hair and pale complexion. Hap sat to Weston's right while darkness shrouded the fringes of the cold room.

Weston folded his hands on the glossy table. He slowly turned to Hap whose anxious gaze met the Chairman's closed eyes. Weston maintained that pose for several seconds before raising his chins. His puffy gray eyes opened. "My horses don't know me anymore."

Befuddled, Hap's mind raced for meaning and context. Failing, he asked, "Your horses?"

"The world is too much with us." Weston's words dripped with pathos.

In the stale air, Hap smelled Weston's breath, a mixture of egg and coffee. The moment seemed surreal. He didn't know how to respond so he waited.

Weston cleared his throat. "You and I are captains of industry," he said. "A maligned breed. We've sacrificed much… ourselves and if we're honest, friend and foe."

Hap thought of his wives and children whose sadness always gave way to hurtful invectives. And the faces of shock and betrayal on those he fired, not to mention his old pal Charlie whose words of abandonment he couldn't shake. Examples of sacrifice flashed in his mind. That's why Jim's work was so important, for the airline yes, but also for his conscience. All that hope would vanish if he were summarily dismissed.

Weston's eyes stared past Hap, to some distant object in the darkness. "Some might say we sacrificed for career. Others, for ego." Weston paused. He turned again toward Hap who felt his expression scrutinized. Weston continued. "But, you and I know otherwise." His lips curled, forming a grin.

Hap's eyes narrowed. Weston's suggestion of kindred natures and aligned paths captivated and consoled him. Yet, uncertainty gnawed. Kinship hadn't spared Abel, he thought.

Weston inhaled, his chest thrust forward. "*Noblesse oblige,*" he said raising his nose in the air. "Wouldn't expect you to know the term. People like us are driven by duty. We see our moral obligation to lead companies and people. Weighty responsibilities, my boy. My years here have extracted a heavy price. Endless trips to Washington to fend off the likes of Congressman Klein and others, clamoring for regulation. Glad-handing shareholders and bureaucrats. New York, London, and Tokyo to court suitors." Weston tapped the table as he recited his litany. He stopped, leaned back in his chair and raised an eyebrow. Hap was mesmerized. Weston continued. "Pitiful to be titled but destitute, whoring for a wealthy mate." He sighed. "Yes, duty keeps me from my beloved horses. I've become a stranger, indistinguishable from itinerant stable hands. You know about horses?"

Hap felt as if Weston's eyes bore into his own. He froze; his breathing stalled. Had Weston gone mad? At last, he answered. "Not really."

Weston's face warmed. His eyes came alive. "Wonderful creatures: majestic, empathetic. Independent, yet appreciative for a strong and decisive hand. Once tamed, unquestionably loyal. Submissive to a firm voice." His eyes closed again. When they reopened, all animation vanished, his tone now somber. "Horses listen, they listen. My horses bring me peace. What brings you peace?"

Hap didn't anticipate the question. No one ever asked him that and he certainly never considered it. Running an airline didn't allow him to luxuriate in such indulgences. He entered the conversation with the reticence of one reasoning with a crazy man. "Not sure I crave peace. Jet fuel and airports seduce me. Where some see chaos, I see beauty."

"Yes, chaos can be a powerful stimulus," Weston said, looking into Hap's eyes. "In situations like this, one must choose words carefully."

Hap scrutinized Weston, resting his chin on his clasped hands. He grew weary of the ramblings and wanted answers. "You can cut the crap. Am I being fired?"

Weston winced as if pierced by pain. Creases formed around his eyes. "Heaven's no! Your services are still in demand, for now. I won't banish you from your Valhalla. You hear me?" A faint grin appeared on his face when he wheedled Hap's nod.

Hap rubbed a hand across his warming face. "Perhaps I'm overreacting. You're closer to realizing your vision of selling Intercontinental. Getting out of the airline business, but--"

Weston cut him off. "You make me sound mercenary. My *vision* is industry consolidation. A noble aspiration. The fate of one airline is inconsequential. Intercontinental's disappearance, merely an unfortunate outcome of a bold and selfless plan to save an ailing industry. A vibrant airline sector is key to our nation's economic might and to our national security." Weston projected his words boldly to the empty chamber. He concluded with fists pounding the polished wood.

Hap pushed himself away from the table as Weston's tirade exploded. The Chairman paused to catch his breath. He turned a cold and unwavering stare toward Hap. Suddenly Weston's face muscles relaxed. His countenance transformed back to a creaseless marshmallow. With voice lowered and cadence slowed, he asked, "How does that sound? You buy it?"

Hap clasped his hands tightly in front of him. "I don't understand. Buy what?"

"My angle. Selling the airline to restore industry health. My altruistic act to protect the country. Patriotism and all that crap. Ingrid's masterful creation. Thought I'd indulge in a dress rehearsal to get your reaction." Weston ran his fingers down his lapel. "Damn! Forgot the flag pin, a guaranteed crowd pleaser. I threw in that tone of righteous indignation on my own. So?"

Hap sighed. The man had gone mad. "Employees will feel betrayed no matter how you spin it."

"Employees?" The word delivered with a scoff. "I'm not referring to employees. No matter how we spin, they'll respond with emotionally charged prattle. Ingrid's team won't waste time creating a sympathetic employee message. That's an exercise in futility. But Cabinet material, yes?"

Hap felt dizzy. He felt his forehead vein throb. His hand shook and his lips quivered. These were the times when he wanted to wring Weston's fat neck. He inhaled to fuel his response when Weston added, patting the table, "Don't get me wrong, employee messaging will be tasteful. We won't embarrass ourselves with anything fancy that smacks of insincerity. Tubs of Chanel couldn't perfume this pig."

Hap clenched his hands under the table. "Speaking of Dagger, I suspect he's been cleaned, pressed and perfumed to assume a role in your production."

Weston's palm swatted the air. "Let's talk about Hap Sweeny—a man vital to this airline, now and during the TransSky integration. Full harmonization could take years. You need not look far to see examples." He smiled and winked at Hap. "I've asked the Board to promote you."

Hap gasped. "Promote me? To what? CEO is taken." He poked his finger toward Weston's barrel chest.

Weston laughed, seeming to scorn Hap's wagging finger. "I won't be returning to my horses for some time. TransSky won't assume complete control of this behemoth for a year or more. I'm promoting you to Chief Integration Officer."

Hap flinched. He'd never heard of such a title. "What's that?"

"You'll have far-reaching powers to impose our seamless absorption into TransSky. Your influence will calm the FAA's jitters during the two or three years necessary to merge the operating certificates."

Hap smiled, his muscles relaxed. "You need me." The childish tone of his own words struck him. He felt his face warm.

Weston patted his arm. "Never any doubt, my boy. Of course we need you. Comes with a hefty pay raise and other enticements of secondary importance to your beloved jet fuel and airport chaos."

"What about my Chief Operating Officer duties?" Hap asked, although Dagger's appearance primed his suspicions.

"I'll always think of you as the industry's premier Chief Operating Officer. None better. But, you're more valuable elsewhere. TransSky demands a credible company veteran to drive herd on the integration. The sale is contingent upon that appointment. You should be flattered."

Hap didn't care about that. He had a single focus. "You're advancing Dagger as Chief Operating Officer, aren't you?"

After a lengthy pause, Weston stood up. He inhaled. "*Sacrifice*. Both of our paths are littered with sacrifices, my boy."

"But Dagger?" Hap groaned.

Weston shrugged. "He's the only member of the team who can pull it off."

"I thought Wilkerson was your golden, go-to boy?"

"A popinjay." Spittle sprayed from Weston's pallid lips.

"A what?"

"A prick. A foppish little gnat who's only capable of bandying about my name to bully people into action. He's screwing Ingrid. Assumes she'll provide power and access, but she's just fucking with him." Weston leaned forward. He rested both hands on the table. "He's done nothing to learn the business. Your disdain for him is obvious."

"I've shown the same dislike for Dagger, yet you put your faith in him."

"You're transparent, predictable. Dagger has been your rival since I hired him. Your dislike is mere jealously, not disapproval of his abilities. Dislike and envy don't disqualify him. In fact, they bolster his credentials."

"But he's never overseen an operation, especially one as complex as ours," Hap protested.

"Dagger keeps Planning. Doesn't that make it better? The two of you have been at each other's throats like squabbling brats, vying for daddy's attention. Blaming *his* Planning or *your* Operations for our failures."

Hap's head cocked. "So now he's responsible for both?"

"Hard to cast blame when both accusatory fingers are your own." The tips of Weston's index fingers met in front of him. "Uncomfortable for Dagger, isn't it?"

Hap stroked his chin. "Poetic."

"Business schools will be teaching case studies about our success—inspiring legions of Weston and Sweeny disciples. The Weston School of Business has a nice ring."

Hap wasn't listening. He leaned forward, palms resting on the table. "I'm to have authority, emergency powers over Dagger."

"Absolute authority for integration efforts, not day-to-day operations. I won't have two Chief Operating Officers," Weston said, his tone sharp.

Hap nodded. "I understand," he replied, although he began to plot a broader definition of integration. He could make Dagger's life difficult. The repudiation of Wilkerson and the pay raise were sweet consolations.

"What about Jim?" Hap asked, recalling Weston's earlier rebuke.

Weston sneered. "Stirring up populist banter. Employees continue to focus on what's wrong with the company. I wanted to tame the beast, not agitate it."

"A matter of validation. The first step toward recovery is recognizing your demons. Venting is part of the process or so Richter tells me."

Weston slapped his hand on the table. "We don't need that kind of publicity with TransSky. They're already jumpy about integrating our spoiled brood with their contented angels. They fret about introducing a Trojan horse filled with cancerous discontent into their culture."

"But that's exactly why you authorized me to hire Jim."

"I'll say this once. Harness your wild horse or cut him loose."

Chapter 39

Jim is Briefed

After he left Hap at the hotel, Jim tried to connect with Richter, but reached voice mail. Surely the consultant would find further assault on resources frustrating. He'd likely have choice words for Tavistock and their *Lights Out* exercise. Jim felt his own light flickering.

He had fifteen minutes to grab lunch before his meeting with Dave Ramirez. Reaching the airport's food court, Jim played rancid roulette, a term he coined for using the shortest line to determine meal choice. Chance brought him chicken fried hangar steak while the *flyer upgrade* added chips and soda. Airport value pricing was an oxymoron he thought as he forked over his cash and grabbed his tray.

A jumbo jet nosed the window beside his table. Biting into his sandwich, Jim felt a slap on his back and recognized the south side Irish accent. "Airport food'll kill you or your wallet." He turned to find Tom Brophy, a company veteran who managed the airport for Wilkerson.

"You must mean the tainted food you serve employees," Jim said. He still suffered snide remarks from peers and his boss over the food poisoning incident.

"Ouch!" Brophy reeled backward. "Wilkerson already ripped me a new one for that fiasco despite recommendin' the vendor." Brophy kicked out the chair and sat down placing his cell phone and pager on the table. "You got blasted by that mess too. Sorry."

Jim bit into a potato chip. "No worries. Goes with the territory."

"But you were only the bag man. Deserved thanks, not blame. Wilkerson fingered your team. Told Hap and Weston you shoulda scrubbed the vendor list."

Jim gasped. "My buddy Wilky did that? Probably left out the part about picking the vendor."

"He's a prick. Master deflecter," Brophy said.

Jim nodded. "And if all else fails, he takes others down with him."

"For Chad the cad, blame's a team sport while glory's a solo performance," Brophy said as he leaned forward. "Don't repeat that, please."

Jim winked. "No one to tell."

"He's not happy that I sent Hap a note peggin' the incident as local, minor at that. Most of our folks loved the picnic. Embarrassed by calls to the media. By the way, no one's admitted makin' the calls."

"Thanks for telling my boss, but that wasn't necessary." Jim sucked on his straw.

Brophy shrugged. "I knew Hap when he was a reg'lar guy. You've experienced his grillings. It's a game. He already knows the answers."

"Wasted energy," Jim said, scraping crumbs to the floor.

"More like a trust test. My advice. With Hap, throw yourself on the sword, before bein' skewered."

"Thanks for the advice. He's a hard one to figure out," Jim said.

"A riddle alright. Eyes and scowl that repel like porcupine quills. Wasn't always like that. No one gets close now. Not even three Mrs. Sweenys, so I've been told." Brophy checked his watch as his gaze moved from Jim to the window.

"Patty Thorsen told him he scares people. Still, he's better than Wilkerson. That skunk envelops others in his stink." Jim pinched his nose and both men chuckled.

Brophy rose. "Speakin' of stench, gotta run to see my budget manager. We're slashin' supervisors and customer frills."

"I'm sorry," Jim said, reminded of *Lights Out.*

"We're guinea pigs for a new tool that fingers employees who dole out too many goodies to unhappy passengers. In the sacred name of accountability," Brophy said, crossing himself, "supervisors and probably managers will be crucified too!"

Jim shook his head. "Bless you. Good luck."

"Budgets have nothin' to do with luck. Slights of hand and out-finessing your boss. Failin' that we merely out-maneuver the weakest peer."

"A little luck couldn't hurt."

Brophy's blue eyes twinkled. "Need luck for my goals, all ninety four of 'em. Only a fly can focus on ninety-four things."

Jim turned to the window. His gaze took in the scores of workers from a dozen departments that came together to turn one airplane. The choreography was a thing of beauty. "We pit employees against each other every day."

Brophy pointed to the workers below. "Like gladiators. Ask any of 'em if they feel they're on the same team. They call Weston, Nero—fiddlin' while the airline collapses." He patted Jim's shoulder. "Watch your back, Jimmy. Hap better watch his too from what I hear." Brophy winked as he grabbed his pager and phone.

Jim finished his lunch absorbed by the activity surrounding the jumbo jet. He mumbled, "Down there, you're above miserable politics. Lucky bastards."

❧❖❧

As Brophy's secretary led Jim to a vacant office, she motioned to a closed door and whispered, "Frida Sallinger's using that office. She's catching a flight to New York. Walls are paper thin," she added with a wink.

"Appreciate the head's up," Jim said with a smile, wondering what business sent Weston's backdoor fixer to New York. He took a seat behind the gunmetal gray desk and scanned his messages. Sallinger's voice bore through the wall, her Long Island accent detectable despite decades in Chicago.

Meeting headhunters. Babysitting HR while searching for a new VP.... Bobble-headed Patterson crossed Shattenworter one too many times. Weston's through—said her bloated lips felt like a party balloon on his penis—feared they'd pop during... She shrieked with laughter. *Heavens no! Absolutely zero interest. Weston wants the seat warm while the sale plays out. Don't want to get stuck with a real job if the deal collapses...* She groaned. *I'd stand on Michigan Avenue with a sandwich board sourcing candidates... My current job? Excruciatingly laborious darling—Executive VP, mollycoddling Weston and kowtowing to her royal highness, Ingrid Shattenworter...Ha, yes a very high-priced...*

The call ended with the walls reverberating with Sallinger's uproarious laughter. Jim held his breath. His heart raced as the door opened then slammed shut. A sharp knock on the doorframe stirred him. He looked up to find Dave Ramirez smiling. Jim rose and extended his hand across the desk. "Thanks for trekking out to the airport to meet me. Sorry about the mix up."

Scrambling to adjust Jim's appointments after Hap's urgent call to the airport, his secretary transposed numbers sending people to a broom closet in the VIP lounge. Brophy's secretary came to the rescue but the episode furthered Jim's opinion that Mona must go. Dave sat on the stiff vinyl chair, his brow furrowed as Jim finished his tirade about Mona's incompetence. "Her mistakes make us look bad." Jim's tone, defensive. He rapped the desk with his knuckles, the rattle of empty drawers echoed through the Spartan office.

Dave inched forward. He sat on the edge of his chair. "Let me go out on a limb." Jim folded his arms. He stared across the desk as Dave continued. "Firing Mona doesn't exactly represent the kind of culture our team champions."

Jim bristled. "Careful. Ignoring poor performers like Mona isn't only bad business, it fuels critics who call us pixie-dust people. We can't protect mediocrity," Jim said, catching his reflection in the wall poster behind Dave. Piercing eyes, the frown, and creased brow reminded him of Hap Sweeny. He winced.

Dave tapped the desk. "We have to do what's right, regardless of how we look. Employees expect us to model integrity. Your words. Pardon me for saying it, but you sound like a torchbearer of our old culture."

Jim scowled. The allegation cut. Dave added, "Why not get Mona back into one of her former jobs where she was successful?"

Dave's kind face was a stark contrast to the reflection staring back at Jim from the poster. He unfolded his arms, leaned forward, and took a deep breath. "Something to think about. Thanks," Jim said with a wink. "Tell me about your work. Are our facilities and equipment as deplorable as employees say?"

"Worse! We have fifty-year-old tractors. HDQ instructs managers to borrow from other airlines. Employees sneak into competitors' bathrooms to save refurbishment costs." Dave spoke with animation.

Jim sighed. "Our idea of a refresh is shuffling old equipment between locations and adding air fresheners to dilapidated break rooms."

"How about a contest to identify the worst offenders? We could call it the *Top Ten Shames*. Just like late night TV. Employees select the best submissions. Doing the prioritizing for us."

Jim smiled. "Brilliant. Our people are involved and see results."

Dave blushed. "We can't replace everything, everywhere.

It's a start. We go until the money runs out."

Jim cupped his chin. "Maybe Finance and Purchasing will be shamed into funding more fixes." He paused. Both men shook their heads and uttered in unison. "No!"

Dave's hand waved the air. "But God forbid if bean counters can't park their asses in ergonomic chairs."

For the next hour, the two reviewed Dave's work. Jim was pleased with the progress despite limited resources. At the conclusion, he patted Dave's arm. "You're right, of course."

Dave tilted his head. "Good to hear boss, but right about what?"

"Mona. Guess I'm a product of Intercontinental's culture. It's in my blood. I settled for expediency. Instead of discarding her, I'll get her back on track."

Dave leaned back. "You had me worried."

Jim wiped his brow. "Promise to keep pulling me from the brink."

"Wouldn't be comfortable talking like this to any other leader. That's a compliment to you. We sink or swim together," Dave said. As he rose, he remarked, "Your buddy Cal Gladden contacted me. Says you approved a bigger office and a key to the executive washroom. He's kidding, right?"

Jim burst out with laughter. "What chutzpah," he said. Tell Cal you messed up. I told you to shrink his office in proportion to his productivity. And, revoke his urinal privileges for overtaxing the system with his super-size soda addiction." Dave laughed as he backed over the threshold. Jim added, "Great work. Fantastic ideas." Dave glowed.

"Hard act to follow," Evy Dial said as she entered on Dave's heels. She waited for an invitation to sit, a formality Jim tried to tame. With impeccable posture, Evy perched on the chair's edge, her crisp blouse buttoned to the neck.

Jim wanted to loosen her up, sensing great humor and wit

lurking below the rigid veneer of an engineering PhD. Evy would give his team credibility among the cynics who considered the work, fool-hearted fluff. Hap beamed, calling the recruit a conquest. With the internal war for talent a zero sum game, Hap coveted the technical prowess poached from Jacobs' Finance organization. Hap never asked about Evy's passion for employees or her burning desire to help people she confessed to Jim.

For all that Evy could bring the team. Jim saw a way to help her. He wanted to humanize her, help her transform from industrial engineer to a leader of people as well as ideas. He loved watching her grow with Lindy, Patty, and Dave as positive influences.

Jim leaned forward and gently tapped both hands on the desk. "Tell me about your work. You hired your team quickly."

She cocked her head, her expression serious, hands clenched tightly on her lap. "I assure you I employed a methodical selection process."

Jim smiled. "That wasn't a criticism. On the contrary, kudos for jumpstarting your work. Impressed with your discipline. Never seen anything like it." He didn't exaggerate. Evy spent hours reviewing applicants. Checklists, screening questions, skill and attitude matrices and a battery of round-robin interviews with her peers put HR to shame. Lindy joked, "Good thing Evy didn't recruit me. I couldn't land a job fluffin' pillows or flushin' lavs."

Evy exhaled. "I'm relieved." She pointed and added, "Be honest though if you see me doing anything wrong."

"You're doing great. Honest." He coaxed a smile. "My job's to get out of your way and let you learn. You won't always hit a homerun. That's how you grow. I give you permission to fail." Evy wrung her hands. Concern returned to her face. Jim responded. "No worries. I'll grab you before you fall. Take risks, work outside your comfort zone, and push the envelope to the edge of that cliff."

She rubbed her hands on her thighs. "Nobody's ever said that. I've always been warned not to fail."

Jim shook his head. "That's not how I operate. Mistakes are okay. In fact, I'm expecting them. That's an order."

Evy sat back, shook her long brown hair outstretched her legs and sighed. "Okay then, let's get down to business." She described plans to develop tools to validate employee investments. "My models will allow us to compete for budget."

"And cling to the scant resources we've managed to scavenge," Jim said, his mind wandering to Hap's warnings about impending cuts—*Lights Out* and the dire *for now*.

An animated tone revealed Evy's excitement. "I'll go even deeper. We'll identify programs with the greatest impact, link employee initiatives and business outcomes."

Jim threw up his hands and winked. "You make it sound so simple."

She winked back. "Necessity breeds invention."

"We got loads of necessities," Jim said.

"You said survival depends on playing Finance's game."

"I like your approach," he added.

"I'm optimistic." Evy paused. She adopted a serious expression. "Of course, I'm bound to make mistakes, even fail, but that meets your expectations—right?" They both laughed. Her finger thrust forward. "If Finance demands a return on investment, we'll give it to them."

Jim flinched. "Good thinkin' kid. I'm proud of you."

She blushed. "I'm encouraged, but I'll need some outside expertise. You budgeted for that, right?"

"I've squirreled away some money—safe, *for now*." Jim recoiled as he repeated Hap's phrase. Would the money survive *Lights Out*? The irony didn't escape him. Evy's work could be doomed without the very model to set its value. He didn't share his fears but encouraged the enthusiastic architect to continue the groundbreaking work.

Evy reached across the desk and touched Jim's arm. "I'm honored to have your faith. I love this work. I can make a difference for employees. Friends in Finance scoffed when I told them I took this job. Called me foolish. Accused me of dumbing-down to join a bunch of cake cutters and party people."

Although he winced at the familiar snipe, Jim chuckled. "Love to taste a piece of all the cake we're accused of serving up. How do you feel?"

Evy's voice trembled. "No doubt I made the right decision. I have a noble purpose for the first time in my career." She inhaled and shot him an endearing grin before adding, "The icing on that cake."

After Evy left, Jim sat in the office and reflected on yet another rollercoaster of a day. Chaos and uncertainty became the new norms. Yet with all the angst over axed resources, mysterious meetings, and the ominous sounding *Lights Out*, the passions and energy of his team gave him hope. They had faith in him, so why shouldn't he have faith in Hap, the very man who created the dragon slayers? He only hoped the lights wouldn't dim too much, making the dragons hard to find or friend indistinguishable from foe.

His phone vibrated on the metal desk. He looked down and felt relieved to see Richter's number.

Chapter 40

Jim Seeks Richter

"Caught you at last. What's up, young man?" Richter greeted Jim with the exuberance of a doting uncle.

"I needed to vent. Hap issued new guidance," Jim said. "I downed Cal's bottle of antacids." Hell, Jim thought, digesting the news served up by Hap and Frida Sallinger. Rat poison would be quicker.

"You've faced headwinds since takeoff." It sounded to Jim as if Richter was shouting into a speakerphone.

"The percentage plummets. If that even matters anymore," Jim said with a frown as he recalled Sallinger's flip comments about an imminent sale.

Richter stammered. "Per... percentage? Oh... *that* percentage."

"Hap summoned me to the airport. Informed me that your old firm, Tavistock," Jim said the name with disdain, "has been commissioned to slash costs—*including staff*."

"Don't tell me, their signature *Lights Out*. Let the inquisition begin," Richter said.

Jim welcomed the sarcasm in the consultant's voice. He needed the humor and the ally. "Figured you'd understand consultant-speak. Without so much as a shrug or a sorry, Hap carved another chunk of budget from recognition. Warned me to brace for more, Cal's ole BOHICA."

"Dare I ask?"

Jim chuckled. "Bend over, here it comes again. And that was before I heard Frida Sallinger." Jim didn't mention the sale rumblings. As a company officer, he couldn't divulge that kind of information. Better to let Hap violate SEC laws.

"What about Sallinger?" Richter asked.

"Oh, nothing," Jim said, trying to hide his embarrassment. "It's the budget slashing I'm concerned about."

"I'm sorry. You need resources, a *big bang*, especially if they want fast, dramatic results. Hap didn't pull the whole plug, did he?" Richter's voice was sympathetic.

"No, but his qualifier, *for now,* raised my hackles. Crisis excites him. It's in his eyes—a mixture of menace and megalomania."

"And fear?" Richter offered.

"Possibly. You know him better than me. Fire fighting is what Hap does best. He sucks energy from chaos." Jim closed his eyes, leaning back in his chair.

"But he still backs you. That's good."

"Yeah. He seems committed to employees. He birthed the work."

"So ego is at stake," Richter interjected. "He's gotta understand you can't perform miracle cures without resources."

Jim spoke in monotone. "Resources yanked before the treatment begins."

Richter's response was filled with empathy. "This is incredibly hard. You recruited an A-team. They signed on because of you."

"I'm trying to keep them motivated, focused. Their passion inspires *me.*"

"So their spirits are still okay," Richter said.

"Most have endured booms and busts. I'm not giving up. Can't let them down." After a few seconds of dead air, Jim spoke loudly into the phone. "You still there?"

Richter spoke. "Digesting the setback. I'll talk to Hap. I've had experience with *Lights Out.* Hang in there. I'll be in

Chicago, day after tomorrow. We'll connect."

"Wait!" Jim shouted. "The percentage. Where do you place our odds, now?"

"Safe to say it's not fifty/fifty anymore. I'll know more after I see Hap," Richter said before hanging up.

Jim looked up hoping the freaky reflection he noticed when meeting with Dave was gone. Although they may prove to be better survival tools, he drew comfort seeing his familiar face replace the piercing eyes, frown, and creased brow of Hap Sweeny. Slowly, however the picture came into focus. Why hadn't he noticed it before? The shopping mall poster depicted *Teamwork* as a group of yellow-clad skydivers plummeting to earth, hands interlocked. He shook his head. Intercontinental would eliminate parachutes. He didn't know whether to laugh or cry.

Chapter 41
Hap Seeks Richter

From the airport, Hap decided to skip a rush hour trek back into the city. He headed home instead. After a day of surprises with the Board Meeting and Weston's bizarre soliloquies, he needed time to breathe, absorb the news and soak his brain in alcohol. A jazz station provided background noise as he settled in for the long drive from O'Hare to the North Shore. He aimed the BMW east, seeming to put it on autopilot as his mind raced.

Weston played him for a fool. Or maybe he did that to himself. Instead of sticking to his principles, he caved at the first whiff of being fired. He recalled his words, worse the childish tone when Weston pulled him from the abyss—*you need me.* He cringed. How pathetic! He sounded like an insecure actor or worse, a neurotic lover embracing an adulterous partner's return.

Had he intertwined his identity so entirely into Intercontinental that the prospect of expulsion terrified him? Did he measure relevance by a fortieth floor office, a reserved parking spot and the unflinching submission of an army of underlings? Did people like Pete the country club starter scare him, empty lives once the power went out?

And for all the griping, didn't the Charlie's of the world have it easy? Nice, tidy lives outside the tornado's vortex. Get up, go to work, collect a paycheck, go home, eat dinner, and watch TV with a beer before sleeping like a baby—blissfully ignorant of the pressures that brought ulcers, heart attacks, night sweats, and broken marriages. Damn Charlie had four good decades with his sweetheart. Hell, the fool probably lived in a house with a picket fence, giggling kids, and a shaggy dog—the real American dream. Yet even poor ole Charlie wasn't satisfied.

Hap shook his head. The vein on his forehead throbbed. He cracked the car window to let in some air. Yep, bet it was the six million dollar pay package that got Charlie's blood boilin', thinkin' how rotten he had it. Hap could hear the bitterness. *I'll get me a piece a Hap's pie or make him wretch, reminded of the starving masses.* Yep, everyone had an angle and he'd finally figured out Charlie's.

The voices in his head were making him crazy. He had to talk to someone. He dialed Richter's number.

"He's selling the goddamned airline." Hap's voice quivered. He described to Richter how Weston broke the news moments before TransSky's CEO and President arrived in the conference room. After venting, he added, "He's shaking up senior leadership. Patterson's an early casualty but there'll be more. Made it crystal clear that Jim's work is out of tolerance. Drumming up outcries instead of smothering dissent."

"Weston wanted Valium and instead got crack," Richter said.

Hap was appreciative for the sarcasm. He needed laughs and an ally. "Weston named me Chief Integration Officer," he said before inhaling deeply. "Dagger succeeds me as COO." The words sounded as horrible as he imagined.

"Weston seems confident the sale will happen," Richter said.

"He and Jacobs are comparing erections. They say only a fool would pass up the discounted price and millions in cost synergies." Hap sighed. "On paper, it's a slam-dunk—little overlap, similar airplanes and oodles of customers to squeeze for more business at lower discounts."

"And you?"

"Maybe I'm a fool. I got my doubts. The buyer runs a great airline, consistently profitable with high scores from customers and employees," Hap said, casting his eyes to the horizon. He admired the Intercontinental jet climbing, banking to the northwest. *Tokyo. On-time,* he thought. "Get this, the buyer refuses to outsource or displace a single employee."

Hap heard the chuckle. "I would've waived my fee to see their faces when they got that juicy morsel," Richter said.

"*Foolishness!* Jacobs cried. *Fiduciary folly,* Weston sneered. Their dicks went limp," Hap said with a hearty laugh. "But TransSky has great labor relations. Unheard of in our business."

"Employee and customer satisfaction usually go hand in hand," Richter said.

"That's why I think the sale is in jeopardy. TransSky pressed for our satisfaction data. Weston and Jacobs don't take the request seriously. Convinced these guys will focus on the financial plums dangled in their faces. I give the sale a fifty/fifty chance."

"Everyone has percentages," Richter mumbled.

Hap wrinkled his nose. "What?"

Richter spoke louder and clearer. "Nothing. Tell me about Jim's work. Won't a sale be the death blow?"

"Not at all. May be the best chance for survival."

"But a buyer will have their own ideas about employee experience," Richter said.

"Absolutely! Jim's focus shifts, that's all. He'll support the integration." After his session with Weston, Hap considered the resources he'd need to be successful in his new role. Jim and his team were naturals to jump-start the work.

"The Achilles heel of most mergers," Richter said. Airline employees are notoriously stubborn. They've been known to cling to allegiances long after their carrier vanished."

"Eastern, Western, Southern, PSA, Piedmont, TWA, et-cetera," Hap said, tapping his fingers to the litany. "Each has legions of employees in denial. That's where Jim comes in. Sale covenants require we support workforce harmonization."

"But you gave the sale a fifty/fifty chance. What happens if it falls through? I can see Jim's team continuing to support Dagger and Operations."

Hap responded without hesitation, his hands clutching the leather steering wheel. He'd been over this in his head. "Absolutely not. I won't set Dagger up for success. Jim's team is my creation." The line went quiet. "Richter? You still there?"

"Still here," Richter answered. "Assuming you want me to help Jim redirect the team toward integration." Hap rolled his eyes at the judgmental tone.

"Start thinking about it, but don't move yet. The sale isn't definite; Jim's in the dark. In the meantime, we're launching an exercise to cut costs," Hap said, sneering at a TransSky Airbus on final approach.

"So I've heard. You're using Tavistock."

Hap grinned at the consultant's access to insider information. "Deal or no deal. We gotta get costs under control to remain an attractive match. And if that fails, we gotta turn over every rock just to survive."

"Is it *Lights Out* for Kyle Richter?"

Hap chuckled to himself. He loved Richter but the man always brought the conversation back to his fees. "Not for now. Jim's work is becoming an irritant to Weston. With a looming sale, people initiatives have diminished in value."

"Why doesn't Weston kill it outright?" Richter asked. "He hooked a buyer."

"He faces a delicate balance in the short term. He's trying

to keep the company an appealing bride. *Lights Out* is a financial diet to squeeze the binging bride into her gown. Jim's effort keeps the homely maiden veiled. Provides convenient cover as Weston thwarts his suitor from peeking at satisfaction scores. The data would show that our bride shouldn't wear white."

He heard Richter's sigh before the consultant spoke. "I've seen the survey results. I suggest scarlet. So the employee effort survives as a diversionary tactic. The promise of a chaste maiden."

"There's something else," Hap said.

"What's that?"

"The lid's been cracked on Pandora's box. The masses are encouraged by talk of employee investments. While Ingrid has attempted to keep Jim's work low-key, word slipped out. Expectations are high."

"Hard to put toys back in the box without a tantrum," Richter said.

Hap scowled at an idling school bus, its stop sign extended as several lackadaisical kids stepped off. The boy in the back seat flipped him off. "Weston's talking outta both sides of his ass. He cites Jim's work to his advantage with the Board and Washington regulators. He can't squash the effort without raising the ire of employees and congressmen."

Richter chuckled. "Threatening to deflower his blushing bride before the *I dos* and ring exchange. You and your cohorts sure know how to complicate things."

An incoming call clicked Hap's phone. Amber's name flashed on the screen. He better take it. His mind jumped to the conversation awaiting him at home. With echoes of the first two Mrs. Sweenys, Amber grew increasingly frustrated. She complained he excluded her from the most enjoyable part of his life, *his work*. Called him, *unavailable,* physically and emotionally. The anonymous caller didn't help matters. Could

Amber really believe he and Ingrid were having an affair? But he couldn't tell her how far off the mark she was. He wasn't screwing Ingrid, rather Weston's secretary Kay.

He tried to get Richter off the phone. "Gotta go," he barked. "Schedule visits with leaders, especially my… I mean Dagger's Ops people. Ask if they still value Jim's initiative." Hap expected to hang up but the consultant cleared his throat with exaggeration. "Okay Richter. I know that signal. What's on your mind?"

"You could influence the outcome by stating your strong support for Jim. COO or not, you're still one of the most powerful people at Intercontinental."

Hap swallowed hard. He'd have to come clean. "If Jim's work must disappear due to cost pressures, Weston's fickle whims--"

"Or Dagger's elevation to Chief Operating Officer," Richter interrupted.

Hap sighed. "Yes, that too. With likely employee backlash, better to frame the decision as a broad consensus among company leaders—"

"Than as the embarrassing surrender of its powerful sponsor. I get it," Richter interrupted. "Collaboration at last," he mumbled.

Hap furrowed his brow. "What?"

Richter added boldly, "I can predict the outcome. Could save you time and money given the cost pressures and rhetoric coming from the executive suite."

Hap's forehead vein throbbed more intensely. Since when did Richter care about saving time and money? He wasn't in any mood to let Richter stoke the fires of his conscience. His survival instincts never let him down. "I'm counting on that result. The dog and pony show gives legitimacy. We won't release your findings until we have to."

"You mean, *unless* you have to. Isn't that right?" Richter asked.

Hap's tone sharpened. "Yes, yes, for now." He hung up the phone. But it was too late for Amber's call.

The car put distance between him and the embarrassing episode at the hotel. As for Weston, two can play at shock and awe. Hap Sweeny wasn't about to play second fiddle to that idiot Dagger. Damned if either of them would get the better of him. Next time, he'd tell Weston to fuck off.

He reached into his breast pocket as he had done dozens of time since getting Charlie's letter those many months ago. He scoffed. How foolish he'd been to tote it around like a scarlet letter. He could free himself of the unfair burden. His fingers tugged at the tattered paper. A feeling of liberation swelled within him as he pulled the letter and let it flutter to the passenger seat.

Chapter 42

Richter's Confessions

The sun filtered into Kyle Richter's North End townhouse where he sat at the kitchen table picking at his laptop and the remnants of a late lunch, leftovers in Styrofoam from some prior meal. He wore trousers found draped over the banister while the matching jacket remained balled on the sofa where the consultant tossed it on his return from Logan.

The house provided refuge from lengthy road trips, although an actuary joked that the clumsy consultant tempted fate since statistics proved most accidents occurred at home. Antiques complemented the colonial pedigree while fabrics, survivors of his shuttered family business, crafted curtains, upholstery, and wallpaper, reminders that beauty, honor, and tradition were easily lost to hubris and greed.

With hair uncombed, Richter rubbed his bare feet to ward off the chill that rose through the well-worn floorboards. He faced the multi-paned window, glancing into the backyard common, dominated by two massive chestnut trees as he pondered the calls in rapid succession from two desperate men.

First Jim. Richter had grown fond of the younger man who he saw as a visionary, able to build consensus through respect and hard work. Now, he felt sorry for him. The traits that made Jim an ideal candidate—sympathetic, collaborative, creative, thoughtful—were the qualities that doomed him. The current culture was rebelling. Company leaders were making things difficult. Ingrid and HR weren't alone. One executive even told Jim to *shit in his own litter box,* but Jim was too professional to repeat the slight or complain to Hap. Now he had to work under the specter of Lights Out.

Richter looked down at the words scribbled and underscored in his notebook, mentioned by Jim and repeated by Hap. He knew the routine. Zealous Tavistock ingénues eager to earn their six-figure salaries would seek redundant heads with the passion of big game hunters. Even if Jim survived, would he find receptive recruits among the scarred battlefield willing to listen? Richter shook his head, envisioning the classic hierarchy of human needs. Between *Lights Out* and a sale, the organization would be reeling at the bottom of the pyramid clamoring for survival basics. Jim's message would fall on deaf ears.

Richter rose from the table and poured coffee that sloshed over the cup's rim. Stains too stubborn for the cleaning lady marked the trail from pot to workspace. He sat again tugging his eyebrows as his thoughts turned to Hap. With eyes bored into the scribble, *LIGHTS OUT,* he clenched his jaw recalling Hap's assurances to Jim's anxious team at their first meeting. In an emphatic tone, Hap pledged: *Your work is our top priority. You must succeed if we are to succeed. My reputation and career are on the line. You have my unyielding support.* Richter shook his head; why wasn't Hap fighting?

Maybe Hap was right. Diverting Jim's mission toward integration might be his salvation. But Hap wasn't a selfless humanitarian. He made his motives clear. Jim would either help Hap or be discarded as a political liability. And like armies that destroy bridges and supply depots in their wake, Hap would sacrifice Jim instead of letting Dagger get hold of the valuable resource.

Richter detected something in Hap's voice. Was fear poisoning his thinking? Perhaps as the dust settled and Hap's position stabilized, he'd honor his pledges to Jim and his team.

Richter would help Jim as much as he could, maybe until Hap came to his senses. But fear was the most dangerous of emotions because it was unpredictable. Would there be enough time? He sighed. Is this how a priest felt—sins heard but judgment withheld?

Richter lost track of time. Evening produced longer shadows across the floor planks. A chill stung his feet. His coffee was stone cold. "Won't take a wooly caterpillar to predict an early winter." He spoke, gazing toward the chestnut trees animated by a breeze. The leaves glittered with silver hues. "I saw those trees leaf in spring when Hap began this effort. I'll be surprised if Jim lasts until autumn bares every branch. Unbelievable!"

His ringing cell phone startled him—another Chicago area code. "Richter here." Ambient noise suggested a speakerphone.

A deep voice boomed across the line. "Richard Weston of Intercontinental Airlines."

Richter sat up. Rubbing his feet together, he felt naked. His hand flew to his chest for a tie but grasped only a cotton T-shirt. "Yes sir."

"You perform substantial work for my airline or should I say, we receive huge invoices from your firm." The words of the patrician voice came as a statement, not a question.

Richter detected the muffled snicker of a woman. He responded, "I've been privileged to work with Intercontinental for many years."

"And hope to continue that relationship well into the future. That could happen."

"I certainly hope so," Richter said, fearing *Lights Out*.

"Good. Then we're on the same page. This is what I need you to do…"

Chapter 43

Weston in Manhattan

Marathon negotiating sessions began the Thursday before the long Labor Day weekend. Manhattan, seen as neutral ground, provided anonymity as well as easy access to cadres of merger and acquisition specialists, many of whom groused about surrendering the season's last hurrah in the Hamptons— gin and tonics sipped by the *Fabulous* set attired in linen jackets and smart black dresses on well-manicured lawns.

But anguish proved transitory. The parade of imported sports cars along Further Lane and weekend visitors to quaint million dollar retreats would have to wait. A bonanza of billable hours, rich fees and the promise of sweetened year-end bonuses induced euphoria, cheaper and more sustainable than artificial highs, legal or otherwise, found on the end of Long Island.

The Intercontinental team anchored by Weston and CFO Bryce Jacobs padded their ranks with Wall Street's best, brightest and most expensive hired guns. Chief Counsel, Lyle Pavlis, Ingrid Shattenworter and SWAT teams from finance, law and communications also hunkered down for the duration. The battalion encamped at the Mandarin Hotel at Columbus Circle, ceding mid-town to TransSky Airlines who bivouacked at the Waldorf-Astoria. Couriers shuttled documents between camps all weekend while the Rockefeller Center offices of the nation's top M&A attorneys served as ground zero for face-to-face negotiations. Skirmishes between lawyers and scuffles among consultants flared and abated as the deal inched forward.

By late Sunday, the battle weary adversaries forged an agreement. While the transaction smelled in every way like an acquisition of Intercontinental by TransSky, both sides ultimately agreed to the term *merger*.

Weston argued the point with passion. "Semantics cost neither of us one cent. The modest concession placates labor, calms customers and quiets communities." He glared menacingly from puffy, bloodshot eyes at his TransSky sparring partner who had suggested with a boarding school sneer, "The rhetoric's only value is to soothe the battered egos of Intercontinental leaders."

Both teams used Labor Day morning to brief respective boards and union leaders, harmonize messages and finalize communication plans. The nuptials would be announced publicly, before the market opened on Tuesday. Weston and his counterpart, Steve Ridgeway, TransSky's CEO, would remain in New York. In a show of solidarity, the two commanders would hold a joint news conference at the Wall Street offices of TransSky's financial advisors at 8am. The symbolic gesture intended to show the business community and traveling public that the union was amicable.

The plans then called for the two CEOs, sporting fraternity brother grins, to fly to Washington for a dinner with DOT officials to loosen their ties before a Wednesday morning meeting with the same stiff-collared bureaucrats. A reception with Congressman Klein would follow before courtesy calls to the FAA and Department of Justice. Blessings from the government agencies augured well for the union's approval.

Klein had been labeled a media nuisance rather than decision maker. Ingrid advised the two CEO's, "With his Capitol Hill platform, the man can screw us. Stroking his ego for sixty minutes serves us all well for the mere cost of a Cobb salad and coke."

"To cement the deal, I'd gladly stroke something else," an ebullient Weston replied, gesturing obscenely with his pudgy hand. Ridgeway's jaw dropped while Ingrid squealed.

Ingrid laughed, telling Weston that her lieutenant, Scott Underlicht, went sleepless for three days. "Kept him busy. Washington will be ready for our visit." Intercontinental's brass would camp at the Willard Hotel. Underlicht had orders to provision Weston's favorite sheets, shampoo, and cognac in the usual suite.

Meg Orkin, Ingrid's cackling aide-de-camp, with a script scrubbed and sanctioned by her boss, began calling senior company executives Labor Day morning. The need-to-knows included heads of major operating divisions like Wilkerson and junior officers who oversaw large contingents of employees. Jim's name was not on that list. A dour Hap Sweeny in his role as Chief Integration Officer placed the exclusive group on high alert in secret briefings, feeding them talking points and instructions at the same time for visiting key company installations.

Secrecy shrouded the mission. Flight reservations were booked under dummy names. Implementation would commence Labor Day evening with officers moved into position for employee briefings beginning Tuesday. The idea of fanning out company leaders to inform and calm employees came from TransSky who shared their comprehensive communication playbook.

Flipping the document with eyebrows arched Ingrid sighed. "Workable," she said in a monotone voice. "With modifications of course. Tone down employee assurances and augment shareholder benefits. Then, yes, quite adequate."

Weston spent Labor Day sharing anecdotes, even finding humor in some of the most horrific times marking his Intercontinental career. Uncharacteristically chipper, he went out of his way to thank lower level staff for sacrificing their long weekends. Shadowed by an aid whispering names into his ear, Weston delivered hearty slaps on the back and shoulder jabs to the slack-jawed staffers.

⚜

By late Monday afternoon with plans set and the Board's rubber stamp obtained, launch sequence initiated. Weston and Jacobs sank into chairs beside the floor-to-ceiling windows of the Mandarin's lobby lounge, thirty-five floors above Columbus Circle. From that perch, the views of Manhattan and a bustling Central Park impressed and distracted.

Weston's shirt sported platinum cufflinks fashioned into globes with diamonds marking his birthplace but in a bow to holiday informality, he shed his tie. He sipped single malt scotch as his mind catalogued his accomplishments. Heck, many said it couldn't be done, but he did it. He sold the old mare as if she were a derby winner. All he had to do now was sit back and wait. The call to serve in the cabinet would come.

Jacobs, slurping through his second gin and tonic reclined, practically supine, his timber-like legs outstretched. Upon the duo's return from their lawyer's office where the Board convened in secret, the CFO traded his suit for khakis, a yellow polo and topsiders. He sighed. "I'm spent. This deal's been more of a ball buster than two rounds of bankruptcy." He beckoned a server with a wave of an empty nut dish.

"Bankruptcy gave us leverage. Anyone owed a dime, banks, lessors, aircraft manufacturers, airports, unions," Weston said, using fingers to track the list, "sat with sweaty palms and knocking knees afraid we'd fold." He chuckled. "The end of the gravy train. An ounce of fat better than none at all."

"And praying for more to come," Jacobs added, his drink resting on his stomach.

"Tables are turned. We'd be toast if TransSky balked." And although he didn't say it to Jacobs, his political aspirations would be over. He'd face ridicule and a chorus of told-you-soers as he rode into the sunset a failure. But success was his. His chest puffed.

Jacobs grinned, picking a peanut shell from his teeth with his pinkie. "Masterful maneuvering. Your impassioned plea for the teetering industry's future and that dramatic soliloquy touting TransSky's destiny as savior. Yep, you clinched the deal," Jacobs said with bobbing head. "Richard Weston's too big to fail."

Weston postured, seeking his reflection in the window. "Can't take all of the credit. Your proposal to clean house on our watch polished the deal."

"Employees will be infuriated," Jacobs said with a shrug. "Not a criticism, merely fact."

Weston turned from the window with an air of grandeur. "We will be vilified. Every titan is. But I won't be bullied. History will be kind, even if employees aren't."

"Hell if that matters. The deal makes us rich." Jacobs jiggled his drink, ice clanking, before downing the remainder and snapping his fingers for a third.

Weston toyed with a cufflink. "History rewards victors and clever men." The two sat in silence before Weston added, "Something Ridgeway said keeps eating at me."

"Yeah, what's that?"

"Rubbed our Chief Employee and Passenger Officers in my face. I've never been so humiliated."

Jacobs nodded. "Yep, you turned beat red. Thought you'd have a stroke," he said before popping cashews into his mouth.

"Condescending crap!" Clutching his drink, Weston exaggerated the TransSky CEO's southern accent. "*Take Japan Motors, tops in customer ayand employee satisfaction. Emagine thayat!*"

Qualitee isn't ayan afterthought thayat needs to be policed, eet's paht of every process. No qualitee control department ayand no employee or customer happiness ayat TransSky because employees ayand customers aren't afterthoughts. Well fiddle dee dee! Aargh!" Agitated hands splattered scotch onto his trousers.

"Ridgeway didn't bait you intentionally. Seems like a decent chap." Jacobs spoke with his mouth full. He missed Weston's glare by looking toward the park as he gulped his drink.

Weston didn't protest. He knew that Jacobs checked out. Probably sat there with that shit-faced grin thinkin' how he only had to endure the bullshit until the deal closed. In a few short months Jacobs would be free. Even confessed a hankerin' to move to Manhattan to join a venture capital firm. Weston followed Jacobs' stare to a banner advertising park view condos from $3.5 Million.

Weston's cell phone rang. He recognized Ridgeway's number. They traded calls for weeks. "Hello Steven. Hope you're enjoying a little down time before our big cavalcade commences in the morning," he said as he snatched his drink from the side table. Seconds later, it dropped. Glass rattled glass. Jacobs jumped, his eyes turned toward the noise.

Weston's jaw dropped, his heart pounded. Girth impeded his ability to lean forward. His flailing legs unintentionally kicked Jacobs in both shins. "What? I don't understand—not comfortable? We've been over that. Your Board supports your decision... Is there no way? Very disappointing." Weston closed his eyes. His cadence slowed. "Yes, we both have many things to do. Touch base later in the week."

Jacobs sat up. He leaned toward Weston as his hands rubbed his ankles. "You okay? Not a stroke, is it?" he asked with a frantic expression.

Weston inhaled. His lips curled slowly into a grin. Before his cell phone returned to his pocket, an alternate scheme popped into his head. He wasn't about to let the deal get away. Skittish, that's all, like a nervous filly he thought. He winked at Jacobs. "Merely a case of cold feet," he said. "If TransSky won't wed, we'll be fuck buddies—friends with benefits." He pulsed his eyebrows. "Code share buys us time to woo with guile. We'll show them we're still a good catch."

Weston spent the next two hours on the phone briefing his board and calling his executive team to rally the troops. He instructed Hap and Dagger to eliminate the subjects of Ridgeway's scorn, *immediately*.

He yelled into the phone. "We gotta get TransSky into bed, gotta make them want to fuck. These positions make us look bad. Like hanging a freakin' student pilot sign on a plane— *amateur*. Tell Abernathy and Presto, officers must go... I don't care what you say... blame fuel, blame global warming, pull out the violins and hankies. Call it noble given the sacrifices we'll be asking of employees."

Weston covered the phone and said to Jacobs, "Shit, now I'm doing Ingrid's work. That mawkish sap will spin well with employees. Officer sackings always do." Back into the phone, he screamed. "Get it done, or I'll do it myself."

Reinvigorated, Weston declared, "I'll be damned if I get stuck running this airline."

Chapter 44

Jim Gets Surprise News

The day after Labor Day usually generates little news. Heaving a collective sigh, Americans pack away summer whites and holiday attitudes to refocus on ambitious pursuits. Airline finance managers lament revenue dives while their employees celebrate the survival of another season of full airports and airplanes, doe-eyed travelers with oversized expectations and suitcases, squeezed-out business flyers, and irritable co-workers frustrated by the clamor of customers and thunderstorms.

This sunny Tuesday after two hits of the snooze button, Jim grabbed the TV remote off the nightstand. He scanned the morning news as he eased out of bed. Even though Julie slept in the guest room, he lowered the volume to avoid waking her. In the weeks since she returned home, the couple had established domestic routines that adapted to their new détente. Having her under the same roof gave him peace and hope that he could find a way to change her mind.

Jim hoped that working less weekends and catching earlier trains established a pattern of normalcy that Julie would warm to. He kept secret, the sent-out resumes and the contacted headhunters, not wanting to raise her expectations, especially since he hadn't even gotten a nibble. He planned to wait until he had something tangible to share, reminding himself that *talk is cheap*. Lack of interest by prospective employers, he wanted to believe, was merely the summer doldrums and not his lopsided career spent exclusively with a twice-bankrupt airline with a poor track record of leaders. Things would pick up after Labor

Day, he told himself. He still had time before the baby arrived.

His ears perked at the end of the business report hearing a reference to Intercontinental. He moved to the edge of the bed, pet the dog with one hand and channel surfed through news reports with the other. The story pieced together. After the info became repetitive, he turned to email where he found a terse company message to employees. In addition, Patty, Lindy, Cal, and Kelly Green among others forwarded a lengthy letter apparently sent by TransSky management to its employees. From the dozen or so other emails, Jim assumed the competitor's more comprehensive note exploded like buckshot throughout Intercontinental.

TransSky employees, Jim gathered from all the bits of information, reported to work greeted by the following letter.

Dear Colleagues,

We want to inform you about a series of events concerning our company that will soon be reported by the media. Over the past several months, we've entertained merger discussions with Intercontinental Airlines. Negotiations reached a critical stage over the weekend. Last night after much deliberation, we notified their CEO, Richard Weston III, we couldn't consummate the transaction.

Your leaders decided the proposed combination wouldn't serve the best interests of our employees, customers and consequently, shareholders. You've transformed TransSky into a world-class airline. Your dedication and loyalty to customers and each other have made us strong. Our team is the industry leader in customer satisfaction. The merger compromised that good work.

We recognize the pressures on our industry. Rest assured, we won't take any action that compromises corporate values or weakens our company. We remain proud of you and honored to serve as your CEO and President. Steve & Alex

The airline notified media outlets that a press release would be issued late morning, the delay intended to give the

TransSky family opportunity to digest the news.

Intercontinental released a statement, simultaneously to the media and employees at one minute after midnight, that Tuesday:

Merger negotiations with TransSky Airlines have been suspended. Intercontinental management and its Board of Directors believe consolidation within the US airline industry is necessary to restore financial health to the ailing sector, vital to the nation's commerce and security. Intercontinental continues to oppose regulations, including foreign ownership limitations, which tie our hands. Chairman, Richard Weston III affirms his commitment to shareholders. Protecting and enhancing their investment is his primary goal. Inquiries can be made to Investor Relations.

Jim cradled his head. The adrenaline rush from the news reports swept away any lingering sleepiness. He was surprised at his relief. The talks, speculated for months, were exposed at last. Leaders kept junior vice presidents like him in the dark, no doubt bowing to SEC requirements. Still, he sat amazed at the terse statement. "Employees will be shell shocked," he mumbled. He considered TransSky's message, *brilliant,* informational, and inspirational. "Masterful," he said aloud. "TransSky's too good to associate with us. From the glaring disparity in messages, they're right."

He imagined Weston and Ingrid applauding their words while snickering at TransSky. He could hear them—*Emotional rot. Greeting card drivel.* A chuckle quickly gave way to anxiety. Now what would Weston do?

As he pulled on trousers and eyed his tie rack, he knew his team would want answers. He wished he had more information but he wasn't scheduled to meet Hap until 9am.

Blocks from the office, the vibration in his pocket signaled an incoming email. *Morning. Left VM on office phone. Hap meeting moved to 5pm. The place is up for grabs—Winny.*

Chapter 45

Jim Gets an Offer

As Jim waited outside Hap's office, he struck up a conversation with Winny, the white-haired pixie with a terrier personality. Although always pleasant to him, she seemed extra chatty this afternoon asking about his wife, mother, and the family's preparations for a newborn. As he spoke, squinting at the sun-glittered river out the window behind her, he almost forgot the anxiety of his impending meeting.

News of the failed TransSky merger shocked the workforce. Worry consumed everyone. Productivity tanked as gossip surged. Jim spent the morning calming his team although the terse press release offered the only information. Ingrid promised FAQs, but they remained undistributed by day's end, an apparent victim of surprise and a Byzantine approval process. The building was deserted. People sulked home early or clustered in bars to fret over scenarios of the next shoe to drop. Was Hap about to drop a wingtip on him?

Winny pushed her candy dish toward him as he adjusted his tie. "Shouldn't be much longer," she said. "Sallinger's just wrapping up."

"I'm sure he's had quite a day." Jim said, making small talk. But the mention of Frida Sallinger, Weston's shadowy enforcer, unsettled him like a shard of glass boring through his stomach. His imagination went wild manufacturing reasons for her visit. "The mood around here's bleak," he added. That assessment included his feelings.

Winny nodded. "Felt it the second I walked through the

revolving door. Sullen faces, whispers and people huddled in hallways." She shrugged her shoulders. "But, que sera, sera— no sense worrying about something that hasn't happened."

Or that we can't control, Jim thought. He motioned toward his boss's closed door. "Hope he's in a good mood."

Winny peered over her glasses. "No telling. Been holed up all day. Ventured out only for a meeting with…" Her eyes veered toward Weston's office. "Other than your buddy Richter and Sallinger, no other visitors."

So Richter was already in Chicago. Why hadn't he said anything? He usually called or texted as a courtesy should Jim need to meet. He pushed aside the surprise as a logical consequence of Richter's influence and the likely confusion sweeping through the executive suite at TransSky's rebuff.

A brooding figure with stooped shoulders entered Jim's peripheral vision. He turned to see Wilkerson trudging from the direction of Weston's office. Avoiding eye contact with Winny or Jim, Wilkerson grunted. Jim discerned the mumble as, "He can go fuck himself." Wilkerson walked away pinching his bottom lip.

Jim whispered to Winny, "Tough day for everyone." His eyes followed Wilkerson plod down the hall. "People are anxious, torn. Happy with the status quo, but aware it's only a temporary bump in Weston's plan. Lots of outrageous rumors."

Winny cleared her throat. "Even those against a merger are infuriated by TransSky's snub." They both chuckled before she added. "Fear has an odor. Smelled it after nine-eleven and when we declared bankruptcy. This too shall pass."

"You're probably right, but they'll need to hear reassurances from leaders." Jim nodded toward Weston's isolated bunker.

Fingering the buttons of her pink sweater, Winny rolled her eyes. "Still the optimist, I see."

A buzz of activity at Weston's end of the floor drew his attention. Weston's secretary was directing a team from building maintenance. "What's up?" Jim asked reaching for another foiled chocolate.

"They're dismantling a wall."

"I thought Weston craved seclusion. Doesn't that compromise privacy?"

"Wants better access to Dagger. Ours is not to question why." Her face flashed a firm but pleasant expression. Jim understood the cue. The terrier exercised patience with one she liked, but a friendly growl signaled the limit of her candor.

He winked. "We'll find out soon enough."

Sallinger emerged from Hap's office. She carried a leather portfolio and sported the day's grim expression, a poor accessory for the canary yellow suit. She shouted over her shoulder as her black Prada pumps crossed the threshold. "Whoever called airlines glamorous was neither investor, customer, nor employee. If I didn't have three mortgages, I'd retire. Weston won't let me go." Jim met Winny's eyes suggesting a shared opinion about the comment's absurdity.

Sallinger bowed her head. "Hap's expecting you."

Jim nodded to both women and disappeared into the office. Inside the sanctum, he shivered. Shades had been drawn against sun and city. Hap sat, seemingly dwarfed by the massive desk. His blank stare unsettled more than his usual scowl. The amber lampshade and desk's cherry hues provided the room's only warmth.

Speechless, Jim remained standing. He waited for his boss to break the silence. Hap looked pale, his laurel of hair more silver and his features worn like the face on an old coin. The eyes blinked lifeless and gray. The isolation Jim perceived in that first meeting months before, felt more pervasive.

Hap sputtered to life. He rose from the desk, disappearing

into the shadows before emerging with outstretched hand. Thin, pursed lips looked blue as they formed a smile. He motioned Jim to a table where a single spotlight reflected off the glass top. Jim remembered the corner seat against the window as the exact spot where Hap pressed him into service.

Hap spoke as he lowered himself into a chair. He appeared brittle, his voice weak. "Another banner day at Intercontinental. Your team's probably asking the same questions as every employee. Same goes for everyone in the executive suite, *every one*." Hap's eyes drifted toward the closed door.

"People are stunned," Jim said, folding his arms across his chest to ward off the cold air blown by ceiling vents.

Hap slouched as he spoke from the opposite chair. "A cruel business. Labor strife, fuel shocks, high capital costs and La Guardia delays, the only constants."

Jim studied Hap's face, trying to identify the prevailing emotion -- sadness, anger, fear or defeat. As usual, the man was a riddle. It could have been any or all of those or something entirely different. Jim mustered an encouraging tone. "Yet, you've been at Intercontinental forty years and I've logged over twenty—second generation. The industry's addictive, impossible to abandon."

Hap's eyes seemed to study Jim's face. He cupped his chin. "An unhealthy obsession."

The words sounded eerily similar to their conversation when Hap asked Jim to tackle the employee initiative. "Although Intercontinental has suffered more than most, it hangs on as do people like us," Jim said.

Hap shrugged. His fingers tapped the table as he leaned into the spotlight. "Not without casualties."

"Too many, I'm afraid," Jim said. He noticed Hap's wrinkled shirt. For the first time he ever remembered, the spit and polished COO looked tarnished.

Hap ran his hand over his scalp and inhaled. "I originally scheduled a morning meeting."

Jim nodded. "I'm sure the merger news kept you busy."

Hap's tongue clicked against his palate. "Blindsided. Changed everything. I planned to tell you of my appointment to lead the integration."

"Logical, given your background and company knowledge," Jim said, grabbing the table edge. It felt like ice to his touch.

Hap looked into his eyes, holding the gaze without blinking. "I intended to redeploy your team to workforce harmonization."

"I'm flattered, but guess that's now moot. Assuming we stay the course, for now." Jim noticed Hap stiffen, hands dropping to his lap. Had *for now* just expired? "Fair assumption?"

Hap looked over Jim's shoulder to the window. "I'm sorry for our employees."

Jim leaned forward, both arms on the table. His boss's pained countenance perplexed him. Unease rose. "Many are happy the merger fell through."

"TransSky runs a great airline," Hap said. "In terms of employees, *they get it*. Our people would have been better off."

Jim froze, astounded by the declaration. The all-powerful Hap Sweeny admitted failure. Surely Hap realized the self-incriminating pronouncement. As second in command, he was a chief architect of the status quo.

Hap continued. "But, that's yesterday's diversion. Today we file a new flight plan."

"And, that would be?" Jim asked, cocking his head.

"Instead of integration, I assume the role of Chief Administration Officer. Divine retribution. Weston is bestowing HR, Public Relations and Communications on me."

Jim's mouth fell open. "They'll report to you?"

"Ironic. My disdain for those organizations is no secret. Now they're mine, all mine."

"What about Operations?" Jim's eyes narrowed.

Hap gritted his teeth; hands clutched thighs. "Dagger adds COO to his current responsibilities. Merger or no merger, Weston decided."

Jim now understood Wilkerson's sour mood. He banked on the job that went to Dagger. Surely he felt Weston betrayed him.

Hap's eyes turned metallic. "Richter will coach Dagger. Don't be surprised to see our silk-suited COO shaking hands and kissing babies. Weston will spare no expense on the metamorphosis. Ingrid will mount a sweeping campaign to paint Dagger as an enlightened leader and Intercontinental as a cutting-edge company."

Hap's candor surprised Jim. "Where does my team fit... and me?"

Hap sat up. He inhaled and held a deep breath before responding. "In the short time you've been vice president, you've made much progress. The officer title gave your work credibility. We've spent millions on equipment and employee facilities. You've resurrected recognition. Leadership initiatives are gelling. Remarkable given the obstacles you've faced."

"Headwinds and brick walls," Jim said with a nod. This was the first time Hap acknowledged the challenges and the accomplishments for that matter. Still, Jim's shoulders tensed, his hands clenched on his lap. He braced for the *but*.

Hap spoke with what Jim felt was a forced smile. "You can be proud."

"Thanks. Wish we could do—"

Hap interrupted him. "But with soaring oil prices and employee sacrifices..." Hap paused. He fidgeted. "We can't justify... the current number of vice presidents."

Jim's heart sank. He took a moment to recover from the blow. Hap sat silent his expression frozen. Finally Jim asked. "You're eliminating my position?"

"Not just yours. Presto's job is gone as well as vp's in finance and project management."

The fact that the latter two positions were vacant and Presto was a gazillionaire with little company loyalty offered no consolation. Jim fought swelling emotions. "And my team?"

Hap pushed himself from the table. "Safe, *for now*. Your pal Richter convinced me they fill a void. We'll study that decision. But the team will merge into HR now that I have that responsibility. Sallinger tells me job candidates balked at a renegade team performing traditional HR functions."

Jim was confused. His renegade team was okay when HR didn't report to Hap. He pressed an index finger to the corner of his eye. "Does Richter know I'm being dismissed?"

Hap held up a palm. "Slow down. While we gotta cut your vice presidency, I'm hoping you stay."

Now he was even more confused. Hap was talking in riddles. "What do you mean?"

"I want you to be a Director reporting to the new head of HR."

Jim's head snapped back. "Doing what?"

"Exactly what you're doing now—with everything in tact. And I do mean *everything*—salary, perks, benefits." Hap leaned forward. His expression conveyed excitement like the bingo emcee convinced the just-plucked ball would prompt a winning shriek.

"*Everything?*" Jim asked, rubbing his forehead. "Except the title."

"Precisely! You keep your team." Hap rubbed his hands together. He watched Jim process the offer as if anticipation mounted for a shout of *BINGO*.

Jim shook his head. "I don't understand. You said we have to cut costs, *to survive*. Lights Out unplugged my position yet your offer carries the same financial burden to the company."

Hap nodded. "A reflection of your years of contributions."

"And all I have to give up is the title?"

"Consider it a reward. Think of the employees you'd continue to help. Think of your wife."

Hap's encouraging smile and head bob made Jim feel like a floundering swimmer being coaxed into the lifeboat. His mind flashed to a scene from his favorite Christmas movie, *It's a Wonderful Life*. Wide-eyed idealist George Bailey nearly submits to Potter's cunning seduction, tempted with money, position and security. Drawing strength from his values, George steps back from the moral abyss.

You sit around here and spin your little webs and you think the whole world revolves around you and your money. Well it doesn't, Mr. Potter. In the whole vast configuration of things I'd say you're nothing but a scurvy little spider.

While such a declaration appealed to Jim, the prospect of a new baby, and financial considerations tempered his response. It was easier to land a job when you had a job and he was already nervous about his marketability. He needed time to consider his options. "When do you need an answer?" He asked.

Hap's smile vanished, transforming into a scowl. He rose from the table and looked to his desk. "Friday. I want this wrapped up before the new HR head arrives. It would be unfair to make him deal with this."

Jim couldn't speak. He merely nodded as he rose from the table. As he opened the door, Hap's voice shouted after him.

"One more thing for Friday. Identify another head for *Lights Out*."

Chapter 46
Jim Gets Advice

Jim had to escape. He felt like running and never stopping.
The lakefront? No, too far. The coffee shop, yes—quiet,
empty at this hour. Then he'd return to his office, grab his coat
and briefcase with zero chance of running into anyone from
his team. "Beats heading to the bar," he mumbled to himself
as the freight elevator opened on the fortieth floor. But as he
descended, he wondered how long he could hold out before
desperation drove him to alcohol, or worse.

He darted through the marble lobby with eyes focused on
the revolving door. He didn't want to get caught in a conversation; he wouldn't know what to say. Turning toward the coffee
shop with city stride and glazed eyes, the urge to confide in
someone swept over him. But who? Not his mom or Patty
Thorsen whose numbers flashed on his cell phone, and certainly not Julie. There was plenty of time to let her gloat about
predicting Hap's fickle loyalty. That left one person.

"You win." Jim spoke into the phone, slumped in a corner banquette. He tried to dilute the sadness in his voice with
sarcasm.

"You okay?" Cal replied.

With head pounding, Jim mussed his hair. "I scooped the
master scooper?" Even he knew his laugh sounded forced.
"Got a big decision to make."

"Where are you?" Cal asked.

Hearing concern in his pal's voice, Jim realized his sarcasm failed to veil his discouragement. He had to get his head

together before he talked to Julie or anyone from his team. "That artsy coffee shop," he spoke into the phone. "A few blocks from the office. I needed space." Jim's eyes absorbed the normalcy of his surroundings—the smell of coffee, the sounds of Copeland and the banter of mundane conversations.

"You're being cryptic. Want me to meet you?"

"No, I'm fine. Don't mean to speak in riddles. Just confused, that's all."

"Jimmy boy, I don't like your tone. Stay where you are. I'll be there in five," Cal said, hanging up the phone before Jim had a chance to reject the offer.

As he waited, Jim buried his head in his hands. What should he do? A muffled chime signaled an email. He fished his phone out of his pocket out of habit and scrolled through his messages -- something to take his mind off of the meeting with Hap and the decision in front of him.

His smile grew to a full-blown grin as he scrolled through the latest message.

You restored my faith. I'd been banging my head against the wall, telling myself what an idiot I was to give my life to this god-damned airline. Now I can retire with my head held high, proud of my years of service and proud of my company. God Bless You.

Maybe Jim Abernathy wasn't a complete fuck up. He remembered the guy. Initially bitter, more like a cornered dog than a grandfather of sixty plus. After a couple of calls and a meeting, the gnarly ramper calmed, and became downright charming. Jim and his team went to work.

He recalled Lindy, like a dog with a pork chop, and the insurance staffer who couldn't wait to shake the curly-haired pit bull from his ankle. Lindy learned that the company had incorrectly denied hospice coverage for the man's wife. Then Evy, she found errors in the man's pension estimate including the exclusion of overtime from the calculation. And Mary reviewed his work history with airport management. Turned out the guy was eligible for several awards including a safety commendation. She in turn partnered with Dave who sourced a new tractor in time for the guy's fortieth company anniversary. Jim's entire team attended the ceremony. The guy broke down, cried when they unveiled the shiny new tractor with his name—*Charlie Weber*. Jim's eyes teared at the memory, especially the image of Charlie's kids and grandkids beaming with pride.

Even now, Jim wondered if there was any truth in Patty's comment – Charlie Weber and Hap started with the company on the same day. In the grand scheme of things, it didn't matter.

A kick to the shin recalled Jim to the present. His eyes moved from his phone to the figure of Cal staring down at him. The huge soda cup in his buddy's hands amused him.

"I'm lookin' for the optimist, the valiant crusader, our romantic hero," Cal said, plopping into a chair. "This merger SNAFU hasn't put him out of a job?"

Despite the sarcasm, Jim was glad to see Cal. He wiggled upright. "That's the odd part -- not sure. Depends on perspective."

"Now you've piqued my curiosity. Talk!"

Jim inhaled. He collected his thoughts. He decided against filtering any of the account. "Hap called me into his office. Sat me in the very chair where he promoted me." Jim wondered if he'd ever be able to shake the image of that moment from his brain. He cut to the bone. "The company's shedding vice presidents."

Cal's mouth fell open. "The ole heave ho, huh? Boxes at the curb already?"

Jim chuckled at Cal's irreverence. "Such empathy!" he said, poking his pal in the chest. "Not that simple. My position was eliminated. However, I can stay."

"Lucky you. Flight attendant, pilot, floor sweeper," Cal said, before slurping his straw.

Jim stuck his tongue out. "Funny. No. My current job with everything in tact. And I do mean *everything*. Except one tiny little thing." Jim measured an inch with his thumb and index finger as Cal's brow furrowed.

"Lemme guess. Your first born or maybe your soul."

Jim swatted the air. "My title, my *vice president* title."

Cal scratched his temple. "I'm the rational republican, remember. Takin' stripes away but not cuttin' the perks makes no sense. Especially given our financial woes. Did you hear correctly?"

Jim nodded. "Repeated it back to make sure."

Cal looked down and tapped the table for several seconds before responding. "Hap feels guilty as hell. Got you into this mess with false promises. That, or he fears a mutiny for sacking employees' advocate."

Jim shrugged. "I don't know, Cal. The man's as much a mystery today as he was months ago."

"Yeah, but he's savvy. Knows you're respected and what's more, *loved*," Cal said, pinching Jim's cheek. "Yep Jimmy boy, guilt and fear are big motivators especially if your name is Sweeny. Thank stern priests, ruler-toting nuns and purgatory for your salvation. If not those guilt peddlers, then lawyers. All scare the crap outta me. I'm assuming you'll jump at the sweetheart deal."

❦

With Cal convinced he wasn't suicidal, Jim's buddy left the coffee shop in search of something stronger to take the edge off of the day. They parted company at the door under the screeching brakes of an L train.

The sound of bells and horns drew Jim to the river where

he stood on the wide promenade across from Intercontinental Tower. The rising iron span mesmerized him. He leaned over the concrete balustrade watching a flotilla of sailboats head to dry dock. Another season over, he thought recalling yesterday's Labor Day holiday.

He almost didn't hear the cell phone over the din of bridge alarm bells. Richter's name appeared on the display—safe to answer. Jim assumed Hap's confidante knew everything.

"How you doing buddy?" Richter's tone was empathetic.

Jim gave him points for not pretending to be in the dark. He answered, staring at the river. "Better than an hour ago. But still stunned."

Richter paused before speaking. "I'm so sorry young man. Hap asked me to interview division heads. Wanted to know how they felt about continuing your mission in the face of cost pressures."

Jim rolled his eyes. It didn't take a high-priced consultant to know the answer. Hell, precious little support existed before *Lights Out*. And Hap, for all of his assurances, was a student of the sink or swim school of mentoring.

"I was flabbergasted. Support vanished," Richter said. "The same people heralding your arrival turned a cold shoulder in the face of Lights Out."

Jim scoffed. "No surprise. Better me than them. We claw each other for resources. Survival's the game. Neither pretty, nor compassionate. Kindness is a handicap." A single boat drew Jim's eyes. It failed to advance with the others before the bridge descended and floated back-and-forth, trapped between lowered spans.

Jim detected a sigh before Richter responded. "The odds went against us, especially when Hap's passion waned. You can't drive culture change with the Chairman in the backseat."

Jim let out a scornful laugh. "Hell no, Weston drove. Just

happened to be another car. Pedal to the metal in a completely different direction."

"I know about Hap's offer, Jim. Any initial thoughts how you're leaning?"

"Too early to tell."

"Let me know if I can help."

Jim inhaled. He recalled Richter's help over the last several months. "We made a great team. Hap tells me you're responsible for saving my people, at least until the dust settles. Thanks. I've got to consider what's best for them."

Richter's voice lowered. Jim imagined the consultant huddled in the hall outside Dagger's office waiting for a coaching session. The consultant's tone was more emphatic, his tempo more deliberate. "Admirable. But my advice, young man—as a friend, not a consultant. Do what's best for Jim Abernathy. Hap Sweeny survives by that creed."

Chapter 47

Jim Gets Disturbing News

Still reeling from Hap's unexpected blow, Jim hoped to avoid his team, at least for one night. He wanted to digest the news and cycle through his own emotions before facing people who'd study his face for answers. He was surprised therefore, when the elevator opened on his floor to see the somber face of Patty Thorsen. He took a deep breath mustering the strength to present a stoic façade.

Patty's face was red and she wrung her hands. Her usually perfect hair was mussed. "Oh... oh thank God," she stammered. "Winny said you'd be down over an hour ago."

From her distressed expression and frantic tone, he guessed she knew everything about his meeting. While her killer intuition may have figured things out, he felt it more likely that Hap resorted to his old tricks. Probably took Patty into his confidence to monitor and report on Jim's reaction to the offer.

"Can you wait until tomorrow? It's after six. Got a lot on my mind right now," he said, avoiding eye contact. "I'm awfully sorry." He didn't want to be rude, but he couldn't let down his guard. A medley of emotions bubbled just below the surface.

Patty grabbed his arm. "No, Jim. This can't wait."

Her tone drew his eyes. He tried to pull away. "Let's go to my office, then."

But Patty held her ground. Her expression remained resolute. "No. Dave will meet us here with your things," she said pulling her phone from a pocket and punching in a text.

"What's wrong? Why all the drama?" He cringed hearing the harshness in his tone.

Patty squeezed his arm. "It's Julie," she said with a sniffle. His heart sank. Blood drained from his head. He felt dizzy remembering the calls he let go to voice mail. How much time had he wasted? Patty's grip got tighter. Her tone was soft, calm. "Your mom called. She's with Julie—at the hospital, your hospital."

Panic swelled. His voice echoed in the empty corridor. "Hospital! What happened?"

"You should go, right away. Your mom will meet you there. Julie's mother's on her way down from Wisconsin. We offered to put her on a flight from Oshkosh or Milwaukee, but she insisted on driving." Patty shook her head. "Afraid of puddle jumpers."

Jim tugged at Patty's sleeve, comforted at holding onto something. "What's wrong?"

"Your mom said Julie collapsed."

"My poor darling," he said, wincing at the image that jumped into his head.

Patty grabbed both of his hands. "Listen, she had enough sense to call your mom when she started to feel faint. Your mom rushed to your house. Found her unconscious."

Jim couldn't keep still. He figured he'd pass out if he did. He pulled one hand from Patty's grasp to rub his forehead. It was clammy. "Is Julie okay? What about the baby?"

Patty didn't answer. She hugged him with tears swelling in her eyes. Finally she stammered, "Julie's... awake. She's... asking for you."

His hands pressed against his temples. Was he trying to soothe his pounding head or push the terrifying images from his mind? "But the baby. Tell me the truth."

Patty shook her head. "They're running tests. They don't know. That's the truth."

He took a deep breath as his heart raced. Thank God he didn't chuck his job into Hap's face or he'd have to go crawling back. Unlike Bedford Falls, hospitals and doctors cost a fortune. If he quit, there'd be no insurance, no security for his family, *nothing*. Right now, Julie and the baby were his priorities. God only knew what lay ahead.

"Do you have your car?" Patty asked.

He nodded. "Yes, yes. I drove. Got the keys here." But as his nervous fingers fumbled through his trouser pockets, he turned up only spare change. Frenzied, he patted every one of his pockets, once, twice, three times.

"Maybe they're in your jacket," Patty said in a soft tone as she grabbed his arm.

"Yes, yes, of course. In my office."

She smiled. "Dave will have them then. Why don't I go with you? You shouldn't be alone."

"No, but thanks. I wouldn't want to risk anyone else's life." He jerked his head toward his office. His foot started tapping the floor. What could be keeping Dave?

Patty grabbed his arms; she looked him straight in the eyes. "Jim, we don't need you in the hospital too. You hear me? Promise you won't do anything stupid. Julie needs you. We all need you."

Dave finally appeared in the corridor. He hustled, his hands filled with Jim's briefcase and jacket. As he approached, Jim saw concern and sympathy in his face. Dave squeezed Jim's arm. "Let me know if you need anything. Day or night."

Jim winked. "Will do," he said, turning to the elevator, the button already pressed. He retrieved his keys from the jacket and jangled them in the air with a wink to Patty.

"I didn't say anything to Lindy or Mona," Patty said. "Your mom's call came after five so Mona was long gone. Besides, the news would have been all over the building by now—my bad." Patty's palm covered her mouth as she mimicked their secretary. "As for Lindy—"

Dave finished her sentence. "She'd require medical attention, herself."

The banter provided needed levity. Jim chuckled as he pressed the button a second and third time. "Thanks you guys. You're the best."

Patty hugged him. "Call me," she whispered in his ear. "I'll call your mom. Tell her you're on your way."

"Tell Julie were thinking about her," Dave added as he embraced Jim in a bear hug.

Jim choked back the tears. "I'll do that," he said backing into the elevator.

"We love you, Jim," Patty mouthed as the doors closed.

⤞✧⤝

As Jim drove out of the building's garage, he listened to his mom's messages. The first one urgent; by the third, she assured him Julie was okay. Like Patty, she begged him to be careful for Julie's and her sake. She ended the call expressing her love for a wonderful son. He cried for most of the drive to the hospital, praying for Julie and the baby and making all sorts of bargains in return for their wellbeing. His mind in a fog, he didn't remember anything about the drive or parking the car. He bolted through the parking garage and barked his wife's name to the receptionist.

As he opened the door to his wife's room, his mother rose to greet him with a finger to her lips. The concern etched into her face melted as she reached for him. She offered a hug and gently pushed him into the corridor. "Oh sweetie, I'm so glad to see you." She dabbed her eyes with a soaked handkerchief.

"How's Julie?" Jim asked. His eyes wandered to the closed door.

"She's fine sweetie. Just fell asleep. I didn't want you to wake her. The doctors say she needs rest. She struggled to stay awake. Wanted to see you, but she's exhausted. Lost a lot of blood."

Jim's shoulders sank. He moaned. "Oh Mom. I did this to her. That damned job and all that stress. You warned me. You *both* warned me."

His mom grabbed his shoulders. She shook him as her voice rose. "Listen to me. That's nonsense. Don't blame yourself. I don't give a flippin' fig for Weston, Hap, or the rest of those assholes. But, don't blame yourself."

Jim rubbed his eyes. He stared into his mother's face trying to see if she hid horrible news. He had to ask the question but it pained him to do so. "What about the baby? Did we lose the baby?"

She hugged him. "No, no—there's still a heartbeat. But they're not sure if the baby was harmed... too early to tell. The doctors ran tests. They're waiting for results."

He felt like his head would pop. Where were the damn doctors? He wanted to talk to them. But first he had to see Julie. His groan surprised himself.

His mom brushed the hair from his forehead. "Sweetie, the baby's a fighter, just like you. We'll know more in a few hours."

"Where's Julie's mom?"

"Should be here in an hour. Told her she's staying with me. The last thing you need is a mother-in-law at home right now." They both managed a laugh. His mom caressed his cheek. Her voice lowered but her words were firm. "Sweetie, whatever happens, Julie's gonna need you."

His gaze dropped to the floor. "Truth is, Mom, I'm not sure she wants me."

She pressed his arm. "Why do you say that? She tell you that?"

His eyes looked into his mother's. "I don't know if I can stomach myself. She's the one paying the price for my stupidity."

His mom straightened her back and poked him in the chest. "You weren't here, honey. *You* were on her mind. Julie didn't want to let *you* down."

"Oh my poor Julie. She never disappointed me, not once. It's me. I let her down. I shoulda listened to her." The image of Hap, alone and scowling in his tomb-like office, flashed in his mind.

"Sweetie, Julie loves you. I saw it in her eyes. A mother knows." She kissed his cheek.

"I hope you're right."

"Your wife needs you, one-hundred percent of you. Whatever happens."

Jim stepped into the room alone and stood beside his wife. He grabbed her hand and spoke. "Julie, I love you so much, so very, very much." His head bowed as tears swelled in his eyes. "I'm so sorry. Forgive me. You're the best thing in my life. I promise I'll leave Intercontinental as soon as I can." He leaned over and laid his face on her hand.

After a few minutes he stood upright, still squeezing her hand. He didn't ever want to let it go. "You were right about Hap," he said. "Please, please be okay."

Julie moved her head but didn't open her eyes. Jim thought he detected a smile. Still holding her hand, he caressed her head and kissed her cheek.

Chapter 48

Weston's Christmas List

Waves of holiday goers inundated the airport. The mass exodus began one week before Christmas. Early birds led the tide followed by the succession of universities and other schools that disgorged for winter break. Procrastinators brought up the rear.

Navigating the peak was an annual challenge for Intercontinental's scheduling department, an exercise in art, science and seat-of-the-pants guesswork. Employee absences and passenger volumes surged in tandem. Schedulers of flight attendants and pilots organized sick-call pools, the payoff—a poor man's holiday bonus. Seasoned front-liners abandoned posts for coveted vacations, adding an invisible layer of complexity. Christmas, the airline's Super Bowl, fielded benchwarmers and the B-squad.

Fickle weather and morale along with an aging infrastructure, kept the airline jittery. Baggage systems, carts, tractors, and containers groaned and bulged as luggage, cargo, and mail swelled simultaneously. Arctic blasts kneecapped the company's geriatric equipment.

Company executives, especially those in operations, inhaled in early December and held their breaths until January. Many careers crash-landed because of catastrophes on their watch. Front line staff approached the rush with the same gallows humor marshaled for thunderstorms and summer hordes—heads down, game faces on and I-pods blaring.

✎✦✐

A small army of nervous managers huddled in the ops nerve center as Weston swooped from HDQ in a black cashmere coat and fedora to catch flight 930 to Frankfurt. The broad conspiracy that insulated him from the cruel realities of air travel was difficult to maintain during December. His declaration raised anxiety levels. "This trip will define my legacy. *Fuck ups* won't be tolerated."

Weston's grand plan that reached a critical head this Christmas began its incubation on Labor Day in Manhattan's Mandarin Hotel. In the weeks following their altar jilt, Weston and Jacobs secured a marketing agreement with their runaway bride, TransSky. They traveled overseas seeking capital, finding a European airline willing to buy a twenty-five percent stake. Unloading the remainder would require a change of law or a change of heart. Weston hatched another scheme to fix domestic operations that bled from high labor costs.

Light snow began falling just after noon. The National Weather Service predicted minimal accumulation and company meteorologists advised Weston's secretary that the event shouldn't disrupt the *big guy's* flight. However, a shift in wind direction off Lake Michigan, they cautioned, would bring more snow and impact airport operations.

Weston's limousine snaked through late afternoon traffic destined for O'Hare. Progress was swift on the expressway, but the blue Lincoln got snarled in traffic, one mile from the terminal. Slick roads and curbside congestion slowed the convoy of cars, taxis and courtesy vans to a crawl.

"Damn snow," muttered Ingrid, who sat wedged beside Weston in the town car's back seat. "We'll miss our goddamned flight. We should have demanded they come to us. Flying off at Christmas smacks of desperation."

Weston's pudgy fingers tapped the rim of his hat that rested on his lap. "Flexibility costs us nothing. We're desperate. Not every day you find a partner willing to snatch up a quarter of your business, *for cash*. Assinine limits."

"A temporary hurdle. Underlicht works Washington. Even Klein is more receptive since your generous contribution and his landslide victory. Then there's your Cabinet post." Ingrid's eyebrows arched. "All in good time. Trust me."

He studied her face. "I trust you too much."

She puckered her lips and kissed the air. "Maybe you do. But I haven't disappointed."

"Not yet," he said, eliciting a sneer and a flick of Ingrid's hand.

She pawed her fur coat. "Changing the law will be a snap when you're in the administration."

He winked, his tone mischievous. "I'd have to recuse myself from decisions."

Ingrid purred. "Recuse, but influence. Blind trusts silence accusatory tongues. In the end, same outcome. Your plan to stop the domestic hemorrhage buys us time."

He puffed up his chest. "More than one way to skin a rabbit. Our new friends won't be the first foreigners to birth a US airline. Then we sell domestic operations to the upstart." Lawyers, he knew, would correct his semantics. Intercontinental would sell *assets:* planes, slots, gates, facilities, etc... Buyers didn't want legacy employees with bloated salaries and benefits. The nasty task of sweeping away surplus workers was a pittance to pay to unload a chunk of the airline. "Once the work disappears, we announce layoffs. The new airline plump with our assets feeds us passengers. That's all we care about anyway."

Ingrid fluffed the fur with a puff of breath. "Like magic, a low cost airline is born."

He reached across the seat and squeezed her arm. "Cost

slashing and the TransSky alliance boost our cash flow. We'll be sittin' pretty just waitin' for a proposal."

"Like a baby-faced virgin behind bars," she said, rubbing the ermine against her cheek.

"I'm guessin' TransSky pops the question again. That, or another suitor sweeps our gussied up maiden off her feet. God and superpacs willin', we'll win Washington's support to open our industry to foreign investors. If this country can mortgage itself to the Chinese, why shouldn't foreign wallets pluck up airlines?"

Ingrid writhed. "Oh, the pitiful moans of *national security*."

He scoffed. "Bullshit! Supremacy of the skies and all that rubbish. This century's battleground is the marketplace. Ask the Chinese."

He caught her staring at him with curled up lips. "You'll unyoke this albatross at last," she said. "One would think it's Christmas and Richy's been a very, very good little boy." She pinched his cheek and tossed her head back in laughter.

His co-conspirator still had the power to excite him. He found her knee under the folds of her white cashmere skirt. Stirred by nostalgia for their amorous past and zeal of the current mission, his puffy hand glided up her inner thigh.

Her shudder slowed his progress. Her bark, "Nein!" halted his advance.

Weston looked to the rearview mirror in anticipation of curious eyes. After staring down the chauffeur, he turned to find Ingrid's legs, sheathed in patent leather, crossed and her coat tugged across her lap. Although her ermine-covered head turned from him with dramatic exaggeration, he grinned upon sensing gratification in the face reflected in the car's window.

Chapter 49

Hap's Christmas List

Fearing a rush hour from hell on the Kennedy expressway, Hap drove out to O'Hare in the early afternoon. Even though scheduled to fly to LA thirty minutes after Weston's Frankfurt departure, he had another reason for getting to the airport early. He wanted a good seat for the fireworks. With scores of tasks necessary to give Weston a flawless experience, something was bound to go wrong. Some errant rocket perhaps, falling into the unsuspecting crowd.

Hap reacted to Weston's announcement of the critical trip to Germany with mischievous delight since he no longer served as chief babysitter when Weston took to the skies. The fact that the trip plopped in the middle of seam-bursting Christmas gave him added pleasure. He secretly wished for some catastrophe to befall Dagger, ninety-day Ops wunderkind. *Tapped the info into a smart phone for Christ's sake*, Hap thought at the time. *No respect for the ball-busting preparations.* He felt cheated by Dagger's poker face; wanted the thrill of seeing his rival squirm but suspected Richter's hand in molding his successor.

Weston's Atlantic crossing would be tracked by more eyes than Santa's sleigh, with one notable difference. Santa's bag bulged with gifts for others while Weston flew to Europe to bag his own goodies. "Visions of euros dance in his head. Lump of coal's more like it," Hap mumbled as he rode to the top of the concourse escalator.

A life-size velvet Santa commanding a sleigh trimmed with lighted evergreen boughs drew his eyes to the ceiling. His memory flashed to last Christmas. An electric short sparked a fire, triggering a terminal evacuation. He could laugh now, but his forehead vein almost burst that night. Horrified children watched Santa smolder. A crisp Kringle didn't inspire confidence among flyers. The media hadn't been kind. They exaggerated with news teasers and headlines: *Santa's Flight Cancelled*; *Kris Kringle Kalamity*; *St. Nick Fired*. After days of interrogations, management pinned the debacle on City crews. *Otherwise Brophy would be toast, just like Santa*, Hap thought as his Adam's apple pulsed.

"It's Dagger's funeral now," he muttered, elbowing his way toward a coffee kiosk. A choral group donned in Dickensian costumes sang *Here We Come A Caroling*. Hap scowled at spectators congregated in a bottleneck. His groan of "Bah humbug!" set a toddler sobbing.

Under a pretense of pre-holiday chats, Hap visited each of the airport department heads to get the dirt on Dagger *and flight 930 to Frankfurt*.

The Inflight manager welcomed him into her office. She bristled at the mention of Dagger but hemmed and hawed when pressed for details.

"Aw come on," Hap said with a wink. He knew she wouldn't have opened up when he was COO. "Spill the beans. I'm just an Admin. puke."

She sat back in her chair and exhaled. "Dagger called six times with the same warning," she moaned. "Must have forgot we have hundreds of other departures and tens of thousands of other passengers. I get it. I'll be fired if I screw up. Motivational don't you think? Happy Holidays and all that."

She reported that her division would be well staffed although sick calls climbed. "Got plenty in reserve tonight but that shortchanges Christmas," she added with a shrug.

"More snow would cause problems," Hap said with a nod

as if urging on a blizzard. "What about flight 930?"

"Full. Only last row of coach empty. Unless it fills with employees on stand-by."

"And the caterers?" he asked, narrowing his eyes.

"Adequate staffing, functional equipment. They assigned an experienced manager to 930—our employee for decades until we outsourced his job." She pulled a paper from her desk. "Hmm…"

"Hmm what?" Hap shot back.

"Don't often see this. Four of the nine First Class passengers ordered special meals—religious."

She went on to explain that she added extra flight attendants to 930 to ensure good service. The flight's purser, Samantha D. a recent transfer from Boston, had a work history containing numerous accolades. Other veterans rounded out the crew with one exception that piqued Hap's interest. "Tell me about him."

"Roger something or other. Like the purser, he traded into the flight within the last day. A blemished record…" Her words trailed off as she scanned her notes.

Hap leaned across her desk. "Don't keep it to yourself."

"Recent transfer from Newark. Steps ahead of discipline, probably termination."

"I hope he's not a problem," Hap said, wishing otherwise.

"With any luck," she said, "he'll work Economy or merchandise sales. We'll advise the purser to watch him."

"Sounds like you got things covered," Hap said as he rose hiding his gritted teeth.

"One more thing," she said.

Hap froze at the door. "What's that?"

"I prepped the return journey. Ingrid Shattenworter cancelled her booking."

Hap found the detail curious. Didn't jive with Weston's

plan. He'd check it out, but told the inflight manager. "Probably nothing. O Tannenbauming with her family."

He stepped across the hall to meet with the Chief Pilot. After jokes about Hap's six-million-dollar contract including a Steve Austin dig, they sat in the man's office with the door closed. The pilot offered a cigar.

Hap furrowed his brow. "Terminal's non-smoking."

"It is?" the pilot said with a laugh and *what-the-fuck* shrug. Hap recognized the cigar pulled from the drawer as Cuban.

Because of scheduled flight time, 930 required an extra first officer. "Ordered two management pilots to stand-by just in case," the pilot said, lighting his cigar.

"Tell me about the crew," Hap said, picking up a jet model from the man's desk.

The pilot leaned back in his chair and blew smoke toward the ceiling. "Top notch techies. Safety records beyond reproach."

"So nothing out of the ordinary," Hap said, pretending to study the model's winglet.

"Hate to even mention it," the pilot said, sitting forward.

Hap's eyes moved to the man's face. He sat up. "Go ahead."

"One of the first officers is a rabble-rouser. The one behind all the petitions to oust Weston."

Hap surged with curiosity and delight. "You're not thinking of replacing him?"

The pilot shook his head as his fingers tapped his desk. He avoided Hap's stare. "Weston doesn't talk to crew and that Shattenworter woman's a match for the burliest of pilots— male or female."

"Good call," Hap said, rising to go.

The sight of several workers shuffling out of the maintenance manager's office with heads bowed and hands in their pockets encouraged Hap. The manager himself was red-faced with hair disheveled. His hoarse voice offered Hap a chair.

"Trouble?" Hap asked, trying to look empathetic.

"Christ I hope not. Told my guys to pray like hell though."

Hap wriggled in his seat. "Weston's airplane?"

All color vanished from the pockmarked face. The man looked like he might vomit. "How'd you know?" He must have caught himself as he shook his head and lowered his voice. "Yeah... I mean... I hope not."

The manager explained that a mechanical problem grounded flight 930's original airplane in Tokyo. The tattered substitute that now represented 930 to Frankfurt didn't have the lie-flat private compartments or sparkling new interior. "It's a dog," he said.

"New-plane scent air fresheners might do the trick," Hap said, trying to crack the man's deathly expression.

The manager remained grim. "Had Dagger callin' me every thirty minutes. 'I'm no fuckin' magician,' I says to him. 'Can't wave a wand and make a shiny plane appear on the O'Hare tarmac.' I says."

"I'm sorry," Hap said, his foot tapping the floor with excitement. "Wish there was something I could do."

"How about a good reference?" the manager said. "Just kiddin'. We'll fix what we can. Dagger lifted *Lights Out* overtime curbs for tonight."

Hap scowled at the precaution. "That's mighty nice of him."

The manager sighed. "930 mustn't be delayed. We'll just have to cross our fingers, hope for the best."

Hap flashed a thumb's up on his way out. "I'm rooting for you."

Airport manager Brophy was candid with his old buddy. "Place has gone to hell since you been gone."

Hap couldn't contain his grin. "That's too bad."

"Yeah, you're sobbin' in your scotch," Brophy chuckled. "Shoulda been here this morning. Had Wilkerson bellowin' at me." Brophy pointed to the speakerphone before imitating Wilkerson's high-pitched frat boy accent. "'Don't give a rat's ass what happens onboard,' ole Wilky said. 'When Weston's at O'Hare, he's your headache. Make sure the lounge food is fresh and Santa keeps a cool head,' blah, blah, blah." Brophy concluded by twirling his finger in the air.

Hap nearly doubled over in laughter. "I'd love to see Wilkerson or Dagger try to do better."

"Thanks boss," Brophy said. "You know the drill. Assigned my best agents to flight 930. Only one landmine."

"What's that," Hap said, leaning forward.

"Our version of the dragon tattoo. Girl named Kelly Green. One of swing's best agents. Tech whiz. Warned her to cover skin, de-spike the red hair and ditch the faux leopard cat's eye glasses even if she's blind."

Hap slapped the desk. "Your dragon lady's no match for Ingrid."

Brophy shook his head. "C-note says your wrong." His phone began to ring. "Sorry Hap," he said, picking up the receiver.

Hap swatted the air. "No worries. The place is rumbling like a volcano."

Brophy spoke into the phone. "Like I could eat off the floor... lounge and Frankfurt gate. Rovin' crews... yeah in spotless uniforms. Tidy for the duration... Of course restrooms... how do I know where his highness might decide to take a royal crap... Yeah all of 'em. Got the Countess with him so ladies' heads too. Jenny Cooya." He hung up the phone and turned to Hap. "Polish for thank you."

Hap snickered. "In Brophski's world. Hope all goes smooth tonight."

Brophy rolled his eyes. "Yeah, sure you do." They both laughed. "If it's any consolation," Brophy added. "Dagger and Wilky are shakin' in their Bruno Maglis."

Hap liked the sound of that. "Poor things."

Brophy chuckled. "Wilky's sending over a couple of his HDQ goons. *Lend me a helpin' hand*, he says."

Hap nodded. "Spies and enforcers."

Brophy shot him a piercing look. "You taught him well, boss. Well if they wanna stick their nose in my skivvies, maybe I'll just have a steamin' surprise waitin' for them." He sighed. "Wouldn't life be easier if we crammed Weston's fat ass into a FedEx envelope?"

Hap shook his head. "Overweight fees and bubble wrap would get pricey."

Hap left Brophy's office dreaming about the disasters that could imperil Weston's trip on Dagger's watch. His eyes wandered out the window to the parking lot reserved for company execs. He flinched. Dagger's silver Porsche sat in its reserved spot next to his own black Beamer. "What's he doing here?"

"Referring to me?" the voice laced with sarcastic overtones.

Hap felt the hot breath on his neck and smelled the cologne. He turned. His eyes inventoried the four hundred dollar haircut, shiny silk suit, Italian loafers and Swiss watch. "Hmm, Dagger. What's the going rate for babysitters these days?"

"A bit higher than Chief Administrative Assistants."

Hap scoffed although the poke at his title smarted. "Really think being here will make a difference?"

"Sure hope so. I'm a last minute add to Frankfurt 930," Dagger said, brushing his hand through his hair. "Weston's request." His face took on an exaggerated pout. "Didn't someone get an invite?" Then he grinned and clicked his tongue.

Hap wouldn't give Dagger the satisfaction of showing

surprise. "Enjoy your trip. Get rested. The FAA will be all over your Armani ass when you return."

Dagger shook his head. "Your threats don't scare me. Intend to use my bonding time with Weston to share your antics. Wilkerson's got a great eye *and ear* for detail." He tapped his briefcase before disappearing into Brophy's office.

Hap seethed. Weston and Dagger were getting too chummy, pushing him aside. After forty years maybe he was nothing more than a glorified clerk. *The castrated bull put out to pasture,* he thought. "I'll show them who has balls."

Chapter 50
Jim's First Class Memories

"Come with me, sir."

Jim felt the tug on his tweed overcoat before his head turned toward the firm voice. But anxiety melted when he saw the face of an old acquaintance, a supervisor with whom he once worked. "Jean!" he shouted, dropping his shoulder bag to the terrazzo floor. Outstretched arms embraced the middle-aged woman.

Picking up his smaller duffel, she nodded toward a quiet corner of the massive hall. "I'm weedin' the lines. Takin' you to the Inner Circle."

"That's service!" he said, gathering up his remaining bags. Jim was conscious of the stares the exchange drew from nearby passengers.

His husky friend navigated through the crowded lobby like a pro, stepping over and around the overstuffed bags of customers who shuffled forward toward haggard looking check-in agents like zombies. He cringed at the snipes of line cutting but watched as Jean ignored them with the stone face of a secret service agent. Her ear-piece and radio wire made the comparison complete.

"Gotta love the holidays. Ten pounds in a five pound sack," she shouted over her shoulder to him. "Where you headin'?"

"Frankfurt. Snared the last Business Class seat. Then hopping a train to Nuremberg for the Christmas Market."

"Lucky you. Welcome to my Christmas bazaar!" The Chicago native with a tamed south-side accent waved her free hand before ushering him into the private lobby.

For the first time since stepping inside the teeming hall, the piped-in seasonal music reached his ears. He wondered how the carols inspired peace and goodwill among the holiday horde unable to hear it.

Jean stopped and pivoted. Her expression turned serious. "I heard through the grapevine you—" A shriek truncated her words. Both turned to see another agent waving at them with a dimpled smile.

After bidding a customer *good flight* and *Merry Christmas*, the other agent bounded over. She pushed Jim backward with her bear hug and kisses. "I told Jean to fetch some business," she said. "And she drags in my favorite VIP."

His cheeks warmed. "How you been?" he asked.

He figured she must have caught him eyeing the scores of poinsettias covering floor and counter. "A freakin' florist shop," she said with bobbing head. "Showed up two hours ago. If I could snare a husband, I'd get married right here. It's so purdy." She elbowed him before introducing two other agents who stood behind podiums, faces hidden by red flowers trimmed with gold angels and silver airplanes. "This is Jim, a *real* VIP. One of my favorites."

Jim shook the hands of the smartly dressed men, too young he guessed to have worked with him at the airport. A raucous chorus of expletives from outside the sanctuary riddled Silent Night's refrain. Jean cleared her throat, threw back her shoulders and inhaled. "Duty calls. Gotta love the holidays." She gave Jim a peck on the cheek and left.

Jim turned back toward the animated agent whose fingers frantically tapped at a keyboard. Her rosy round face shot up from the computer. "Richard the Third's on your flight."

Jim chuckled, recalling the vulgar variant, *King Dick* bandied about during bitter labor disputes. "Weston, that so?" he said without looking up from his passport.

"Hasn't checked in yet. Brophy's wading through the masses—search and rescue. Shouldn't be too hard to spot." She leaned across the desk and whispered. "He's huge, you know. Make a great Santa Claus if he wasn't such an asshole." She snorted, then blushed. After a few more clicks at the computer, she spoke. "You're seated in the first row of Business, next to the galley. Flight's full but I can try to move you."

"Don't bother. I like the aisle. Plan on sleeping most of the trip. At least my loafers can fly first class," he said, pointing toward his shoes, still damp from the snow.

"Tell you what," she said with a firm nod. "Even though you're flying Business, I'll call the first class lounge. They'd probably admit the beloved Jim Abernathy anyway. You can wait, sipping champagne if you don't mind slumming with King Dic—I mean Richard the Third." She slapped the podium, snorted and blushed.

Jim smiled his acceptance as she came around the podium.

"You're the best," she said, looking up into his eyes. "Worked beside us when we needed support and left us alone when we didn't." She squeezed his arm and lowered her voice. "Can you confirm the horrific rumors I've heard?"

Brophy's booming voice and the unmistakable patrician patter of Weston heralded their entrance into the private enclosure. Jim didn't turn. Instead, he winked at the agent, hugged her and mouthed *Merry Christmas*. As he hustled away with his boarding pass, he recognized Ingrid's German accent command, "Careful! Those bags are Vuitton. And not those cheap knock-offs our flight attendants peddle, either."

Jim sensed exasperation in the voice when Weston spoke. "I still ask why you need *five* suitcases for a *three*-day trip."

Ingrid's haughty laugh echoed behind him, as he made his way toward security.

≈❖≈

As he entered the lounge, Jim felt holiday sensory over-load. Fresh evergreen in every shape bunted with satin ribbons, holly sprigs and dozens of flowers trimmed the room. Holiday hits arranged for harp streamed from the speakers.

"There can't possibly be a poinsettia left in Chicago," he said to the two impeccably groomed receptionists.

After rushing from the desk to extend a hug, one starched agent raised an eyebrow. As he fluffed his Santa boutonniere, he spoke with bitchy tone. "Impressing our special guest. Bit over the top even for me. But, no one ever asks the help." His tongue clicked his palate.

After some personal chitchat with the pair, Jim settled into a corner. He declined an offer of champagne, choosing instead, a cabernet. He paired the wine with a selection of cheeses and a ramekin of nuts. After surveying the half-empty room's other occupants, he sat back and closed his eyes.

The combo of cushy chair and wine provided the perfect mood inducer to contemplate the past nine months. Was his career's defining moment that spring afternoon when Hap pro-moted him to vice president? Perhaps, that sunny September morning, the day he rendered his decision as Hap doused the embers of his once burning platform, employee alignment? His dilemma was daunting. Remain betrothed to his beloved company as an officer in *all* but name, or fight to save his frag-ile family. He risked losing both.

He turned toward the window. Against spotlights illuminating jumbo jets, snowflakes got bigger and fell more rapidly. Rampers in parkas scurried across the glistening apron while de-icing trucks nicknamed *elephants,* sprayed glycol from mechanical trunks.

Paris and London were called. Passengers roused. A whirl-ing dervish of an attendant stirred up whiffs of spruce and pine as she filled Jim's crystal tumbler. Pages announced early boarding for Buenos Aires and Moscow. A handsome couple and a cluster of bald businessmen rose. Outside, baggage carts and a posse of service vehicles surrounded the planes.

Jim's mind wandered back to early September.

Hap had set the Friday after Labor Day as the deadline to deliver an answer. At the time, Jim questioned the arbitrary hard stop. In retrospect, he wondered why he needed any time at all. Of course, he reasoned, his mind then was elsewhere. Julie's medical crisis consumed him.

When he accepted Hap's proposal in spring, he had his doubts. He half-expected the culture to reject him, a radical cell introduced to fight a destructive cancer. But the swiftness of the deathblow surprised him. Delivered by the very person who, with bold guarantees, introduced the change agent.

Jim remembered telling friends early on how he viewed the promotion as a win-win. Changing the company to a place where he could proudly serve as an officer—victory. Likewise, rejection by the dysfunctional culture would free him from the toxic environment to pursue other dreams like his wife implored.

That Thursday, deadline eve, Hap texted a reminder of the decision due. A phone call, he added, would suffice. With a laugh, Jim remembered how he flipped off the phone screen. Did Hap think he forgot? Anger and anxiety kept him awake most of that night.

On Friday as Hap ordained, Jim placed the call. Maybe the phone was better than face-to-face, but at the time Jim considered it disrespectful. Even defendants got to face their accusers and stare down jurors as the verdict was read.

The conversation lasted two minutes, max.

"I made up my mind," he said, knots in his stomach.

"And?" Hap's voice anticipatory, expecting good news -- maybe
Bingo.

"Not an easy decision."

"No." Hap's voice less certain.

"It's best…best I leave." Jim choked.

Hap paused, his tone changed. *"Oh… disappointing. But if that's
your final answer…"* Silence. Perhaps time to reconsider.

"It is." Jim's tone emphatic.

*"Not much to say, then. I'll notify HR. You should have the paper-
work before you leave today."*

"Efficient. I have one request."

"Okay." Hap's voice tentative.

*"I'd like you to author the departure message. Your new HR head
knows me less than you."* Now over the hump, Jim found his sarcasm.

"Sure." Tone, cold.

Silence ended the call. Short and simple, Jim thought. Hap
apparently wasn't interested in how he reached his decision.
Did Hap expect an apology for turning down the generous offer? His tone indicted—*stupidity, arrogance.* If he had asked, Jim
would have said that leaving was best for the company. Using
Richter's vernacular, the odds of success for an employee effort would be higher, even fifty/fifty under new stewardship
untainted by the stigma of a demoted leader.

In the end, Jim clung to his core values. He couldn't accept the sham. And title? An irrelevant measure of Hap's and
Weston's value systems, not his. Sometime after that call, he
didn't remember when, he told Hap he erred in creating the
position in the first place. An executive advocate raised expectations, set false hopes. Maybe Hap didn't like the rebuke or
maybe he thought Jim was being sarcastic. He sneered when
Jim said he could find satisfaction as a barista or airport supervisor. *Aim higher*, Hap said.

"Hap Sweeny never understood me—never attempted to try." Jim spoke aloud in the lounge. An elderly couple, Lake Forest types, looked at him out of the corners of their eyes.

After rendering his decision, Jim agreed to stick around at the request of the new head of HR. Saved him from the officer walk of shame, a hasty exit under a rent-a-cop's glare, carting away a career in a box. He wrangled two extra months of pay and more importantly, a say in his team's future. He felt an obligation to them. After all, they left secure jobs and put their faith in him.

"Strayed too far from the metal," Jim said, raising his wine-glass to his lips. "Expendable." The gray-bunned lady with the Hermes scarf rolled her eyes.

Of course, Julie came first. She could divorce him if she wanted. He wouldn't stand in her way. But he wouldn't abandon her when she needed him most. He spent every hour at the hospital, day and night for four days. Together, they made the decision to accept the doctor's recommendation. The morning of the procedure, they held onto each other as the nurse administered the first sedative.

He paced the floor of the waiting room and held her hand until she awakened from the anesthesia. He brushed the golden hair from her eyes then squeezed her hand as he told her about their son. He kissed her then choked up when he said he didn't know whether the baby suffered any permanent defects.

Clutching hands, they waited. They held on even tighter as the doctor delivered the news. They both sobbed when they heard that their baby appeared normal, but weak, small and susceptible to infection. Weeks would pass before their baby could go home.

After the doctor left, Julie looked up into his eyes. "I made a decision." His breathing stalled. "I want our baby to be called, Jim."

Shortly after the baby's birth, Jim was floored when he got a call from TransSky. They wanted him for a job in Europe. With their reputation for investing in employees he jumped at the opportunity, after consulting Julie.

Despite grave reservations voiced by Hap, Wilkerson, and Sallinger who dismissed Patty Thorsen as too compassionate, he convinced them she could drive the work forward as long as she retained Lindy, Dave, and the others. Richter proved a reliable ally. Took reams of PowerPoints to wear them down. "Maybe they granted the last wish of a dying career." His whisper drew glares and cleared throats from the Lake Foresters.

He never offered up another *Lights Out* head. If Hap, Tavistock, Weston, or another greedy headhunter wanted a sacrifice, they could sharpen their machetes and lob it off themselves.

His last officer dinner played out more uncomfortably than the first. Weston, Jacobs, and Hap kept their distance. No last-minute speech this time, either. Probably would have been gagged if he even tried. Colleagues hurried past, few stopped. Having been marked for thinning, no one strayed into the sharp shooter's sight. Hap flicked his palm as he raced to the bar where Wilkerson pouted and polished off a bottle of vodka, alone.

Dagger surprised. Made a point of shaking his hand and asked for a meeting before Jim departed for good—*A* for effort. Richter was a damn good coach. Dagger's assistant later canceled the requested audience. *F* for execution.

Hap last communicated a week before Jim's final day. The meeting Jim requested to say good-bye lasted five minutes. Hap never left his desk. It was awkward for both.

Jim's finale took place on a beautiful fall day. In typical October fashion, the sun warmed while a crisp breeze fanned the air. The lake mirrored the brilliant blue sky while the river hid its murkiness under a shimmering green coat.

"Comforting when the Universe speaks. Some people don't listen," Jim said, stroking his chin.

The Lake Foresters frowned, gathered their things and rose. The gray bun muttered. "The Universe, we'd listen to. You? You're annoying."

Employees aware of his departure visited or sent encouraging messages. His team brought cookies and cakes. Tears flowed.

Even Nelly Connors showed up with chocolate chip cookies, breaking a vow not to set foot in the building again. Showered with hugs and greeted with news that her former skunk of a manager fell victim to Lights Out, a beaming Nelly spoke of her new job purchasing air travel for a conglomerate. "My first task put the screws to Intercontinental," she gloated. "I demanded big discounts or I'd move our multi-million dollar account to TransSky." Her audience clapped. "Intercontinental caved," she added. "I got a bonus."

Hap didn't stop by or even call. His final scowl was symbolic. A terse email announced Jim's leaving, signed by the slick new head of HR whisked from the unemployment line by Sallinger. The legendary transparency of Ingrid's communication department triumphed. The stealth departure notice prevented flames of employee discontent. He still ran across many employees, surprised to learn he no longer worked for the company. Perhaps a part of him would always belong to Intercontinental. Yet, walking out the door for the last time, he felt liberated.

He looked out the window at the airplane. Julie and the baby left on the same flight one week earlier. She wanted to spend time with her sister and brother-in-law, a military family who lived outside Frankfurt. She could scope out new houses.

In the meantime, he looked forward to a relaxing family weekend at the Christmas markets before starting his new assignment.

"Ironic to be flying with Weston and Ingrid," he said. "Of course, they're first class…"

Chapter 51

Jim's Fantasy Flight

Sixty minutes before Intercontinental 930's departure, with scores of hands conjuring up a flawless flight, nobody guessed that the aircraft would never make it to Frankfurt.

Weston and Ingrid gusted into the first class lounge drawing glances from the normally aloof sophisticates. Weston wheezed and Ingrid's fur hat bobbed above a half-wall topped with poinsettias as Brophy escorted them to a velvet-roped corner. Once settled, they buried themselves in mobile phones.

A few minutes later, Ingrid excused herself. With Weston alone, Jim rose, smoothed his wool trousers and stepped past the gold stanchion. Extending his arm, he cleared his throat before speaking. "I'm Jim Abernathy."

Weston's feet twitched, a sign he was startled. Yet he looked up from his phone with poise. Instinctively, he grabbed for Jim's hand and pressed it into his own fleshy, perspiring palm. "Oh…hello."

As the flint-gray eyes behind the rimless glasses raced, Jim guessed Weston didn't recognize the name or face. "I used to work for you," Jim added.

"Yes…yes. Where are you off to?"

"Weekending in Nuremberg. Christmas markets," Jim said, although tapping fingers and a furtive glance to a Breguet watch keyed him into Weston's growing impatience.

"And, how are you?" Jim asked.

Weston became animated, almost jiggling as he droned on about the company's revenue performance. Jim noted the grin, exuberant tone and superlatives as he talked about the airline's ability to deal with fuel prices and the recession. The eyes came alive at mention of the millions saved by layoffs. "Our outlook is positive. An attractive investment, indeed! Wouldn't be surprised to see a competitor on bended knees," Weston added with a wink.

Jim's stomach knotted. He'd almost forgotten the stress. "Apologies for monopolizing your time." He backed out of the enclosure. His parting words of, "Merry Christmas and a successful New Year," drew a nod.

Ingrid soon returned. Whooshing into the chair beside Weston, she dropped her phone on the table and called for caviar. Weston declined all food except a bowl of nuts. He emptied several glasses of champagne while Ingrid sipped chilled vodka from glasses fished from a bowl of crushed ice by the hovering room attendant in pressed white shirt and crimson vest with matching bowtie.

Twenty minutes later, Hap entered the lounge as crisp as Jim remembered from their first meetings. As Hap proceeded to their corner with determined stride, Jim noticed the bottle with the gold-shield label he carried along with three glasses. The cork was pulled without the expected pop. Hap poured, remained standing and led the three in a toast. "To your success and a very prosperous new year for us all." He left abruptly, even forgetting to leave his glass or the bottle of champagne.

"Flat," Ingrid cried with puckered lips as she pushed her glass away.

Sometime during the next ten minutes, Weston experienced a coughing jag. "Filbert... wind... pipe," he gasped. Flailing hands sent Ingrid for water. She returned with shaking head and raised eyebrows. Jim thought he saw menace in her eyes as she pushed away the room attendant and slapped Weston on the back several times. Although she looked in his

direction and walked past him twice, Ingrid never acknowledged Jim's presence.

Final boarding, 930 to Frankfurt.

As if on cue, a pack of spotless employees appeared to usher the entourage to the aircraft. The rosy-cheeked agent who
checked Jim in was among them. He waited for the tornado
of activity to abate before he gathered his things. Discovering
his travel documents missing, he called for help. A red-faced
cleaning lady mumbled something in Polish that he took for
an apology. In her zeal to keep the room clean, she had picked
them up from the side table and tossed them in the trash. Jim
hurried to the gate.

The nearly full flight boarded without incident through two
jet bridges, the forward door reserved for First and Business.
Jim passed through First Class unnoticed as Ingrid instructed
a nose-flaring flight attendant on proper stowage for her *genuine* ermine coat and Weston received assistance with a seatbelt
extender from the purser.

Jim found his seat in the first row of Business, behind and
kitty-corner to Weston's right shoulder. He exchanged pleasantries with his row mate, an Austrian businessman in a hunter
green suit who spoke broken English. Jim did a double take
when the flight attendant bending over Weston stood up. It was
Samantha, Richter's favorite flight attendant out of Boston.
He tried to catch her eye, but wasn't certain she remembered
him. He continued watching with interest, peering over the
top of a magazine.

First Class seated nine, a tenth spot reserved for crew rest.
Six single seats including the curtained pilot rest area lined the
windows in three rows. Between the aircraft's aisles, two rows
contained pairs of seats.

Weston and Ingrid settled beside each other in the middle
section's second row, the galley wall immediately behind. In

front of them, two women in full headscarves chatted. A pair of bearded men Jim assumed to be the husbands, sat across the aisles on either side. One spoke into his cell phone, the other clicked a laptop. The seventh and eighth passengers consisted of a deadheading pilot in uniform, who split time between the cockpit and galley, and a burly man dressed in blue jeans and tightly-zipped denim jacket. Jim first noticed the odd man in the lounge where he drew attention for loitering around the bar and knocking a wine bottle to the ground.

The ninth and last First Class customer to board surprised him. Tyler Dagger, wearing a tailored silk suit, slipped into 1A, escorted by a brooding Wilkerson who toted his new boss's hand luggage.

Even after leaving the airline, Jim kept up on company gossip especially that pertaining to former bosses. Wilkerson didn't disguise his disappointment in being passed over for Hap's job. Dagger put him on a short leash, shrewdly aware of a Pit Bull's value. The new COO, perhaps coached by Richter, suggested he portray an elf at the children's Christmas party to soften his image. Wilkerson declined.

Wilkerson's presence in the aisle disturbed the pre-departure service. After an exchange with Samantha, he disappeared into the galley only to emerge with champagne. He delivered the drinks to Ingrid and Weston with a smirk. "Here's to *your* bright futures." Turning crimson after Ingrid ran a hand up his inseam, he deplaned.

Flight attendants offered pre-departure drinks to First and Business Class customers—water, juice, or champagne. Weston and Ingrid clanked glasses repeatedly. Having witnessed their lounge consumption, Jim understood their giddy mood. During one of these toasts, the deadheading pilot bent over Weston and whispered something before slipping into the galley. Then, a male attendant Jim recognized but couldn't place appeared.

"French perfume, English tobacco and Swiss chocolate," he said, fanning catalogues into Ingrid's and Weston's faces.

Swatting him away, Ingrid delivered a gruff rebuke. "I don't buy from brochures and I certainly wouldn't purchase goods peddled from a cart. No different than a filthy falafel vendor." The two scarved heads in front of her came together in chatter as their husbands glared over their shoulders.

Jim gasped with delight to see Kelly Green board the plane. She marched down the aisle in army boots and gave him a farewell kiss on the cheek. Brushing past Weston as she returned to the aircraft door, she shot him a dirty look and mumbled, "Ask me, they got rid of the wrong guy."

Weston's head followed her up the aisle. "Tattoos!" He blurted as his neck jerked toward Ingrid.

The purser asked one of the bearded passengers to turn off his phone after Kelly closed the aircraft door. He complied only after a threat to involve the cockpit.

Taxi and takeoff were normal. Once the plane reached cruising altitude, the service proceeded smoothly with only one disruption. Samantha chased the hawking male attendant out of the galley. A succession of cocktails, appetizers, soup, salad, entrée, cheese, and dessert accompanied by wines, water, port, and coffee sequenced flawlessly. The party of four received special meals accompanied by soft drinks. Weston, Ingrid and Dagger were the only forward cabin passengers who consumed alcohol.

Near the end of the dinner service, Jim watched as Dagger approached Weston, document in hand. He couldn't tell whether the paper dropped or was knocked to the floor. As Weston and Ingrid bent down to retrieve it, Dagger plucked teetering port glasses from their trays with the reflexes of a cat. An inaudible discussion followed, characterized as tense given jabbing fingers, bobbing heads and tapping feet. Weston tried to rise, maybe to pursue a retreating Dagger. But Ingrid pulled him back with a yank to his belt. Through gritted teeth, she snarled, "Let Hap fight his own battles. He's inconsequential. Too dangerous to protect."

After the less elaborate service concluded in Business, Jim slept. Harsh words awoke him an hour later. Weston and Ingrid argued in whispers. With the cabin dark and passengers sleeping or watching movies with headphones, no one else could confirm the conversation. Jim leaned toward the pair.

"My decision's final. I'm doing you a favor telling you tonight. Would you rather have found out tomorrow at GlobalEurope's offices when I introduced you to my new boss?" The German accent was pronounced.

"Outrageous! I won't stand for it. You know our entire negotiating strategy—deceptive, unethical. I'll sue you for breach of contract. After all I've done." Words delivered through labored breathing.

"Done for me? Drivel. Success you always said, is reserved for the rational. If you want to inventory gives and takes, fine. You won't win that game. I know things. Things you wouldn't want aired in court, the newspapers or at the White House. That's my sandbox."

"You can't leave me Ingrid." Weston's head bobbed. A quivering hand wiped his forehead with a handkerchief.

"It's done. My resignation is on Pavlis' desk. Effective before we set foot in GlobalEurope's lobby."

"You...you can't...can't leave me." The tone riddled with fear.

A laugh, then, "I won't be straying far. As head of U.S. operations and your largest shareholder, you'll be working for me."

"I'll ruin you." The gruff voice seethed.

"Ladies first. Underlicht is GlobalEurope's future communications head by the way. He has an envelope with instructions should that be necessary. Now go to sleep and shut up."

The conversation ceased. Weston's shaking fingers pressed his call button. He barked for a cognac to the responding attendant. Jim drifted back to sleep, but used the forward lavatory twice during the next few hours. Both times, Weston sat in the dark, a vise-like grip on the glass in one hand and clenched fist in the other. He stared straight ahead with vacant eyes and quivering lips. Ingrid slept like a baby.

Four hours out of Frankfurt, Weston again rang his call button. "I'm sick," he told the yawning attendant. "It's my stomach. And my travel companion's missing."

Ingrid returned ten minutes later to a seat surrounded by the purser and first officer. They gave Weston antacid and paged for a doctor. A middle-aged woman responded, presenting her credentials as a mid-wife from Stuttgart. She offered to monitor his vital signs, but could render little additional assistance.

Ingrid remained vague about her lengthy absence. Finally, after firm questioning by the first officer, she huffed. "I had diarrhea. White cashmere's a bitch in one of those dirty, little toilets. Shall I be more graphic?"

Weston calmed, but three hours out of Frankfurt, he purged his crepe suzette, Stilton, beef tenderloin, asparagus risotto, arugula, and crab cakes in the reverse order in which he ate his first class meal. When the convulsions began, Ingrid plucked the ermine hat from her lap and threw it across the aisle where it landed in the crotch of the passenger in 2A. Sequenced heaves of lobster bisque, champagne, and nuts finally emptied Weston's stomach. His seat was unusable.

Awakened by the clamor, the resting Captain parted the privacy curtain around his seat. After consulting the purser and mid-wife, he wanted Weston moved to the last row of coach—vacant and with easy access to the large aft lavatory designed to accommodate special needs customers. He could rest, laying flat. The first officer, deadheading pilot and denim-jacketed passenger who identified himself as an air marshal moved Weston. Ingrid recovered her hat and plopped into the seat vacated by the air marshal. She yelled at the flight attendants cleaning up the mess. "Grab perfume from the merchandise cart—douse that stench. The sky cop can have my seat. He flies free."

As tranquility settled in First Class, the Captain declared an emergency and diverted toward Glasgow, Scotland. Despite Weston's penchant for first class living, he lay unconscious covered in champagne vomit in a middle seat in coach.

Upon landing in Glasgow, a cargo forklift removed Richard Weston III, wrapped in polyester blankets from the aircraft's rear service door.